Also by Sara Fraser

SARA FRASER
— TILDY: —
POORHOUSE WOMAN

Futura

A Futura Book

Copyright © Roy Clews 1986

First published in Great Britain in 1986
by Futura Publications, a Division of
Macdonald & Co (Publishers) Ltd
London & Sydney
Reprinted 1987, 1988

ISBN 0 7088 2672 5

Typeset in Baskerville by Fleet Graphics, Enfield, Middlesex

Reproduced, printed and bound in Great Britain by
Hazell Watson & Viney Limited
Member of BPCC plc
Aylesbury, Bucks, England

Futura Publications
A Division of
Macdonald & Co (Publishers) Ltd
Greater London House
Hampstead Road
London NW1 7QX
A member of Maxwell Pergamon Publishing Corporation plc

Introduction

In the England of 1821, to be a Poorhouse Woman, was to wear a badge of shame. Tildy Crawford was forced to wear the badge. But she refused to bow her head, and accept the shame . . .

Chapter One

The Parish of Bromsgrove, Worcestershire.
June 1821.

Although it was not yet nine o'clock in the morning the sun blazed from a cloudless sky upon the long straight street that comprised the centre of Bromsgrove Town. Aproned shopmen were taking down the shutters from the bulls-eyed windows of their premises, while mob-capped housewives came hurrying with wickerbaskets on their arms to buy their domestic necessaries. Small children carried writing slates and chalk pencils reluctantly schoolwards. Two- and four-wheeled carts drawn by horses and oxen lurched over the ruts of the road, and fat William Bunegar, parish constable and surveyor of roads, waddled painfully towards the Golden Lion Hotel, the main coach and posting inn of the district.

Despite the threatened heat of the day the constable wore a caped greatcoat and tricorn hat, and sweat oozed from beneath his dirty-white tie-wig to trickle down his puce-complexioned jowls. He cursed beneath his breath and swung his long staff of office to clear a scrawny hen from his path, and the bird's squawk of fright momentarily soothed his irritation.

'You're in a hurry, Master Bunegar?' A shopman accosted him.

The constable scowled. 'Indeed I am, Master Stilman. There's a vestry meeting bin called, and I knew naught of it until seven o' the clock this morn. They'm agoing to call over the paupers, and the last man to know of it was me.'

His scowl deepened. 'Me! Constable o' this parish, the last one to be told.'

The other nodded in commiseration. 'Just so, Master Bunegar, just so. It's always that way, the most important men gets left 'til last to be told of events concerning them. Well, I'll not delay thee longer. I know they'll not be able to start wi'out you.'

Bungar waddled on, momentarily soothed by the man's sycophancy, but when he reached the Golden Lion Inn his irritation returned abruptly as he saw the noisy crowd of men, women and children clustering around the great double doors. For the most part their clothes were ragged and threadbare, the children barefoot, with the stench of unwashed flesh emanating like a miasma to saturate the air about them.

The crowd fell silent as Bunegar approached, and moved back from the doors to give him a clear way. Self-importantly he waddled past, not deigning to answer those who greeted him and refusing to meet their eyes. As he reached the door he ponderously turned and shouted.

'Stay silent, all on you. Don't be disturbing your betters wi' your bloody rattle. Iffen any on you makes a commotion you'll get no relief this day. I'll promise you that.'

For the first time he stared directly into their eyes, visually challenging any one of them to dispute his order. No one dared, and satisfied with their apparent submissiveness Bunegar entered the inn.

In the main bar-parlour awaiting him were seated six men, ranged behind a long polished oak table at one end of the room. These men were the select vestry of Bromsgrove Parish, the governing body of the district. Two were church wardens, three were overseers of the poor, and the sixth, who had a large leather-bound ledger on the table before him, was the vestry clerk. This was Joseph Blackwell, attorney-at-law, a fussy-mannered, pedantic little man, whose black coat was forever powdered with the dust of the ancient documents he perused.

Now he acknowledged William Bunegar's arrival by addressing the vestry in his reedy voice.

'Gentlemen, before we begin the business of the day, I would like to inform you that the measures we intend to take have the full support, nay indeed, the approbation, of our district magistrates, Reverend the Lord Aston and the Reverend Mark Pyndar. They have both assured me that any pauper who lays complaint before them as to the treatment we mete out, will be given short shrift. I can tell you further that Reverend the Lord Aston is highly gratified that the newly appointed vestrymen, namely yourselves, Gentlemen, are determined to put an end to the abuses of the system of Poor Relief perpetrated by previous vestries. In his Lordship's own words, "Charity must be tempered with sound sense and good management to avoid bringing ruin upon this parish". The poor rates presently imposed upon this parish are fast rising to amounts too great to be borne by those who have to pay them. Namely, Gentlemen, the people such as ourselves, the manufacturers, the farmers, the leading tradesmen and the gentlefolk.' He paused as a murmur of agreement sounded from his listeners, then continued.

'You are all of you doubtless familiar with the system of Outdoor Relief we apply here. But it does no harm to briefly remind ourselves. A scale of relief has been drawn up by previous vestries, which is designed to ensure that every pauper and pauper child in the parish have their incomes made up to a sufficient sum to provide them with adequate foodstuffs. In many cases rent is also paid for the pauper, and occasional grants of money can be made for the purchases of fuel and clothing.' Blackwell paused again and frowned.

'It is well known what are the evils this system has brought about. Certain unscrupulous manufacturers and farmers deliberately pay such low wages that the main cost of providing for their labourers is provided by the poor rate. The labourers themselves have become accustomed to receiving a guaranteed income from the parish, and do not

9

trouble to seek employment or to render satisfactory service to their masters. With an insufferable insolence, they tell their betters, "Why should we toil, when the parish will support us anyway". Not only that, Gentlemen, but most of the money we so charitably subscribe towards their relief, is taken by them and spent on drink, and debaucheries of the most evil descriptions.' Blackwell's pale face was visibly reddening as his indignation fuelled upon itself, and the faces of the vestrymen mirrored that indignation.

The clerk suddenly slapped his palms down on the ledger and spread his fingers wide across the leather binding, then hooked them as if to draw the book's contents into his hands.

'We must carefully examine every pauper who comes before us this day, Gentlemen, and do our utmost to ensure that they shall not be enabled to continue this abuse of our charity. Are we agreed?'

The answer came almost in unison. 'We are so agreed, Master Blackwell.'

'Call Martin Duffil.' Joseph Blackwell's reedy voice echoed through the entrance passageway, and William Bunegar waddled to the inn doors and repeated in a hoarse bellow. 'Call Martin Duffil.'

A lean-bodied, savage looking man with a great shock of tow-coloured hair hanging low on his forehead stepped out from the crowd of paupers. 'I'm to be first, am I, Bunegar. That's a rare honour, arn't it?'

The constable scowled. Duffil was an old acquaintance, a hard-drinking, fierce-brawling nailer, whom he had put in the parish stocks many times for disturbing the peace.

'You just watch your tongue in front o' the vestry today, Duffil.' He growled in reply, and motioned with his many-folded chin towards the passageway. 'Now get on in 'ere, and don't keep the gennulmen waiting.'

Inside the bar-parlour the nailer came to a halt before the

10

table and sullenly returned the hard stares of the vestry-men.

Joseph Blackwell studied the ledger before him for some moments, then stated accusingly. 'I see you've been claiming relief since February the tenth, Duffil. Why is that?'

Incredulity appeared on Duffil's gaunt features. 'Why be I claiming relief?' He questioned rhetorically. 'That's bloody clear to see, arn't it? I carn't earn enough at the nailing to feed me childer. You knows well enough that the trade's gone flat. I'm lucky iffen I gets two days work in the week.' He flung out one sinewy arm to point at the face of the man sitting to Blackwell's right side. 'Ask Joseph Rutter theer what the state o' the trade is. He knows well enough.'

Joseph Rutter, churchwarden and nail master, stirred uneasily on his chair, and rubbed his huge beak of a nose with the back of his hand.

'Well, Rutter, why wunt you spake out?' The nailer demanded angrily.

Rutter again stirred uneasily, and then answered in a pettish tone. 'The trade is a trifle slack at present, but is improving.'

'That's bloody rubbish, that is,' Duffil shouted.

The constable was quick to intervene. 'I'se warned you afore to watch your tongue, Duffil. I shan't tell you agen.'

Rutter spoke in a whisper to the clerk. 'This man takes no iron from my warehouse, Master Blackwell. He works for George Hobbs, and if Hobbs don't have sufficient orders, then that's a judgement on him for being a poor man o' business.'

Blackwell nodded brusquely, and again turned his attention to the ledger. He ran ink stained fingers down a column of figures, his thin lips moving soundlessly as he computed totals.

'You have been claiming for your wife and five children under the age of fourteen years, Duffil. You receive weekly, eleven shillings and fourpence ha'penny, that

11

being the scale of allowance for fourteen quartern loaves, at a price per loaf of ninepence and three-farthings. I see also that you allege paying three shillings and sixpence a week rent for your cottage and workshop, and you lay claim to such sum accordingly.' He lifted his head to look directly at the nailer. 'That makes a grand total of fourteen shillings and tenpence ha'penny for each week. 'Pon my soul, Duffil! That's a goodly income for sitting on your arse in the beerhouses all day, is it not?'

The nailer's gaunt face flushed deeply, and his voice thickened with anger. 'Look agen at your figures, Blackwell. I can't read nor write, but I can tot up what's due me. You'se never given me fourteen and tenpence, never. Even in me wust week I manages to blow enough nails to earn six or seven shillings. You only makes me money up to the bread-scale, and I pays for me breeze and tools and rent out o' that.' He drew a deep breath before going on. 'Does you think I enjoys coming here week arter week to beg charity offen you fine gentlemen. Does you think that?' His voice rose as his temper flared higher. 'Look at me clothes, and then look at your own.' With a sweeping gesture he contrasted his rags with the fine broadcloth coats and ruffled white linen of the vestry. 'Does it look as if I'm living on the fat o' the bloody land?'

'That's enough, Duffil.' The constable broke in, and grabbed the nailer's shoulders with his meaty hands. 'I'll remove you from here iffen you don't shut that big mouth o' yourn this minute.'

'You needn't bother to drag me out, Bunegar. I'll goo meself, and bollocks to you, and your bleedin' charity!' the nailer shouted, as he tore free from the constable's restraining hands and flung himself out of the room.

The vestrymen looked at each other in stunned silence, and then Blackwell chuckled mirthlessly.

'I'll warrant an empty belly will soon cool his temper, Gentlemen. He'll be back shortly begging forgiveness, that you may depend upon. Let us get on now, and waste no more time. Call Ephraim Cull . . . '

12

Chapter Two

The Sidemoor was a mile to the west of Bromsgrove's centre. A sprawling settlement of terraces and squares of two-storied, red-brick hovels. Each hovel with its lean-to workshop at its rear, where men, women and children plied their trade of nail-making. Normally at this hour of the morning the district would be resounding with the deafening clangour of metal on metal, and the heavy thuds of the treadle-hammers, the olivers, smashing down upon the great blocks of solid iron which held the nail-dies. The workshops' hearths of breeze-coke would be flaring, white-hot shards of metal flying, bellows wheezing and panting, and men, women and children from six years to sixty, sweating, swearing, aching, as they slaved to earn their daily bread.

But today it was only here and there that metal rang upon metal. Most of the workshops were still and silent. The trade for nails had slumped, and there was little work to be had. Men and women lounged in the yards and alleys, talking in low, dispirited voices, trying to ignore the rumblings of their empty stomachs. Only the children, released from the tyranny of incessant labour, ran and shouted and played in joyous freedom.

Martin Duffil, still seething with anger, strode through the filthy streets towards the close-huddled square known as the tinyard, where he lived with his wife and children. People called out to him as he passed, asking what the newly-appointed vestrymen were like. To all who asked he grunted the same reply.

'They'm bad buggers.' And strode on, leaving the

questioners staring after him, a dawning apprehension in their eyes. Apprehension engendered from the bitter experience of what a hard-hearted vestry could mean for them and their families in times of distress.

Lean-to workshops comprised the inner face of Tinyard Square, crammed between each pair of workshops was a tiny brewhouse with a copper and firehole, and at the corners of the rows were the communal privies and midden-heaps, foul smelling and infested with rats and vermin. In the centre of the yard was the well, the only water supply available, with a crumbling brick surround and broken wooden roofing. In fine weather and on the rare rest days the well served as the social meeting place of the square, and the women would sit on the low surround and gossip while the infants and smaller children played in the rubbish-strewn dust at their feet.

Martin Duffil came through the narrow covered passage-way that was the sole entrance to the tinyard and found his wife sitting with some other women around the well. All the women were toilworn, with lack-lustre hair and dirt-grimed skin. Some had made attempts to patch and darn worn-out dresses and aprons, others were uncaring of the rents and holes in their clothing. Alice Duffil looked at her husband's face, and what she saw there brought her to her feet.

'What's happened, Marty? What's amiss?' she questioned nervously.

He glared at her. 'The bloody new vestry, that's what's happened.' He spat the words. 'But I'se told 'um what they can do wi' their bloody charity. I'll not be blaggarded by them bastards. Not I.'

Alice Duffil's face blanched, and her sunken eyes welled with sudden tears. 'You'se not been give any money then?' she quavered.

The man's anger subsided at the sight of his wife's distress, and his shoulders slumped dejectedly. 'No, my wench,' he muttered despondently. 'I lost me temper, and had to go from there, or else I'd ha' swung for the buggers.'

14

'Oh dear Christ! What'll we do now?' The tears spilled from Alice Duffil's eyes, and her voice choked with sobs. 'What's we going to feed the childer wi' now?'

Awkwardly the nailer reached out and patted his wife's heaving shoulders. 'Theer now, my wench, don't take on so. I'll goo back in a bit and ate dirt afore 'um. They'll gi' me summat if I does that. Stop skrawkin' now, 'ull you.'

'Her's got good reason to skrawk, Martin Duffil.' A tall rawboned woman strode from the workshop door facing the nailer. Her face badly pitted with the blue scars of small-pox, a man's battered billycock hat perched on her tousled mass of grey hair. Her only clothing a torn bodice which displayed one shrivelled breast, a long sack apron stretching from her middle to her iron-tipped clogs and a pair of man's breeches. Her name was Hester Lammas, and she was the uncrowned Queen of the tinyard.

'Now what's amiss wi' the new vestry?' She demanded to know, and Duffil, for all his savagery, dropped his head and mumbled his account of the morning's happenings like some dejected schoolboy.

While he was speaking another younger woman appeared in the doorway behind Hester Lammas. She also was toilworn and thin, but her grey dress, although old, was neatly patched. Her dark hair worn in coiled plaits was glossy with brushing, and her pale skin shone with cleanli-ness. With wide luminous brown eyes she studied the scene before her, and her smooth brow creased with a growing anxiety as she listened to the man's story.

'I knew we'd have trouble when the bloody farmers took over the vestry,' Hester Lammas complained bitterly.

'Rutter's no farmer,' Duffil disputed.

'No, but all the other bleeders be,' the woman overrode him. 'I knew us nailers'd have trouble getting our allow-ances from the parish. We'd be alright, iffen we was bloody chawbacons. The bloody farmers 'ud give us our dues then, just to save themselves having to pay us a living wage for doing their stinkin' work. But because we'em naught to

15

do wi' them, then they'll not gi' us a penny-piece if they can help it.'

She swung about and spoke to the young woman in the doorway behind her. 'Come on, Tildy, let's get down to Bromsgrove and see what's happening.'

The younger woman, who was little more than a girl, nodded agreement. 'I'll just fetch the baby, Hester.' Her voice was low-pitched and tuneful, and her accent tinged with a soft rustic burr, distinct from the harsher tones of those around her.

'I'll keep me eye on little Davy, Tildy. That'll save you mawling yourself wi' carrying him all that way,' a woman offered.

Matilda Crawford hesitated a moment, then smiled, showing even white teeth. 'My thanks to you, Maggie, but I'd best take him. He'll fret if he wakes, and I'm not there.' She disappeared inside the workshop and returned moments later carrying a shawl-wrapped child in her arms.

'Right then!' Hester Lammas pulled her wide-brimmed hat low down on her head. 'Let's be away. And you'd best come down as soon as your temper's cooled, Martin.' Her toothless gums glistened pinkly as she cackled with wide-mouthed laughter. 'I'll need you to pick the yeds o' the bloody vestry offa the floor arter I'se got through wi' 'um.'

Hester Lammas didn't complete the journey. A few hundred yards from the Bromsgrove High Street a man called to her from a wayside cottage.

'Hester, you'd best come and get your man. He's alaying in the ditch out the back and canna stir a leg he's so bloody drunk. Iffen the constable see's him, he'll have him in the stocks for sure, he's making such a racket, and cursing the King and Church summat awful.'

The woman's toothless mouth gaped wide, and she spewed out a torrent of vituperation. 'That barstard 'usband o' mine, up to his bleedin' tricks agen! That whoreson! That useless bugger! Wheer's he got money for drink? The stinking pig told me this morn that he hadn't a

16

penny-piece to bless hisself wi'. I'll swing for the bastard, so I will. I'll bloody well kill 'im!'

She gently pushed Tildy onwards. 'You get on down to the Lion, Girl. I'll have to come later arter I'se got this bugger home and settled.'

The younger woman smiled a farewell, and trudged on to join the crowd of paupers at the inn.

It was three hours before Tildy Crawford was called in by the vestry, and during that time her anxieties had burgeoned ever greater as pauper after pauper came out of the Golden Lion cursing or crying in anger and despair. The new vestry was proving itself to be assiduous in cutting the cost of the poor rates by reducing the relief granted to the very minimum, and refusing any relief at all if any pretext – no matter how slight – to do so could be found.

The crowd, growing ever more dejected, had not appreciably diminished, being continually augmented by fresh arrivals, but the newcomers very quickly quietened and merged into the prevailing mood as the day wore on. At last, weary with the burden of the sleeping child, Tildy was brought to stand before the long, polished oak table. As she came into the bar-parlour a vestryman leaned across to his neighbour to whisper.

'My Oath! Her's a rare sweet piece for a pauper wench, arn't her.'

His colleague's eyes lingered hungrily on the girl's full breasts jutting out the thin fabric of her bodice, the slender waist and rounded hips, and the thin, yet pretty face.

'Ahhrr,' he breathed gustily in agreement. 'She can share my bed anytime she wants.'

Joseph Blackwell ahhemmed pointedly to quell such unseemly whisperings and, unmoved by any sexual desires, addressed the vestrymen.

'This young woman, Matilda Crawford, has a some-what unusual history, Gentlemen. She came to this parish in the month of April, the year past, to work at the nailing trade with her new-wed husband, one Thomas Crawford, who had been born a native of this parish, but had at the

17

time of his wedding, been in service to the vicar of the Ipsley Parish, Warwickshire, for some three years or more. Thomas Crawford was discharged from his post for insolence, and bears a bad character. One could also wonder as to the character of a woman who joins herself in wedlock to such a man . . . '

Tildy felt herself becoming hot with embarrassment as the clerk talked about her as if she were an inanimate object. An embarrassment compounded by the lascivious faces staring at her. Summoning her pride, she hugged her child closer to her breasts and kept her gaze firmly fixed on the blank wall behind the head of the clerk.

'The infant she carries was not born in this parish. Although the said Thomas Crawford is alleged to be the father. This girl, for some unexplained motives of her own, wickedly ran away from her husband just prior to her confinement, and the child was birthed in our neighbouring parish, Tardebigge. In the poorhouse there, so I believe, another damned pauper brat.'

Tildy's embarrassment heightened and her flush deepened uncontrollably, causing her pale cheeks and neck to glow with colour, but her pride kept her face expressionless, and her eyes did not waver.

'She returned to this parish following the birth, and resumed working with her husband at the nailing trade. Again sharing his bed and hearth. You will well remember the Strike of the nailers when they wickedly refused work during the winter months, Gentlemen. To her credit, Matilda Crawford did not join those misguided nailers who struck work. She was then attacked by the evil ruffians known as Belly Hoggers, whose object was to bring ruin to the trade. After that attack Thomas Crawford ran away from this parish, abandoning his wife and child. During a further attack by Belly Hoggers, Matilda Crawford was again physically injured. But that was in early February of this year, and dammee, if she ain't lived solely on parish relief since then. A long time to recover from a bullet-wound and some trifling burns, in my opinion.'

18

'And her husband. Wheer's he at ?' The most greedy-eyed of the vestrymen wanted to know.

'His whereabouts are not known, Gentlemen,' Blackwell answered. 'However, that is not important. What is important is whether this woman and her child have any lawful claim to continue drawing relief in this parish. Whether, in fact, she has any right to a settlement here at all?'

One of the men with greedy eyes, John Dolton, was the acting Chairman of the Vestry. His bulky, well-fed body, weather-reddened face and hands, leather boots and gaiters, cord breeches and crude-cut broadcloth coat denoted him as the successful farmer he was. His small eyes now flickered over Tildy's body, and he swallowed hard as his throat tightened with lust.

'And iffen her's no right to settlement, what then, Master Blackwell?'

'Then, Master Chairman, we must examine her carefully to determine her rightful parish of settlement, and have her conveyed there as soon as possible.'

'What say you to that, Young 'Ooman?' the chairman questioned.

Tildy took a deep breath, causing her breasts to rise and fall, and fought to control the fear that had coursed through her when she had heard the vestry clerk speaking about her settlement. It was not for herself that she was afraid, but for her child. At least here, hard and comfortless though life was in the Sidemoor, Davy, her baby, had a roof above his head, and food to sustain him should her own bountiful milk not suffice. If she was sent out of this parish then God only knew what might become of her. And how could her child survive if anything was to happen to her in a strange parish where she would be completely friendless.

'Come now, Young 'Ooman,' Dolton urged impatiently. 'Let's hear what you've got to say for yourself.'

Fighting to appear confident and unafraid, Tildy met his eyes squarely. 'I believe I have a right to a settlement here, Sir.' She inwardly berated herself for the nervous tremor in

19

her voice, and willed it to steadiness. 'I have lived at the Sidemoor for more than a year now, and that gives me the right to a settlement in this parish.'

'That is not so, Crawford.' Blackwell's reedy voice challenged. 'There are three failings here. Firstly, you did not stay in the Sidemoor for an unbroken stretch of time. You ran away from this parish, and remained away for more than forty nights. Secondly, when you first came here with Thomas Crawford, he failed to deliver into the hands of the churchwardens, a written notice of his intention to live and work here, and so gain a settlement. He having forfeited his previous right to settlement by birth, by being gone from the parish for more than three years, and not being gone in the service of His Majesty as a soldier or sailor. Thirdly, a sojourn of a year in service or residence in a parish, must be a full year without making application for any form of relief. You applied for relief after only ten months. Thus you forfeit any claim to a settlement on those grounds.'

'But I've paid rental on a cottage and workshop since April of last year,' Tildy argued spiritedly.

The clerk smiled mirthlessly and shook his narrow head slowly from side to side. 'That story will not serve, Crawford. It will not serve at all. The rent you speak of was paid on a cottage and workshop belonging to the notorious Belly Hogger, Richard Suffield. Since February last he has been a convicted felon and under sentence of transportation. You have paid no rent to anyone from that month, since the ownership of the cottage and workshop is under dispute.'

'Thomas Crawford or myself paid three shillings a week rent from April to the following February.' Tildy's growing desperation forced her to stubbornly persist. 'T'was not my fault that Dick Suffield was sent to the hulks. He shot me, not I him. And 'tis not my fault that there's no landlord to pay the rent to. I'm willing to pay, 'tis not my fault there's no landlord at present.'

The sneer in Blackwell's voice openly transferred to his

face. 'As the law now stands, Crawford, a person must rent a tenement at £10 per annum to qualify for a settlement. Your rent for a full year amounts only to £8-4 shillings . . . ' He paused, and glanced round the vestrymen. 'The only other way this pauper could have qualified for settlement, Gentlemen, was to have served as a parish officer.' He looked at Tildy. 'Have you done so, Crawford? Have you been a constable or churchwarden or overseer to the poor, or even surveyor or roads?'

Tormented by her fears for her child, and driven by her intense resentment of his sneering, hectoring manner, Tildy could not stop herself from striking back.

'You know well I have not been, so why must you bait me? Is it because I am a woman and alone in the world, is that why you dare use me so? You are too much the coward to serve a man in this way . . . ' Her overstrung control suddenly snapped, and to her utter chagrin she burst into tears.

The sight of her tears touched a softer chord in some of the vestrymen, but Joseph Blackwell was unmoved. He had seen too many tears from too many paupers to be affected.

'Our course of action is quite clear under the law, Gentlemen. We must determine her rightful parish of settlement, and I shall immediately make application to the magistrates on behalf of the overseers for her removal to that parish.'

He spoke sharply to Tildy. 'For pity's sake dry your eyes and cease this unseemly display, Crawford. I do assure you that a veritable ocean of false tears will not alter our decision in this matter.'

Tildy, balancing her child on one arm, dashed the tears from her eyes with her free hand, angry at herself for weeping.

'I'm not crying because you have distressed me,' she blurted out defiantly. 'I'm crying because you make me so angry with your baiting and bullying.'

'Tchhaa!' The clerk ejaculated with an air of disgust. 'You've a sight too much wicked insolence in you, Girl.

21

You would be well advised to curb that insolence when you address your betters.'

Though her eyes were still wet with tears Tildy met the clerk's hard glare unwaveringly and her voice was firm and steady.

'You are not my "better", Master Blackwell, and I don't care a damn for your removal order. I'll leave the parish this day, and not because I'm feared of you. But because I'll not lower myself any more before you by begging for your charity. I'd sooner die of starvation in a ditch rather than . . . '

The baby in her arms woke up and with all the force of his lungs emitted an ear-splitting howl of protest. Tildy, cut off in full flow, became flustered, lost the thread of her words, coloured furiously, and ran from the room.

After a few seconds of silence, Blackwell snorted indignantly, 'There now, Gentlemen, you see how the gutter-snipes so quickly turn and bite the very hands that feed them. Mark that woman well, Master Bunegar. You will ascertain her parish of origin before this night is out, and we'll have the removal order for her by tomorrow. Now, let us get on. Call Widow Brown . . . '

Chapter Three

'But wheer 'ull you go, Tildy?' Hester Lammas asked yet again, and yet again Tildy could only shake her head.

'I haven't decided, but go I will.'

The two women were in the tiny living room of Tildy's cottage, which adjoined that of Hester Lammas' in the tinyard. On the table between their stools the baby whimpered fretfully in the lidless wooden box which served as its cradle.

'And how about this little 'un?' The older woman's work-gnarled hand tapped the side of the box. 'It's all very well for you to lose your temper wi' the vestry and leave this parish. But what's to become o' this little morsel when youm on the road like a bloody tramper 'ooman?'

A troubled frown imprinted the girl's smooth features. Then she sighed heavily. 'Oh, Hester, do you think that I am not troubled by those same thoughts? But what's to become of him if I wait for Blackwell to put removal upon me? We'll be sent to the poorhouse at Tardebigge Parish, and once I'm in there I'll not get the chance to find work and a home for us both. The poor little mite is sickly enough as it is, and in the poorhouse most babies die within a few months.'

'Most babbies die wherever they be, Tildy,' Hester Lammas told her bluntly. 'The Lord gives 'um and the Lord takes 'um away agen. That's nature, that is. I'se birthed fifteen in me time, and only three live still.' She shook her frowsty mass of grey hair. 'No, my wench, iffen anybody wants to be sure of having childer to support 'um

23

when they'm too old to work themselves, then they'd best breed a score or more o' the little buggers to start wi'. That way they might have four or five grow to manhood.'

Sudden dread clouded Tildy's soft brown eyes. 'Don't say such things, Hester. My baby's all I have in the world. He'll live, I know he will.'

The older woman pursed her toothless mouth and offered bleak comfort. 'Ahrr, so he might, wench. We can but hope so. He's no sicklier than the other babbies hereabouts anyways, so that's summat to the good I suppose.'

As if understanding her words the baby cried for attention, a thin high-pitched keening, and Tildy unbuttoned her bodice, freeing her breasts, before lifting the rag-swathed bundle from the box. She felt the tiny teeth fasten and bite sharply on her erect, dark-ringed nipple and experienced the familiar rush of love toward her child as he sucked greedily to draw the rich, life-giving sustenance from her body. She stared down at the tight-screwed eyes with their dark clouds of lashes, and the soft black hair clustered tight-capped upon the delicately moulded head, and her lips curved in a tender smile.

Hester Lammas, battered and hardened by life as she was, smiled also. Remembering those days long past when she too had suckled her first-born with the same tender joy. For a brief while the three of them remained cocooned in peaceful contentment, the only noise the gentle breathing of the women and the muted sounds of the tiny lips seeking and finding comfort.

The banging of a wooden staff on the outer door shattered that cocoon of peace, and William Bunegar's hoarse wheezing voice preceded him into the room.

'Well now, Young 'Ooman, you knows why I'm here.' His eyes, almost buried in puffs of fat, dwelt appreciatively on the smooth white roundness of Tildy's breasts, and flustered, she hastened to draw her shawl about her to hide them from his view. Bunegar coughed noisily, shielding his disappointment at the loss of such a pleasurable sight, and came straight to the point.

'I'm to find out your rightful parish, Girl. So let's be hearing what you'se got to tell me, without any more ado.'

Tildy hesitated, then realizing the futility of argument answered. 'I think that my rightful parish must then be Tardebigge. Because until I was eighteen years I lived with my aunt and uncle in the Brockhill Woods, just a few miles out of Redditch Town. That would put me in Tardebigge Parish, wouldn't it?' Memory carried her back through the years, and visual pictures flooded her mind . . . *'Orphaned before I was yet three years, taken by my father's eldest sister and her husband, that raving religious maniac who regarded a smiling face as a mortal sin. My little brother put out to service when he was seven. Carried off to the North Country, and for all I know dead and buried, for I've not heard anything of him since. And I, drudging out my years, watching my aunt weep and my uncle rant and rave, knowing only blows and kicks and hungry nights and days. And then, when I was eighteen years, running off to Redditch Fair, and meeting my husband, Tom Crawford* . . . ' Her lips trembled uncontrollably as the pain of her past overwhelmed her, and she was grateful when the constable's wheezing voice dragged her back to the present.

'Be your relatives still living?'

She shook her head. 'I don't know, Master Bunegar. But whether they live, or are dead, it makes no odds. I'll find neither welcome nor shelter under their roof. I must make my own way in the world.'

Bunegar's gaze flickered about the room. Despite its poverty its confined area was well swept and free from stench, and the young woman herself was clean, her hair tidily dressed and her worn faded clothes neatly darned and patched. He experienced a surge of sympathy, and tried to speak kindly.

'Well, Tildy Crawford, you knows already that the vestry clerk is getting a removal order from the justices. There's naught I can do to stop that. But is there no one who might give you shelter in Tardebigge or Redditch? I could see that a message was sent to them tonight to let 'um know you was acoming.'

25

He waited for her to reply, but she remained silent, only shaking her glossy head and keeping her sad eyes downcast.

A sudden inspiration struck Hester Lammas. 'O' course there's someone, Tildy. How about that young cove you told me about? Him 'as gi' you and the babby shelter arter the bloody poor'us master had you put on the cart and taken to the parish line.'

Again memories crowded Tildy's mind bringing with them poignant pleasure and regret. *'Davy Nokes. Laughing, generous Davy Nokes. My sweet, gentle Davy. On whom I brought trouble and misfortune. As I brought it on Tom Crawford, and Dick Suffield, and as I'm feared I'm doomed to bring it on any man who becomes involved with me . . . '*

Aloud she snapped sharply. 'No Hester! He can't help me. So leave it lie.'

The other woman was piqued by her friend's sharpness. 'No call for you to bite me bleedin' yed off.' She sniffed.

'I'm sorry, Hester. I didn't mean it that way,' Tildy was quick to apologize. 'I know that you're my true friend, and you mean only to help. But I wish to make my own way through this trouble. I'll not drag anyone else into it with me.'

'Suit yourself, my wench,' Hester refused to be so easily placated, and lapsed into a surly silence.

'Listen to me for a minute, Tildy Crawford,' Bunegar wheezed solemnly. 'Don't you be so stupid-proud. If you goes on the road by yourself, then you'll be naught but a tramper. And all you'll get for your pains is the Bridewell and a whipping, whenever youm seen to be begging. And you'll surely have to beg, unless you tries being a hedge-whore.' His eyes were shrewd as he measured the effects of his words. 'Youm not the type to be a tanner-whore, Tildy. I know that youm a good-living young 'ooman. So why . . . '

'I'll find work,' Tildy interrupted vehemently. 'I'm young and healthy and willing to do any task.'

The constable's jowls quivered as he ponderously shook

his head. 'Times are sore hard, Girl. If there's no work for you here, then what makes you think that there'll be work elsewhere. Your best bet is to let the overseers remove you to Tardebigge. That way, you'll at least have a proper settlement theer. Oh, I knows what youm agoing to say.' He lifted a meaty hand to forestall her protests. 'You don't want the shame o' being in the poorhouse. Well, bugger the shame, Girl! You'll do no better at present than that. It'll gi' you shelter for you and the babby, and you can look about for work while youm theer. They'll not stop you from doing that, 'ull they. It's better for them if you can find summat for yourself, arn't it.'

'He's right, Tildy,' Hester Lammas added her support to the man's argument. 'What odds are a few weeks in the poor'us?'

'But it's the shame of it!' Tildy burst out, and her face burned hotly. 'My baby was born in the Tardebigge poorhouse, and I swore then that I'd never put that shame on his innocent head again. God knows it's shaming enough to take the Outdoor Relief, but it's twice as shaming to be in the house. I've never wanted charity, and until last February I never asked for it. You know well enough that it's through no fault of mine that I must live off the parish. I worked until the Belly Hoggers fired the roof over my head and put a pistol-ball in my body . . . '

'We all knows that, Tildy,' her friend spoke bluntly. 'But pride makes a bad bedfellow when you've naught to buy food with. You must just swallow that pride o' yourn, Tildy Crawford, and bite on your tongue.'

The sickening realization that the woman was right filled Tildy's being, and even while her emotions battled against that realization, her deeper instinct knew that in the end she could only accept the inevitable with whatever good grace and courage she could muster. She sighed chokingly, and unshed tears glistened in her dark eyes. Unable to speak, she nodded, and the constable took the gesture for surrender.

'Now youm being sensible, Girl. Here.' From the

27

capricious pocket of his greacoat he took some thick copper coins and placed them on the table. 'The vestry has allowed you fourpence to buy a bit o' grub to see you through until tomorrow. I'll have the removal order then, and I'll be coming to fetch you. So you'd best make your farewells early.' He stared hard at her for a moment, then patted her shoulder commiseratingly. 'It'll be for the best, Girl, you'll see. And God blast me, youm leaving precious little o' good behind you, when you leaves the bloody Sidemoor . . .'

Chapter Four

Tildy left the Sidemoor at noon next day, carrying her baby in her arms, and all her worldly possessions tied in a small bundle upon her back. The farewells of her neighbours were brief and perfunctory. It seemed as if they were afraid to come near her, in case her misfortune was contagious. Only Hester Lammas hugged her, and pushed a small piece of cone-sugar into her apron pocket.

'Here, my wench, here's some sweet-suck for the babby.'

Tildy gazed fondly at the battered, pock-marked face surmounted by the mass of frowsty grey hair and billycock hat, and could not hold back her tears. 'I'll miss you, Hester,' she whispered.

The older woman gulped hard, and rubbed her faded eyes with the corner of her sack apron. 'Theer now, youm amaking me act like some soft silly cow!' she scolded harshly, and leant forward to kiss Tildy's cheek. 'God keep you, Tildy. I'll miss you sore as well.' Unable to control her own sobs she turned and ran into her workshop.

'Come now, Girl, we've got a long walk ahead of us,' Bunegar urged, hiding his sympathy under a brusque manner.

Tildy dried her eyes and dutifully followed the bulky figure out of the tinyard and along the Broad Street. A group of urchins ran alongside her, excited by this unlooked for entertainment.

'What's you done, Missus?'

'Has you killed somebody?'

'Be you a robber? Be you going to the Bridewell?'

29

'Is he gooing to lock you up?'

'Be off, you young jackanapes!' The constable's long staff swung with unerring aim, and yelping with fright and pain the urchins scattered. The adults they met along the way averted their eyes until the ill-matched couple had passed, then stared greedily after them, wondering loudly what the young woman had done for the constable to be taking her off.

Tildy, despite her embarrassment at being made into a travelling show, could not help commenting. 'Why don't they ever look directly at us, Master Bunegar? Even in the tinyard my neighbours wouldn't meet my eyes.'

The fat man chuckled wheezily. 'I've seen it many the time, Girl. I reckon it's a sort of superstition. They thinks that if they catches your eye, then they'll be unlucky themselves.'

Tildy thought about it for a few seconds, then dismissed the subject from her mind and looked at Davy. The blue eyes were wide and as Tildy smiled down into them she felt a sense of disquiet. The small body lolled in her arms as if it had no strength, and the eyes themselves seemed to have a peculiar vacancy of expression.

'I wonder why he's so still?' Tildy's disquiet became a foreboding. The small body abruptly tensed and stiffened, but then a thin whimpering came from deep in the child's throat. 'He's alright,' she hastened to reassure herself. 'There's naught wrong with him. He'll be tired, that's all, and it's the heat that makes him so listless.' Breaking off a tiny piece of the cone-sugar in her apron pocket, she pushed it gently between the pursed lips, and the baby's whimpering changed into a contented mewing as he tasted the sweetness.

By the time they reached the end of Broad Street, where it joined the road that led into Bromsgrove Town, Tildy's embarrassment at being a public spectacle had increased unbearably.

'Master Bunegar?' She halted, and the constable turned to face her.

'What's amiss?' he demanded.

'Where exactly do we travel to now?'

'We'll have to goo into Redditch Town,' he told her. I've to deliver you to Joseph Cashmore, he's the constable there.'

'Must we then have to go through Bromsgrove?' she asked, and felt her neck and cheeks begin to flush. 'Only I'm feeling so shamed, being led like some dumb beast through the people.'

He scowled irritably, and taking a voluminous grubby handkerchief from his sleeve, wiped at the trickles of sweat on his face. 'God save us, Girl! Does you think that anyone is taking notice o' you?' he demanded harshly. 'God save us! They sees me taking paupers out from this parish nearly every bloody week. It's naught new to anybody. They'm not caring about you, or any other bloody pauper. They'm just glad to see the back on you.'

Tildy's streak of stubbornness came to the fore. '*No!*' she told herself fiercely. '*I've been humiliated by others too many times in my life. They might not care about me, but I care about myself, and for my baby. I'll not let us be made a spectacle of any longer.*' She faced the fat, scowling features before her, forcing down her inner nervousness, so that no trace of it betrayed her.

'If we've to go first to Redditch Town, and not directly to the poorhouse, then it's a better way across the heath-land to Broad Green, and then into the Hewell Woods and through the Brockhill Road. I know the bridle paths well, Master Bunegar, and in this heat it'll surely be a cooler way to take, than to go by the roads.'

Bunegar again mopped his puce-coloured jowls, and stared briefly up at the brazen furnace of the sun. His feet were already swollen and beginning to pain him, and the thought of the six miles hike along the rutted, dusty cart tracks to Redditch made him accept the girl's argument.

'Lead the way then,' he ordered. 'And let's get into a bit o' shade.'

They crossed the dry-baked scrubland of the heath, and

31

the woodlands welcomed and enfolded them with a fresh green coolness. From the edges of the bridle paths great carpets of slender-stalked bluebells stretched beneath the high branches of ancient oaks and elms, and the clustered heads of yellow Golden Rods waved in the soft breeze to keep measure with the white blossoms of wild cherry trees amid their massed guards of thorned brambles. Birds fluttered and sang, squirrels chattered and jumped in the high treetops, and tall grasses rustled and swayed to mark the passage of small wild animals. Tildy felt the peace of the woodlands enter her soul, and her weary spirit was eased. Inevitably she thought of the young man who had found her in these same woods, then lashed with rain and rent by lightning, the wind shrieking among the massive trunks and bending the shrubs to the ground. For it was on that terrible night when, the birth pangs upon her, she had run from her brutal husband to seek any refuge.

She felt a sudden intense yearning to see Davy Nokes again, to hear his soft rustic burr, and share his gay, infectious laughter. '*I should have stayed with him. Shared his life in that little cottage along by the canal,*' she thought regretfully. Then she berated herself for her foolish longings, '*I couldn't stay. I was a married woman with a new-born child. I couldn't stay and live in a state of sin all my days. It was my duty to take little Davy back to his father.*' Her full lips twisted in a rueful grimace, tinged with bitterness. '*And what happened when I did return. Only more misery, both for myself and for Tom Crawford. But then, it wasn't all his fault, I suppose. God knows I never loved or wanted him and he had little enough reason to remain with me in the Sidemoor and slave his days away at the nailing.*'

'Which way now, Girl?' William Bunegar's mood had also improved in the coolness of the woods, and he smiled at her as he pointed to the forked paths ahead of them. 'Which one does we take?'

'We go left, Master Bunegar.' Tildy led the way forwards until at last they came through the woods and saw in front of them a wide shallow cultivated valley, beyond

32

which rose the steep hillsides of Redditch in the parish of Tardebigge.

The town was a peculiar industrial/pastoral menage. Tall chimneys of needle mills belching clouds of oily black smoke over groves of fine trees. Red-brick clusters of alleys, courts and terraces divided from each other by stretches of green pasture and flowered gardens.

'Does you know that place well, Girl?' William Bunegar questioned.

Tildy shook her head. 'No, not at all really. I've not been there more than four or five times in my life,' her lips tightened, 'and the last time I was there was on my wedding day when my husband was put in the stocks and bombarded with filth by the locals and all our money was stolen. So it holds no fond memories for me.'

'Nor me neither,' the constable grunted dourly. 'I was here a few years since wi' the Bromsgrove Volunteers, when the bread riots was agoing on, and these bloody needle makers was trying to burn the whole town down. They'm like bloody wild animals, so they be.' He put his forefinger to his eye. 'Near got that knocked out, so I did. A bloody old 'ooman chucked a lump o' grate iron at me. Couldn't see through it for a bloody month.' He hawked and spat on the ground. 'That's what I thinks to Redditch. Cummon, Girl, the sooner we gets theer, the sooner we can leave it.'

They crossed the valley by way of a soft-surfaced grassy path and started to ascend. As she toiled up the long steep hill behind the puffing fat man, Tildy's body began to ache with weariness and the weight of the child seemed to increase with every step and every gasping breath. All she had eaten in two days was a single lump of stale bread. The fourpence the vestry had given her she had given in turn to a neighbour in payment of a small debt. The lack of food engendered a fast growing bodily weakness as Tildy's hunger gnawed at her, and the sun beating down on her bare head caused a dull pain to throb behind her eyes.

The road was almost empty except for a pair of mangy

dogs snarling across a stinking bone, and here and there tiny children playing about the doorways of the tumble-down houses watched over by ancient crones.

William Bunegar came to a standstill. 'God blast me! I'll ha' to catch me breath. This hill 'ull be the death o' me.'

Tildy gratefully seized the opportunity to sink down upon a doorstep. She loosened little Davy's shawl and checked to see that his rag clout was dry. The child's blue eyes stared vacantly up at her, and his body was hot to the touch. Tildy felt anxiety tug at her.

'You don't seem well, my lamb,' she crooned the words. 'Are you too hot in this shawl, is that why you lie so still?' For a brief moment she considered taking the shawl from around him, but feeling the soreness of her own face from the sun's burning, she was afraid to let the child's delicate skin be exposed to its fierce rays. The misery of despair threatened to whelm over her, but doggedly she fought the dark mood back, refusing to surrender to it.

'We'll soon be in a nice cool place, Davy,' she whispered soothingly. 'You shall soon have some nice pap to suck, and a comfortable bed to lie on. Mammy will care for you.' Ever since his conception the baby had been the focal point of Tildy's life. The helpless, needing creature upon whom she could lavish all the love that her bleak, affection-starved life had pent up within her.

'God blast it! You've not time to gi' that little bugger suck now.' William Bunegar's uncertain temper had again been soured by the heat and the hill. 'Let's get on and find bloody Cashmore.'

It was three hours later, and nearly twice that number of miles when Tildy, for the second time in her life, stood in front of the doors of the large decayed building that served as the poorhouse of the Tardebigge Parish. Light-headed with hunger, throat parched from the dust of the road, her body aching with weariness, she watched Joseph Cashmore, the taciturn parish constable, tug the bell-pull, and heard the discordant janglings echo within the entrance hall. At her side William Bunegar grumbled wheezily.

'God blast me, Cashmore, there was no need for me to ha' come here wi' you. I could ha' took my bloody quittance back in Redditch. You was harder to find than a bloody needle in the hay, as it was. Walked bloody miles looking for you, so I did. The least you could ha' done wa to bring the wench here yourself.'

Cashmore sniffed loudly, and grunted, 'It's the new arrangements. You needs both mine and his signings now.' Then ignored his companions.

The weather-beaten door creaked open, and a young shabbily-dressed, heavily-pregnant girl eyed them. 'New arrivals is it, Master Cashmore?' She grinned at Tildy. 'It'll be you and the babby, no doubt, me duck.' She pointed her hand towards Bunegar. 'I reckon there's a deal too much meat on that 'un there, for him to be wanting shelter.'

The girl's pert manner and bright laughing eyes made Tildy warm to her immediately, and despite her near exhaustion she smiled back. 'Yes, it's me and my baby who're come to stay.'

'Wheer's the master?' Cashmore grunted.

The girl held a finger to her lips. 'Shhh! He's otherwise engaged at the moment. He's giving Bible instruction to one o' the girls. Don't you goo disturbing him now, he'll get really roiled if you does.'

Her gamin-like cheekiness made Tildy want to chuckle, but Cashmore only loured dourly, and growled, 'You get him here right now, Girl. And button them lips o' yourn, or you'll be tasting the back o' me hand across your chops.'

The young girl squealed in mock fright, and fled back into the dark hallway shouting, 'Master Morris, the constable's here, and if you doon't come this instant he says he'll kill us all. Come quick, Master Morris. Come quick for Christ's sake, come quick.'

Her strong young voice resounded through the house and brought the tall cadaverous figure of the poorhouse master hurrying to the door. His rusty-black clothing was disarranged and he struggled to re-tie his cravat as he pettishly demanded. 'What's amiss, Master Cashmore? What's amiss?'

'Naught's amiss, Master Morris, except your britches be still undone.' The constable's heavy features were contemptuous as he handed the man the folded Notice of Removal. 'I'se brought you a fresh pupil for your Bible class.'

Ebenezer Morris scowled, and quickly fastened the fly-piece of his breeches, then took the paper in his spatulate fingers and scanned the fine copper-plate writing upon it. Recognition gleamed in his close-set eyes as he examined Tildy, and the tip of his tongue ran backwards and forwards along his thin lips. 'I knows this wench, Master Cashmore, she birthed that babby she's carrying in this very house.' He swung his eyes to the constable, 'Be the Tardebigge overseers agoing to make an appeal against this order?'

'No, they'll not do that,' Cashmore asserted positively. 'Lord Aston signed it hisself, so he arn't agoing to contradict his own order at the next sessions, is he. Now give Master Bunegar here a receipt for this 'un and her babby, and don't waste any more of our time. We'em busy men and have much to attend to, not like some hereabouts.'

The poorhouse master glared. 'I've much to attend to I'll have you know Master Cashmore.'

For the first time since she had met him Tildy saw Cashmore smile.

'Oh aye, I knows that well enough, Master Morris. No doubt you've got to gi' Bible lessons to all the rest o' the females in the house.'

The other man's thin lips worked furiously, but he thought better of making any retort, and only nodded to Bunegar.

'Please to step into my parlour, Master Bunegar, and I'll make out the receipt for you.'

'I'll step in as well, Master Morris,' Cashmore declared,

36

and again smiled broadly. 'No doubt you'll offer us a glass o' summat refreshing to help lay the dust of our journey.'

'No doubt I must,' Morris rejoined, with obvious bad grace. And the three men went into the house, leaving Tildy standing outside the closed door.

She stared at the cracked, warped panels and bitter resentment coursed through her mind. 'They treat us as if we were less than dirt, Davy,' she muttered to the sleeping child. 'Murderers and thieves are not served with such contempt. In their eyes we are lower than criminals because we have nothing. No home, no possessions, no money, no one to protect us. But it will not always be so, Davy. I swear upon my mother's grave, it'll not always be like this for us. Somehow I'll obtain all that we lack, and you shall become a gentleman.' She hugged the child fiercely, and he woke but made no complaint, only gazed blankly up at her.

'Hey? Young 'ooman?' The pregnant girl was beckoning from the end corner of the house. 'Come this way, youm not allowed to go through the front door. That's only for our lords and masters to use. We has to goo round the back way. What's your name, anyway?'

'Tildy . . . er, that is Matilda. Matilda Crawford. But they all call me Tildy.'

'I'm Hannah Knight,' the girl's pleasant face radiated friendliness, and again Tildy warmed towards her, 'and they all calls me Hannah. That's when they'm not calling me Dirty Whore or Lazy Slut or Loose-living Tail.' Seeing the shock on Tildy's face, the girl burst out laughing. 'And that's only what me Mam calls me. You should hear what the bloody preacher says.'

This time Tildy could not help but join in the girl's infectious laughter. She followed her new companion round to the rear of the house, which was a large cobbled courtyard with ramshackle outhouses enclosing it. Above the rear entrance door hung a big brass bell, and Hannah pointed at it.

'That's what we lives by here, my duck. It fetches us

from our beds in the morning, and sends us to work, and to pray, and to ate and to bed agen. The only thing it don't do, is to tell us when to shit.'

She kicked the rear door open and led Tildy into a big stone-flagged kitchen. It was the smell in that room which would always remain in Tildy's memory. A thick, heavy, all-pervading rancidity that seemed to fill and clog her throat.

Two withered, bent-bodied, mobcapped old women were standing at the long wooden table which dominated the centre of the room, cutting up a great chunk of rotting, fly-blown meat. Their mishapen, arthritic hands were thick with blood and filth and strong-stomached though Tildy had become during her sojourn in the Sidemoor, still the combination of nasal and visual assaults caused her to swallow queasily.

Hannah Knight grinned at her new friend's discomfort. 'You'll get used to the stink, Tildy. The meat arn't always so tod-rotten as this. Only Old Morris found a bargain. One o' Farmer Buckley's cows died, and the Marster bought it cheap. Only trouble was, it took a time afore it could be fetched here. All the carts was at the haymaking see. O' course, it being so hot lately the old cow had gone a bit stinking by the time we got it here. Still, Phoebe 'ull enjoy it. Won't you, Phoebe?' She shouted into the ear of the nearer of the two women. 'I say you'll enjoy this bit o' mate, won't you, Phoebe.'

The watery, red-rimmed eyes blinked hard as the old woman cackled with delight. 'Corst I shall. It'll taste as swate and tender as a babby's bum.'

'You sit here, Tildy, and rest yourself,' Hannah indicated a rough hewn wooden bench before the smoke-blackened inglenook. There a timber fire sparked and spat beneath a great chain-hung iron cauldron filled with grease-scummed water that bubbled out a strong fishy smell. 'Does you want a bit o' bread?'

'I'd like a drink of water first.' Tildy thankfully seated herself and welcomed the easement of her overstrained muscles as she rested the baby on her knees. She greedily drained the horn-tot of water that Hannah gave her, and as greedily drank two more fillings of the tot until her raging thirst was quenched. Then ate the thick slice of gritty brown bread. Heartened by the food, she smiled her thanks at Hannah, who had perched on the small side-seat of the inglenook.

'Where are the others? Or are we all who live here?'

'God love you, no, Tildy. There must be nigh on forty souls in Happiness Hall. Only they'm nearly all on 'um out working. Morris farms us out you see, to anybody who wants a bit o' cheap labour. The only ones left inside here today are the bed-ridden, the babbies and the Mad 'ooman. Old Phoebe here is the cook, and Old Sarah is the kids' night nurse, so they doon't goo outside to work. And me, well . . . .' She patted her swollen stomach, 'I felt real queer earlier on, so the mistress said I could stay inside today and rest a bit.' She paused for a while, and then added, 'Oh, and there's me friend Liza, Liza Parker. Her that Ebenezer Morris was giving the Bible instruction to.' She winked salaciously. 'I expect she'll be down presently.'

'I fear he's a hard master, Ebenezer Morris.' Tildy was remembering the previous brief interlude she had spent in this house. When she had seen no-one but the doctor, the overseers and Ebenezer Morris himself.

Momentarily Hannah Knight's youthful features transformed themselves into an older, harder, bitter mask, then the mask vanished as she laughed and winked again. 'Old Ebenezer is hard to some, my duck, and soft to others, it depends on which side of him you gets.'

'It arn't his side you young sluts gets by, is it. It's under the bugger,' a deep-timbred voice declared harshly.

A hatchet-featured, thick-bodied, middle-aged woman had come through the open door from the courtyard. She wore a black dress, white mobcap and a stiff-starched white apron that crackled audibly as she strode past the table and came to a halt by Tildy.

'You'll be the new 'un.' It was more statement than question. 'And youm a pretty 'un, I see. You'll be to Morris's taste, right enough. Another hedge-whore for him to rut with. You'll enjoy that no doubt.'

'I'm no whore!' Tildy met the cold eyes above her without fear. 'I've never sported with any man, and this child was born in wedlock. So I'll thank you to stop insulting me, whoever you might be!'

The woman's eyes narrowed menacingly, and the big hands tensed and moved to the massive bunch of keys that dangled from her waist. 'I'm Anna Morris, Girl. Wife to the master o' this poorhouse, and the first thing you'd do well to learn, is to keep a civil tongue in your head, and treat those who God has put above you with respect. If you don't, you'll likely get summat to lift the skin off your back.'

Although Tildy was gentle by nature she had ample courage and a fiery temper, and the implied threat of violence didn't deter her from speaking out against an injustice.

'I am civil to those who use me with civility, Mistress. But I'll not be called a whore by you or anyone else. I'm good-living, and always have been.'

Before the woman could reply a terrible throat-wrenching scream erupted from the room above, and the ceiling shook, casting flakes of rotting plaster as a thunderous pounding came down on the floorboards above it.

'Oh mistress, the mad 'ooman's got loose agen!' Hannah shrieked in sudden terror, and Anna Morris snatched the long iron poker from the inglenook and hurried from the kitchen, her urgent shouts resounding behind her. 'Morris! Morris! The madwoman's loose! Morris, wheer be you? The madwoman's got loose!'

Tildy heard doors slamming and the raised voices of both the Morrises and the constables. Then the frantic clumping of heavy boots up the stairs and along corridors. A young girl wearing only a thin shift, her long hair streaming about her almost naked shoulders burst from the house into the kitchen. She flung herself into Hannah's

40

arms, and the pair of them crouched in a corner, clutching each other tightly, whimpering and moaning.

The door of the room above crashed back against a wall and a series of the terrible screams volleyed through the house. Shocked and frightened, Tildy could hear the dull thudding of blows and kicks, and the gasping curses of the constables. The pounding on the floorboards became a maniacal drumming, the plaster flakes showered down from the ceiling and again and again the terrible screams split the air.

Tildy clutched her baby to her, and readied herself to flee. Then suddenly the screams were cut short, and a heavier impact shook the ceiling, and a repetition of hammer-blows against the floorboards. Then only the sounds of shuffling feet and Anna Morris's voice giving instructions to the men was heard.

'Thank God, it's over.' Tildy drew in a shuddering breath of relief, and for the first time old Phoebe and her colleague ceased cutting the meat and stared wonderingly at the ceiling. As they did so a large flake of plaster fell squarely on to old Phoebe's nose, and her expression of aggrieved amazement caused Tildy's jangled nerves to erupt in a brief fit of hysterical giggles. *Oh God, what have you brought me to?*' she questioned silently. '*What have I come to here?*'

Later, when everyone had calmed down and finally recovered from their frights, Hannah introduced Tildy to her friend, Liza Parker. The girl was not more than fourteen years, yet her breasts were those of a full-grown woman, and her manner far older than her age. She examined Tildy with knowing eyes, and repeated Anna Morris's sentiments.

'Youm really pretty, arn't you. Old Ebenezer 'ull be fancying you like mad, so he 'ull. You'll have a soft life here alright, wunt she, Hannah.'

The pregnant girl answered with a touch of malice.

41

'What if she does, Liza? Be you feeling jealous already? Does you want to keep the marster's little treats all to yourself?'

The other's face twisted spitefully. 'It's you who'se the jealous one, Hannah Knight. Jealous o' my small belly! No man 'ud look at you wi' that great lump youm carrying in front of you.' She flounced from the room, her breasts swinging and hips rolling, as she flaunted her body.

'Morris tries to make free with the women here, does he?' Tildy asked.

Hannah Knight's cheeky grin was forced. 'Well, you must know yourself, my duck, that us jolly poor'us girls be always willing for to open our legs, arn't us.' The grin faltered and fled, and the girl's bravado dissolved into a sad hopelessness. 'Once youm in this place, Tildy, youm reckoned fair game for any man who's got an itch between his legs. When we'em farmed out for work, then the contractors tries to have us, when we'em in here, then the men paupers tries to have us. We gets no peace from men's hungers, no matter wheer we be. Old Morris arn't so bad compared to a lot o' the buggers. At least he never tries to force us or serve us cruel, like some I could name. And his missis watches him like a stoat watches the rabbit, so he don't get too many chances to try and make free wi' us anyway. But the mistress can be a cruel bitch, at times. Her's strapped many a poor wench to the whipping-tree up in the attics, and beat her until the blood's run from her back.'

Tildy listened with a fast-growing pity. She didn't doubt this young girl's story, knowing from her own bitter experiences how cruel life could be for any young girl or boy who lacked parents or friends to protect them.

'Crawford? Crawford? Come along here,' Anna Morris's deep shouts sounded clearly in the kitchen.

'You'd best go quick,' Hannah advised. 'She don't like to be kept waiting. Here, gi' me the babby,' she held out her arms beseechingly. 'I needs to cuddle summat sweet and innocent.'

42

Tildy, normally so reluctant to give her child into another's keeping, recognized the deep-seated needs of the girl and gently handed Davy to her.

Anna and Ebenezer Morris were waiting at the open front door with the two constables.

'Master Bunegar wants a word wi' you, Crawford.' The poorhouse mistress seemed resentful of that fact.

Tildy looked enquiringly at the fat man, who was regarding her with a troubled expression.

'Well, Crawford, I just wanted to tell you, that I'se given Master and Mistress Morris a full account of your character, and how you'se come to be brought here. I'se told 'um that youm a good young 'ooman, and it's through no fault of your own that you'se come to such a sad pass.'

Sensing that the man truly meant her well, Tildy smiled at him. 'I thank you for that, Master Bunegar.'

Pulling the grubby handkerchief from his sleeve Bunegar wiped the gin-induced sweat from his face. 'It arn't brought me no pleasure to remove you to this parish, Girl, but there's naught else could be done. It's the law o' the land, so it is . . . the law.'

'The law. I know that, Master Bunegar,' Tildy's voice was detached, as though she were speaking mainly to herself. 'The law, no matter how cruel and unjust it is, has always to be obeyed. *The law*.' She spat the final words with such contempt and loathing that all those with her gazed at her in surprise.

'Well, that's that. I'll bid you all farewell, and wish you God Save, Tildy Crawford,' Bunegar wheezed, and made his departure in company with Cashmore.

Tildy stared after their bulky bodies, and the constable's parting wish re-echoed in her mind. 'God Save, God Save, God Save . . . ' She smiled bitterly. '*God won't save you, Tildy*,' she told herself. '*He's too busy caring for the rich and powerful. He's their God, not yours. You'll have to save yourself, Girl*.'

'Come with me, Crawford,' the mistress ordered and Tildy followed the woman up the wide staircase to the first

43

floor. They walked along the carpetless corridors past many closed doors, and up other narrower stairs to the attics beneath the roof-trees. In the end attic lit by a skylight was a wooden crate in which were piled musty smelling clothing, both male and female.

'Stand there, Crawford,' the mistress pointed to the floor space directly underneath the skylight. 'Strip your clothes off.'

'Why?' Tildy was instantly defensive.

Anna Morris frowned. 'It's the rules, Crawford. I has to check you for lice and crabs.'

'I've neither. I keep my body clean,' Tildy protested indignantly, but the other woman was obdurate.

'Just do as youm told Crawford, and get them clothes off. Because if you don't, I'll fetch Mister Morris and the porter, and they'll soon strip 'um off you.'

When Tildy still didn't move, the woman's manner softened a trifle. 'Look, Girl, rules is rules, and I has to obey them, just like you must do so. Youm in the poorhouse now, and in our charge, and if you trys to disobey us, then we has the power to make you obey. So stop acting like a silly young bitch, and let me gerron and do my job.'

'I can always walk out of this place,' Tildy said defiantly, and Anna Morris slowly shook her head.

'No, Girl, you can't walk out just as you please. You didn't come here, you was committed here. We'se signed for you, and youm parish property now, in a manner o' speaking, and so is your babby. The only way you can leave here, unless you got enough money to keep yourself, is with our Ticket of Release. If you trys to run away and beg a living, then you'll be whipped when youm caught. If you tries it twice, then you'll get the whipping and a sentence to hard labour at the Bridewell.'

'That's awful harsh. I didn't know that my case would be such,' Tildy argued as the full realization of her position struck home. 'I might as well be a criminal, as be treated this way. There's little difference between the two, it seems.'

The hatchet features creased into a joyless grimace.

44

'This is a hard parish to be a pauper in, my wench. You ought to have gained a settlement in an easier one if you chooses to be a pauper, and then be too soft to bear it.'

The aspersion on her courage stung Tildy. 'I can bear whatever I must,' she snapped, and took off her clothing. Naked, she stood proudly erect refusing to show how degraded she felt as the mistress scrutinized her intimate body for infestation. The bodily inspection was done, and the mistress lifted Tildy's gown and shift and carefully checked the inner seams of the garments for the eggs of lice. Then handed the clothing to the girl.

'Youm a clean wench, Crawford,' she admitted grudgingly. 'That's rare to find among them who comes here. You can keep your own clothes on, they'll not need burning arter all, like most on 'um does.'

While Tildy dressed, Anna Morris rummaged in the crate and pulled out a piece of grey cloth on which was painted two large letters in red, a capital 'T' and a capital 'P'.

'Here's your badge, Girl. You'll pin it on your right shoulder whenever you goes out from the house for any reason. If youm ever caught outside and not wearing it, then it's a whipping you'll get.'

For the first time Tildy's face began to burn. This cloth badge was to her truly the 'badge of shame'! The scarlet letters proclaiming for all the world to see that here was a pauper of the Tardebigge Parish. She turned the letters in her fingers, her eyes studying them, and a sickness growing in her soul as Anna Morris continued speaking.

'Whenever you meets the parson, or any o' the gentry or parish officers youm to halt and drop 'um a curtsey, and treat 'um with the utmost of respect. If they wants you to do a service for 'um, then you must do it cheerfully and willingly. That can stand for any o' the respectable farmers or suchlike as well.' She paused, and regarded Tildy's downcast head with an ambiguous expression. 'Look at me when I'm talking to you, Crawford. Don't act so sulky and shifty.'

Tildy forced herself to meet the other's eyes with a steady gaze, and tried not to betray in her face any of the humiliation she was feeling.

'Master Bunegar give you a very good character, Crawford. That's why I'm taking such trouble to explain things to you. If you does what youm told and behaves yourself, then you'll not find the life in here too bad, and we might even be able to help you to find a situation o' some sort to enable you to support yourself and your babby, and be free o' parish relief.

'But I'll warn you straight. Them, who in their wickedness tries to defy us gets their spirits broke, just as sure as I'm standing here before you. There's a lot of the wicked in here, as well as the poor souls who God has afflicted. Don't you go mixing in with the wicked ones, Tildy Crawford, because they'll surely drag you down to ruin.'

Tildy's sense of humour lanced through her sickness of soul. 'Some might say that I've already been dragged down to my ruin by my entry here, Mistress Morris.'

There was no spark of reciprocating humour in the poorhouse mistress, as she replied stonily, 'Oh no, Crawford. There's lower levels than this 'un, that's certain sure.'

Tildy dropped her eyes, and her lips quirked as a tiny voice in her mind whispered, '*Maybe so, but you'd need to use a shovel to find them.*'

'Follow me.' The Mistress led the way back down to the first floor, and Tildy dutifully trailed after her, clutching the pauper's badge in her hand. As they passed along the corridors of the rambling house Anna Morris tapped on the doors, identifying what lay behind. 'That's the master's room. My room. The women's dormitory. The sick room. The children's room. The men's dormitory. Storeroom. Storeroom. Spare room. The porter's room. The laying-in room . . . ' At one door she halted. 'This door is always kept locked, and you must never go inside this room unless me or the master tells you expressly to go in.'

'Is this the room where the noise came from earlier?' Tildy asked.

46

Anna Morris nodded. 'It's a sad case, Crawford. A young woman from a very respectable family. They'm all dead or gone abroad now, and her's got nobody to look arter her, until her brother comes back from Ameriky. I tried to persuade the vestry to pay for her to be kept in one o' the proper madhouses at Henley in Arden, but they says it would cost the poor rate too much, and it's a lot cheaper to keep her here. So here we must keep her.' Again the ambiguous expression came into her eyes, as she asked Tildy. 'Does you want to have a look at her?' Without waiting for any reply, and still with that unreadable expression as she stared at Tildy, the woman inserted a key into the lock, turned it, and gently pushed the door wide open.

The room was empty of all furnishings except for a canvas sheet placed on the bare boards against the wall to the right of the door. Sitting on the sheet was a young woman, naked except for a soiled night-shift now rucked up about her thighs. Her feet were bare, and a broad leather belt was strapped around her waist from which a heavy iron chain led to a staple in the floor next to the sheet. Her blonde hair was raggedly cropped close to her skull, and on her lap was a large feather which she continually stroked and turned, stroked and turned, stroked and turned. For some moments she seemed unaware of the opened door, then her head jerked up. Her face was layered with grimed-in dirt, and dried blood crusted her forehead and cheeks where it had fallen from the big, fresh-swollen cut in her hairline.

Tildy gasped audibly in surprise, 'But she is beautiful!'

She spoke truly, for beneath the layers of filth and blood and bruises was a delicately lovely face, with brilliant green eyes that glowed like jewelled orbs.

The green eyes stared at Tildy, and puzzlement flooded them, then they switched to Anna Morris, and the puzzlement turned to fear. The woman drew up her legs and cowered back against the wall, her broken-nailed hands pressed against her whimpering mouth.

'The poor thing! The poor suffering thing!' Tildy felt immeasurably saddened. 'Let's leave her be, Mistress Morris. She's frightened by us.'

Anna Morris gently drew the door closed, and relocked it. 'She's afraid of me because she remembered that I used the poker on her this afternoon.' There was no trace of any emotion in the woman's tone, merely factual statement. 'You saw that chain that's stapled to the floor?'

Tildy nodded, but Anna Morris had continued without pausing for any answer. 'She pulled it clean out of the floor this afternoon. It happens every now and again. She throws one of her fits and tugs and tugs at the chain until the staple gives way. You'd have to see her to believe it, her being such a frail looking cratur. Her's got the strength o' ten men when she gets violent, and given half a chance she'd kill anybody she could lay her hands on. That's why we had to handle her so rough today.' She shook her head regretfully. 'We don't do it for badness, Crawford. Although there's some in here who'll tell you that we does. It gives me no pleasure to hurt the poor soul.'

With startling abruptness her manner again became brusque and harsh. 'Go back down to the kitchen, Crawford. You can ask Hannah Knight to show you the way o' things in here. You'll be her bedfellow, so you may as well get used to each other. I'll put you to work tomorrow.' With that she was gone, rustling along the corridor and disappearing through a door midway along its length.

Tildy slowly walked downstairs to the kitchen, her mind struggling to come to terms with this strange environment she had entered.

In the kitchen Hannah Knight and the two old crones had been joined by a middle-aged man lounging on the bench at the table where the two crones still hacked at the stinking meat. When Tildy came in the man stared hard, then whistled through his decaying teeth.

'God fuck me, I knows this 'un here.'

48

Tildy returned his scrutiny, but did not recognize the dirty-red face, the thick mop of greasy grey hair and the burly, smock-clad body with the red pauper's badge on the right shoulder.

'I don't know you,' she answered. 'How is it you know me?'

He tapped his head with a black-nailed forefinger. 'They says that Crump is stupid, but Crump never forgets faces. I seen you wi' Davy Nokes last year. I seen you wi' him many's the time awalking the lanes.'

The mention of Davy Nokes gave Tildy an unexpected jolt, and her throat tightened.

The man's green-black teeth glistened, and his blood-shot eyes were only slits in his broad face as he wheezed with hoarse laughter. 'Oh I knows you alright, my duck. Crump arn't a man who forgets a fine pair o' tits. And you'se got a fine pair alright. Crump remembers them.'

His manner and words caused acute distaste to Tildy, but impelled by her own curiosity she could not help but ask. 'And Davy Nokes, have you seen him lately. How is he?'

The man leered at her body. 'He arn't wheer he can do you any good. But you doon't need to goo short, Girl. I'll gi' you what you needs atween your legs, and more besides.' He dropped a hand to his groin, and began to knead himself there. 'Crump's got just the thing for you, Girl. Crump 'ull make you scream.'

'Pay that bastard no heed, Tildy,' Hannah Knight called from the inglenook, where she nursed little Davy in her arms. 'Crump's the house porter, and he's the filthiest, randiest sod in the bloody parish. He'd block a sow-pig if he got half a chance. And that's about all he'll ever get to block as well, because no 'ooman in her right mind 'ud ever have him in her bed.'

The man scowled threateningly. 'You wants to watch your mouth, Slut, afore I punches it into a different shape for you.'

The pregnant girl was unafraid, and spat back fero-

49

ciously. 'You just try it, you filthy bastard, and I'll scream the bloody house down. If I tells the mistress that you bin trying to get into the window o' the mad 'ooman's room agen, then you knows what you'll get.' She turned to Tildy, 'That's why the door o' that room is always kept locked, Tildy, because this filthy sod used to goo in theer and get up to his tricks wi' the poor benighted soul.'

The man stared vacuously at the girl, and a slime of saliva dribbled from the corner of his loose-lipped mouth. Tildy suddenly realized that he was a 'natural', a simpleton. Hannah Knight noted the other girl's change of expression, and grinned.

'Yes Tildy, that's right. Crump here is a bloody natural. He's got a strong back and a weak yed. Only he's a nasty, filthy bastard wi' it. Arn't you, Crump?'

The man cursed vilely, but made no further threats of violence.

Hannan Knight cocked her head curiously at Tildy. 'What's this about Davy Nokes, Tildy?'

'Did you know him also?' Tildy met question with question.

The young girl nodded vigorously. 'O' course I did. Davy was well known in these parts, on account of him being a "lord o' the harvest". My old Dad was in his "company". Was you the woman who Davy took to live wi' him last year afore the harvest? There was talk that he'd took a good-looking woman, but not many ever got to see her.'

Tildy could only nod, her heart was momentarily too full of memories for her to speak.

'Why did you part from him? He was a real nice chap, and real handsome.'

Tildy shook her head. 'That makes no matter now, Hannah. But how is he?'

The girl's pert features became solemn. 'He's gone, Tildy. Got transported in the last sessions. Him and his mate, Tommy Gibson. They both got took up for poaching by the constable over Worcester way, and the next thing we

50

heard was that they'd both bin sent to Botany Bay for seven years. It must be true, because there's a family o' tinkers living in his old cottage now.'

Tildy made no reply, instead she walked out into the courtyard and paced up and down its cobbles while she struggled to come to terms with the shock of what she had heard. She refused to allow herself to give way to the futility of 'if only'. To some extent at least she was a fatalist, and accepted that the main pathway of life was pre-determined. It was God's Will that Davy Nokes should have been transported. Just as it was God's Will that she should now be here in the poorhouse. She drew a deep breath. 'So be it. Davy Nokes can now only ever be a sweet and tender memory. I pray that he will find happiness, wherever he might be. But my future still lies before me, and I've little Davy to think about. I can't spend my time grieving for what might have been.'

She went back into the kitchen, and smiled at Hannah Knight. 'I've no wish to talk any more about Davy Nokes, Hannah. Some day perhaps, but not now. So, come, tell me what I have to do to survive here.'

The girl cocked her head in that mannerism so peculiarly her own. 'By the looks on you, Tildy, the first thing you needs to do in order to survive in here, is to get to your bed and have a good sleep, afore you falls down.'

At her words Tildy realized she did indeed feel utterly spent.

'Come on, Tildy,' Hannah Knight cradled little Davy in one arm, and used her free hand to pull Tildy with her. 'Don't you argue back. Youm going up the wooden hills to Bedfordshire.'

'But my baby . . . ' Tildy protested weakly as they mounted the wide staircase.

'It's me that'll feed him and put him to bed. He has to sleep in the room next-door to our dormitory,' she cut off Tildy's protest before it was half-uttered. 'There's no use you argufying about that, my duck. That's a hard and fast rule, and not one o' the women in here has ever been let

51

break it. The kids goes into their room, and we goes into our'n.'

By now they were moving along the corridor, and resentful though she was at the rule of separation from her child, Tildy was forced into surrender by her own hopeless exhaustion. For the moment she was too tired and weak to be able to fight against this new stricture.

'Don't you fret about your babby, my duck. I'll care for him as if he was me own.'

Tildy found herself trusting and believing the younger girl, and experienced a wave of gratitude that she could, at least for a few hours, let herself forget the world.

'I think that you and I will become good friends, Hannah,' she said quietly, and the pert features beside her beamed radiantly.

'I reckon we'em that already, Tildy.'

The next few minutes were a dazed succession of having her gown drawn over her head, and her clogs and cotton stockings stripped from feet and legs; of being gently lowered onto a bed and covers being drawn over her; of her head sinking into a pillow, the ache of muscles soothing into relaxation; and of the sweet onset of dark, welcoming oblivion.

Chapter Five

The rising sun was an orange sliver on the mist-shrouded eastern horizon when Edward Watts shuffled into the darkness of the courtyard. He shivered in the chill air and sibilantly cursed the aching of his seventy-year-old bones as he took hold of the long hanging rope and tugged hard. The bell's clangour shattered the peace of the morning, and another day had begun.

Tildy reluctantly dragged herself to consciousness, and opened her eyes. Around her the women's dormitory came awake, coughing, hawking, spitting. Grumbling, scratching, belching, farting, in the cold, evil-smelling darkness. Beside her on the straw-filled mattress of the low wooden bed, Hannah Knight pushed her ponderous body upright and shook Tildy's shoulder.

A sudden sense of loss made Tildy's heart thump wildly, and frantically she felt around her, her eyes straining to pierce the gloom. Then, suddenly, remembrance came, and her pent-up breath vented in a gusty sigh of relief. Davy was in the children's room.

'Come on, my duck,' cooed Hannah. 'If we'em late for prayers, we'll get no breakfast.'

Hastily she threw aside the coarse sheet and coverlet and lifted her dress from the hanging nail at the head of the bed. Pulling it over her head she fumbled her way from the room and along the dark passageway. She was about to lift the catch of the children's room door, when she heard foot-steps, and saw the white apron of Anna Morris luminous in the light of the lantern she carried.

'What are you doing there, Crawford?' The lantern was

53

lifted high so that its yellow rays shone upon Tildy's face.

'I'm going to see my baby,' Tildy answered, quick resentment causing her to add, 'There's no law against that, is there?'

The other woman's grim face seemed to soften momentarily, but perhaps it was only a trick of the light, for when she spoke her tone was harsh.

'You've no cause to worry about your brat, Crawford. We provides a night nurse to watch over the babbies.'

This information caused Tildy's lips to curl scornfully. She had seen old Sarah the nurse the previous afternoon. A dribbling, half-senile wreck, who could barely totter upright.

Anna Morris brushed past and led the way through the door. The children's room was a shorter narrower version of the rectangular women's dormitory. Only instead of truckle beds its two long walls were lined with what looked like shallow wooden troughs, compartmented into individual boxes.

The night nurse was slumped on a low stool by the side of the fireless grate at the far end of the room. Her mob-capped head sunk upon her chest, snuffling in her sleep. On the floor by her side was a guttering stub of candle in its holder.

'Sarah Chapman!' the poorhouse mistress hissed angrily. And the shrivelled skull jerked upright, wobbling on its withered stalk of neck.

'You've all day to sleep in, you old besom. You should be awake now, that's what youm here for.'

Even while she scolded Anna Morris was moving along the wooden troughs, shining the lantern on the children in their boxes.

Peeping over her shoulder Tildy smiled as she saw Davy's wide blue eyes blinking into the light.

'There, your babby's alright, Crawford,' the mistress snapped curtly. 'You'd best get on downstairs and wash yourself before prayers. You can come and see to him directly after.'

54

The lantern's rays moved on, and then swung back to shine again into the box next to Davy's.

'Sarah Chapman, get here this instant,' Anna Morris's voice cracked out, and the old woman rose shakily to her feet and tottered to where the mistress waited. 'Look there, you old bat.'

Tildy moved also so that she could see into the box. A small boy, not more than four-years-old, was lying on his back with his lips drawn back into a feral grin, and his lifeless eyes fixed glassily on the light.

'Hold this, Crawford.' Anna Morris gave the lantern to Tildy and bent over the child, her hands gently straightening the already stiffening limbs, and moving to close the eyes. She pulled the coverlet up to cover the small face, and then turned to confront the night nurse.

'That kid has been gone hours since, he's got the rigor setting in,' she hissed furiously. 'You've bin sleeping all night, you useless old cow.'

The crone's toothless mouth trembled, and she quavered, 'No, I arn't bin sleeping. I knowed he was gone, but I didn't want to fetch you from your bed. There was naught you could do for him, when he was already dead, was there.'

'Youm a liar, Sarah Chapman. A bloody liar.' The mistress's big hands grabbed the front of the old woman's bodice, and shook the frail body until the shrivelled skull jerked backwards and forwards. 'I'se told you time and time agen to fetch me when one o' these kids looks near to death. I wunt have them dying alone. I wunt have it. Does you hear me, Sarah Chapman, I wunt ha' them dying alone.' Her voice rose until she was almost shouting the last words, and then she dropped her hands, and jerked her head in dismissal. 'Goo on. Get put o' my sight, afore I breaks your bones for you . . . '

The sight of death had not unduly shocked Tildy. She was a woman of her time, and death was an ever-present companion. A familiar dark reaper who cut down the youngest and tenderest in multitudes, and no one, no matter how strong, could know when they might not become part of his harvest. She gazed at the grey sheet moulding to the small still form, and a prayer formed on her lips.

'Oh Lord God, take pity on this poor child. Bring him to you to dwell in everlasting peace at your side, and forgive him whatever little sins he may have committed. For he was only a child, Lord, and knew nothing of evil and wickedness. Amen.'

'Amen,' Anna Morris's deep voice repeated, and she studied Tildy curiously. 'I didn't take you to be a God-fearing woman.'

Tildy gave a slight shake of her head. 'Truth to tell, Mistress Morris, I don't count myself to be a God-fearing woman. I suppose it's only my upbringing that causes me to pray, for I've no real faith that God ever listens to the poor. But then, I'm so ignorant I can't pass a judgement on these matters. I can't read nor write, I've never had schooling, you see.' She lapsed into silence.

For the second time that morning Anna Morris's grim features seemed to soften, but yet again her harsh voice dispelled the illusion.

'You'd best get on and make ready for prayers, Crawford. Don't sadden yourself about this child. Death's mark was already on him when his slut of a mother come into this place. When you goes downstairs send her up to me. Her name is Kate Reeves.'

Tildy had gone to her bed before the inmates had returned from their work, so now in the grey light of dawn she saw her fellows for the first time. They were gathered in the communal day room. It was a large, bleak oblong room with wooden benches ranged around its walls, now filled with the mob-caps and grey beards of aged men and women, while the younger people grouped in the room's centre, talking volubly, laughing and disputing. Curious stares and whispers greeted Tildy's entrance, but she ignored the comments directed at her, and instead searched for Hannah Knight. She saw the girl sitting on a bench across the room, and went quickly to her.

'Listen Hannah, which one is Kate Reeves? She's to go upstairs and see Mistress Morris in the children's room,' Tildy deliberately kept her voice low, aware of the cocked ears around her. 'God pity the poor woman. Her child died in the night.'

Hannah grimaced at Tildy's obvious concern. 'Don't you fret yourself for that whore, Tildy. It's good that God finally took pity on poor little Charlie and carried him off. The cow's got another two lying up there who'd be better dead, as well.' Ignoring Tildy's shocked face, Hannah shouted loudly. 'Katey Reeves? Youm to goo up to the kids' room. You'se just lost another half-crown a week.'

A woman, whose belly showed the first swelling of pregnancy, pushed through the crowd to stand in front of Hannah Knight. 'Be you making mock o' me, Girl?' she demanded. ''Cos if you be, I'll take the bleedin' eyes out o' your yed.' Kate Reeves was a handsome, wild-haired slattern. Gypsy-like with her gaudy coloured dress and shawl, and swarthy complexion.

'No, she's not making mock of you,' Tildy intervened, puzzled by the woman's aggression. 'I brought the message from Mistress Morris. She wants you to go to the children's room.' Her voice dropped, and she explained gently, 'I fear that your child died in the night.'

Reeves's eyes measured Tildy, and she sneered to the room at large. 'We've got a proper lady come among us, arn't we. Look how neat her is, and how nice her spakes. Well, Lady Muck, I'll goo up to the kids' room, but if youm making mock o' me, then it's your eyes that'll be bleeding.'

The woman's manner disgusted Tildy, and she merely nodded, then ignored her.

With a final muttered oath Kate Reeves left them and Tildy turned her attention to her fellow inmates. The women ranged through all the age groups, from the very young, to the very old, and several were obviously pregnant. But the males were nearly all mere boys or

57

elderly greybeards, only one or two of them were mature men. Tildy queried Hannah Knight about this discrepancy, and the girl grinned pertly.

'Well it's bloody simple to see. They gives the proper men Outdoor Relief. They won't have 'um in here, if they can help it. They causes too much upset among the women.' The girl giggled. 'Old Ebenezer likes to keep us all to hisself, worse luck. I could enjoy a handsome young buck now and agen.'

Tildy smiled, and again looked about her. She saw that the clothing, although shabby and worn, was at least patched and darned, and that everyone had clogs or boots on their feet. The strident red shoulder badge was universal on smocks, coats and gowns. She whispered to Hannah. 'The people here look more comfortable than our paupers back at the Sidemoor.'

The girl wrinkled her nose and quipped. 'I bet they doon't smell no sweeter though.'

Both of them giggled, and then Hannah Knight said seriously. 'It arn't really so bad here, Tildy. At least we ates regular, and in the winter we has fires in the grates. It's better than lying out under the hedges in the cold and rain.'

Tildy looked pensively around her, heard the foul language, smelled the fouler air, saw the sadness and hopeless resignation, and gently shook her head.

Ebenezer Morris came into the room, followed by Crump the porter.

'Be silent, all on you.' The poorhouse master stood on one of the benches so that he could overlook the congregation. The coughs and snuffles and whispering hushed for only a moment, then seemed to redouble their intensity.

'Let us pray,' Morris glared about him until every head was bowed in the posture of submission. 'Oh Lord God, look down upon these miserable sinners, these sinners who have fallen by the wayside of the Christian road to Heaven . . .' Ebenezer Morris addressed the Deity as an equal, and saw no reason to include himself among the sinners. 'Cast

58

the wickedness from their hearts, Lord, and wash the evil blackness from their immortal souls. Teach them to be humble, and to be grateful for the kindness and charity of their betters. Teach them to be industrious, and to show a glad obedience to those set above them . . . ' A particularly loud and harrowing bout of coughing caused Morris to glare at the offender and point towards the door. 'Get out into the yard, John Roberts, youm not fit to stand in the sight o' God, making such a shameful commotion.'

The old man singled out, shuffled shamefacedly away, and Morris went on, 'Do not be too hard on John Roberts for interrupting our prayers, Lord. The old fool knows not what he does. He's gone senile these last weeks . . . '

A spluttering of laughter came from the younger women at his words, and Morris scowled at them. 'I'll be warming your backsides wi' my stick iffen you don't shut your rattle this instant. Forgive these harlots, Lord, and help those you have set above them to bring them into the paths of righteousness.'

Tildy bit hard on her lips, fighting the overwhelming impulse to join in the laughter.

'Blessed be your name, Lord, for ever and ever, Amen.'

Morris finished with a flourish, and shouted, 'Shift yourselves and get your breakfast ate. There's work waiting for you.'

A gust of chattering and laughter swept across the room as the master stalked out, and the younger people ran to fetch their eating bowls and spoons, and pushed and jostled to be first in the queue at the kitchen door.

On the long table was set a great iron cauldron, half-filled with oat gruel, and next to it were piled chunks of brown bread. Wielding a ladle Anna Morris stood behind the cauldron flanked by the old cook-woman. One by one the paupers filed past, holding out their earthenware bowls to be filled with gruel, and taking a chunk of bread from old Phoebe's dirty hands. They settled to eat wherever the fancy took them. Some to the day room, some to the dormitories, others into the courtyard.

59

Tildy went to the children's room. The box next to Davy's was now empty. Laying aside her bread and bowl of oat-gruel, Tildy lifted her child and kissed his soft cheeks, mouth and forehead. 'Don't take him from me, God.' She murmured. 'Don't take him, as you took that poor little soul in the night.'

She became aware of other small children sitting up in their boxes. They stared at her with wide, curious eyes, and apart from the crying of a baby further along the room, not a sound came from any of them. She smiled at the child nearest to her, a tiny girl. 'This is Davy, and I'm his mother,' she explained to the solemn-faced mite. 'And what's your name, Honey?'

The child made no reply, only remained silent, her large eyes fixed on Tildy's face. The sounds of footsteps echoed hollowly from the corridor, and the children who were sitting up in their boxes, now lay back and closed their eyes. Tildy frowned uneasily.

Anna Morris came into the room, and nodded at the empty box where Charlie Reeves had died. 'I never let the dead 'uns stay in the same room wi' the living, if I can help it. There's some poorhouses that I knows of where they leaves the body lying for days. But I don't approve of that.' She clapped her hands sharply, and like disciplined soldiers the children tumbled out of their boxes and stood stiffly in front of them. The woman clapped again, and the children filed silently out of the room and along the corridor to the stairs.

'I always make them wash their heads and feet under the yard pump,' Anna Morris remarked. 'Then they says their morning prayers and has their breakfast in the kitchen. We only got a couple o' babbies here at present, and I makes their mothers tend to them. Unless they'm orphans 'o course, then I gets a wet-nurse for them.' She looked at little Davy. 'I see by the look of him, that youm a caring mother, Crawford. That's not so common in here as you might expect it to be. Some of the bitches we gets in here don't care a damnall for their kids.'

60

'The little boy who died?' Tildy asked. 'What was it that ailed him?'

The other woman shrugged. 'Well, he'd got a fever, but I don't reckon that it was that what he died from. Like I said afore, Katey Reeves had crippled the cratur wi' beating him. It 'udden't surprise me none, if it warn't a result of her beatings.'

Tildy found it hard to credit her own hearing. The woman before her appeared totally unmoved.

'But that would be murder!' She burst out. 'How could you let a child be served so? Surely the doctor should have been called to him, and the constable told what had happened?'

Anna Morris's hatchet features were bleak. 'Youm talking foolish, Crawford. Who gives a damnall what happens to a pauper child? D'you think that the doctor 'ud give a bugger? Or the constable? And like I said, he had a fever. So that's what 'ull be noted as the cause o' death.'

A sudden fear loomed in Tildy's mind. 'What about my baby? Fevers can spread, he could take it as well, and so could the other kids in here.'

The thick shoulders shrugged once more. 'Kids can be took sick anywhere, Crawford. So can we all. There's naught we can do about that, no matter where we be, it's God's will if we'em struck down by disease. And when you asks me how I could let a child be served so ill by its mother, then you'd best be able to tell me how I could prevent that? Kids have to be taught their place, and how to keep good conduct. And if they sometimes gets hurt in the teaching, then that's the way of it. It's always bin like that, and always will be. God sees fit to let some get beaten worse than others. Mothers can do what they wants wi' their own children, just as husbands can do what they wants wi' their own wives. No one has the right to interfere in them matters. I'm not saying that I'd stand by and let a kid be beat to death in front of my eyes, but even in here, I can't watch over them all the hours of the week . . . ' She hesitated, and once again it seemed she softened. 'I do what

I can for them that's in here, Crawford. But in all truth, there's not much that I can do, most o' the time.' The momentary softening was replaced by the bleakness. 'Soon as you've tended your babby, come downstairs. You'll be going out wi' the weeding gang today.'

Chapter Six

The horseman reined in his mount and regarded the peaceful country scene. The fields were somnolent beneath the hot sun, cows fed placidly under the shade of hedgerow trees, their long tails swishing to drive off voracious tormenting flies, and in the distance a shepherd slowly walked among his browsing flock, his dogs slinking low to the ground at his heels. More than twenty miles to the south the blue humps of the Malvern Hills dominated the Worcestershire Plain – to those who had seen no others, these ancient hills were veritable mountains, but the horseman had spent part of his childhood among the Highlands of Scotland, and to him the Malvern Hills were not impressive. The countryside also was too soft, too verdant for his taste. He preferred the wild stark beauty of moor and crag.

A labourer came trudging up the track towards the horseman. He wore the ubiquitous smock and billycock hat, and balanced a long-handled shovel and mattock across his shoulder. As he neared the mounted man he slyly studied the funereal black clothing and top hat, noting that the material was shiny and threadbare with age, the cuffs and high-winged collar of the white shirt frayed, and the highlow boots cracked on top and broken-soled beneath. He evaluated the spavined horse and the thin, under-nourished body of the man astride its splay back, and lastly took notice of the ancient leather bag strapped on top of the worn canvas saddlebags.

'*He'll be a bloody quack!*' He dismissed the stranger

scathingly, and would have passed without acknowledgement if the horseman had not hailed him.

'Tell me, Man, where's the road for Redditch? I seem to have missed my way.' The speech held an accent which the labourer recognized. '*He'll be a bloody scotch quack!*' Not halting, he jerked his thumb rearwards.

'Many thanks,' Lucas Royston said aloud, and added in his mind. '*Surly hound!*'

The manners displayed by the English labouring population towards strangers had irritated the young medical man ever since he had crossed the border on his long journey from Edinburgh to the small Midlands town he now sought. A wave of homesickness coursed through him as he kneed his mount into plodding motion and continued his journey. Many weary miles later, the hilly town came into view. He sighed gratefully and patted his mount's drooping neck.

'That'll be it, I'm thinking. Not much further now, my friend, and then you shall rest, and I shall relieve my thirst.' He used his tongue to explore the dry, stale-tasting insides of his mouth. 'This damn English gin leaves a man terrible dry and sour,' he told his horse. 'I don't know why the damned surly bastards cannot take whisky, like civilized men.'

As he neared the clusters of buildings on their steep slopes he came to a bridge, before which roughly-dressed men were lethargically using hammers to break piles of stones into smaller fragments, which more men strewed into the ruts of the road with their long-handled shovels. Beyond the bridge the road ran on between rows of trees and occasional buildings, then rose sharply upwards between closely packed roofs, high chimneys and crooked gables.

Royston reined in beside the men. 'This is Redditch, I take it.'

Unshaven, sweating faces peered at him with hostility. He suppressed the irritation their expressions roused within him. '*I should be accustomed enough by now to these English bastards not to let them rile me,*' he told himself, and singling out a burly heavily-muscled man from the group he asked. 'If this is Redditch, then can you direct me to the house of Doctor Alexander Pratt?'

'Who might you be? And what d'you want wi' old Pratt?' The man thrust his bullet head forwards aggressively, and his companions left off working and watched with an air of pleasurable anticipation.

Lucas Royston's thin, pale face was saved from plainness by a pair of well-shaped lips and remarkably fine dark eyes. Now those lips tightened and wariness crept into the dark eyes. There was an atmosphere about this group which made him uneasy. 'No matter,' he snapped, and kneed his horse to move on, but the bullet-headed man stepped forwards and gripped the horse's bridle with his hairy hands, bringing it to a halt.

'I asked you a question,' he growled. 'We likes to know who foreigners be, when they comes here, arn't that so, Lads?' He grinned at his workmates, who in their turn moved to cluster close around the mounted man.

Lucas Royston was now acutely uneasy as he glanced about him. These men were a ferocious looking bunch, even allowing for the normal low standards of physical delicacy and refinement among the labouring classes. He blustered to hide his unease.

'You'd be wise to let my horse's head go free, Man, and stand aside. Or I might be forced to crack your head.'

Bullet Head laughed grimly. 'This cove's a regular dung-hill cock, arn't he, Lads. Look at him ruffling his hackles, and crowing so bold.'

The young Scot's fiery spirit rose. 'I told you to let go,' he spat out, and leaned forwards in his saddle to strike the man's hands from the bridle. But even as his out-stretched arm fell, so Bullet Head's hands moved faster. Lucas felt his wrist painfully gripped and twisted, and before he could react he was jerked head first from the saddle and brought thumping heavily down onto the dust of the road. His horse squealed in shock as a shovel-blade smacked hard against

65

its bony hindquarters, and it bolted into an ungainly gallop across the bridge, followed by a barrage of shouts and stones.

On hands and knees Lucas looked down at his top hat in the dirt beneath his eyes, and his pale face flamed with anger. 'Bloody barbarians!' he howled. 'Bloody savages!' He came to his feet and threw himself at the bullet-headed man. The blade of a shovel speared between his legs and he tripped and came sprawling again, the breath exploding from his lungs as he hit the road hard with his chest. Jeering laughter filled his ears, and blood-red rage filled his head. Again he came to his feet, again launched himself at Bullet Head, and again was tripped and sent sprawling before his fists could find their target. Almost sobbing with fury and frustration he sprang up once more, swinging his fists wildly at the taunting laughing faces tormenting him on all sides.

'He needs cooling down, Lads.' A voice shouted, and in seconds he was flattened beneath a swarm of heavy bodies, then lifted effortlessly by a score of hands, and he shouted in terror as those hands swung in unison and pitched him bodily through the air. Earth and sky span giddily, then he hit cold water. His mouth and throat filled and in blind panic he fought desperately to find air, thrashing with arms and legs against thick fronds of weeds and soft yielding mud. His head broke surface, his feet found purchase and he coughed and retched and struggled to drag air into his straining lungs. He shook his head to clear his confused senses, and realized that he stood in waist deep water a few feet downstream of the low stone parapet of the bridge. His attackers lined that parapet, howling hysterically with laughter, some with eyes streaming, others doubled over holding their stomachs as they jeered at their saturated victim.

Clawing the slimy green tendrils from his hair and eyes, Lucas waded to the bank and pulled himself from the water. He stood on the grassy bank and fast-spreading puddles formed around his feet.

'Welcome to Redditch, Cully.' Bullet Head yelled. 'You'll find old Pratt's house across the road from the Unicorn Inn. Goo up the hill theer, and when you reaches the chapel, then take the road west from the crossroads. You can't miss the Unicorn, it's only a few yards down along theer. Pratt lives across from it in the house wi' four steps.'

Still laughing and applauding the men left the bridge and went to resume their work.

Lucas squelched back onto the road and picking his battered top hat from the dirt, crammed it onto his head. Slowly he removed his boots and poured the water from them, scraping out the mud that had oozed into them with his fingers. He glared furiously at his assailants, but knew that he could do nothing against the weight of numbers, and contented himself with muttered insults and promises of future revenge before dejectedly beginning to trudge towards the town centre. A hundred yards on he found his horse, standing with a drooping head under a roadside tree, and saw thankfully that his meagre belongings were still intact in their various bags. Remounting he slowly ambled up the steep hill, keeping his eyes frontwards, and his expression stonily indifferent to the grins and comments of loungers and passers-by as they saw his bedraggled appearance.

He found Pratt's house and left his horse hitched to the post at the side of the four steps that led up to the ornately porticoed front door. Water still dripped from his clothes as he hammered with the brightly burnished brass knocker until the door shook under the force of his blows.

'Goddamn me, d'you want to break the blasted door?' Sallow-faced, lanky-bodied, Alexander Pratt opened the door and his jaw dropped in surprise. 'Goddamn me, is it you, Lucas Royston? What . . . in Hell's name . . . has befallen you?' He spoke in clipped staccato bursts.

The young man angrily told him, and the full-bottomed tie-wig on Pratt's narrow head slipped slightly as he clapped his hand to it. 'Damn worthless scum . . , Every man-jack of them . . . Damned yard-land men . . . Ought to be whipped and put to proper work . . . Damn parish pays their wages for 'em . . . Damned scum!' He paused, and tutted his disgust at his caller's appearance. 'Goddamn me . . . you look like a drowned rat . . . Come in, Boy . . . don't stand there, like a booby . . . Tom? Tom? Take the gentleman's horse round to the stable .... Take his baggage to the guestroom . . . And you, Sir, go upstairs with him . . . When you've changed yourself . . . come to my study.'

Some time later, wearing his only other suit of clothing, as shabby and threadbare as his first, Lucas Royston faced his maternal uncle in the booklined study with its leather-topped table, two wooden armchairs and assorted glass jars of gruesome looking anatomical specimens.

Alexander Pratt regarded his deceased sister's son, and only living relative, with mingled doubt and distaste, pursing his thin lips and rubbing his long nose with steepled forefingers. 'Be seated, Nephew.' He indicated the chair facing his own across the desk. 'Now, what is to be done about you?'

The younger man stared with surprise. 'I do not understand you, Uncle. What do you mean, what is to be done? My mother, only scant weeks before her death, said that you had intimated in your letters to her, that I could always be sure of obtaining the post of your assistant here in Redditch!'

'How could you be that?' Alexander Pratt snapped. 'There are scarce enough respectable patients for a decent living to be got by we doctors who are long established in the town. Plenty of poor patients to be had . . . that's for sure . . . But that sort of practice we don't serve . . . It don't serve at all . . . Doctor Taylor has a son . . . name of Hugh . . . he is his father's apprentice to the profession . . . But I've no need of an apprentice . . . No need at all.'

Lucas Royston's pale face flushed. 'Then why did you write to my mother, that you would employ me, Uncle? And why indeed, did you reply to my own letter of last month, and invite me here?'

The edge in his voice caused the older man to look more sharply at him. 'Don't use that tone with me, Nephew . . . It won't serve . . . It won't serve at all.'

Lucas forced himself to speak placatingly. 'I mean no offence, Uncle. But I confess, that I am grievously disappointed in your reception of me. I am sure, that if they were still living, my parents would share that disappointment.'

'Then understand one thing, Nephew . . . That disappointment that you mewl of . . . would be caused to them by your own follies.' From a drawer in his desk he took out a sheet of folded letter pages. 'These are some of your mother's letters to me.' He tossed the sheaf onto the desktop. 'They detail how your father's assets were squandered by you . . . Dissipated in less than three years . . . to pay your gambling debts . . . and all those other debts created by your drunken roisterings!' He leaned back in his chair and drummed his fingers upon the faded brown leather of the desk. 'When I suggested to my dear sister that I might someday offer you employment . . . It was on the understanding . . . that you would bring capital . . . into the practice . . . But now you have no capital . . . You have wasted all the monies your father left . . . and what is more . . . you have not gained your Degree in either Medicine or Surgery from the University of Edinburgh . . . Over the years . . . you broke your poor mother's heart . . . and for my part . . . I firmly believe that through your wicked follies . . . you helped to drive your mother into her untimely grave . . . That is why I invited you here, Nephew, to tell you that fact in person.'

The flush on Lucas Royston's thin face was now engendered by shame. 'I fully accept that your strictures upon my conduct are justified, Uncle. And truly I have great remorse for what I have done, or failed to do . . . ' He faltered, and tears shone in his dark eyes. 'But my dear mother's death cannot be blamed on me. It was a malignant quinsy of the throat that occasioned her demise, not I.

Several others took it and died also in her village. There was naught that I or anyone else could do to save her. It was God's will . . . ' He coughed long and hard, and regained full control of his emotions. 'But she is gone to be with father, and that is an end to the matter . . . God rest their souls.'

Sorrow also patterned Alexander Pratt's features. 'Amen to that,' he breathed softly. 'It is a sadness to me that although my sister and I were close when young, we grew apart in later life.' He looked speculatively at his nephew. 'It is the remembrance of that closeness that your mother and I once shared, that prompts me to consider if I might still help you in some way, Nephew. Despite your previous misconduct.'

Sudden hope emboldened Lucas Royston. 'Only hear me out, Uncle. I know that I have not gained my Degrees from the University, but I am still more than competent as both Physician and Surgeon. After all, I have at times studied under Gregory, Duncan, Monro, Rutherford and Hamilton. This last year I worked as an assistant in the dissecting room under Andrew Fyfe, the "Prosector" himself. And also I have walked the wards at the Royal Infirmary, the Dispensary and the Lying-In Hospital. But I've been near to starving these last months, Uncle. I could not physically remain any longer in Edinburgh without funds. But I'll wager that I'm as good a doctor as any country apprentice. Surely there must be something for me somewhere.' His eyes glistened with urgent intensity. 'I am asking you to help me, Uncle, not only for myself, but also for the sake of my parents' memory. I know that I have been a drunken sot, and a waster. But only help me now to make a fresh start in my life, so that I may not shame the memory of my parents by miserable failure . . . ' His voice faltered, and again he coughed, then went on. 'I want only the opportunity to redeem my past sins, and in my mother's memory do some good in this world . . . '

He fell silent, his eyes fixed on the other man.

Alexander Pratt's steepled forefingers rubbed up and

down his long nose for a while longer, then he emitted a short dry chuckle. 'Goddamm me, Nephew, you'd do well to try the theatre for a profession.' The cynicism in his voice was matched by that in his eyes. 'But I always remember what Shakespeare had to say . . . "Methinks he doth protest too much". Or was it, "She doth protest too much" . . . No matter . . . Either gender would fit the bill.'

Some inner prompting caused Lucas Royston to bite back the hot protestations of sincerity that his relative's words would normally have provoked from him. He inwardly acknowledged the older man's perception. He had admitted to himself many years past that he did possess all the dramatic instincts of an actor, and that his sentiments of remorse, and desire to make amends for his misconduct, while sincerely felt at the time of his expressing them, normally only lasted just so long as it took him to recover physically from his excesses, and to restore his financial resources.

Now he met Pratt's cynicism with what he hoped was an air of wounded nobility, but said nothing, waiting for what was to follow.

Pratt's short dry chuckle came again. 'I see that you know when it is best for you to keep a still tongue in your head, Nephew. That is a strong point in your favour.' His shrewd eyes flicked over Royston's face and figure. 'You've that poetic air about you that women so extravagantly admire. Especially foolish Old Maids . . . and lusty widows. That also could be a strong point in your favour . . . if it were to be used wisely.' His steepled forefingers were all the time rubbing his nose, and now, as new ideas came to him, the tempo of that motion quickened. 'Taylor and his son . . . they've improved their practice lately . . . Acquired some wealthy patients. It's the son that's the attraction for the women . . . young peacock that he is . . . No good as a surgeon . . . but quite the dandy . . . All stays, scents and whiskers . . . You might well check his gallop though, Nephew . . . Yes, indeed you might.' Suddenly the doctor jumped to his feet. 'You will wait

71

here, until I return . . . Call for Tom if you need anything in the way of refreshment . . . I'll not be away above an hour.'

As soon as he heard the street door open and close, and saw his top-hatted uncle pass before the study window, Lucas shouted for the manservant. 'Have you any whisky in the house, Tom?'

The man shook his head. 'Only spirits we'se got be rum and brandy.'

'Then bring the brandy,' Lucas ordered grandly. 'And make haste, Man. You move slower than a tradesman's hearse.'

A little later, with two glassfulls of finest French already warming his throat and belly and a third glassful nestling in his hand, Lucas was pondering what his uncle might have in mind for him.

'Whatever it might be, it'll not enable me to enjoy too much of this, that I'll wager on.' He took a sip of his drink, savouring the delightful hot bite on his tongue and the rich aftertaste it left in his mouth. 'Uncle Alex must do well enough though, if the quality of his cellar is anything to go by.'

A pretty girl twirling a silk pagoda parasol over her poke-bonneted curls tripped daintily past the window, and the young man softly whistled his appreciation. 'D'you know, Lucas, I cannot help but feel that in some aspects this town might prove to be to your taste,' he murmured. 'And face it, Man, you've precious little to hope for elsewhere. At this point in your misspent life, you really do require Uncle Alexander's help, no matter how grudgingly he might bestow it, or how scant it may prove to be.'

Lucas knew only too well that the profession of medicine did not automatically bring wealth to its practitioners. It took long years and much good fortune to establish a lucrative practice, and the more wealthy patients tended to be reluctant to employ a young man to treat their ills, when so many older, and thus more experienced practitioners were available. Not to mention the swarms of quacks, wise-women, cunning-men and charlatans who by promising miracle cures attracted the desperate and the credulous.

Lucas Royston could never be classed as an altruist concerning his profession. Yet he truly did have interest, and an inherent ability in its practice. But he enjoyed wine, women and song, good food, good horses and the excitements of gambling, and to ensure himself those things was capable of exercising both the utmost selfishness and the utmost self-discipline.

His hand reached for the bottle on the desk by his side – then withdrew.

'I'd best not risk upsetting the old fellow by drinking all his fine brandy,' he muttered. 'I fear he wouldn't take too kindly to coming back to an empty bottle and a full nephew.' He chuckled.

Before the hour had elapsed Alexander Pratt returned, and Lucas Royston congratulated himself on his forebearance as he saw his uncle's eyes measuring the amount left in the bottle. He decided to strike first, and display some show of independence of spirit.

'Well now, Uncle, shall I make my farewells and march on to seek my fortune elsewhere? I've sufficient pride left not to beg for your charity.'

The cynical smile twitched at the older man's thin lips as he reseated himself, and shouted for the manservant to bring him a glass and a fresh bottle of brandy. But he waited until they were alone again before answering.

'You may help yourself to what remains in that bottle before you, Nephew. And while doing so . . . pay careful heed to what I say . . . I am prepared to aid you . . . for my sister's sake.' He lifted his own glass in the air. 'Here's to her memory.' He drank deeply, and smacked his lips in satisfaction, then centred all his attention on the young man in front of him.

'There has lately been displayed a great concern in this area . . . about the plight of the poor . . . during this time of distress in trade and industry . . . The Earl's lady herself has given much thought to that plight . . . and so have

73

many other gentlefolk . . . At their request the select vestry of Tardebigge Parish, has decided to re-establish the position of "Surgeon to the Poor", and has advertised this post some weeks since . . . which means that they will contract a doctor . . . to care for the paupers hereabouts . . . and pay his fees from a poor rate.'

Noting his nephew's dawning expression of rejection, Pratt hurried on. 'Wait, take thought before you spurn this idea . . . the income is small of necessity . . . after all, paupers are of little or no value to the parish . . . But at this time . . . with the interest of the countess and the other gentlefolk . . . so engaged with the plight of the poor . . . a poetic-looking young doctor . . . who performed sterling service . . . and created a good personal impression . . . might well lay the foundations of very powerful local connections.'

'If that is the case, Uncle, why do you not apply for the post yourself? And has the younger Doctor Taylor made application, I wonder?' Lucas was totally unenthused by Pratt's words. He had seen in Edinburgh what it meant to be a surgeon to the poor. Filth, little money, hopeless cases. The unfortunate man so engaged jeered at and scorned by those of his brethren with more respectable and lucrative practices.

Pratt was scathingly contemptuous. 'What a worldy-wise young rogue, you think yourself to be, Nephew . . . Of course none of we established men want this post . . . for obvious reasons . . . but if I were in your shoes . . . I'd jump at it . . . Because of the reasons I have already given to you . . . And what do you have to lose? Nothing! And what could you gain? Why, the favourable notice of the local gentry . . . even perhaps, the attention of the countess herself . . . Also, it will keep your belly filled . . . and clothes on your back . . . and a roof above your head . . . Remember, Boy . . . beggars can never be choosers.'

Lucas was already reluctantly recognizing that he had no real choice. If he refused this chance, then he would not easily find any other work, and he was already in desperate straits. But stubbornness caused him to make a further objection.

'If, as you say, Uncle, the select vestry have advertized this post, then there will surely be other applicants, with perhaps their degrees obtained. After all, I am not the only young doctor with empty pockets and holes in his shoes.'

His uncle's dry chuckle rasped out. 'There are indeed many young doctors with ragged britches, many older ones as well, come to that. But you are the only one of them who is my nephew, are you not . . . And I have good influence . . . with the select vestry . . . They meet to decide the issue in four days time . . . Do you wish to apply for the position, Nephew?'

Lucas took a long swallow of brandy, and replaced his empty glass on the table. He grinned ruefully. 'Of course, Uncle. Here's one beggar at least, who cannot attempt to be a chooser.'

The older man's head bobbed in satisfaction. 'So be it, Nephew. I suggest that you spend the next four days in familiarizing yourself with the parish . . . Also, I own a house in a street called Silver Street, quite close to the Chapel Green. You will rent it from me, and it will serve both as your home and your surgery.'

'I am most grateful,' Lucas told him, with veiled irony.

His uncle airily waved aside those thanks. 'No need to try and gammon me, Nephew. I'm too old and wise a bird to be so easily decoyed. However, I wish to impress upon you, that as far as public knowledge goes, you hold your degrees from the University of Edinburgh.' He paused meaningfully. 'Degrees in both medicine and surgery . . . Is that understood, Nephew?'

Lucas could not help but laugh aloud, and silently applaud his uncle's slyness. 'Of course, Uncle, and yet again, I am most grateful for your advancement of my qualifications!'

Chapter Seven

'I am in truth a country youth,
unused to Lon--don fashhhions.
Yet virtue guides and still presides
O'er all my steps and passshhhions.'

The large fat singer strained deafeningly for the high
notes until beads of sweat stood out on his purpling face.
Lucas Royston, sitting bolt upright on a straight-backed
wooden chair, tried to maintain a smile of pleasure on his
lips as he endured the tuneless cacophony assaulting his
eardrums.

'No courtly leer, but all sincere.
No bribe shall evveeer blind me.
If you can like a country wight,
An honest maaan you'll find meeeeee.'

Lucas glanced surreptitiously at his fellow guests in the
stifling hot drawing room. They all, old and young, male
and female, bore the same expression of strained appreciation, and even as he looked two of the younger women
lifted their fans to hide irrepressible yawns.

'Tho' Envy's tongue with slander hung,
Do oft beeelie the countreee,
No men on earrth, boast greater worrrth,
Or more extend their bounteeeee.'

Seemingly endlessly the fat man roared on, and Lucas
tried to ease his torment by letting his mind wander.
The select vestry had interviewed the candidates for the
post of 'Surgeon to the Parish Poor' that morning. There
had been five of them including Lucas. All uniform in their

threadbare seediness. Lucas's own interview had been ludicrously brief. The vestrymen had merely ascertained that he was the nephew of Alexander Pratt. Had accepted without any questioning his own claims of professional competence and experience, and had handed him the certificate of contract binding him for a period of twelve months on his part, but not binding them to guarantee his retention in the post.

The vestry chairman, a hard-featured needle master, told him bluntly. 'We'se bin made to employ a surgeon agen our better judgement. In my opinion we'em only mollycoddling a lot o' shiftless idle scoundrels by doing so. So listen well. We pays you only for the time you spends on our business. We pays only for the simplest and plainest medicines. We doon't pay for high-diets and port wine and brandy and such like. You must keep the costs down as low as can be done. You only gets paid for treating the paupers in the poor'us or them outside it who brings you a ticket written and signed by us allowing for you to treat 'um.

'You presents your reckonings on the last Sat'day in each month to the vestry, and we looks 'um over and settles our accounts wi' you on the fust Sat'day o' the month following. That's all for now. I'll bid you good day.'

Lucas had left the meeting, contract in hand, with the glum certainty that in the eyes of the select vestry of the Tardebigge Parish he counted only as a necessary evil. That afternoon a messenger had come to his uncle's house bearing an invitation to this musical evening he was presently enduring. His uncle had insisted he attend, since the hostess was one of the gentleladies who had forced the vestry to employ him.

'After all,' his uncle had sneered. 'She has the right to see what sort of fish her and the other cats have brought in.'

Lucas sensed eyes upon him, and for a brief embarrassed moment wondered if he had been talking aloud to himself in his reverie.

The eyes belonged to a woman sitting opposite him on

77

the far side of the singer and his fiddle-playing accompanist.

> 'A noble mind is ne'er confined,
> To any shire or natiiooonnn.
> He gains most praaiiisse,
> Who best displaaayyysss,
> A gen-ner-ous edoooocaaationnnnnn.'

The singer was now sweating so heavily that visible rills trickled down his purple face and dripped from his multiple chins onto the vast bulge of his white waistcoat, creating sodden spreading patches. By keeping his gaze on the man, Lucas was able to switch his focus repeatedly to the woman opposite. She looked to be about thirty years old. Too strong-featured to be pretty, yet she was not un-handsome and her lowcut green evening gown displayed her fine breasts to advantage. A small white-lace cap sat on her hair, which she wore in the antique Roman style, its dark tresses brought together, pinned at the back of her head and terminating in ringlets falling to her neck.

She sat erect, her hands holding a small folding fan on her thighs, and her body seemed tensed, as if she were about to spring up and commit some act of violence. Again her eyes sought him, and this time he met and held them with his own. The candles' light wavered, casting shadows across her broad brow, and Lucas sensed rather than saw, contempt in her steady gaze. Surprised, he broke contact and looked downwards at the polished oak floor.

'Why contempt?' he wondered. 'Why should she feel contempt for me?'

> 'While ran---cour rolls,
> In nar---row souls,
> By nar---row view discerniiinnng.
> The tru--ly wise, will only priiiizzzze,
> Good man---ners, sense and larnnnniiinngggg.'

A burst of relieved applause greeted the ending of the song, and a middle-aged lady rose from her armchair and faced the audience. She was Mrs Amelia Boulton, the doyen of the artistically inclined among Redditch society.

A be-feathered, over-rouged, overweight, very wealthy widow, who despite her affectations possessed a kind heart and a generous spirit. Her myopic, belladonned eyes fluttered furiously as she held out her plump, be-ringed, white-enamelled hands, gesturing for silence.

'Ladies and gentleman, honoured guests, dear friends,' her voice was breathy and gushing. 'I know by your applause that the singing of Signore Botecellano was as delightfully pleasing to your ears, as it was to my own.' She smiled roguishly at her audience, displaying porcelain-white false teeth, and again fluttered her eyelids furiously. 'Therefore, I intend to presume upon the Signore's kindness, and insist that he regale us with one song more from his immense repertoire.' Too short-sighted to see the visible despair her words engendered, she waggled a finger playfully at the sweating fat man. 'No, Sir, you shall not say me nay.'

She curtseyed daintily, and begged coquettishly. 'I beg of you, Signore, do pray oblige your humble supplicant.'

Signore Alfredo Botecellano, born Alfred Botts of Huddersfield, bowed low, swore vilely beneath his breath, and graciously consented to oblige. He stroked the velvet lapels of his lavender-coloured coat, ran both hands through his long, thinning Italianate curls, struck a dramatic pose and wheezily began.

'It was a lov--ver and his lass.
With a Heeyyy and a Ho, with a Hey Non Ne No,
And a Hey Non Ne No . . .'

At last the song was done, and Signore Botecellano bowed his farewells. Card tables were set up by the maids, and some of the company settled to play whist. The remainder took refreshments from the laden buffet table, and congregated in small groups, exchanging smalltalk and laboured witticisms.

Lucas Royston stood against the heavy drapes of the windows and toyed with a glass of wine. Waiting for the tedious hours to pass until he could politely take his leave.

The company were mainly local minor gentry with their womenfolk, their coats and gowns a rainbow of colours in the light of many candles. The young doctor knew that he should make an effort to mix, that these were the people he needed to become his patients, but he could not bring himself to make that effort. The low spirits engendered by the morning's interview still weighed upon him.

Amelia Boulton noticed him standing alone and came fluttering her way to his side. 'I declare, Doctor Royston, what must you think of me? So shamefully neglecting my duties as your hostess in this manner. Let me introduce you to someone.'

He allowed himself to be led in her wake and found himself bowing to the woman in green.

'Allow me to present Doctor Lucas Royston, Anna my dear.' Amelia Boulton gushed. 'Our new-come medical gentleman. Doctor Royston, allow me to present, Mrs Anna Coldericke.'

'Your servant, Ma'am.' Lucas bowed low, as the seated woman regarded him with calm grey eyes, and when Amelia Boulton fluttered away, she observed.

'You did not enjoy Signore Botecellano's singing, Doctor Royston, are you not then a lover of music? Or conversely, are you a lover of music, and for that reason rightly thought the man ungifted?'

For a moment he was taken aback by her directness. Ladies in polite society normally waited for the man to initiate conversation. He opened his mouth to reply, but unable to think of any truthful words which would not make him appear contemptuous of his hostess's choice of entertainment, only coughed, and closed his mouth again.

The grey eyes glinted with pleasure. 'I see you are lacking the adroitness of a diplomat, Doctor Royston.'

A quick resentment, fuelled by the memory of her previous contemptuous regard of him, caused Lucas to rejoin stiffly. 'I lack the ill-manners to criticize an entertainment that my hostess has been gracious enough to provide for my own entertainment, Ma'am.'

'Are you implying by that statement, Sir, that I lack good manners?' she asked tartly, yet still the grey eyes glinted mischievously.

He found himself becoming flustered. 'No, I do no such thing, Ma'am.'

'Indeed, Sir, the sincerity of your denial is hard to credit.'

He struggled to maintain a calm dignity. 'My sincerity has never before been inpugned, Ma'am.'

'Has it not, indeed?' She smiled with an acid sweetness. 'I'll wager that there are those now lying in their final resting places, who could indeed give good reason for doubting your sincerity.'

'What do you mean?' His resentment overflowed and he spoke forcefully enough to attract curious glances from those nearest him.

'Pray, Sir, be good enough to modulate your tone. You are drawing attention to us.' Anna Coldericke smiled mockingly at him, and then went on in a low voice. 'What I mean, Doctor Royston, is that many who have believed in the sincerity of physicians and surgeons promises to cure their ailments, find themselves in their graves as a result of those cures.'

With an immense effort Lucas controlled his temper and his voice, and answered her with a careful softness. 'You seem determined to force a quarrel on me, Ma'am. For what reason I cannot begin to conceive. Therefore, I think it best that I take my leave of you.'

A fleeting expression of disappointment crossed her face. 'No, Doctor Royston, I pray you do not do so. I meant you no offence. My tongue is always sharper than my intentions.'

Her suddenly apologetic manner unbalanced Lucas. He had never met anyone who could in such a short space of time, reduce him to such confusion. 'Then why, Ma'am, do you act towards me in such a manner?'

Sadness clouded her grey eyes and she shook her head. 'I confess, Sir, that at times I find it hard to understand why I

81

behave as I do. It was not always so. Mayhap it is simply boredom. Boredom with myself, and my life, and with all these good, honest, dull dull dull people who now surround us.'

She rose to her feet, and Lucas found that she was tall enough to meet his eyes on level terms. 'I'll bid you goodnight, Doctor Royston. I pray you make my excuses to our hostess. You may tell her that I am assailed with a sudden megrim.'

Then she was gone, moving swiftly and gracefully through the crowded room and out of his sight. He stared after her, unsettled by their brief encounter, until a pleasant-timbered male voice sounded in his ear.

'I fear that our Mrs Coldericke has left you somewhat bemused, Sir.'

A young sombrely clothed man, wearing the short-queued wig, plain white front and neck-stock of a cleric was smiling at him.

'John Clayton, curate to Reverend the Lord Aston, vicar of this parish. Your servant, Sir.' The young man bowed as he introduced himself, and Lucas returned the bow.

'Lucas Royston. I am honoured to make your acquaintance, Reverend Clayton. I intended to leave my calling-cards later this week, when I had settled my lodgings sufficiently to receive visitors.' He regarded the cleric with a professional interest. The man appeared to be an exceptionally fine physical specimen. Ruddy-complexioned, deep-chested, broad-shouldered, the muscles of his thighs and calves bulging out against black breeches and stockings. 'You mentioned Mrs Coldericke?' Lucas hinted, hoping to learn more about the woman.

'Oh yes, the widow Coldericke,' Clayton laughed softly. 'I could not help but hear your exchanges with her. Forgive me for it, I beg of you. She is a most interesting lady, is she not. Our local blue stocking. But I fear that her views on the deity and His servants here on earth would not meet with the illustrious Hannah More's approval.' His attractive-ugly face became animated with pleasure. 'I must confess that the widow Coldericke's views on most matters do not meet with the approval of our town's leading citizens either, but for my own part I greatly admire the lady. She is unique amongst us in that she will openly voice her opinions, no matter how unpopular those opinions might make her within polite society.'

'She is fortunate that she does not have to depend on that society for her income,' Lucas observed, a trifle grimly. 'I personally could not afford to offend in that manner.'

Clayton again laughed softly. 'But that is precisely one of the reasons why I admire the lady. In all truth, she cannot really afford to do so either. She has a small Ladies' Academy of which she is sole proprietress. Whenever she offends one or other of our local people of influence, they invariably withdraw their daughters from her establishment.'

Lucas smiled, his mood lightening under the influence of his companion's good temper. 'Then how does the lady continue to function as a teacher?'

'Oh, the withdrawal never lasts for too great a length of time. The young women hereabouts adore the lady, and give their Pas no peace until they relent and permit them to renew their attendance.'

'She sounds a most pernicious influence.' Lucas was only half-joking.

'Indeed she is, Sir,' Clayton admitted delightedly. 'A veritable Jacobin, who constantly rants of the Rights of Man, on the one hand, and on the other advocates something she terms the Rights of Women, and rails against the iniquities of man concerning his mate. Do you know, when the news came of the King's divorce action, the widow Coldericke hung an illumination in her window, wishing long life, happiness and a successful defence to Queen Caroline.'

Lucas's shocked disapproval, hid his desire to laugh. 'I consider that to be most unseemly, Sir. It does not befit a lady to behave in such a way. It was an insult to His Majesty.'

The cleric grinned like some mischievous schoolboy. 'Indeed it was, Sir. But not unjust, for all that.'

Despite his attempt to maintain a disapproving air, Lucas was forced to grin himself. 'That I will admit, Reverend Clayton. Loyal subject of the Crown though I am. You really do have a warm regard for her, do you not.'

The other nodded. 'I do, Sir. She has a warm heart, and a truly Christian sense of charity. She is ever ready to help the fallen and the afflicted. I myself have a small Academy for Gentlemen and she aided me greatly when I first mooted my intentions of this venture. There is not an ounce of real malice or cruelty in her. I count myself her friend and am honoured to do so.'

'I hope that I shall be able to express similar sentiments concerning the lady before too long.' Lucas told him politely.

Clayton hesitated a moment, then said. 'I understand that you are our newly-appointed Surgeon to the Poor.'

Lucas mockingly half-bowed. 'I hold that doubtful honour, Sir.'

The other's face was now very serious, and his words came hesitantly. 'Forgive any suggestion of presumption on my part, Doctor Royston, I intend none, I do assure you. But gossip travels fast in this town, and gossip has it, that you hold your degrees from the University of Edinburgh.'

Again Lucas half-bowed. 'I have that honour, Sir. I hold degrees both as Surgeon and Physician.'

'Hmmm.' Clayton appeared to ponder on this for a moment. 'But that is a most prestigious School of Medicine, Sir, and held in the highest esteem throughout the whole of Europe.'

Lucas grinned in malicious enjoyment. 'In other words, Sir, how can it be that a man holding such prestigious degrees, is now holding the lowly post of a pauper's surgeon.' He grinned again at the other man's obvious discomfiture. 'It is easily answered, Sir. In one word. Drink! That wicked demon drink!'

84

John Clayton's mouth rounded, and his rugged features displayed his shocked embarrassment. 'Ohhh, I see.'

'I am happy that you do, most Reverend Sir.' Feeling greatly cheered, Lucas Royston bowed low, and took his leave. 'That's one in the eye for you, Uncle dear,' he chuckled silently. 'You lying old bugger.'

Chapter Eight

The field was foul with weeds, its six acres bestrewed with
couch grass, thistles and docks, their tough roots raping the
soil, and choking the softer clovers and grasses.

The twenty-odd human beings spread out in a line
moved slowly across the surface of the land, bent low to the
earth, grubbing up the strangling weeds with their bare
hands.

By the gate that gave access to the top of the sloping field
two men stood watching the toiling line inching its way
upwards towards them.

'Just look at 'um, 'ull you. Bloody Paupers! They arn't
got a good hour's work in 'um, let alone a day's.'

It was the older man who complained so disgustedly.
Grey-haired and lined with sixty years of hard living, but
still erect and strong-bodied, carrying little excess fat
beneath his brown riding jacket and gaitered, cord
breeches. He lifted his hand to the brim of his squat-
crowned top hat to shield his gaze from the sun.

'Look at that bugger on the bloody end theer – if he
moves any slower he'll be mistook for a dead 'un. They's
bin here since seven o' the clock, and they's not claned
more than a squared rood measure yet.'

He pulled a brass-cased hunter watch from his waistcoat
pocket and stared at it, muttering calculations beneath his
breath.

'It'll take the idle buggers until bloody Michaelmas to
clane this field the rate they'm gooing at it,' he grumbled.

His companion regarded him with ill-concealed
amusement.

The older man saw the smile. 'Oh, it's all very well for you to laugh, Caleb Hawkes, but it arn't you that has to pay the buggers, is it.'

Hawkes's light-blue eyes danced with inner laughter – '*You don't pay 'um a penny-piece, you bloody old miser*,' he thought – but made no reply. He was a tall man and rangily-built, wearing similar clothing and headgear to the farmer, but his white linen collar was open and instead of a cravat and neck-stock, he wore a bright red kerchief loosely knotted around his sun-browned throat. A long scar ran down his forehead, bisecting his left eyebrow and furrowing his cheek, imparting to his lean face a piratical quality which many women found sexually attractive.

Near the centre of the weeders Tildy worked beside Hannah Knight who, despite her advanced pregnancy, had been sent to the weeding gang that morning as a punishment for being cheeky to Ebenezer Morris. The girl straightened and massaged the small of her back. 'I'll be bloody glad when I'se birthed this little 'un,' she complained. 'The weight makes me back ache summat chronic.'

Tildy looked sideways at her friend, and brushed away a loose wisp of hair from her eyes, leaving reddish smears of dust on her sweat-damp skin. 'Rest yourself a while, Hannah. It's not good for you or the baby to overwork yourself at this time.'

'Overwork herself? That lazy cow? You both wants to get a bit o' bloody work done.' The elderly smock-clad man on his hands and knees next to Tildy glared at them irascibly. 'Can't you two lazy bitches see that George Holyoake is standing up at the top theer? Does you want to gi' him cause for anger by lazing about while he's awatching us? Gerron wi' your work, both on you.'

The women and girls who made up the majority of the line, instantly reacted to his words.

'Who the bloody hell does you think you am, Tommy Snipe, acalling us lazy bitches?' Kate Reeves led the onslaught.

87

'Yes, you stupid old sod, just shut your cakehole!'

'What's bloody old Holyoake agoing to do then, Snipe? Bloody gi' us the sack?'

'He canna sack us, Snipe. He arn't our master, only your'n.'

'We doon't get paid for this, you old bastard!'

'No! We 'as to do it for bleedin' sour beer. That's all we gets out on it, sour beer, mouldy cheese and stale bread.'

'So you shut your rattle, you old bugger!' Kate Reeves hurled a clump of docks at him. The clump caught the man on his ear and knocked his shapeless hat flying.

He creakily clambered to his feet, his face flaming with anger. 'I'll knock your bloody yed orf for that, you slut!'

'Does you hear him, girls?' Kate Reeves shouted. 'Does you hear the old bugger athreatening me?' She also rose to her feet, and mockingly squared up to Tommy Snipe, fists raised like a pugilist. 'Come on then, you bullying sod. Come on and try it,' she challenged, half-laughing, half-serious. 'I'll tap your bloody claret for you. Just you come on.'

The women laughed and jeered at the old man. 'Goo it, Snipe! Put your fists wheer your mouth was! Let's see you show your mettle!'

One of the younger women crept up behind Snipe, and rammed a great bunch of weeds into his face. He coughed and spluttered and shouted in rage as the dirt of the roots went into his mouth, nose and eyes.

'Get him, girls!' Kate Reeves screeched, and hooting and shrieking with excited laughter the women danced around the old man, showering him with weeds and dirt. He cursed and bellowed and staggered in pursuit, blindly lashing out at his tormentors. Tildy found herself laughing also, so comically grotesque were Tommy Snipe's contortions as he fought the empty air. He swung a mighty roundhouse blow with such force that he spun round and tripped and went sprawling. Immediately the women were on him. Smothering him with their weight, stuffing his mouth full of docks and grass, and rolling away almost helpless with laughter.

'Look what the buggers be doing to my servant!' George Holyoake couldn't contain himself, and set off down the field, bawling at the women to stop. Caleb Hawkes, laughing uproariously followed the farmer down.

Tom Snipe was on his knees, spitting dirt and shreds of weed from his mouth and George Holyoake savagely cuffed the balding grey head.

'You damned old fool!' Putting his hands on his hips he glowered at the paupers, all women and girls except for a few old men and small boys. 'You'll be laughing the other side o' your ugly faces when I gets through wi' you,' he threatened furiously.

Intimidated by his mood, the women exchanged nervous glances and remained silent.

'You'd best tell me who started this. You knows that I'm an overseer o' this parish. It'll only take a word from me, and you'll be treading the mill in the Bridewell,' Holyoake fumed. 'Iffen I don't find the one who started this, then it'll goo hard wi' all on you. I'll promise you that.'

Caleb Hawkes strolled to join the group. 'Hold hard, George, t'was only a bit of a skylark they was having.' He smiled broadly. 'They'll work all the better for it.' He was conscious of the female eyes upon him, and he swaggered a little. 'Come up, Tom.' He lifted the ganger easily, showing off his strength. 'There now, George, here's Tom Snipe back on his feet, and as good as new. The finest gangerman in the county. There's no harm bin done.' The light blue eyes scanned the women's faces and his teeth gleamed as he saw in some of them the softness of admiring invitation. There was one pair of dark eyes, however, that held only a quizzical amusement. His vanity piqued, Hawkes asked, 'And who might you be, Pretty 'Un?'

Tildy met his question with silence. Instead she spoke to George Holyoake, telling him politely. 'Your servant brought this upon himself, Master Holyoake. He insulted us for no reason. The girls were only funning with him anyway.'

The Farmer's beef-red face was contemptuous. 'Insulted you, did he? Well let me tell you summat. Poor'us sluts can't be insulted, my wench. They'm too low in the world to be insulted.'

His cruel words reverberated in Tildy's head, and sheer impulse caused her to reply sharply. 'Well, I'm not yet low enough to continue working for the likes of you.' She turned to Hannah Knight. 'I'm going back to the house, Hannah, I'll do no more work for this man. Are you coming with me?'

The girl's eyes wavered, and Tildy recognized her fear. She patted the slender shoulder. 'I'll see you back there later.'

Without another word she pushed past the farmer and walked up the field towards the gate.

For a few seconds Holyoake was motionless, his mouth gaping in stupefaction, not able to believe that a poor'us woman could so calmly treat him in this manner. Then he turned and bellowed after her.

'You get back here, you pauper slut! Get back here this instant!'

Tildy walked on, giving no sign that she had heard him.

He shook his clenched fist at her back. 'You'll get a bloody thrashing if you leaves your work, Slut! I'll make sure o' that. You'll get the bloody skin flayed off your back.'

Tildy continued to walk steadily on, through the gates and along the rutted cart track which would take her westwards over the Shadow Hill past the ancient Bentley House through the tiny hamlet of Bank Green and on to the Webheath Liberty some two miles distant. As the shouts behind her grew fainter and died away she began to feel nervous about the retribution her impulsive action might bring down upon her head. For a brief moment she slowed, wondering whether she should return to the field and ask the farmer's forgiveness. Then angrily thrust the notion from her mind.

'No, I'll not go back. I swore to myself in the Sidemoor that I'd never again willingly submit to other people degrading me. I've had too much of that already in my life. No matter what George Holyoake threatened me with, I'll not bow my head to him. He cannot hang me, can he. And I'm not feared of a whipping.'

Bolstering her courage by summoning her inner resources of pride, she again lengthened her stride and went on.

In a field to the right she saw a party of haymakers at work. The scythesmen, smockless and shirt-sleeved, tumbling the lush, heady-scented grasses in great swathes with their long curved blades. The straw-bonneted women following close behind their menfolk, tending the crop with wooden rakes, singing in unison beneath the sun, while under the great elms of the hedgerow the small children and babies played or slept. Memories of how she and Davy Nokes had spent long happiness-filled days working thus, brought nostalgic yearnings.

'*I'd love to see him again. He was the kindest, sweetest man I've ever known. I wonder where he is at this moment. He's swinging a scythe somewheres, that I'll warrant. Laughing and golden in the sun.*'

She came to a dip across the track where a small stream gurgled gaily down from a low hill. Hot and thirsty, Tildy left the roadway and climbed up the hill to the shady clump of woodland where the spring which fed the stream welled upwards in limpid coldness among ancient-lichened rocks. She cupped her hands and drank deeply, then slipped off her clogs and rolled up the skirts and sleeves of her dress, so that she could wash herself. She gasped at the chill shock of the water on her hot skin, revelling in the sense of clean freshness that it imparted. Then lay back on a patch of greensward, letting the hot rays of the sun dry her.

Myriads of insects hummed in the air, mingling in soothing melody with the songs of birds and the gentle

91

soughing of breezes among the leaves. The peace of the day entered her, and imperceptibly she drifted into sleep . . .

'Wheer in Hell's name 'as you bin?' Ebenezer Morris's tallowy face was greasy, and the blackheads and pustules around his nose magnified as he thrust his face aggressively close to Tildy's. 'I said, wheer 'as you bin? Whoring wi' some man, is that what you bin adoing?'

His breath filled her nostrils, and she jerked her head back from its foulness.

'I sat down to rest, and fell asleep,' she explained.

They were standing in the kitchen of the poorhouse, and behind the master, George Holyoake was glowering at her. Caleb Hawkes was sitting on the bench in front of the ingle-nook, his back to the room, hands locked together, arms bridging his parted knees as he leaned forwards, staring into the smouldering fire. Anna Morris stood, a silent onlooker, with her back to the courtyard door.

'Master Holyoake has bin waiting here for nigh on three hours,' Morris growled. 'And he's got more important things to do wi' his time, than to hang about waiting for the likes o' you to show your face.'

'I'm sorry he's had to wait. I didn't mean to fall asleep.' Tildy, confused by this attack which had begun the moment she had entered the kitchen, tried to excuse herself, but Morris didn't want to listen.

'Hold your tongue! Youm in trouble enough, wi'out making it worse by giving me a pack o' lies.'

'I'm not lying!' Tildy's spirit rebelled against his brutal hectoring. 'And I've committed no sin by falling asleep. That isn't a crime, is it?'

'Hark to the saucy bitch, Master Morris.' George Holyoake invited indignantly. 'She's got more badness inside her than Newgate's knocker holds in.'

'Don't worry about it, Master Holyoake. We knows how to deal wi' that sort here. We'll soon beat the badness out of her bones,' the Poorhouse Master promised grimly. 'And if she persists in defying us, then she'll find herself in the house o' correction for a few months. There'll be no starch left in her arter that!'

'But what have I done that is so bad?' There was genuine puzzlement in Tildy's question. 'I refused to continue working because that man there insulted me for no reason. That's all I've done.' She pointed at the farmer. 'Ask him yourself, if you don't believe me.'

Morris's close-set eyes were merciless. 'Master Holyoake has already given me a full account of what happened this day, girl. And I knows him to be a Godfearing, honest man. So you'se got two choices in front of you.' His tone held a hint of pleasurable anticipation. 'We can either whip you here, for your badness. Or we can send for the constable and have you brought in front of the justices. That'll cost you a whipping and twenty-one days' hard labour in the house o' correction.' He paused, measuring the effect of his threats, then added spitefully. 'And your babby stays here.'

'No!' Tildy burst out, and a sickening dread washed over her. Her throat went dry and she swallowed hard. 'You could not do that,' she uttered. 'You could not separate me from my child.'

The master's eyes glowed with triumph. 'It's the law, Girl,' the triumph entered his voice. 'Your babby's old enough to be full-weaned, arn't he. And we 'udden't be doing our Christian duty by him if we was to let him be taken into such a den o' wickedness as a jail, 'ud we. The justices 'ull make an order that he stays here in Tardebigge Parish while youm in Worcester Jail. They knows that he'll be well cared for here.' He paused once more, savouring his sense of victory, then demanded. 'So what's it to be, Girl. Does we whip you here for your badness, or does you goo in front o' the justices? Spit it out, what's it to be?'

'Neither!' Caleb Hawkes came twisting lithely off the bench to confront the master. 'Youm doing neither of them things to her.'

All four stared at him in shock. George Holyoake was the first to recover.

'What's you mean by this, Caleb? This is naught to do wi' you. She's no kin o' yourn.'

Hawkes's lean face was hard and challenging. 'No George, the wench is no kin o' mine. But I'm making this summat to do wi' me.'

Tildy, her mind still grappling with the dreadful prospect of being forcibly separated from her child, could only stare bemusedly at her new defender.

'But why be you sticking up for her?' Ebenezer Morris wanted to know.

'Because she's done nothing to deserve being sent to jail nor being whipped neither. I listened to what George Holyoake told you when we came here, and I held me peace, because I thought you'd have sense enough to see that he was exaggerating everything. That's the sort o' cove he is, and youse known him long enough to know that he always makes bloody great mountains out o' molehills.'

'But you was theer,' Holyoake protested furiously. 'You saw this hell-bitch attacking poor old Tom Snipe. And you heard her atrying to get all the others to stop working. You was theer, right behind me, you heard her becalling me.'

'That's right, George,' Caleb Hawkes suddenly grinned, but the grin didn't reach his cold eyes. 'I was right behind you, and I never saw this wench lift a finger against Old Tom, and the ones that did were only having a bit o' fun wi' him. He never come to no harm, did he? And I heard what you said to her wi'out cause, as well. She was right to walk off from you. Because I'll tell you straight, iffen she'd bin kin to me, and I heard you speak to her like you did, then I'd ha' broke your jaw for you, make no mistake about that. So far as I'm concerned, she's done naught to deserve any punishment at all, and I'll not stand by and see her served badly for doing nothing wrong. If that means that I'll have to be a witness afore the magistrates, then I'll do just that.'

'Hark to me, all on you,' Anna Morris broke her silence.

'It arn't seemly to be rowing with each other in front of a pauper wench.' The woman's strength of character was such, that all three men fell silent. 'You, Girl, come wi' me.'

Tildy also felt the force of the woman's dominance, and followed her out into the courtyard.

'Now then,' the hatchet features were expressionless. 'I'm only going to arsk you the once, Girl, and you'll gi' me the truth. What happened?'

Tildy told her, simply and briefly.

Anna Morris listened without comment until the girl had finished her story. Then said. 'You did refuse to work then, didn't you, Crawford. That's a whipping matter, that is.' She lifted one large hand to forestall any argument. 'But I'm not going to let them whip you, Girl. To my way o' thinking, George Holyoake lets self-pride overrule his yed at times. But I'm still going to punish you for refusing to work like you did. Iffen I lets you get off scot-free, then the other trouble-makers in here 'ull begin to think that they can do as they please with us.'

Tildy sensed that the feared separation from little Davy would not now take place, and her relief was such that she was ready to accept any punishment that Anna Morris chose to inflict upon her.

The woman stared at her speculatively. 'Be you ready to accept my punishment, Crawford?'

Tildy nodded slowly.

'Right. You'll spend the night in the hole. That'll cool your hot temper for you.'

She took hold of Tildy's arm and led her unresisting to an outhouse in the corner of the yard. She opened the heavy door and thrust the girl into the windowless room. The fading light of the day lanced the musty, clammy interior, and Tildy had only brief seconds to glance about her before the door slammed shut, the key turned in the lock and darkness veiled her sight.

She moved backwards until her shoulders rested against the rough, unplaned door-planks and drew a deep breath to

95

steady her jangled nerves. The room was barely nine feet square, and she knew that two paces forwards would bring her to its sole furnishing. The long, lead-lined trough against the far wall, in which lay the naked corpse of little Charlie Reeves, a large onion forced into his mouth because it was thought it would prevent the smell of death's decay.

Chapter Nine

Clang, clang, clang, clang, Tildy awoke with a start as the bell rang out. The blackness of the hole was total, and sitting with her back to the door Tildy lifted her head from her bent knees and blinked blindly about her. Her body was stiff and cold, and her joints creaked painfully as she clambered to her feet. She heard the clatter of wooden-soled clogs on the cobblestones of the yard, and then a key rattled in the lock and the door swung open. Tildy squinted at the dark figure silhouetted against the faint dawn paling of the eastern sky.

'Come on, Crawford.'

She followed Anna Morris past the bent body of Edward Watts tugging at the bell-rope, and into the fuggy, odorous kitchen. An oil lamp hung from one of the ceiling beams cast a dull light over the room, and Anna Morris, her face shadowed by her capacious mobcap, pointed to a small earthenware bowl on the table.

'Drink that, Girl. You looks perished wi' cold.'

Tildy was cold, shivering involuntarily, and she lifted the bowl and gratefully sipped its steaming hot contents of milkless, sugarless tea, welcoming the warmth it brought spreading through her body. She could not help but feel a sense of gratitude towards this dour, forbidding woman for this unasked for kindness.

'Thank you for the tea, Mistress Morris.'

'That's not needful, Crawford. I'm only doing my duty.' The woman brusquely rejected her thanks. 'Sup it quick now, and join the others.'

97

The sounds of voices and movement showed that the paupers were gathering for morning prayers.

The day room was also dimly lit by a solitary oil lamp, but there was sufficient light for Tildy to see the curious stares directed at her as she entered the room.

'Be you alright, Tildy?' Hannah Knight whispered, and Tildy nodded and moved to stand beside her friend.

Kate Reeves tugged her sleeve. 'Wheer was you? In the hole?'

Tildy stared at the swarthy, boldly-handsome face and could not hide the distaste she felt for this woman. To Tildy the callousness that Kate Reeves had displayed on her child's death was an evil thing. Visions of the pathetic little corpse lying unmourned in the hole came before her mind's eye, and shaking off the woman's hand, she turned her back on her.

Kate Reeves's lips drew back in a snarl. 'Acting like Lady Muck agen, be you,' she hissed savagely. 'Well I'll soon drag you off your high horse, Crawford, you see if I doon't.'

Tildy ignored the threat, and instead asked Hannah, 'Who is Caleb Hawkes?'

The younger girl was eager to tell her. 'He's a higgler, Tildy. He goes round the farms buying eggs and poultry and different things. They say that he's got other dealings as well, wi' the poachers and suchlike.' She grinned archly. 'Why d'you want to know about him?'

'He stuck up for me yesterday, against Morris and George Holyoake,' Tildy told her, and the memory caused a warm glow to course through her as she added reflectively, 'and there's precious few men ever stuck up for me before.'

The younger girl was avidly curious. 'What did he do?'

'He wouldn't let them whip me.'

Envy and excitement throbbed in Hannah's voice. 'I wish I'd bin you, Tildy. I think he's a lovely man. A really proper man. D'you reckon he's took a fancy for you, Tildy? I wish he'd take a fancy for me. Though, they do

98

say as how he's got women all over the county. He's real free and easy wi' his money. Spends it like a lord, they reckons. I bet he'd be real good to you, Tildy. 'Ull you goo wi' him iffen he asks you to?'

'Hush now and stop building dream castles. Here's Morris come.' Tildy was relieved to see the poorhouse master enter the room. Her friend's eager questioning was beginning to embarrass her, forcing her to admit to herself that similar thoughts had passed through her own mind during the long cold hours of the night.

After prayers Tildy collected her breakfast of bread and gruel from the kitchen and went straight to the children's room, and took little Davy with her into the female dormitory. She tried to give him suck, but his normally eager tugging at her nipples was done long before her milk ran out. She offered him a spoonful of gruel, but he spat it out, dribbling it down his chin. Then he vomited the milk he had taken. A sense of disquietude assailed her. Running down into the yard she drew water from the pump into a wooden bucket and brought it back with her to the dormitory. Stripping off the baby's soiled clout she gently bathed his body, examining it closely, and frowned as she noticed some flea-bites on his chest and buttocks.

'God's curse on this filthy place,' she muttered angrily, and wrapped a fresh clout around him. He was flaccid and lethargic, and his skin was hot to the touch. Neither his face or eyes held any expression as he stared blankly upwards.

'Oh Davy, what's the matter with you?' Tildy whispered aloud. 'What is it that ails you, my Honey-Lamb?'

'Let me see him, Crawford.' Unheard by Tildy, Anna Morris had come to the door of the room. She moved to Tildy's side and stood for a moment staring down at the child. Gently she took him from the younger woman's arms and stripping the clout from him, laid him on the bed. She also noted the flea-bites, and frowned as she saw them. Tildy saw the frown, and cried out anxiously.

'What is it? What ails him?'

Anna Morris shrugged. 'Could be any one of a lot o'

99

things, Girl. And then again, it could be next to naught. Mind you, kids whom are weakly to begin with doon't last long in here.'

'But he's not weakly,' Tildy protested fearfully. 'I've always been strong and healthy, and his father the same. He can't be weakly.'

'That's sarft talk,' Anna Morris told her sternly. 'Strong parents can sometimes breed weakly kids, and weak parents breed strong 'uns. It all depends on God's will. We can only pray to Him to give us . . .'

Before she could finish, Tildy broke in on her. 'Pray, is it?' For the first time in her present distress she had found some target to strike back at. 'What good did praying ever do for the likes o' me? Tell me that, can you? If God is so good, why is he afflicting my baby in this way? When did that good Lord, you prate of ever stretch his hand out to help the crippled and the blind? When did he ever save any of the poor from their sufferings? Never!' She spat the last word out with a vicious finality.

The bell in the courtyard rang out to call the paupers to their various tasks. Anna Morris sighed heavily.

'I must go down. You stay here, Crawford. I'll find you other work, rather than send you to the fields today. Stay here with your babby for now.'

She left the room, her starched apron rustling as she walked, and the great bunch of keys clinking against her heavy thighs.

Left alone, Tildy felt the hot scalding of tears in her eyes, and tenderly cuddling her child to her, she let those tears fall.

'I'll take you from here someday, Davy,' she whispered. 'There'll come a chance for us to get out from this place, and live clean and decent like other people. I must be strong,' she told herself. 'I must be strong.'

Chapter Ten

It was not the clanging of bells that awoke Caleb Hawkes, but warm soft hands gently fondling his manhood, teasing it to a throbbing erectness. He stirred lazily and his hands reached for the firm breasts and hard-swollen nipples of the woman beside him. Greedily he clamped his mouth on the silk-smoothness of pulsing flesh, his tongue probing the nipple's dark hardness, and moved so that he lay on top of the woman, enfolding tender yielding hips and thighs, belly against belly, mouth against mouth. She moaned in pleasure as his muscular thighs parted hers and she guided him into her hungry wetness. Driven by mindless needs Caleb Hawkes thrust savagely into the soft body beneath him, and moaned in his turn as tremors of delight shivered through his loins. With a force akin to brutality he drove his hips into a faster and faster pounding, and the woman beneath him clutched his hard buttocks, digging her finger-nails deep, kneading the spasming muscles, gasping his name over and over again.

His excitement mounted unbearably and his breath rasped in his throat.

'Don't stop! Don't stop! Don't stop!' she panted, and he felt her hot moist lips sucking at his ears and throat. The wooden bed creaked and shook and he cried out in a final paroxysm of ecstasy as his seed exploded into her heaving hips and he slumped upon her, the sweat of their bodies mingling to create a liquid bonding.

Slowly his rasping breathing eased and quietened, and he rolled off her, then lay close, holding her in a gentle embrace.

'Was I nice, Caleb?' she whispered, and he smiled acknowledgement, his teeth a white gleam in the twilight of the room.

'Oh Caleb, I wish we was married,' the woman took his face between her hands and covered his cheeks, eyes and mouth with fleeting kisses. 'I knows we carn't never be married.' Sadness was in her voice. 'I'm just a whore to you, arn't I. I'se had too many men atween me legs for you to ever marry me, arn't I.'

'Hush now,' Caleb Hawkes spoke gently and kindly. 'I've never called you whore, has I. You do what you have to do to survive, Honey. I arn't the type o' man to blaggard you for that. I never has done, has I.'

'I knows you doon't, Caleb. That's why I loves you so. Youm always nice to me. You always treats me tender. When I goes wi' you it's like a paradise arter some of the others. Wi' them I doon't feel a thing. But wi' you it's like I was a young maid agen, going wi' me first sweetheart. Is it like that for you, Caleb?'

He kissed her tenderly, touched by her words. 'Sure it is, Honey. Now let me sleep for a while.'

'I'se got to go now,' she told him. 'The kids 'ull be screaming for some breakfast.'

'Here.' He leaned across her to take his breeches from the bedside stool.

'No Caleb! You doon't have to pay me.' She sounded hurt. 'I doon't go wi' you every time just for the money.'

He grinned down at her. 'I knows you don't. But I likes to give you a little present. I don't gi' it to you as payment, Honey, but because I cares for you. Here now.' He opened her hand and put some coins on her flattened palm, then closed her fingers firmly over them. 'You buy your kids a nice breakfast wi' that, as a favour to me.'

She sniffed emotionally, and kissed him again, hugging him fiercely. 'Youm a good man, Caleb. Truly a good man.'

When the woman had dressed and gone, Hawkes tried to

102

settle himself once more, but sleep eluded him, and instead he could only lie and listen to the sounds of the morning, and let his thoughts drift wherever they might.

'*Matilda Crawford . . . Tildy. A rare sweet-looking piece, that one, and spirited too. Not foul-mouthed, but soft-voiced and almost like a lady for all her shabby clothes and country accent. Got a fair character too, by all accounts. Not a hedge-whore like so many poorhouse women be.*' The man grinned to himself. 'Youm getting obsessed wi' the wench, Hawkes,' he muttered aloud. 'Seems like she's in your thoughts more than she's out of them.'

Caleb Hawkes was ambivalent in his views on women. Although he did not condemn or despise those who slept with many men, for he was himself an avid hunter of woman-flesh, yet he could never allow himself to become emotionally involved with any woman who was as promiscuous as he himself was. Like most men he believed in the dual-standard. If he fell in love with a woman he wanted her to possess an approximation of chasteness. He recognized the essential injustice of his own attitudes, yet was incapable of altering them.

It was this quality of chasteness that he thought he perceived in Tildy, and it was that that attracted him so strongly to her. But he had mixed feelings about that attraction: one part of him fearing any emotional involvement. Caleb Hawkes had buried one wife, together with the baby she had died giving birth to, and he had no wish to risk again the heartbreak he had known on that occasion.

'*No, it's no good*,' he told himself now, for perhaps the hundredth time. '*I'm better as I am. Finding my loving with the whores and the tails. I like them well enough, and there's no disturbance of my peace of mind when I leave them. I don't want to break my heart again over a woman. It was enough that I lost Susan.*'

His eyes clouded, as for a brief while he relived that loss which had left him grieving and bereft. Yet try as he might to dispel it, the image of Tildy Crawford's sweet face and luminous brown eyes persisted in haunting his memory. Becoming impatient with his own weakness, he threw aside his coverings and dressed himself in his lower garments, then taking a strip of rough towelling went downstairs.

Even this early in the morning the keeper of the Red Lion Inn at Redditch was bustling about. Herbert Willis, a bluff-featured, plump-bellied man winked at Hawkes.

'I didn't think you'd be rising so early, Cully. I reckoned you might need to rest most o' the day, arter the labours o' the night.'

Caleb laughed, and went out to the back of the inn, where a long-handled pump and stone horse-trough stood against the wall of the stables. He tossed a penny to one of the ostlers.

'Here, Jake, work the handle will you.'

The man pumped with a will and the cold clear water gouted out of the iron nozzle. Caleb doused his head and lean muscular torso in the gushing water, hissing at its impact. When done, he towelled his short-cropped, thinning fair hair and rubbed his body until his skin glowed with the friction. The ostler sidled up to him and whispered from the corner of his mouth. 'Richie Bint is in the tap room, he wants a word wi' you.'

Caleb nodded. 'Tell him I'll be in presently.' Then went back upstairs to finish dressing.

'You'se took your time,' Richard Bint grumbled, and reaching for the pewter tankard of ale drained it dry, then clumped it down on the table.

'Herbert, send in the wench, 'ull you,' Caleb shouted, and seated himself opposite the other man. Bint was a needle pointer, and like the rest of that hard-living breed showed the effects of his brawling, drunken life, looking far older than his thirty years. He wore a square-shaped hat fashioned from tough brown paper on his thick uncombed sandy hair, a leather waistcoat and red flannel shirt, breeches, ribbed stockings and iron-studded clogs, and around his waist a rolled white apron. His body was squat and solid, and his nose flattened by the prize-fighting he loved to indulge in.

The small serving-girl came, and went, and returned again with fresh tankards of ale, a dish of broiled beefsteaks and a loaf of new-baked bread. Both men ate without talk, using their fingers to portion the tender steaks, soaking hunks of fragrant-smelling bread in the rich gravy and cramming them into mouths already full of meat. Only when they had both finished their meal, and were puffing clouds of strong-smelling smoke from long clay church-warden pipes, did Caleb Hawkes break the silence.

'What have you got for me, Richie?'

The pointer grinned, disclosing stained teeth made crooked and broken by knuckled fists. From his waistcoast pocket he took a small, very pale olive-coloured egg.

Caleb's eyes showed momentary surprise. 'Pheasant? They'm a bit late, arn't they?'

'Bit late am they?' Bint's sandy head rocked on his shoulders as he jeered the higgler. 'My oath, Hawkes, how long you bin dealing? Them old birds lays right up to the last week in June, and into July sometimes as well, I'm damned if they don't. Jesus Christ on the Cross, they didn't learn you much when you was a soldier, did they. No wonder it took so long to beat the Frenchies.'

Caleb accepted the jeering in good humour. 'How many have you got, Richie?'

Again the sandy head rocked, and the broken teeth showed in a grin of anticipation of the higgler's reaction. 'I'se got three gross.'

'Jesus!' Caleb's jaw dropped, and Bint howled with delighted laughter.

'Ahr, I thought that 'ud take you back a bit.' He dropped his voice. 'It'll take the bloody keepers back as well when they next checks the coverts.' His laughter stilled and he got to business. 'So, what price?'

The higgler pondered, then offered: 'A florin the dozen.'

The other man snorted in disgust. 'I were thinking of a crown the dozen.'

'A crown? Where does my bloody profit come from if I pays you a crown?'

'The carrier told me they was afetching eight shillings the dozen in London.'

'That was last month, Richie, and that was in London. There's bin a change since then. They'll not fetch more than six bob now, and I've to pay the carrier's bill, and sweeten the poulterer, arn't I. Don't forget that.'

'I still reckons a florin is too low,' Bint grumbled.

'Alright then, because I trusts you, and I knows that they'll be fresh and sweet, I'll give you half-a-crown the dozen. But that's my final price, Richie. I'll not pay a penny more.'

'Throw in a couple of flasks o' gin to be drunk now, and they'm yourn.' The pointer grinned, and Caleb matched the grin.

'Done!'

They spat on the palms of their right hands and slapped them hard together to seal their bargain.

As the higgler went to fetch the money, he mentally computed his expected profit. 'They'll sell at Leadenhall for eight bob the dozen, so that's fourteen pounds and eight shillings. Allow two guineas for the carrier, two guineas for the poulterers sweetener, four pounds and ten shillings to Richie Bint, and the food and drink plus a few bob off-reckonings. That leaves me five guineas at the least. That's a fair enough return for today.'

Once re-seated in the tap room Caleb counted out four golden guineas and six shillings. Richard Bint pocketed the coins, then glancing out of the window that fronted the road outside the inn, uttered a curse and immediately popped the pheasant's egg into his mouth, crunched it and swallowed hard. Heavy boots crashed on the flags of the entrance and then the room suddenly filled with men.

'I told you we'd find the thievin' bugger here, Master Cashmore.' The speaker was the head gamekeeper of the Earl of Plymouth's Tardebigge estate. A tall ruddy-cheeked countryman, with a moleskin cap, fustian clothes and canvas gaiters. In his hands he carried a long-barrelled sporting gun, which he swung about as if he wished to fire it then and there. The taciturn Joseph Cashmore bore his staff of office, and behind him were three underkeepers, dressed like their headman, and also wielding long-barrelled guns.

Richard Bint hawked and spat on to the sanded floor at the head keeper's booted feet. 'And who be you referring to as a thievin' bugger, Tom Davis?'

'You, Bint, it's you I'm calling.' The man was trembling with barely suppressed rage. 'You been at my coverts down along the Tack Farm lower edge, arn't you. There's not a bloody egg left theer.'

Bint wasn't cowed by rage or numbers. He rose to his feet challenging. 'You can step outside into the yard right now, Davis, and I'll close that lying mouth o' yourn in double-quick time. Ahr, and bring your bullyboys wi' you and all. You'll be needin' 'um. Theer arn't a good fighting man to be made out o' the lot of you put together.'

'That's enough of that sort o' talk, Bint.' Joseph Cashmore intervened. 'Youm in trouble enough already.'

'Why? What's I done?'

'You were seen poaching pheasants' eggs last night in the coverts by the Tack Farm.'

'Who's supposed to have sin me?' Bint demanded truculently. 'Let's be hearing from your witness afore you goes making more false accusations.'

Drawn by the noise, Herbert Willis pushed his way into the room. 'What's this then, Master Cashmore?'

'It's Richard Bint here,' the constable told him. 'He was poaching last night.'

'That's a bloody lie, Cashmore, and you knows it is.' The pointer shouted. 'I spent last night in me bed along o' me missus. She'll bear witness to that. I never left home from the time I come back from me work, until I come here this morning.'

'You was seen at the coverts,' Cashmore reiterated.

'Who by?' Bint challenged.

Unable to restrain himself, Thomas Davis bawled. 'By Tucker Smith, that's who.'

Richard Bint burst into raucous laughter, and the constable scowled angrily at the keeper. 'Why did you have to open your mouth?'

Davis, realizing his blunder, could only stammer out lame excuses.

'Tucker Smith?' The pointer jeered incredulously, and slapped his thighs resoundingly as again his laughter pealed out.

Caleb Hawkes and Herbert Willis couldn't hide their own smiles. Tucker Smith was famous for having only one eye, and that one was nearly blind. Unable to see more than a couple of yards in front of him, Smith was usually led about by a small child.

'Which eye did Tucker see me wi', Davis, the one that's missing?' The pointer questioned mockingly, knowing now that the constable's bluff had failed miserably. Not even the most ferociously pro-game law magistrate could risk commiting him to the sessions for trial with Tucker Smith as the sole eye-witness.

Joseph Cashmore jerked his head at the group of keepers. 'Wait for me outside.'

Sullenly they trooped from the room, and as the last one went through the door, the constable swung to Caleb Hawkes.

'Right, Higgler, I'll tell you straight. I knows for a fact that Richie Bint here took them eggs, even though at this moment I can't prove it in a court o' law. And I knows that he's come here to sell them self-same eggs to you. I knows that you has dealings wi' every bloody poacher within ten miles o' this town.

'I don't begrudge any poor man an occasional hare or rabbit for his stewpot, or even a brace o' birds or nest of eggs. But you be taking all on us who holds office in this parish for bloody fools, and I'll tell you now, that the justices be determined to make you smart for it. They'm the law, and I'm their servant, and I shall do their bidding.

And I shall do it wi' pleasure in your case, Hawkes. Because I reckons you to be a flash cove who needs to be taught his lessons.

'It's the likes o' crafty villains such as you, who encourages these silly buggers to goo poaching. But it's them who gets caught, and you who goes scot-free. Well, I'm agoing to change that. Does I make meself clear?'

Caleb nodded slowly. 'Yes, Cashmore, you make it clear. But you're wrong about one thing. It's not me that encourages the lads to go poaching, but the bloody farmers and manufacturers who won't pay labouring men enough to live on. O' course they'll goo poaching. Any man wi' courage will go poaching sooner than see his wife and kids crying wi' hunger.'

The constable's heavy features assumed an exaggerated expression of scorn. 'That's hogwash, that is. That's bloody rubbish. Bint, theer, is a pointer. He can earn himself more bloody rhino in a week at his trade than most labouring men can earn in a month. So don't you tell me that it's bloody starvation that causes the likes of him to poach. He does it just for badness, so he does. He'd sooner steal than do a day's honest toil.'

'Honest toil, you say!' The pointer's hands balled into fists and his aggressive reaction to the words impelled him forwards as if he were going to physically assault the other man. 'Us pointers earns good money because we pays with our health and lives for the work. You name me five men who've lasted more than a dozen years at the pointing and kept their health and strength, Cashmore.' He paused, breathing heavily. 'You bloody well can't, can you, because there arn't a single one who has, let alone five.

'I'll tell you wheer all the old pointer lads be, shall I. They'm in their graves, because none that I ever knew of lived to be more than two-score years old. There's none that I ever knew of who was able to work more than a dozen years at the trade afore they was laying in their beds coughing the blood up by the bucketful.

'If you reckon that the pointing is so good, then why

arn't you and the other fat-bellied bastards like you working at it? I'll tell you why you arn't, because youm bloody feared to!' He was bellowing now, and the veins in his temples throbbed visibly as he worked himself into blind rage. 'That's why the lads goo poaching. Because a shilling earned that way don't have to be payed for wi' blood from our lungs.'

Caleb Hawkes saw that the man's anger would soon land him in serious trouble. He came round the table and physically restrained the pointer. Pushing him down on to the bench and holding him until he had calmed sufficiently to regain control over his tongue. Once satisfied that Bint was alright, Caleb swung on the constable.

'Has you got anything more to say, Cashmore?'

The man was not disturbed by the narrowly averted violence. 'Yes, Hawkes, I got summat more to say,' he growled. 'I knows that youm dealing in poached game, and I'm going to make sure that I catches you at it, and gets your transported for seven years.'

Caleb laughed mirthlessly, and his light-blue eyes were hard. 'You do that, Cashmore. Because the day I let a bloody chaw-bacon like you get me transported, is the day I no longer deserve to be called a man.'

Their eyes locked and held, each conscious of the fact that in the other he had made a dangerous enemy.

It was Cashmore who broke the contact. 'I'll be looking out for you, my flash buck. Don't doubt it for a fact.'

'I won't doubt it, Cashmore. But have a care that you don't find more than youm looking for,' Caleb warned him quietly.

The constable grinned contemptuously, and strode away.

'You've made a bad enemy in that 'un, Caleb.' Herbert Willis's bluff features were troubled.

Once more the mirthless grin bared Caleb's teeth. 'He's made a worse enemy in me, if he don't leave me well alone,' he whispered, and the long scar on his face was a scarlet streak against the sun-tanned skin. The other two men, recognizing the depth of his hidden fury, left the

110

higgler to his thoughts, until he chose to re-enter their desultory conversation.

'I'll be moving,' he finally said quietly. 'I'll see you both later.'

Richard Bint winked at him. 'The usual spot, Caleb.' Referring to the hidden pheasants' eggs. The higgler nodded, and returned the wink.

At the stables he checked his team of donkeys and his bay mare which Jake the ostler had saddled for him. The donkeys carried panniers slung across their backs, and each had a long leading-rein which Caleb fastened in tandem, one to the other, so that he could lead them in single file behind his horse. He mounted the bay mare and heeled her into a trot, drawing the donkeys behind him.

The Red Lion Inn was about two hundred yards to the east of the central green of Redditch, on which stood the single-storied cupolated Chapel of St Stephen. The green was triangular in shape and varied buildings lined its three sides. Shops, terraced cottages, inns, dwelling houses, beer shops, blacksmiths' forges and needlemakers' shops which were easily recognized by their long rows of close-spaced windows to admit maximum daylight for the operatives to see more easily.

Caleb crossed the green, acknowledging the greetings of various acquaintances and plunged westwards down the Bates Hill which would lead him into the Hewell Lane and through the Brockhill Wood. He would load his purchases of poultry and eggs into the donkeys' panniers as he called at farms and cottages on the way to the wharfs of the Worcester to Birmingham Canal at Tardebigge village. He also intended to collect the three gross of pheasants' eggs which Richard Bint had cached in the Brockhill Wood – but that collection would only take place when he was satisfied that no one was spying on his movements to report back to the constable.

At the thought of Cashmore and their long-standing feud, Caleb's scar again engorged with blood, as it always did when his anger was roused.

111

'We've always clashed, him and me,' Caleb mused. 'But he never really hated me until I took Susan from him.' A mingling of pain and pleasure filled his mind. 'I don't really blame the bugger for hating me. He'd been chasing Susan for years, and had some hopes of winning her, until I come back from the war. But once we two met agen Cashmore stood no chance of wedding her . . . Caleb Hawkes had been a Sergeant of Hussars when he first wooed his wife. A dashing vision of sabre-rattling heroism in his blue, scarlet and gold. The piratical scar his own personal battle-honour won on the bloody field of Sahagun during the Peninsular War. Briefly his memories ranged back across the years . . . Sahagun, Mayorga, Benavente, Corrunna, Vittoria, Toulouse, Waterloo, so many battles, so much glory, so much suffering and death . . . 'And wheer was you during all them years, Cashmore?' Caleb muttered scathingly. 'Why, you was sitting safe and sound here in Redditch. And now you thinks to frighten me? Sergeant Hawkes of the Prince o' Wales own Royal Hussars, the glorious Tenth.'

The higgler laughed aloud at his own vainglorying and, his good humour restored, trotted on towards the Brockhill Wood.

At Tardebigge hamlet the Worcester to Birmingham Canal had two separate wharfs and barge basins, each with its work-shops and cottages and storesheds. The northern wharf was the Old Wharf, and it was there that Caleb Hawkes eventually made his way. The Navigation Inn stood opposite the Old Wharf, a sprawling half-timbered Tudor farmhouse that now resounded to the voices of the bargees and the wharfmen, the carriers and the leggers, the artisans and the labourers who kept the narrow boats pouring in both directions from the peaceful green banks of the River Severn to the roaring smoking foundries, pits and factories of the industry-ravaged Black Country.

Caleb dismounted at the Navigation Inn and gave an

urchin a couple of pennies to hold his horse and watch over the donkey's laden panniers. Then he sauntered across to the wharf. A coal barge was being unloaded and even as the wharfmen ran their great triangular barrows down the planks and along to the big weigh-pans, the coal dealers from Redditch and Bromsgrove were haggling prices with the bargee. Their long strings of panniered donkeys stood patiently, their hides as black with coal dust, as the men around them.

Just beyond the wharf itself where the canal curved into the dark mouth of the tunnel a group of young men lounged on the towpath. At first glance they could be taken for farmworkers with their smocks and billycock hats, but instead of boots and gaiters they wore thick-soled clogs on their feet, cleated across the soles with narrow-edged strips of iron. These men were leggers. The Tardebigge tunnel had no towpath, and the tow-horses had to be taken across the top of the tunnel, or into the barge itself as it travelled on. The leggers supplied the motive power for the journey under the earth. They placed planks athwart the bows and stern of the narrow boat, then lay on these planks and pushed with their feet against the tunnel walls, literally walking the barges along. The work was gruelling and only young men possessed the necessary stamina to manage it as a livelihood. It could also be dangerous because the tunnel was wide and this necessitated the leggers lying with nearly all their body outward. Accidents were common as barges hit the sides of the pitch-black tunnel and the planks tipped, throwing the leggers into the water between the hull and the brickwork of the walls. Many were crushed and crippled, some were drowned. They themselves increased the hazards by their habit of drinking in the nearby inns while waiting for their services to be called for. Half-drunk and careless, they all too often paid a terrible price. Most of the leggers practised another sideline to pay for their drinking. They were poachers – and the group that Caleb Hawkes now approached were well known to him in that capacity.

'How bist, higgler?' Their leader, a broad-shouldered man who favoured long sidewhiskers, greeted Caleb warmly. 'Youm just the cove I wanted to see.'

The higgler smiled easily. 'How bist, Jem? I'm glad we're well met.'

The man looked about him with mock wariness. 'There arn't no law around, be there?'

'Why should there be, Jem. I'm an honest man,' Caleb entered the spirit of the game.

'Oh we all knows that well enough, Master Hawkes, but I don't reckon as how the constable would agree wi' us.' He dropped his bantering air and asked seriously, 'Is that right that Cashmore is out to have you? They do say that you and him had high words this morning.'

'They say right, Jem,' Caleb was equally serious, 'but that's for me to worry about. I'm not a man to involve others in my troubles, nor to tell tales to avoid them troubles.'

'That's known well enough, Master Hawkes,' Jem's broad red face split into a wide grin of yellowed teeth. 'We'se had a couple o' good nights. How does eighteen hares sound to you?'

'They sound well enough, Jem. I'll take them the day after tomorrow.' Caleb noted the disappointment on the faces around him, and added, 'If you've a bad thirst I can advance part-payment.'

'What price?' Jem wanted to know.

Caleb considered for a moment or two. 'They'm selling well at present. I'll pay three shillings the nob and risk a loss.'

A rumble of appreciation sounded from the group.

'Theer now, what does I always say?' red-faced Jem beamed at his friends, 'Master Hawkes here gives the best prices in the county, and that's no lie.'

'Indeed it's not,' Caleb agreed somewhat ruefully. It was a fact that he paid well, and even occasionally took a loss. But he accepted this risk because his name as a generous payer always ensured that the majority of poachers in the district gave him first offer of their pickings. 'So that's fifty-

114

four shillings for the batch. I trust they're good?'

'They'm prime, Master Hawkes. I swear on me mother's grave, they'm prime.'

'Right, here's a sovereign. I'll pay the rest after collection. Has Johnny Salt gone through yet?'

'No,' one of the group told him. 'He's picking up a load at Alvechurch, but he'll be through afore dark.'

'Tell him I'll be in the Navigation.' Caleb saluted a farewell, and walked back towards the inn.

In the tap room he called for ale and settled himself to wait for the bargee known as Johnny Salt. It was he who would take the pheasants' eggs and carry them, hidden away in his boat's cargo, to Worcester where he would pass them on to the guard of the Hirondelle Coach, an old regimental comrade of Caleb's. The guard in his turn would carry the eggs to the poulterer at London's Leadenhall Market. The live poultry and eggs that Caleb had bought that day he would sell himself on the morrow in the city of Birmingham, some fourteen miles distant. Caleb could easily have disposed of his illicit game in that same city, but the chances of being betrayed to the local constables were much increased if he did so. So he preferred to deal with London.

There was another drinker in the tap room. A packman resting his weary bones after tramping the local villages with his wares. On impulse Caleb asked him.

'Do you have ribbons?'

The man nodded and opening his canvas pack displayed a handful of brilliantly coloured silks. 'They'm the finest, Master. Fit for a queen.'

Caleb selected several lengths of scarlet silks which shimmered like a living fire as he fashioned them into a nosegay. He paid the man, then added a sixpence to the coins, asking as he did so, 'Does your way take you past the poorhouse at Webheath?'

'I'll be out that way tomorrow or the day arter.' The man grinned, 'Does you want me to pass this fairing on to some wench theer, Master?'

Caleb nodded, visualizing in his mind the scarlet ribbons winding their shimmering brilliance among soft dark hair.

'There's a girl name o' Tildy Crawford there. Give it to her, and tell her it's from her future sweetheart . . .'

Chapter Eleven

The bell still jangled as Anna Morris opened the front door of the poorhouse and faced the caller across its threshold. He lifted his hat from his full-bottomed tie-wig, the white-coloured badge of his profession.

'Good afternoon. You'll be Mistress Morris, I take it. Allow me to present myself. Doctor Lucas Royston.'

The woman bobbed a half-curtsey. 'We bin expecting you, Doctor. Please to step in. Mister Morris will be with you directly.'

Even as she spoke the poorhouse master joined them in the hallway. His manner was effusively ingratiating as he ushered the newcomer into the parlour. The room was comfortably furnished, and despite the warmth of the day a coal fire burned in the black-leaded grate.

'Please be seated, Doctor Royston. Will you take refreshment?' Morris lifted a bottle of gin from the sideboard. 'It's finest Hollands,' he invited.

Lucas was unsure of himself. Wondering if his facetious remarks to Reverend Clayton about drink being his downfall had been spread by that worthy man, and this invitation was a way of testing his readiness to succumb to temptation. He decided to stand on his dignity and refused stiffly.

'No, I thank you, I rarely indulge in strong liquor.'

'Perhaps a dish of tay, then?' Morris was unabashed by any implied disapproval.

'Thank you, no.' The young man shifted uncomfortably, already finding the close heat of the room oppressive.

'Very well, doctor, as you please.' Morris poured a

generous measure of gin into a glass and drained it in one swallow. 'Ahhh, that's better,' he gusted in satisfaction, and winked at the younger man. 'I've a sore throat, doctor, and take this to ease it.' He stared meaningly at his wife. 'Have you no tasks to be getting on with, Mistress Morris?'

Understanding her husband's look, she excused herself and left the two men alone.

Ebenezer Morris wasted no time. 'No doubt your uncle has already explained to you the arrangements between myself and the medical gentlemen, Doctor Royston. They'se served admirably up to now, so seeing as you'll be now the only medical gentleman to be coming here, I've no objections to that same arrangement continuing between ourselves.'

Lucas Royston had no knowledge of any private arrangements but he was not stupid and realizing that it must be some form of graft, he enquired cautiously.

'To what arrangements precisely do you refer, Mister Morris? Doctor Pratt told me of several matters.'

The other man smiled and winked as if to congratulate him on his worldy-wisdom.

'Youm right to be circumspect, Doctor Royston. I'm happy to see that you are so. But we'em both men o' the world, so I'll speak plain. Me and the other medical gentlemen had an understanding about the fees. We shared 'um atween us.'

Lucas's mind raced. 'I see,' he replied simply, and waited

The poorhouse master waited also, and the silence lengthened into tens of seconds then minutes. Lucas finally decided to find out more before committing himself.

'Tell me, Mister Morris, what advantage did the medical gentlemen gain by sharing their fees with you. Surely they would lose by doing so?'

The poorhouse master's smile reminded Lucas of a death's head grimace.

'Surely they didn't, Doctor Royston, that's plain to see arn't it? Here in this house we brings in all the pauper sick o' the parish, who arn't got no one to care for 'um. We gets a lot of the old 'uns coming in just to die, and we gets most o' the bastard birthings. Theer's a lot o' sickness here, Doctor, and a lot o' deaths during the course of a year. And don't forget, we don't employ 'Searchers' in this parish, so you gets paid for giving the cause of death. Why, there's one waiting right now in the Hole, a kid name o' Reeves.'

'But the doctor only has to come here when I sends for him. Of course, he could come anyway, I suppose, but he only gets paid when I sends for him to come. The vestry prefers me and my lady wife to care for the sick ourselves for as long as we can, wi'out calling in the doctor . . . ' He broke off to pour another glass of gin, which he sipped with relish before continuing. 'So it's very simple, arn't it. It's much to your advantage if I sends for you to come twice or thrice weekly, rather than sends for you to come twice or thrice monthly. I knows that as the contract surgeon you can only charge low fees, but little and often can mount to a fair sum, can't it. But, there is a snag. By sending for you frequent, I incurs the anger o' the vestry, because it means they has to levy a poor rate to pay you with.' He shook his head in feigned sadness. 'The gentlemen of the vestry do be hard-hearted at times, I fear. They'm prepared to let the paupers suffer cruelly, rather than pay for treatment. But I do my best for the poor souls in this house, and I stands me ground against the vestry, and insists on calling in the medical gentlemen when I considers it to be necessary.' He rolled his close-set eyes heavenwards. 'The Good Lord sees a sparrow fall, Doctor Royston, and one of these paupers is as precious in His sight as any king or emperor. So I feel that I'm doing His Will, and my own Christian duty when I defys the vestry and sends for the doctor.'

The man's sanctimonious hypocrisy jarred on Lucas, and he asked sharply. 'Does that Christian duty also demand that you share my fees, Mister Morris?'

The death's head grin flickered again. 'It's to everyone's advantage that I does so, Doctor, most particularly those who are suffering. Come up wi' me, now. I'm sure you'd like to see our sick room. There's a few in there at present,

119

that when you sees them I'm certain sure you'll want to attend frequent.'

As he followed the man upstairs Lucas Royston was already recognizing that the other held the whiphand. Lucas knew that without this contract, he himself could well end up completely destitute. Even before he entered the sick room, the young doctor had accepted in his heart that he would be continuing his predecessors' arrangement with the poorhouse master.

Lucas glanced quickly about him and found more or less what he had expected. The sick room held eight truckle beds, each designed to hold two people; the windows were tight-shut, so that no breath of fresh air could enter; the floor was dirty and strewn with rubbish; the bedding looked and smelled as if it had not been changed for weeks; and the patients were mixed without any thought of contagion or suitability: the very old sharing a bed with the very young: the consumptive with the cancerous: the fevered with the scabbed: the dropsical with the bronchial: the dying with the newly ill. All reeking with the smells of their own body-wastes.

The solitary nurse, an old pauper woman who stank of beer and appeared to be drunk, moved her ungainly body about the room, and vented a muttered stream of curses and complaints from her toothless mouth as she ignored all pleas from the patients for attention.

The young doctor didn't need to see more. Even as he had come through the door he had recognized that this poorhouse presented him with the opportunity to make a name for himself locally.

'Let us return to your rooms, Mister Morris. I wish to speak with you and your good wife in private.'

When he again faced the couple in the over-heated parlour, he began without preamble. 'What share of the fees did the other gentlemen pay you?'

'A fifth share,' Morris told him. 'That's a fair amount, I would not consider taking less.'

'I'm not asking you to take less.' Lucas's excitement was

mounting rapidly. 'Indeed, if you are agreeable to what I shall propose, then I will increase your share to a fourth part.'

The poorhouse master's cadaverous features showed surprise, quickly alloyed with suspicion.

Lucas recognized the expression. 'There is no need for suspicion, Mister Morris, but there are certain minor conditions attached to my very generous offer, and you must meet those conditions to the best of your ability. But, I do assure you that they are easily met . . . '

The couple listened as he talked, doubt in their minds, but greed eventually won, and Ebenezer Morris accepted Lucas Royston's plans. He did raise one final objection.

'The thing is, Doctor Royston, I don't know as how there's any woman in here as 'ull suit you in the way o' being a nurse.'

For the first time Anna Morris spoke out. 'I reckon I've got someone as 'ull be suitable for the work. Her name is Crawford, Doctor Royston, Tildy Crawford.'

'This is the wench I told you on, Doctor Royston.' Anna Morris brought Tildy into the parlour where he was waiting alone.

He studied the girl closely. Noting with approval the appearance of bodily cleanliness, and appreciating her good looks.

'I've told her about the work and she's willing,' the Mistress explained. 'She's not experienced, but I think her to be a diligent wench and bright enough, even though she's unlettered.'

Tildy was ill at ease under the searching scrutiny of this thin young man with the remarkable eyes. The very intensity with which he stared at her made her flush uncomfortably.

'So, Crawford, you feel that the work of a nurse will suit you?' He smiled at her with genuine warmth, and she felt immediately more at ease with him.

'Yes, Sir, I've developed an interest in the treatment of the sick. You see my own child is ailing, and I want to know if aught can be done to help him.' She had spoken out on impulse, and for a moment was afraid that the doctor would take offence at her forwardness. But instead his eyes showed sympathy.

'What ails your child?'

'The babby was born weakly, Doctor,' Anna Morris put in positively. 'I knew it as soon as I saw the poor little cratur.'

Lucas rose to his feet. 'I shall examine the child, Crawford. I can see that you are anxious about it, and if you are to work under me then I wish you to have an easy mind so that you may render me the better service.' As the three of them went upstairs, he continued talking to Tildy.

'I'm very much of the modern school of medicine, Crawford. I follow the teachings of the late William Buchan, of the Royal College of Physicians at Edinburgh. He was a great man, and a great healer. That is what I intend to do here, to put his teachings into effect with the pauper sick. If you pay close attention and apply yourself diligently, then you will learn much from me that will prove a boon to you in your future life. Mayhap it can lead to an opportunity for you to make your own way in the world, and cease being dependant on charity.'

His patronizing manner did not irritate Tildy. There was an apparent artless enthusiasm about him that disarmed his listeners.

In the children's room, Royston took off Davy's swaddlings and carefully examined him. 'How long has he been this way, so feverish and listless?'

'More than a week now,' Tildy told him, her anxiety somewhat allayed by the confident air of the man.

He tutted audibly as he noticed the minute papules on the child's breast and arms. Tildy felt embarrassed.

'I keep him clean, Doctor. But those fleabites can't be helped. Some of the people in here are careless about washing themselves, and they bring vermin in with them.'

The next instant Tildy gasped in frightened horror.

Little Davy's flushed skin became pale, and he started to twitch jerkily. His eyes were fixed and even as Tildy bent to him the twitching became more violent, his tiny hands clenched and his body stiffened. Tildy almost cried out in terror as Davy's breathing became shallow and rapid; and as his body became more and more rigid a dusky blueness infused his cheeks and lips. She would have snatched him from the bed, but Lucas Royston held her back.

'Don't alarm yourself, Crawford. He'll come to no harm, I assure you. It is merely a mild convulsion, and a good sign in his present illness.'

'But what ails him?' she demanded frantically. 'What is wrong?'

Royston was calm and appeared very sure of himself. 'Your child has been sluggish and distant because he is infected with the smallpox. Those are not flea bites on his skin, but eruptions of the disease. They will spread to his face and other areas, but their nature will change during the coming days.'

'Smallpox!' Tildy fought for control, knowing that her panic would not help Davy. 'What can we do?' she begged to know.

'Give him cream of tartar in hot water, and put boiled turnips to his feet,' Anna Morris stated positively. 'We needs to make the babby sweat, because then the pox rises better and easier. If the skin is too dry and parched it can't rise so well, and it'll do more damage or even kill him. Everyone knows that, and we can cover him with red flannel to stop the light getting to him. That'll stop the scarring.'

Lucal Royston was visibly angered. 'Mistress Morris! I'll·remind you that I am the doctor here. I'll decide what is to be done.'

'Well that's how I've always treated the pox afore,' the woman argued indignantly, 'and I'se nursed enough who've had it.'

A sarcastic streak surfaced in the young man. 'I need

hardly remind you, Mistress Morris, that the treatments and remedies of the cunning women kill more patients than they cure. Modern medicine is a science, woman, and no longer a form of witchcraft. Let me also remind you that your husband and I have an agreement, and that is that I am in complete charge of the sick in this house, and that my instructions concerning the sick are to be carried out to the letter. Is that fact clear?'

At first it seemed that she would continue the dispute, but then she set her lips and nodded curtly.

'But what is to be done?' Tildy could not understand the man's lack of urgency. The child's cyanosis had receded but still his body was rigid, and his hands tight-clenched.

'Nothing needs to be done immediately, Crawford.' The doctor was enjoying his mastery of the situation. 'These convulsions, although alarming to you, are merely a symptom, not the disease. They require no nostrum, and will cease very shortly. If they should re-occur, then they can be taken as a laudable sign.

'At this stage I want the child kept apart. He must drink freely of weak diluting liquors, and be gently purged. Give him balm-tea or barley water, and for food some whey-gruel, and his feet and legs must be bathed in luke-warm water eight times daily,' he paused, then asked. 'Have you had this pox, Crawford?'

She shook her head.

He lifted his eyebrows interrogatively at Anna Morris.

'I took a mild form years ago,' she informed him.

'Very well. You must not suckle your child any more, Crawford. Fortunately he is old enough to be fully weaned, so he'll take no harm from that. Indeed, it would be better if you did not handle him, or spend time in his breath. The smallpox is very contagious. We are not sure exactly how it spreads, but it could well be 'by bodily contact, or by inhaling foul air from the victim's lungs. If you continue to give him suck, Crawford, then you would most certainly take a most virulent form of the disease from him, and would most probably die.' He again paused, but this time

124

smiled reassuringly at the worried girl. 'Don't be feared. I intend to carry out the inoculation operation on all here who have not had the pox previously. That will ensure protection for you.'

'Mister Morris won't like that,' Anna Morris asserted. 'He says that the inoculation is against the word of God.'

'Then your husband must lump it,' Lucas replied equably. 'For I know of nothing in the Scriptures which forbids us helping those who are sick by any means in our power.'

'But it's a heathen practice.' The woman was not convinced. 'Them Blacks and Moors and Turks does it.'

'And so do many Christians, Mistress Morris. Now let me hear no more on the subject. Do you have a room that can be used for a quarantine?'

Anna Morris thought for a moment. 'There's the one Liza Parker is in. My husband says that she needs to meditate on the word of God, and so must sleep separate for a while . . . ' she suddenly smiled with grim satisfaction, 'but youm paying the piper, Doctor, so can call some of the tunes. I'll tell Morris that you says you must have Parker's room. He'll not argue wi' you this early in the game.'

'Good, get it prepared if you will Mistress Morris, and you Crawford, can accompany me. I shall examine the rest of the children to check for the smallpox, and then explain to you the new arrangements I have in mind for the sick room. This will be the beginnings of your instruction for your new post.'

Involuntarily she looked at her child and stepped towards him, but Lucas Royston gently took her arm.

'No, Crawford, you must not touch him until I say that you can. Please, have trust in me.'

Doubtfully she allowed him to lead her from the room. Further along the corridor a door crashed open and Anna Morris's deep-timbered voice resounded loudly. 'Get out o' that bed, Liza Parker, and get yourself dressed decent. You can meditate on the word o' God, while youm scrubbing some floors for me . . . '

125

Chapter Twelve

Lucas Royston rode away from the poorhouse some hours later well content with what he had achieved. He thought about the young pauper woman, Matilda Crawford. He had spent some considerable time that afternoon instructing her in what he required and had been surprised and pleased by her.

'She is indeed intelligent, and shows much aptitude for the work. Quite ladylike, considering her station in life. Of course, she's been in service to gentry, so that would explain that aspect of her. Even the lowest can acquire some smattering of genteel deportment if they are observant and quick-witted. She has exceptionally fine teeth, good figure and skin as well, and smelt fresh. Damn pretty woman. Once I'm established in the town, and can afford to do so, I might take her into my house as my servant. And if she could be discreet, mayhap into my bed as well.' For a few moments his imagination pictured Tildy lying naked on a bed, and his throat tightened. 'She'd make a rare sweet armful in the night.'

As he neared Redditch he considered his other stroke of good fortune. The child with the smallpox. 'If I can prevent it spreading, and use the inoculation method upon the rest of the paupers in the house, then that would create quite a stir locally.'

The loathesome disease was greatly feared, its mortality rate was high, and its survivors carried the scars of its onslaught to the end of their days. Although the procedure of inoculation had been known in England for more than a hundred years, yet the vast majority of the population ranged themselves against the practice. Some on religious grounds, others through ignorance and superstition.

'If I can be successful at the poorhouse, it would gain me great kudos throughout the parish. Such a success would undoubtedly bring me many patients of the better sort. I might even become wealthy as a result.'

His rosy imaginings accompanied him towards his new home, a tumbledown cottage in the Silver Square. To get there he had to pass through Silver Street, which ran from the square into the main road through an archway abutting on the Red Lion Inn. It was one of the worst slums in the parish, and contained two big lodging houses, each licenced to take in up to forty transients nightly, which guaranteed a constant replenishment of the slum's riotous, drunken, brawling population. The mean hovels and crooked gabled houses crammed tightly together in their broken-doored, rag-stuffed windowed squalor were a seething noisy ferment of humanity by day and night, and a fetid smell hung heavy at all seasons of the year, no matter how hard the winds blew and the rain lashed down on its dirt walkways and red-tiled roofs.

Now, at the end of a working day, rough-looking men lounged and smoked, haggard women nagged and haggled, children played and fought, half-starved dogs hunted rats and manged cats hissed and clawed among the heaps of rotting garbage, human excreta and animal waste that lay on all sides.

Lucas left his horse at the Red Lion stables and made his way on foot under the archway and along the filthy narrow street carrying his ancient leather bag with him. He reached his new home and for a moment regarded its single-storied squalid front with jaundiced eyes.

'Ahhh well, beggars cannot be choosers, as my dear uncle would point out to me,' he sighed, and entered his front room. Its sole furnishings were a straight-backed wooden chair and a rickety table. Behind this room was his bedchamber, containing a narrow bed, and a battered chest of drawers surmounted by a cracked mirror. And leading off from the back wall was a windowless scullery, with a brick shelf for his water jug and washing bowl, but no water supply or even waste pipe.

He sighed again, and placing his bag on the table slumped down on to the creaking chair. For a moment despondency threatened to overwhelm him, but he forced himself to grin.

'Don't be such a sorry dog, Royston. At least now you have your own chambers, and practice, and those are two articles that you did not possess a week ago.'

There came a sharp knocking at the door, and when he answered the summons he was shocked to find Anna Coldericke facing him. Against the background of the dirty street and the equally dirty crowd of curious spectators that her presence had attracted, she was startlingly elegant in her pale-blue walking gown and feathered bonnet, with a silken parasol twirling slowly behind her head.

She smiled at his obvious surprise. 'Pray do not be alarmed, Doctor Lucas, the fact of my calling upon you will not compromise your reputation in the town, I do assure you.'

'Forgive me.' He bowed, and stood aside from the doorway. 'Please come in, Mrs Coldericke. My lodgings are as yet unfurnished, but I can at least offer you a chair to sit upon.'

She deftly furled her parasol, and entered the room, the perfume she wore filling his nostrils and blotting out the foul odours of the street.

'Please,' he indicated the single chair, but she shook her head.

'I thank you, but no . . . I come to you to ask for your professional assistance, Doctor, not to make polite conversation.'

He found himself looking at her clear complexion and full-breasted body with some considerable degree of sexual appreciation, and mentally accepted the fact that he had been celibate too long for his own peace of mind. Now he smiled, and with a touch of gallantry bowed again.

'I will be honoured to aid you in any way that I can.'

Her grey eyes were serious. 'I wish you to examine a small boy child, Doctor Royston. I fear that he is gravely ill, perhaps even near to death. To my own untrained eyes he appears to be suffering from the chin cough, or whooping cough, as the new term has it.'

Lucas's first reaction was to agree immediately to her request, but then his native caution intervened.

'Certainly, I will be happy to oblige you, Mrs Coldericke, but why have you come to me, a newcomer, rather than to one of the established medical gentlemen?'

'Because none of the established medical gentlemen will agree to examine this child.' She told him coolly, and Lucas chuckled in amusement.

'I find your candour refreshing, Ma'am, if not particularly complimentary. For it appears by your words that I am being approached as your last resort.'

The skin around her eyes patterned into laughter creases. 'I find myself liking you, Doctor Royston. I feel that we may have some facets of character that are very alike. Will you accompany me to the child?'

He placed his top hat on his head and tapped it down firmly. 'Lead on, Ma'am.' He danced a few jig-steps. 'Look how you call the tune for me.'

Her laughter pealed out, then a sombreness replaced the merriment. 'I should warn you, Sir, that the child is of pauper parents, there is no fee to be earned for attending it.'

'Is that the reason my colleagues refused your invitation?' Lucas asked dryly, and was a little surprised when she shook her head.

'Not entirely the reason, Sir. In fairness to those other gentlemen, they have many times in the past acceded to my requests of a similar nature. In this case however, the obstacle to their acceptance is the child's father. His name is Danks. Edwin Danks. He is a notorious local ruffian who has at different times insulted most of the principal inhabitants of the parish, and indeed, assaulted some who objected to his insults.' She paused, watching for the young man's reaction to this, with a speculative gleam in her grey eyes. 'To speak frankly, Doctor Royston, I am of the opinion that the other medical gentlemen are feared of what Edwin Danks might do against them if they should intervene in this case and then the child should die.'

It was Lucas Royston's turn to regard the woman with a speculative gleam in his eye. 'And if I intervene, and the child should die, what then, Mrs Coldericke? What might Edwin Danks attempt against me?'

The lucent grey eyes bored into him. 'I hold the opinion, Doctor Royston, that you are a man of courage.' Her voice was innocent of any sarcastic inflection. 'I am convinced that where you perceive it to be your duty as a doctor to act, then nothing will deter you from carrying out that duty.'

Lucas pondered for a moment, then shrugged his thin shoulders and smiled wrly. 'Your words have insured that I can now do naught else but accompany you, Mrs Coldericke.' He lifted his bag from the table. 'If the child is so gravely ill, we'd best waste no more time before making an examination.'

'Danks lives in the Hill Street, down beyond the Unicorn Hill,' she explained as they walked side by side towards the Chapel Green.

'What has brought this particular child to your attention, Mrs Coldericke?' Lucas wanted to know.

'His mother once worked in my house as a maid. She was a good girl, and I grew fond of her.'

'Do you go among the poor a great deal?'

'Do you mean to ask. ''Am I a doer of good deeds and a charitable ornament of society''?' A tartness edged her voice, and Lucas was perceptive enough to understand what had caused it.

'Pray do not misunderstand me, Mrs Coldericke. I know that there are those ladies who disguise less admirable motivation under the guise of charity, and I do not for one moment consider you to be of that type. I was merely enquiring from interest.'

130

She flashed him a rueful smile. 'My apologies, Doctor Royston. I fear, as I once explained to you, that I am over-quick to suspect malice where at times none is intended. To answer your question; I take an interest in the welfare of the poor, but my own circumstances do not permit me to do a great deal to aid the misfortunates of the parish. And to speak bluntly, there is little enough one can do to aid many of their number.' She came to a standstill and faced the young man, and he saw anger in her face.

'Many of the lower orders hereabouts are like brute beasts, Doctor Royston. Indeed they are more ignorant and degraded than the beasts of the fields. They remain unwashed by choice, and would prefer to spend whatever money they have on drink and debauchery rather than food or clothing or household goods. They brawl among themselves like savages, and at times it is unsafe for any respectable person even to pass near to them, and the men serve their womenfolk and children most vilely. It is rare to find one among them who has any conception of the higher things of life. They jeer at learning and culture, and if anything of beauty should come within their grasp, then they seek only to destroy it.'

Lucas was no great lover of the labouring classes of his country, but he felt the urge to defend them against such sweeping condemnation.

'Come now, Mrs Coldericke, surely they cannot be so bad as you make them out to be. Some small proportion of them may be so, but I am convinced that most of the lower orders are possessed of much goodness of heart, and fine qualities of soul.'

Her eyes gleamed with sudden mischievous humour. 'I am so glad to find you well-disposed towards them, Doctor Royston. Because Edwin Danks was the foremost among the men who tumbled you off the Pigeon Bridge and into the stream when you first arrived in this town.'

He gaped at her in astonishment, and her white teeth glistened in laughter as she told him. 'La, Doctor, did you think to keep such a happening hidden from the public knowledge? Gossip has wings in these parts, and it was known all over the parish not an hour after the event.'

He remained silent, and there was a hint of challenge in her voice as she went on, 'Well, Doctor? Now that you know the child's parentage, do you still wish to examine him?'

It was his turn to laugh as he answered with mock ruefulness. 'Would that my heart were not so full of charity, Mrs Coldericke. Then I could refuse, and mayhap save myself another drenching.'

They walked on, talking of other matters, and finding an increasing enjoyment in each other's company.

Hill Street resembled Silver Street in its ramshackle narrowness and swarming life, but here, to compound the general filth, many of the houses were built around enclosed courts. Gloomy, stench-filled pits into which the sun's rays could not penetrate except at the zenith. It was into one of these courts that Anna Coldericke led the way. The high brass pattens strapped to her feet keeping her dainty shoes out of the inches thick liquid ordure that covered the ground. Even as they ducked through the low doorway of the hovel they sought, they could hear the paroxysmal whooping coughing of the child upstairs.

'Molly, it's Anna Coldericke. I've brought the doctor with me,' Anna Coldericke shouted, and beckoned Lucas to follow her up the short dark staircase.

The bedroom was low-ceilinged and minute, the crude wooden bed almost filling the floor space. A young sallow-faced, sunken-eyed woman was sitting on the side of the straw mattress supporting the heaving body of the child. Lucas stayed in the doorway while he waited for the coughing fit to subside. Inured by familiarity he watched the blue face – the watering eyes, protruding tongue with saliva streaming and mucus running nose – and listened to the agonized wheezing of the child's struggles to draw breath, without any emotion other than a clinical interest.

At last the child became exhausted, and the coughing eased, and with the first breaths whistling into the straining lungs, the mother was able to lay the wasted little body back on to the rough blanket.

Molly Danks, whose own body was as thin and wasted as her child's, tried to smile at the doctor.

Satisfied that the attack had fully passed, he moved to look down into the wide frightened eyes of the small boy.

'Lie easy, child, I'll not harm you,' he said softly, and after feeling the pulse in the stick-thin wrist he carefully lifted the soiled nightshirt and glanced at the fragile chest which rose and fell with the rapidity of a pumping-bellows. Apart from the normal spatterings of vermin-bites and pauper-sores there were no sign of buboes or rashes to indicate any other disease being present.

Lucas smiled at the anxious mother. 'Don't fret, Moll. I'll soon have your son well again.'

Her lips trembled, and she whispered. 'I 'opes so, Sir. We'se had Esther Smith in to him, and she give him the spider charms, but it doon't serve at all by the looks on the poor little cratur.'

'Spider charms?' Lucas exclaimed. 'Esther Smith? Who the devil might she be?'

'One of the local cunning women,' Anna Coldericke explained. 'When the people have no money for doctors, they call in the cunning woman or man to treat their sick. Many of the locals prefer them to the doctors anyway. See there, the bag at the head of the bed.'

'Damned witchcraft!' Lucas cursed disgustedly, and snatched the small cloth bag from its hanging nail. He opened it, and poured out the contents of dead and dying spiders onto the floor, where their furry legs twitched and wriggled until he crushed them angrily beneath his boot.

'I've heard of this practice before,' he told Anna Coldericke. 'The dammed witches put the bag into the patient's mouth, then hang it on the head of the bed. They claim that as the spiders die, so the whooping cough disappears. Damned arrant nonsense!'

Molly Danks began to wring her hands in apprehension, and Lucas calmed at the sight of her fear. 'There is no call

133

for you to worry because I've destroyed those filthy insects, Moll. Esther Smith is not able to harm you with her nonsense or spells. It is only superstition.'

Her lips were again trembling slightly. 'It's not so much her as frightens me, Sir. But Edwin, me husband, he swears by Esther Smith. He'll goo bloody mad when he sees what you'se done.'

'Will he now?' Lucas said grimly. 'Where is he at present?'

'I doon't rightly know, Sir,' she answered tremulously. 'He's out wi' his mates somewheres. He'll goo bloody mad when he comes back and sees what you'se done to the spider charms.'

'Then before he returns we must put it back as it was,' Anna Coldericke intervened positively. 'Go and find some spiders and replace them in the bag.' She took it from Lucas and handed it to the other woman. 'Go quickly now.'

As soon as Moll Danks's feet were on the stairs, Anna Coldericke laid her hands on the man's arms. 'Please do not be angry,' she beseeched him. 'I know, as you do, that these charms are worse than useless, but what good would be served by our destroying it? Poor Moll would only get a beating from that brute she is wed to, for not preventing the destruction.'

Lucas reached up to touch her soft warm cheek with his fingers. 'It is you who should be angry with me,' he told her softly, 'I acted impulsively. It will do no harm to let the spiders hang there. God knows, the house is dirty enough for a few more vermin not to be noticed. But how am I to ensure that the child will receive the treatment I shall prescribe, if that man is so enthused by the cunning woman's remedies?'

Her strong jaw jutted. 'I shall do whatsoever is needed,' she said determinedly. 'Edwin Danks will accept that fact.'

As he looked at her, he again noticed her full firm body, and again experienced a powerful frisson of sexual excitement. *'By God, but she'd make a lusty bedmate,'* he told himself. '*And by God, I need such a one. I've been too long without a woman's loving.*'

Now her eyes were warm and soft as she smiled at him. 'Are the instructions for the treatment very complicated, Lucas?'

Her use of his first name promised a potential intimacy which the young man in his present mood of heightened tension, was only too happy to further in its development. 'Indeed they are somewhat, Anna. For the child is very low, I fear, and will require a course of differing treatments.'

'Then might I suggest we take some refreshment at my house and I shall write down the full particulars of what must be done.'

Thinking he saw invitation to something more in her eyes Lucas immediately accepted the proffered suggestion.

Moll Danks came up the stairs, breaking the mood of deepening intimacy, and Anna Coldericke turned from him with a slight moue of irritation, then after Lucas had briefly advised her on the correct care for the child she told the woman. 'I shall return on the morrow, Molly. We'll commence treatment then.' She smiled over her shoulder at Lucas, 'Come then, Doctor Royston, I shall write down your instructions at my house.'

As they picked their way back down the deep-rutted street Anna Coldericke stole side-long glances at her companion, and was powerfully attracted to what she saw. She was a hot-blooded woman, who beneath her cool, controlled façade possessed strong sexual appetites. But deep-grained fastidiousness and self-respect had until now prevented her from indulging in the casual sexual affairs that other women who were in her widowed condition conducted with the available local men: though there were nights when alone in her bed Anna Coldericke wept tears of frustration, and eased her hungers as best she could.

She had been very young when she had wed her dashing soldier, and had loved him with all the fervour and devotion of a first romance. Their time together had been tragically brief. She had still been a newly-wed bride of sixteen years when her husband had sailed for Portugal with his regiment to fight against the armies of Napoleon Bonaparte, and when he had died, whimpering her name on the blood-soaked ridge of Albuera she was left a widow at only nineteen years of age. Her grief had been so intense that for long years she had virtually lived the life of a cloistered nun in her parents' house. It was the same house in which she now dwelt, and it was only their deaths some six years previously that had forced her to face the world once more.

She taught from financial need, having only limited means of her own, but found that although she enjoyed doing so, and it relieved some portion of her terrible loneliness, still that inner loneliness could never be banished. Although she longed to take pleasure in the companionship of others, yet whenever she went out into society the people she met with both bored and irritated her, and because of that irritation she found herself verbally slashing at them with a scornful aggression.

She was honest enough to admit that she had only herself to blame for her loneliness, but to her own dismay found that she could not change her personality. Now, at thirty years of age, she was facing the bleak prospect of a lifetime of loneliness and social solitude stretching before her, in which her only solace would be that which she found in the books that filled her home.

Now she listened to Lucas Royston's talk with an intense pleasure, scarcely daring to hope that in this younger man she had found someone to fill the void her life had become.

'I am a follower of William Buchan's doctrines,' there was an excitement in Lucas Royston's voice which drew her into a sense of identification with him. 'He was a great man, and a truly great physician.'

'I fear I've not heard of the gentleman,' Anna Colderricke confessed.

'Few people outside my profession have,' Lucas admitted. 'It seems that it is only the quacks and self-styled miracle workers who attract widespread attention, and those like James and Godfrey and Daffy who produced patent elixers that do more harm through misuse than any good. But William Buchan will eventually gain the fame to which he was entitled. His doctrines are simplicity itself. He advocated cleanliness, fresh air, exercise, moderation and the isolation of certain diseases, and he believed that many diseases could be avoided altogether by following those simple precepts.' His enthusiasm made him appear very young, and his pale face took colour as his excitement in telling her of these things took hold of him. 'Do you know, Anna, that William Buchan was one of the first medical men to practice inoculation for the smallpox?'

'Oh come now,' she teased gently. 'I fear that you do my own sex a grave injustice. Did not Lady Mary Wortly Montague first introduce that practice into England, I believe as long ago as a century past. And does not Jenner practice a form of it also?

'Yes, that may be so, Anna, but even now in this modern day and age, there are still great numbers of the population who hold out against it. It was men like William Buchan who carried the fight forwards against such ignorance.' He paused. 'Have you, yourself taken inoculation, Anna?'

She shook her head. 'No, I've not taken it. But I am not opposed to it. Indeed, from my reading of such matters it appears to be both laudable and efficacious.'

By now they had completed the short walk to her home, which was situated on the western side of the Redditch Green, obliquely facing the front of St Stephen's chapel. Known as the Ivy House – because its brickwork was literally covered with that tenacious creeper – it's high-gabled front presented a sombre and slightly forbidding aspect to the world. 'Rather like myself, I fear,' Anna Coldericke thought with a sardonic amusement.

Inside the house Lucas looked around the large front sitting-room with interest. It was simply, but comfortably furnished in the heavy Jacobean style with a small blackboard on its easel against one wall, and several additional stools and small tables which Anna Coldericke's pupils utilized as desks.

The hour was now late and the last of the daylight was dying. Anna Coldericke used a phosphorus match to light candles, and as she leaned forward to apply the flame to the wick of the candle in front of Lucas, his eyes were drawn to the dark cleft between the upper globes of her white breasts, and his breath quickened as the heat of sexual wanting engorged his private parts.

She seated herself and made ready paper and a quill pen, then smiled at Lucas.

'Please, give me the full instructions for the treatment.'

With an effort he dragged his imagination back from its erotic visualizing of himself and Anna Coldericke entwined in nakedness. He unconsciously struck a pose, with his hands clasping the lapels of his coat, and his head tilted backwards, as though he sought for inspiration from the Heavens, and Anna bit her lips to prevent herself giggling. She found his stance and manner delightfully endearing for her own vivid imagination was picturing his well-shaped lips greedily kissing her breasts and throat, and the feel of his slender body against her own.

'In this particular case, having due regard for the condition of the patient's living quarters and parentage, I propose the following . . . '

Even his pomposity as he spoke was a delight to Anna, and the aching need for a man that had tormented her for so many long years now centred itself on one man only. The one who stood beside her, and whose lilting Scots voice reverberated in her head.

' . . . the patient's body must be kept gently open, so you shall dose him with two teaspoonfuls of tincture of rhubarb thrice daily. Then I wish you to infuse two ounces of woodlice in one pint of small white wine for one night. Strain the liquor through a cloth, and give the child one tablespoonful thrice or four times daily. At the same time I wish you to use the garlic ointment.'

'How?' Anna found it hard to concentrate on medical

matters while he was close enough for her to smell the faint male acridity of his body.

'It is very simple, my dear. Take hogs lard and garlic in equal quantity, beat it to a paste in a mortar and rub the soles of the boy's feet with it twice or thrice daily. However, if he becomes very hot or feverish, then you must cease using it, for it may well increase those symptoms.

'Finally, bathe his feet in warm water once every three days, and keep a Burgundy pitch plaster constantly between his shoulder-blades.'

He relaxed his pose, and smiled down at her, and again his eyes dwelt on the dark cleft between her swelling breasts.

'If that regimen should fail to affect a full cure within a se'nnight, then I shall recommend another course of treatment.' A hint of smugness crept into his voice. 'However, I think that it will prove salutary.'

She laid down her quill pen and rose to stand facing him, so close as to be almost in bodily contact. 'I shall commence it tomorrow, Lucas.' Her voice was only a whisper as she saw and understood the hunger in his dark eyes.

'And tonight, Anna?' he muttered hoarsely. 'What of tonight?'

Very slowly, as if of their own volition, her hands rose and cupped his thin, flushed face. 'What would you wish of tonight, Lucas?' she whispered.

His arms went around her and pulled her hard against his body, and she met his searching lips with eager pressure.

Without any words exchanged they went with close-pressed limbs to her bedroom, and there she let him strip her clothing from her, and welcomed with soft gasps of delight the exquisite tremors that his mouth sent shuddering through her body as his lips and tongue sought out the secret places. All the suppressed passions of years burst free from their bondage, and with a fervency bordering on savagery she drained the lusts from him, and demanded yet more. For Lucal Royston it was a shattering revelation of

139

the depths of a woman's needs, and long before the dawn paled the night skies he was spent and exhausted – and deep within his being a little afraid. He knew, that as a sexual man, he was no match for the sexuality his body had unleashed from this woman, whose soft lips and hands were even now seeking to arouse his maleness yet again, and use it to satisfy her still voracious hungerings . . .

Chapter Thirteen

'It arn't fair! That old cow is just spiting me, making me do this.' For the twentieth time that morning Liza Parker bemoaned her lot, and Tildy felt her own patience straining.

The two of them were in the brew-house, boiling the soiled clothing and bedding of the sick patients in the great copper. Tildy bent over the bubbling, steaming mess and used a wooden dolly to churn the wash, thrusting down with all her strength to force the foul-smelling dirt from the fibres.

The younger girl let go of her own dolly and went to the door to peer morosely at the cloud-covered sky.

'It's still bloody drizzling! Wheer 'ull we be able to dry the bloody things when we'se done washing 'um. That's what I'd like to know. We wunt be allowed to hang 'um in the bloody kitchen.' Her peevish whinings finally provoked Tildy into a sharp rejoinder.

'Look Liza, I've done naught else but hear your belly-aching all morning. I'm not enjoying this myself, but it's got to be done, and it'll get done sooner if you'd work harder, instead of moaning.'

The girl's snub nose tilted scornfully. 'Youm a real Goody Two Shoes, arn't you. Well wait 'till you'se bin here as long as me. You'll change your tune then, just see if you wunt.'

'How long have you been here, Liza?' Tildy was suddenly curious.

'Years and bloody years, ever since I was a babby. I was brought here by me Mam, but she died pretty quick, and I've got no kin, so I was kept here.' The girl came to lounge against the brickwork surround of the copper. 'I bin put out to service two or three times, but they always sent me back here arter a bit.'

'Why was that?' Although she asked, Tildy could already guess at the answer, and it was no surprise when the girl smiled lasciviously, and ran her hands down across her jutting breasts and full hips.

'Because o' these, Tildy. The men couldn't keep their hands off 'um, and their wives got jealous, so the old cows buggered me off, back to wheer I'd come from. One time I come back wi' a big belly as well. It was a sight to see the cow's face when I told her that her husband had babbied me. She couldn't get me out o' the house quick enough. Theer was blood and snot flew theer that night, I can tell you.

'He thought it was him that had babbied me as well. Went down on his knees, so he did, shouting out for God to forgive him for being snared by a low, dirty harlot. And at the same time he was offering me gold guineas to keep quiet about him being the father. He were a churchwarden, see, and was dead scared o' the parson and his neighbours finding out what a dirty old bastard he really was.'

The girl laughed harshly. 'Mind you, fair play, it probably warn't him as put the babby in me belly. I'd had a few frolics wi' the local lads. So I took the money, and at first kept me mouth shut, but when his old woman started knocking me about for being pregnant, I told her she'd do better to knock her man about, because it was him as had done it to me.'

The harsh laughter came again, but there was no joy in its raucous echoings. 'By the Christ! She didn't 'alf goo for the bugger. Like a wildcat, she was, and I was hauled back here the same night.'

'And the baby?' Tildy queried.

The girl shrugged carelessly. 'Lost it, arter I'd carried it

142

for five months. Good riddance too. What would I ha' done wi' it?' The whining peevishness crept into her voice once more. 'It's alright for the likes o' Katie Reeves to have a bucketful o' kids. She makes a good living out on her bastards. She's got a lot o' kinfolks hereabouts, and they'll always find her a cottage or summat to rent. She comes in here to have her babbies, and then goes out agen and gets half-a-crown a week for each on 'um from the parish. So she goes on the randy wi' the money then, until she's got another on the way, and then she comes back in here for the birthing.' Liza's small pugged features were solemn as she said reflectively, 'I don't reckon as how I'd like to be like her though, Tildy. She's a real hard bugger, so she is. Them kids of her'n only gets fed and clothed when they'm in here. When she's out theer with 'um, the poor little sods be half-perished wi' want, and she don't give a toss about 'um.' Eyes wide, she stared at Tildy with an expression of incredulity. 'Does you know what Katie said to me, Tildy? She said that when she was young, like me, she'd wanted a husband and kids that she could love and care for. She said her hard luck had made her like she is now, and that I'd be exact the same as her when I got to her age. I can't believe that to be true, can you, Tildy? I'll never get like her, will I?'

Tildy's heart went out to this pathetic child-woman. 'No Liza, you'll never be like Katie Reeves,' she hastened to assure her. Inwardly she raged against the fate that seemed so cruelly tilted against the Liza Parkers of this world. Why should young girls be forced to act the whore by those who should protect them? The stones are not thrown at the men who abuse these children, only at the children them-selves . . . A terrible sense of frustration swept over Tildy. *But what can I do to change these things? I'm as useless and helpless as the other women here. I can't even support myself and little Davy, let alone poor souls like Liza.* The emotion reached its apex, then slowly began to ebb, and as it did so the fire of determination and defiance that no wave of hopelessness ever succeeded in completely extinguishing began to flicker. *'I'll do something. I don't know what, but I'll do something to fight back.'*

'Tildy? Tildy? Come here quick.'

Tildy was suddenly back in the present. She went into the courtyard, followed by Liza Parker. Hannah Knight was outside the kitchen door talking volubly with a packman.

'Here she be,' the pregnant girl pointed towards Tildy. 'This is the wench you wants.'

The man looked Tildy up and down, and whistled appreciatively through his gapped teeth. The steaming heat of the brew-house had caused her to undo the top of her bodice, and the rich curves of her breasts swelled visibly. She hastily buttoned the damp cloth as the packman winked cheekily.

'I wish I was twenty years younger, pretty girl. I'd come courting you a bit rapid.'

Tildy took no offence. Honest and open admiration never caused her to feel demeaned. It was the sly glance, and the sniggering innuendo-laden whispers of certain types of men that made her feel soiled and degraded.

'What do you want of me, master?' she asked the man, who unslung his pack and placed it on the cobbles in front of him without answering. He opened its flap and with a flourish held out towards her a glowing bunch of scarlet ribbons.

'I'se bin told to present you wi' this fairing, pretty girl,' the packman grinned. 'And arter seeing you,' he paused and whistled again through his teeth. 'I'm agoing to say right out, that your future sweetheart is a real luck-blessed cove. That's who this is from, your future sweetheart.'

Tildy stared at the bundle of silks with a mingling of conflicting emotions. Surprise, delight, curiosity, suspicion, all battled for dominance.

'Goo on pretty girl, take it,' the packman urged. 'For I'se got to be on me way. I've an urgent call to make.' He pushed the fairing into her hands, shouldered his pack, and was walking away before Tildy had gathered her wits enough to react.

'But who sent it to me?' she called after his disappearing back.

The man shouted over his shoulder without stopping. 'Doon't know his name, pretty girl. He was a tall cove wi' a long scar down his face. Looks to be a dealer o' some sorts, by the cut on him.'

Tildy marshalled the confusion of information, but before she could collate the fragments, Hannah Knight's quick wits reached a conclusion.

'It's Caleb Hawkes, Tildy,' she burst out excitedly. 'It's him that's sent this to you. It's the higgler.'

Tildy's eyes remained fixed on the waves of silks lucently shimmering as she tumbled and turned them in her fingers.

'Caleb Hawkes.' She pictured his light-blue eyes and reckless piratical looks. 'What was the message? Oh yes . . . from her future sweetheart.' Her full lips curved in a smile of pleasure. This was the first fairing she had ever received and its connotations of tender loving brought a tremorous excitement to her breathing and a warmth to her heart.

Anna Morris came into the yard carrying with her some more soiled clothing and bedding. She saw the ribbons and frowned.

'Wheer did they come from?'

'The higgler sent 'um to Tildy,' Hannah Knight said enviously. 'She'll soon be out o' this place with her own house and carriage.'

The mistress sniffed dismissively. 'The only thing she's likely to get from that randy bugger is a bell··ful.'

'Have you been in to Davy?' Tildy asked eagerly.

Anna Morris smiled grimly. 'Yes, girl, Lord love me! You worries about that babby o' yourn too much. I'm taking good care of him, and doing everything that can be done. Like the doctor told me, I opens the window by day, and closes it by night. I'm giving him lots to drink and washing his feet and legs every day.'

'Well why cannot I go in to see him?' Tildy demanded. 'Why must you keep the door locked against me?'

'Because that's what Doctor Royston told me to do.' Anna Morris's heavy features were expressionless. 'He's got all these new-fangled ideas, and he won't have his orders gainsaid.'

'But he's got no right to keep me from my child,' Tildy argued. 'And it's my right to help nurse my baby when he's sick.'

'You'se got no rights in here, girl,' the woman said matter of factly. 'When you comes into the poor'us, then your rights, as you terms 'um, stays outside the door.'

'But that is so unjust,' Tildy protested vigorously.

'Unjust you may think it to be, Crawford, but it's the way o' things and can't be altered by the likes o' you – or by the likes o' me, come to that.' The mistress turned and handed the bundle of dirty linen to Liza Parker. 'Here, get these in the wash.'

With a sullen expression the young girl obeyed and Anna Morris turned again to Tildy. 'Listen Crawford, I've bin patient wi' you and let you keep on nagging me about your babby, because I reckon you to be a good and loving mother, not like a lot o' the whores in here. But enough is enough. You'll get back wi' your babby when the doctor says you can, and not afore. So don't keep on nagging me about it. The doctor 'ull be here later on today. You'd best see him and ask him when you can care for your babby agen. Now get on wi' your work.'

With a bad grace Tildy went back into the brew-house. The fairing, which only moments before had filled her with pleasure, now looked tawdry and cheap in her eyes. 'How could I take delight in such a thing when my Davy is lying ill?' she castigated herself. 'I was acting like a hedge-slut, thinking about a man, when all my thoughts should have been with my child.'

In a sudden surge of self-disgust she hurled the fairing away from her, and it flew through the door and landed on the cobbles of the yard. The breeze stirred the strands causing them to quiver, and for a brief moment it resembled some tiny bloodied animal twitching in its death-throes.

Liza Parker stared in surprise at Tildy's set face, but recognizing the need to leave the other to her own thoughts, said nothing, and went on thrusting at the boiling cloth with her dolly . . .

Chapter Fourteen

Tildy was in the sick room when Lucas Royston arrived. The young man regarded the room with satisfaction. Compared to its previous condition something of a transformation had been effected. The floor was swept, the windows were opened wide and the influx of fresh air had dissipated the thickest of the foul smell. The bedding looked fresh, the patients' night-shifts were clean, and the patients themselves had been allotted as bedfellows with the most suitable of their fellow sufferers. On a sideboard by the door clean bed-pans, bowls, spitting-pots, towels, spare night-shifts and nightcaps were neatly ranged.

'It looks well,' Lucas told himself and then frowned. In the bed next to the sideboard an old man and woman lay side by side. Both were comatose, breathing stertorously. Lucas beckoned Tildy to him and pointed at the shrivelled faces half hidden by the nightcaps pulled low on their heads and tied with large bows beneath their sunken gaping mouths.

'Why are these two sharing? It is wrong for the sexes to be in such close proximity.'

Tildy, still resentful of his stricture against her nursing her own child, answered sharply. 'We did as you bade us to, Doctor Royston.'

He stared harder at her, surprised by the asperity in her voice. 'I did not say that the opposing sexes should be bedfellows, Crawford.'

'No, Doctor, but you did tell us that the dying should be put together. We have no other beds, and no other rooms to enable us to put them apart. And I do not think that in their condition there will be any danger of indecencies occuring.'

His frown deepened. 'I'm not sure that I like your tone, Crawford.'

Tildy's brown eyes met him defiantly. 'And I don't like being kept from my own child, when he is most in need of my care, Doctor Royston.'

Lucas smiled abruptly, and his stiff posture relaxed. 'So that is the reason for your insolence, Crawford. The fact that I have quite correctly isolated your bairn. Well, I have sound medical reasons for doing so, and if you were not such an ignorant and un-lettered woman you would appreciate why isolation is so necessary.'

There was just a hint of malicious delight in teasing this good-looking woman. Subconsciously he resented the fact that she had never displayed any awareness of him as a man, only as a giver of instructions. He watched the distress mounting in her face, and relented.

'I will explain my reasons fully, Crawford, when we have completed our present tasks here. After all, if you are to be a good nurse, then it is necessary that you should know certain medical facts.' He looked again at the two ancients in the bed. 'They're not long for this world. Let them stay as they are. It would be more cruel than kind to disturb them again, immoral though their bed-sharing is. Now, the woman who has Erysipelas?'

'She's been moved down there, Doctor.' Tildy indicated a bed at the far end of the room, in which a pregnant woman was lying beside a young girl.

'I shall want a bowl and clean rags, she'll need to be bled today.'

Tildy fetched the articles to him as he opened his bag at the bedside and took out a small sharp knife. The young girl in the bed saw the knife and her eyes enlarged with fright, but he smiled reassuringly at her.

'It's not intended for you. So rest easy.'

The pregnant woman seemed to be in a daze o. delirium,

149

her head turning from side to side on the pillow, and meaningless jumbles of words slurring from her lips as her laboured breath rasped in and out. Her face was bright red and hugely swollen, the skin covered in liquid-filled pustules, and her eyes mere slits in the puff-balled lids.

'Now, Crawford, do you know how this disease was contracted in this woman's case?' Lucas Royston was irresistibly impelled to show off his expertise. 'Of course, the rustics hereabouts term it a "Blast", and they imagine it is contracted from foul air, the "Ill Wind" as it's known to them.'

Tildy nodded. 'I've always heard that reason given.'

'Do you believe it?' the young man demanded forcefully.

Again Tildy nodded, and he smiled smugly. 'As I said before, Crawford, you are a lamentably ignorant woman. However, I intend to try and impart some knowledge of diseases, their causes and treatments to you. For I believe that you have good natural intelligence, even though you are an illiterate.'

His patronizing insults hurt Tildy, but at the same time she could not help but acknowledge the truth. She was illiterate, she was ignorant, but, she also knew that she was intelligent. And it was that very quality of high intelligence that now enabled her to realize, that this posturing, sneering man before her could begin to fill the void of her knowledge. He could teach her many things and make clear what was now shrouded from her by ignorance. She set herself to endure his insults and absorb his teachings.

'Stated simply, the Erysipelas may at times be occasioned by violent passions of the mind, such as anger, fear, etcetera.' Lucas unconsciously struck his lecturing pose. 'At other times it is contracted when the body has been heated to a great degree, and then is suddenly exposed to the cold air, which abruptly checks the perspiration.

'There have been cases when the Erysipelas has been caused by the victim staying too long in a warm bath.' He shook his head and stared speculatively at the patient. 'But

150

that latter cause does not apply in this case, I'm quite sure.' Again the shake of the head, and the pursed lips of erudite wisdom. 'No, in this case the patient has undoubtedly been drinking spirits to excess. So . . . we now have the cause.'

He gazed at Tildy expectantly, as if waiting for her to applaud him, and when she only remained silently listening, he noisily cleared his throat, and went on. 'We have the cause, an excess of strong drink. We can see that the disease has attacked her head, so to guard against a development of inflammation of the brain, I shall begin a course of bleedings, and other treatments to draw out the foul humours. Blistering plaster must be applied to her neck and feet, and she must be strongly purged also, for by keeping the body open we ensure that no faecal putridity can arise.'

His flow of words ceased momentarily as he removed the woman's nightcap and moved her upper body so that her head protruded over the edge of the bed.

'Put the bowl beneath her,' he instructed Tildy. 'Then place your hands so, and keep her head firmly held.'

He positioned Tildy's hands so that the woman's face was turned sideways, only inches from Tildy's eyes, and her long hair hung downwards towards the bowl. Then rubbed with his thumb over the large vein in her forehead. When the vein had swollen he lifted his lancet and cut into it. The blood gouted and dripped down over Tildy's restraining fingers to spatter into the bowl beneath. She felt an instant shock of nausea, and the head jerked, so that she had to struggle to keep it still. But Lucas Royston went on talking and Tildy, to her own surprise, found herself still absorbed in what he was saying. So much so that the blood she could see and feel and smell ceased to distress her but rather became an object of wonder.

'There, Crawford, there is the Life Force! Miraculous, is it not. Always remember, Crawford, that when the rustics talk of head veins and heart veins and breast veins, and tell you that bleeding from one of those particular veins will cure all diseases of the named parts, then they are fools.

All blood vessels arise from the heart, and return to it again. So, whenever bleeding is carried out, it must be drawn from as near to the infected part as possible. That is the only true method.'

The red rivulet held Tildy's eyes like a hypnotic lure and her mind soared. *How wonderful it must be, to know how to heal. Lucas Royston is only young, and yet he knows how to heal. Why should I not learn to do the same?* The idea came to her with the impact of a blow, causing her throat to constrict and her breath to catch.

And why should not pigs learn to fly? Her self-doubt jeered in her mind. *You're ignorant, you cannot read or write . . . you know nothing!*

But there are women healers. Her stubbornness rallied and counter-attacked. *Midwives and cunning women practice the healing arts.*

Midwives only help at birthings and the cunning women are reckoned by the Church to be numbered among the servants of the devil. Self-doubt riposted. *True doctors are men of education. Men of letters.*

I can learn! Stubbornness suddenly advanced, and like an irresistible army carried all before it as it gathered momentum. *I can learn to read and write. I can learn the arts of the midwives. I can learn of the herbs and plants that the cunning women use. I can learn from the books that the doctors learn from. I can learn . . . and I will . . .*

152

Chapter Fifteen

'Suffer the little children to come unto Me, saith the Lord, and forbid them not, for of such is the Kingdom of God.'

The warm breeze stirred the tails of John Clayton's cravat and ruffled the folds of his long black gown.

'Amen!' A solitary voice intoned, and someone coughed hoarsely. The curate opened his eyes and looked at the small group gathered around the open grave. His lips tightened as he saw Kate Reeves staring about her, trying to catch the attention of the burly young gravedigger.

'Lord God, how can you allow women such as her to bear children?' Clayton silently questioned, and then thrust the unworthy thought from him. The God he worshipped was All Powerful, All Knowing, and had reason for all that He created and caused to come to pass.

' . . . For as much as it has pleased Almighty God to take unto Himself the soul of this child here departed, we therefore commit his body to the ground . . . '

Tildy heard the sonorous words, and their sentiments seemed to her a mockery. If Almighty God had been pleased to take little Charlie Reeves unto Himself, then why had He also been pleased to let the poor little creature suffer so on this earth before He took him?

Beside her, Hannah Knight snuffled noisily and wiped tears from her eyes, and standing before them, Anna Morris sighed heavily and looked sombrely down at the cheap wooden box in which Charlie Reeves lay.

' . . . earth to earth, ashes to ashes, dust to dust . . . '

Kate Reeves finally caught the eye of the burly grave-digger and winked in bold invitation. The young man winked back, and wondered how he could manage to arrange a meeting later.

' . . . in sure and certain hopes of the resurrection to eternal life. Through Jesus Christ, Our Lord. Amen.'

Clods of earth thumped hollowly on the thin planks of the coffin lid as feet shuffled amongst the strewn, sun-dried clay.

John Clayton frowned to quell the restlessness, and intoned. 'Let us pray. Almighty God, our Heavenly Father . . . '

Kate Reeves clucked her tongue impatiently. This was the third child she had buried, so the proceedings held no novelty to entertain her, and she begrudged the time spent here in this peaceful churchyard. The men and laughter of the Plymouth Arms and the Navigation were tantalizingly close, and despite her enlarged belly, she knew well that she would easily find some lusty bargee or wharfman or legger to treat her to ale and gin and to satisfy her other hungers.

Unnoticed by the mourners Caleb Hawkes stood in the sun-cast shadow of the church wall, his hat held between his hands, and his eyes fixed upon Tildy Crawford. He gazed at her slender figure and oval face, and thought her truly beautiful. Unlike many of her companions she did not fidget restlessly and look about her. Instead she was still, and intent upon the curate's prayer. Caleb felt a rush of tenderness for her, and wanted to go to her side and gently stroke back from her brow the lock of dark hair which had come free from beneath her neat mobcap.

The prayer finished, the curate left the graveside, and the gathering began to disperse. The burly gravedigger sliced the blade of his long-handled shovel into the loose soil and tipped it into the dark rectangle where Charlie Reeves would all too quickly become forgotten dust. But Caleb Hawkes had no thoughts to spare for the dead. To his mind they were gone to a better world, and there they would wait for everyone else to join them. Caleb Hawkes's thoughts were centred on one living being, and she was now walking in his direction.

He stepped away from the wall, and as he did so Tildy saw him. She felt a shock of surprise, and to her own mortification was aware that colour was rising from her throat up to her cheeks. That mortification was not eased by Hannah Knight's excited exclamation, and the sharp elbow she poked into Tildy's side.

'Look theer, Tildy. It's him! It's the higgler!'

Anna Morris was leading the group of paupers and she nodded to Caleb Hawkes. 'I bid you good day, Master Hawkes.'

He smiled easily. 'I was passing Mistress Morris, and saw your cart.' He jerked his head towards the wooden-wheeled handcart outside the churchyard gate on which the coffin had been pushed some two miles to Tardebigge church by the paupers from Webheath. 'If you want, I can hitch one of my donkeys to draw it home for you.'

The mistress glanced behind her towards Tildy Crawford, and said in a low voice, 'She's a good girl, Caleb Hawkes, and she's got troubles enough, wi'out you adding to 'um.'

The man answered with deadly seriousness. 'I've no intention of doing that, Anna Morris. You know well enough that I've never bin one to take advantage of women, or to blaggard them.'

The woman nodded. 'Just see that you doon't begin to wi' this one, then.' And walking on, she added, 'and I'll be grateful if you'll draw back the cart wi' the donkey.'

The man smiled at Tildy as she came abreast of him. 'Are you going back directly to the poorhouse, Mistress Crawford?'

'I am.' Her colour was high, but she fought to maintain an outwardly calm demeanour, although his being here flustered her more than she cared to admit to herself.

'Then we're well met.' His white teeth gleamed in his bronzed face, and Tildy acknowledged to herself that she found him very attractive.

'I'm going to hitch one o' my donkeys to the cart, to save you pushing it back over them hills.'

Katie Reeves, surrounded by her cronies, now came up by the trio, and she halted also. 'Well, if it arn't his Royal Highness, Master Caleb Hawkes, come apaying court to our own lovely Tildy.' Jealousy sparked in her eyes as she looked at the couple. 'Arn't I good enough for you anymore then, Hawkes?'

She sneered angrily at Tildy and patted her swollen body. 'This could well be one o' his'n, Lady Muck. He puts hisself about among the women, I can tell you. Aren't that so, Caleb? Youm a regular ram, arn't you.'

Despite her instant recognition that it was jealousy that motivated Kate Reeves's words, still Tildy experienced a sense of disappointment and anger that Caleb Hawkes should be the type of womanizer who would sleep with sluts such as this woman was.

The higgler noted her reaction and wisely made no attempt either to deny Kate Reeves's statement or to shout her down. Instead he merely nodded carelessly. 'I have the reputation of a womanizer, Mistress Crawford. But whether I deserve such a reputation can only be judged by my behaviour concerning yourself. I'll get the donkey hitched.'

He left the women and Kate Reeves, baulked in her object of baiting him into an angry slanging match, turned on Tildy.

'My oath! Youm a proper bloody hypocrite, you am.'

Tildy's heart began to pound, and the rush of adrenalin into her bloodstream caused her face to pale, and her body to tense. She had never brawled willingly in her life, but had endured violence before and was no stranger to – or afraid of – the prospect of physical pain. Possessed of an abundance of courage, she was not unnerved by the threatening attitudes of Kate Reeves and her cronies.

'Why do you call me a hypocrite?' she asked, even-toned.

The woman's swarthy features twisted in a spasm of hatred. 'Does you hear her?' She screeched at her friends. 'Does you hear the mealy-mouthed bitch? She thinks she's

156

better than us, does you know that? She thinks she's too fine a lady to be like us. But see how she's chasing arter the higgler. She's a bloody whore, so she is!'

Tildy saw no point in continuing this confrontation, and started to walk away, but her antagonist grabbed her arm and wrenched her round once more, so that they stood face to face.

'Doon't you turn your back on me, you poxy tail!' Kate Reeves's spittle flecked against Tildy's face, and Tildy's own quick temper rose. Although more slender than Kate Reeves her body had been toughened by long months of nailmaking, of wielding hammer and iron for hour after hour. Beneath her smooth skin pulsed strong lithe muscles, and now, with almost contemptuous ease, Tildy broke the grip on her arm and thrust the woman away from her. Surprise mixed with sudden apprehension showed in Kate Reeves's eyes at this unexpected display of strength.

'Don't force me into disgracing myself by hitting you, Katie Reeves,' Tildy warned, drawing deep breaths in an effort to calm herself. 'Try to remember why we're here in this place, and don't shame yourself so.'

A couple of the less hardened of Reeves's cronies added their voices to the proceedings.

'Come away, Katie, you can't fight today. It wouldn't be decent.'

'No, Katie, it arn't proper. It 'ud count as a mortal sin.'

The swarthy features were almost rabid with hate. 'I'm agoing to drag you down into the gutter, Tildy Crawford.' She flung out her arm, the dirty broken fingernails slashing the air only inches from Tildy's face. 'I'm agoing to tear them bleedin' cow's eyes o' yourn out of your yed. I'm agoing to make you ate my shit! When I'se done wi' you, you'll be begging me for mercy, you poxy tail!'

Tildy did not flinch or show any nervousness, only remained warily poised to defend herself from physical attack. She did not allow the fact of this woman's undeserved hatred for her, to disturb her. Tildy had seen enough of life to know that in this world there are those who hate

157

others without apparent cause or reason. This was the case with her and Kate Reeves, and Tildy knew that no matter what she might do to try to placate this woman, or even win her friendship, nothing would make any difference. Kate Reeves hated her. It was an unalterable state of affairs, and all she could do was to guard herself against it.

'Come away, Tildy!' Hanna Knight begged in frightened whispers. 'Come away from them.'

Tildy's demon of stubbornness would not allow her to give ground, for she felt that to give way to such unprovoked aggression would be utterly wrong. 'You go, Hannah. I'll be alright here,' she urged in a low voice. 'I'm not feared of any of them. You go now.'

Both women continued to face each other. Kate Reeves mouthing threats, Tildy silent, until the impasse was resolved by the return of Caleb Hawkes.

'Here, my duck.' He tossed a gold guinea at one of Kate Reeves's cronies. 'Theer's a couple o' fiddlers down at the Navigation. They'm having a right randy theer. Goo and enjoy yourselves, and take her with you.'

The prospect of music and drink was enough, Kate Reeves's friends grabbed her, and despite her struggles and curses dragged her with them. As the sounds of their progress died away, so Tildy let herself relax, and with that relaxation came a sudden onset of faintness and nausea. She put her hands to her face, and Caleb Hawkes took her arm and led her into the porch of the church, where he seated her upon the stone traveller's stool.

'I was watching you face up to that crew o' harpies, Tildy Crawford,' he told her, and there was admiration in his voice. 'You'se got mettle, girl, no doubt o' that. I wanted to come to your aid, but somehow I sensed that you wouldn't have wanted me to. I reckon youm a woman who must insist on fighting her own battles.'

Tildy smiled wanly, the waves of nausea and faintness were receding and the pounding of her heartbeat was slowing. 'You seem to know me well, Master Hawkes.'

He grinned at Hannah Knight's pale anxious stare.

'Don't fret, honey. Tildy Crawford is alright now, and when she feels able, I'll walk you both back to Webheath. In fact, you needn't walk at all if you'd sooner ride. I've got six donkeys outside that gate, and three on 'um arn't got a pound weight in their panniers.'

Finally it was only Hannah who elected to ride, Tildy preferred to walk, and Caleb Hawkes walked with her. His mare and string of donkeys plodding in single file behind the couple. For a time they continued in silence, and Tildy was content to do so. To the left of the road the great elms of the Hewell Grange woods shaded the travellers from the afternoon sun, to the right the cornfields stretched towards the near horizons. Caleb considered the ripening wheat and remarked.

'It'll be a good harvest this year.'

Tildy smiled acknowledgement and then he asked. 'Did you get my fairing, Tildy Crawford?'

She flushed guiltily, remembering how she had thrown the offering from her. Caleb Hawkes misunderstood her reaction and questioned anxiously.

'It didn't offend you, did it? Me sending you a fairing, and that message wi' it? Theer was no offence meant, and that's the truth.'

She shook her head. 'I took no offence, Master Hawkes,' she hesitated, and then added, 'and in truth I appreciated you sending it to me. It was a kindly thought.'

His involuntary rush of relief caused him to inwardly jeer at his own affected emotions. 'Youm fair gone on this wench, arn't you, Sergeant Hawkes! Youm bloody lovesick!' Aloud, he said quietly, 'I'll speak plain, Tildy. I've tender feelings for you. No! Don't answer yet.' He gently touched her lips with his forefinger, and his expression was very serious, 'I know that you'll find it hard to believe, that arter talking to you once . . . well . . . twice now, I can feel as I do.' He took his high hat off his head and rubbed the back of the same hand against the pale crease that the inner binding had left on his forehead. 'To speak plain, Tildy, I can't really understand it myself, but from the first moment

159

I saw you, it was if I'd known you afore,' he smiled at her. 'Strange, arn't it, Tildy. But even now this minute, walking wi' you like I am, a part o' me seems to have bin doing so for years and years. Everything you do and say seems familiar to me.' He drew a long breath. 'This arn't like me at all, you know, Tildy. I'm not a man who chases arter women, and I've never bin the sort to wear his heart on his sleeve. But when I sees you and when I talks wi' you like now, I just wants to be completely open wi' you. To tell you everything about how I feel for you, and not hold nothing back.'

His transparent honesty touched Tildy's heart, and in return she also felt impelled to speak openly and truthfully, with no coquetry.

'You must know, Master Hawkes, that I'm a married woman.'

'I know that, and more besides. I've spent the last days making enquiries about you. Don't be angered because I've done that,' he beseeched, 'but I couldn't help myself,' he paused, then went on in a rush of words, 'and I'll confess something else, as well. I've been watching the poorhouse these last nights, hoping to get a glimpse of you. It warn't no coincidence, me passing the churchyard today. I knew you was theer. I'd watched you leave the poorhouse and knew wheer you was all going to.'

Tildy listened intently to him. Her own emotions a conflicting maelstrom. She forced her voice to calmness.

'I'm flattered, Master Hawkes, that you should think so highly of me. But I am married. It wouldn't be right for me to give you any cause for thinking that you and I could become united in any way.' A rueful expression wrinkled her brows, and she went on falteringly as if she searched for the words, 'I find it impossible to understand myself, and my actions, Master Hawkes. I don't accept what the parsons tell us, about how we should live our lives. I can't even believe that God is good, and means us well. But yet, there is some force inside me that will never ever allow me to go freely against the teachings of the parsons. I'm still

160

feared of committing sins. And while I'm married, then I cannot let myself think of men in any way other than as acquaintances.'

'You could think of me as a friend, Tildy,' he urged forcefully. 'There 'ud be no sin in that.'

She shook her head bewilderedly. 'I'm afraid to let myself do that, Master Hawkes. It's sin enough that I should find you attractive to my sight. If I let myself begin thinking of you as a friend, then I don't know where it would end.' She came to a standstill and faced him squarely. 'I'm going to be completely honest with you, as I believe you have been with me. I never loved or wanted my husband. He got me drunk, and then pregnant, and there was no other course open to me, or at least I could see no other then – than to wed him. He served me badly, and I can't claim that I ever tried to be a loving wife towards him. There has only ever been one other man in my life. I was very very fond of him, and he was kind and good to me. I loved him with my body only once, and truth to tell, I found it a sweetness doing so, indeed it was the only time that I found sweetness in bodily loving, despite me being a married woman . . . '

Standing before her, Caleb Hawkes felt he was drowning in the huge dark pools of her eyes.

'But it was a sin, Master Hawkes, and because of that sin, I fear that God punished us both for it. The very day it happened, Davy Noakes was badly beaten in a fight that took place because of me. I left him that same night because I'd no wish to bring further troubles upon him. It was the same with Tom Crawford, my husband. From the day he married me, nothing went well for him . . . ' Her lips trembled and tears glistened on the long lashes of her eyes. 'I'm a jinx, Caleb Hawkes! I fear that I'm cursed in some way. I really do believe that any man who wants me for his own, comes to misfortune.' She turned from him, and walked rapidly on.

By the time he had caught up with her, she had recovered herself and was calm once more. Neither spoke until they came into the poorhouse yard. Hannah Knight, eyes wide with curiosity as to what had passed between her companions, thanked Caleb Hawkes for letting her ride the donkey, and scurried into the kitchen, only to peep slyly from the window. When Tildy would have followed her, the man stepped in front of the door.

'I only wants to say one thing, Tildy,' he spoke in a whisper. 'I know that I love you, and while I'll not harass you wi' that, still I'll stand as your friend, and I'll call and see you from time to time, as a friend. Is that alright wi' you?'

Tildy could only nod. 'Yes, Caleb Hawkes, I do need a friend. But there can be no more than friendship between us, at this time. Please be very sure that you understand that. For I've no wish to lead you on in hopes of something more than friendship to bind us.'

He grinned easily. 'That 'ull do me for now, Tildy. I'll just have to keep on hoping that things 'ull change,' he chuckled softly. 'They'se got a way o' doing so, arn't they . . .'

Chapter Sixteen

Tildy stood at the window of the sick room looking southwards across the Worcestershire Plain. In the far distance loomed the blue Malvern Hills, and to her fancy they seemed to undulate in the shimmerings of the heated air like some mythological beast struggling to rise from the imprisoning earth.

'As I am imprisoned,' she thought sombrely, 'imprisoned by this house.'

She leaned her forehead against the leaded panes of the window between the striped shadows cast by the outer bars of iron, that although placed there as a protection against thieves, yet made the house resemble a jail.

'But it is not this house that is really the jail for me. My poverty and my ignorance are my jailers, not these bars and walls. I could leave here today and within hours find some man to give me money and shelter in exchange for the use of my body. But then I would only be adding to my jailers. That man – whoever he might be – would be an extra chain about me, and I would be degrading myself by playing the whore.' She frowned slightly. 'At least up to now although I have been degraded by others, I have never voluntarily degraded myself.' She drew a long shuddering breath as hopeless yearning swept through her. 'Oh God, I wish I was able to be free, to live my own life as I would choose!' Her peripheral vision caught movement on the track that led from the direction of the Tardebigge Church, and she focussed her attention.

It was an open carriage drawn by a fine pair of matched bays, and Tildy knew that the colourfully dressed, parasolled women sitting in the vehicle behind the liveried coachmen, were the expected party of visitors. Behind the carriage rode two black-clad, top-hatted horsemen. Without waiting to identify them Tildy left the window and checked the sick room and its night-capped occupants. Satisfied with what she saw, she went to the corridor to shout downstairs and give warning of the carriage's approach.

Lucas Royston was in high spirits as he rode behind the carriage. It contained three of the most socially powerful ladies in the parish: Elizabeth, the Lady Aston, wife to the Vicar/Magistrate; Mrs Amelia Boulton; and Mrs Letitia Hemming, the wife of the most eminent needle master in the district. There was a fourth female in the carriage, who added yet another fillip to Lucas Royston's spirits: Emma Cutler, a niece of Amelia Boulton's, seventeen years old, pale-blonde hair, blue eyes, rosy-cheeked, slender-waisted and plump-breasted – and in Lucas Royston's opinion, quite the prettiest, most desirable little kitten of a girl that he had ever met in his life.

The Reverend John Clayton winked at his fellow-horseman, and whispered, 'The young lady is gazing at you admiringly yet again, sir. In all truth, I could sometimes wish that I had been born handsome, instead of intelligent.'

Lucas smiled, and looked directly at Emma Cutler, who blushed deliciously, and dropped her blue eyes in apparent confusion.

'Dammee, sir, but you've made a conquest there, no doubt of it,' the clergyman bantered *soto-voce*, and Lucas, secretly delighted with what was happening, kept his own tone light and bantering as he rejoined.

'You possess an overly romantic and fanciful cast of mind, sir. But do I detect the sin of envy, I wonder?'

Clayton's attractively ugly features assumed a mock-dismal expression. 'Indeed you do, sir. Because I wear the Cloth I cannot lie. I am torn asunder by envy, since I know that I am too ugly in my person ever to attract the admiration of such a delightful creature.'

The coachman swung the carriage into the approach lane of the poorhouse, and standing outside the large front doors could be seen the tall cadaverous figure of Ebenezer Morris, and his bulky-bodied wife.

'See there, Doctor Royston,' Clayton whispered, 'Jack Sprat and his good lady await us.'

Lucas spluttered with laughter, but tried to compose his features into a more suitable gravity as he saw the disapproving glare of Lady Aston directed towards him. To redeem himself he made haste to dismount and hand the ladies out of the carriage. The young girl, Emma Cutler, blushed as her small lavender-gloved hand rested briefly upon his flattened palm, and he smiled tenderly and essayed a gentle pressure of his fingers. Her blush heightened, but he felt an unmistakeable squeeze of her own fingers in return, and was well content.

The poorhouse master bowed low, and his wife curtseyed deeply as like three majestic galleons under full sail, the older women swept through the open doors with the remainder of the party trailing after them like escort vessels.

Through her long-handled lorgnette Lady Aston's hard glare raked the length and breadth of the sick room, and her thin lips twisted into a grudging smile of approval.

'You have done well, Doctor Royston. It is clean and stinks only a little – No doubt that'll be the paupers themselves.'

Lucas bowed deeply. 'I am most gratified that my efforts meet with your approval, my Lady. Your sentiments make the arduous task I have undertaken seem even yet more worthy of my endeavours.' Conscious of Emma Cutler's wide-eyed gaze he tried to maintain a balance between manly gratification and gushing servility, but aware of the power of this woman to either make or break him in this parish, he found it difficult not to be utterly servile.

'Why be all them winders open, young man? I'se allus held to the belief that wind and drafts be 'armful to the sick.' The newly acquired wealth and position of Letitia

Hemming's husband had clothed her elegantly and jewelled her expensively, but had done nothing to soften her voice, nor refine her accent.

'That indeed is the case at times, ma'am,' Lucas agreed charmingly, 'but lately there have been made many new discoveries concerning the nature of sickness, and many new advances in its treatment. These days we of the Modern School subscribe to the belief that fresh air is beneficial during the daylight hours in clement weather. But, as you so rightly have pointed out, ma'am, the night air is indeed harmful to the sick. Consequently, I ensure that these windows are opened only when conditions of weather and sunlight warrant it. At all other times they remain closed.'

The woman's broad fat face was bovine as she listened to his explanation, and Tildy pictured her chewing cud. Clad in her grey gown and red shoulder-badge, with a clean white apron and mobcap, Tildy might have been invisible for all the notice taken of her, as indeed might the Morrises. Like mute statues, the three of them stood in line by the dresser, as the party of visitors paraded the room.

'Who acts as nurse during the times you are not here, Doctor Lucas?' Amelia Boulton fluttered.

'I have instructed a pauper woman in those duties,' the young man answered airily. 'She serves well enough.'

No one bothered to glance at Tildy. She was uncaring of being completely ignored, but had experienced a sense of pique as she heard Lady Aston congratulating the doctor on the room's cleanliness. She glanced down at her sore, reddened hands, made so by the harsh lye soap, and the countless hours of immersion in cold water as she had scrubbed floors, walls and furnishings; soaked, pounded and wrung blankets, clothing and bed-linen; washed heads and legs and bodies; tended the sick by day and night with only the minimum of help.

The party moved from bed to bed, and Lucas Royston struck his favourite pose, hands clutching lapels, head thrown back, and lectured on Cancer and Scrofula and

Consumption, the Scab, the Itch, the Ague and the Fevers. The faces of his listeners grew slack and their eyes dulled – but Tildy's eyes were intent, and her ears strained to catch every word that he uttered, and she felt a sense of deprivation when he concluded.

The visit ended, and the party swept out, and Tildy, invisible to the end, watched them go with an envy of their freedom to behave as if they were the captains of the earth. She smiled to herself sardonically. Captains of the earth they might not be. But, captains of the poor, they most surely were.

Ebenezer Morris followed the visitors, but his wife stayed standing where she was. Tildy saw that the older woman was shivering slightly, and her face was working as if she were under great stress, and asked.

'Are you ill, mistress?'

Anna Morris shook her head. 'No, Crawford, I'm not ill. I just feel like burning this place down about our heads.'

'But why? What makes you so upset?'

The mistress let her pent-up breath gust from her, and her shoulders sagged. 'To tell the truth, my wench, I was as angered on your behalf as I was on me own,' she looked directly at Tildy, and her eyes were unusually soft. 'You'se worked like a dog to clean this place, and tend the sick, Crawford – and I'se done little enough to aid you, in all truth – and it makes me angered when them bloody Lady Mucks comes here, and the bloody doctor claims all credit for it.' Her big hands clenched into fists and her indignation fuelled upon itself once again. 'The bloody gentry treats us all as if we'em dirt under their feet. It doon't matter to them that I'm no pauper, and that Mr Morris is a parish officer. They treats us like dirt all the same. Not one on 'um so much as spared us a look, ne'er mind a word o' greeting, or a word o' praise for the work we'se done. He didn't even give your name when they asked about the nurse. Him, who'se naught but a bloody ragged-arse quack! He's changed his tune since the first time he called here at the house, I'll tell you. He warn't so high and

167

mighty then, not be a long chalk he warn't.'

Tildy shrugged and momentarily felt immeasurably old and wise. ''Tis of no importance Mistress. Perhaps we are gaining credit in Heaven for what we are doing here now, and are not meant to have credit for it here on earth.'

Old Sarah Chapman came doddering into the room. 'Please Missis, the higgler's down in the yard, and he wants a word wi' Tildy,' she lisped through toothless gums. 'He's powerful hot for Tildy, arn't he. I reckon it's his oats as he's come for, girl, so you mind he doon't get you somewheers nobody can hear you shout,' she cackled with lewd laughter.

Tildy felt colour rising from her throat to her cheeks, and looked at the mistress, expecting her to make some derogatory comment. But to her surprise Anna Morris only nodded at her.

'You goo on down and see him, Crawford. Me and Old Sarah will look arter here.'

As Tildy stared at her, Anna Morris frowned, and snapped curtly, 'Be you deaf, girl? Goo on and do as I tells you.'

Caleb Hawkes was dressed in his usual manner, with his white shirt opened at the neck, a brightly coloured kerchief knotted loosely around his throat, and his hat tilted rakishly on his short-cropped hair.

Despite herself, Tildy's heart thumped as she saw him smiling at her, and she experienced again the attraction he exerted upon her.

'Hello Tildy.' He reached out his hand, inviting the clasp of her own, but Tildy affected not to notice, and folded her arms to avoid bodily contact.

Aware of eyes eagerly watching them from the windows overlooking the courtyard, Caleb Hawkes sensed what constrained her, and jerked his head towards the gateway. 'Come, Tildy, let's walk awhile. I've something for you.'

She went with him through the gateway, and saw that his horse was standing cropping the grass of the hedgerow in the lane outside. From the saddlebags the higgler took two parcels of brown paper and handed them to Tildy. 'Here, girl. This 'uns for you and this 'uns for little Davy.'

Tildy uttered a faint exclamation of shock. No man had ever given her mysteriously-wrapped presents before.

'Doon't open 'um here,' Caleb Hawkes said quickly. 'Let's goo along the lane aways.' He saw the doubt in her dark eyes, and smiled reassuringly, 'Now doon't you be afeared that I intends to try anything on wi' you, girl,' he lifted his gaze to the windows of the poorhouse, 'but I doon't relish providing a peepshow for them inside theer.'

For the first time she returned his smile. 'No, Master Hawkes, nor me neither.'

They walked slowly out onto the main trackway, he leading his horse by its reins, and he directed her westwards. 'Let's goo up this way, Tildy. Mayhap you'd like to share a pot of ale wi' me. There's an inn not far from here. You can ride pillion.'

'Oh no, Master Hawkes, I couldn't do that.' He frowned impatiently.

'Goddamn it, Tildy, will you just give over calling me Master Hawkes! I'se told you afore, me name is Caleb. Goo on, now you say it – Caleb!' he grinned. 'Come on now, Tildy, say it!'

She grinned also, aware of how ridiculously she was behaving. 'Alright then, Caleb, it is,' she answered. 'And I'm sorry if I'm acting like some silly schoolgirl, but I can't help the way I am.' She lifted the parcels. 'Can I open these now?'

'O' course you can, that's for the boy, remember.'

They came to a standstill as she quickly unwrapped Davy's present, and giggled. It was a wooden soldier – a gaily-uniformed Hussar a full eight inches high, with fierce black eyes and mustachios, and a pelisse and busby fashioned from real cloth and fur. 'He's marvellous!' Tildy's face glowed with delight. 'I do thank you for him.' Sudden doubt clouded her eyes, 'But do you not think that Davy's a little too young to play with soldiers, or even know what they are?'

The man chuckled with a loving amusement. 'Then keep it safe for him until he is old enough. Now unwrap your own present.'

Fingers made clumsy with excitement, Tildy stripped away the brown paper. 'Oh Caleb, it's beautiful! It's really beautiful!' she breathed in heartfelt wonder. It was a silken shawl fringed and tasselled with fine lace, its colour a deep-hued gold that glowed luminously as she spread and held it out before her.

'Do you really like it, sweetheart?' he asked tenderly, and Tildy's eyes glistened as she slowly nodded her head.

'It's beautiful, Caleb. Really and truly beautiful.' Her eyes suddenly scalded, and tears of emotion threatened to spill from the long thick lashes. 'No one has ever in my life given me anything so beautiful.' Her voice was choked. 'But I can't take it from you, Caleb. I can't.'

He frowned bemusedly. 'But why not? I don't ask aught from you in return. Why can't you take it?'

She coughed to ease the tightness in her throat, and told him. 'This should only be given to your true love, Caleb. It's too fine and beautiful a gift for someone who is only a friend. It is a gift for a wife.'

'Why can't you be like a wife to me, Tildy?' angry impatience was in his voice. 'Goddamn it, you know I love you. You'll not find a better or a truer man in these parts. I'll care for you and your babby. You need never again know want in your life.'

She turned from him, as if to walk away, and he held out his arm to prevent her going.

'No Tildy, hear me out . . . Leave that bloody poorhouse and come wi' me. I swear by all that I hold holy that I'll always cherish and protect both you and your babby. I'll be the father that he's never known, and raise him as my own son.'

For a moment the thought of her present existence assailed Tildy, and she wavered on the verge of accepting his offer, of giving in to his wantings and letting herself shelter in his love and protection. Then her earlier thoughts came back to her, thoughts of what comprised her own personal prison, and she thrust her momentary weakening back into retreat.

She took the lovely swathe of silk and gently pushed it into his hands. 'No Caleb, I can't go with you, and I can't accept this. It wouldn't be fair to you, not the way I am inside me at this time. But truly I'm grateful and honoured that you should have asked me. I'll keep the soldier for little Davy, and I thank you for it. But I can't take any present from you for myself.' She saw the baffled hurt in his face, and tried to explain her refusal. 'Please don't think that it's aught wrong with you. It is something only in myself. Something that I know I must do for myself, before I can ever let myself become involved with any man, and take his loving and give him my own.' Her faltering smile was suffused with sadness. 'Please, Caleb, stay my friend until I have come to know myself. If that day should ever come, and you should still want me, then mayhap I will then be worthy to share your life with you.'

Then she was gone, running swiftly back towards the poorhouse, leaving Caleb Hawkes staring miserably after her, the golden shawl clenched in his fingers.

Chapter Seventeen

'Translate the following sentences . . . "Il y a trois ans qu'il est a Paris . . . Y a-t-il long-temps que vous êtes en France? . . . Il y a deux ans que je demeure ici . . . " ' Anna Coldericke repeated the three sentences as she wrote them on the small blackboard in her living room. She spoke French well, with hardly a trace of an English accent.

The class she was taking at this moment consisted of the three Misses Chillingworth, the teenage daughters of a local needle master, who like many of the newly prosperous wished his children to possess the scholastic attainments and social graces that he himself lacked. While the girls laboured with bent heads over their slates, Anna Coldericke moved restlessly about the room.

She had not seen Lucas Royston since their shared night of passion almost a week ago, and was now beginning to regret that she had surrendered so abjectly to her own desires.

'I was a fool to let him use me so. He only wanted to gratify his own sexual appetite,' she thought resentfully and then was honest enough to admit that she had done her own share of using him to gratify her own appetites. She was also honest enough to admit that she had conceived a passion for the young doctor, which made her long to see him again, and to crush his lean body to hers while he filled her hungry emptiness. She coloured, and glanced surreptitiously at the glossy bent heads of the girls. Then scoffed at herself.

'Dear God above, Anna Coldericke, do you think these children can read your carnal thoughts?'

172

The tall grandfather clock whirred noisily and chimed the hour of four and Anna Coldericke sighed with relief.

'It is time to end the lesson, girls,' she smiled at the fresh young faces before her.

The eldest girl, Emily, moued with disappointment, 'But you've not yet talked to us, Mrs Coldericke.'

Anna was puzzled. 'About what, Emily?'

The girls exchanged sly glances, and giggled nervously in concert, then Emily explained. 'About the right of a woman to choose her own way of life.'

Three pairs of bright eyes gazed expectantly at her, and she reluctantly shook her head. 'There is not time, girls, for I see that your Mama is even now crossing towards the house.'

This was true, and the girls vented theatrical groans.

'It's not fair, Mrs Coldericke,' the youngest, Agatha, complained. 'You talked to Hetty Milward about it.'

'Yes, young lady, and Hetty Milward was very quickly removed from my school because I had done so. If that is your purpose, to be removed from my school, then you may tell your Pa that I have indeed talked to you about those matters,' Anna rejoined jokingly. 'But now you must prepare yourselves for the street. Your Mama will not appreciate being forced to wait for you.'

She lifted a small handbell from the mantelshelf and rang it sharply. An older woman in a gingham dress, floppy mobcab and huge apron came in reply.

'Mrs Bray, please fetch the young ladies' cloaks and bonnets.' Anna told her.

'It's such a bore, Mrs Coldericke. We've to go now and take tea with Aunt Sarah Chillingworth.' It was Agatha again. 'All she does is moan on and on about her pains and scold us for things we've not done and tell us how ungrateful we are.'

'Yes, and she always smells most dreadfully like a horse,' chimed Betty, the middle sister.

'That's the liniment she rubs on her pains.' Agatha giggled and Anna could not help but smile with her. The

173

very artlessness of the three girls was appealing, and unlike some of her pupils these were relatively unspoiled by their privileged status in life. Her lips tightened as she thought of the lives of the daughters of the parish poor. Too many of those girls trod bitter paths through life. Grinding poverty, hardship, hunger and cruel treatment was all that some of them would ever know.

'It is to them that I should be preaching the rights of women,' Anna told herself. 'Not to such frivolous and fortunate creatures as these, whose main grievance against life is that they must take tea occasionally with a querulous old woman.'

Alone once more Anna took up a book and tried to read, but found that she was too restless to settle. After several futile attempts to absorb herself in the wisdom of long-dead philosophers, she put the book aside and again rang the handbell.

'I'm going out, Mrs Bray,' she told her servant. 'You may go home now, I'll attend to my own needs when I return.'

She fastened a pea-green walking cloak about her shoulders, but left her head bare. Clouds were massing in the sky, threatening more rain to follow that of the morning, so to avoid saturating her cloth-topped shoes she strapped brass pattens to her feet, increasing her height by a good two inches.

There were few people around the green. At this hour most were working in the various manufactures and cottage workshops. She decided to visit Molly Danks in Hill Street, and see how the small boy's illness was progressing under the course of treatment prescribed by Lucas Royston. She herself had returned to the house as promised, and taken the necessary ingredients, which she had bought and prepared herself. When she had gone there, Edwin Danks had been indoors with his wife, who was nervous and reluctant to carry out the necessary treatment, because of her husband's prejudice against it – he still preferring to place his trust in the charms of the cunning woman. By a mixture of cajolery and bullying, Anna Coldericke had prevailed upon the couple, and Edwin Danks had finally yielded to his wife's pleas and Anna Coldericke's bullying, and had grudgingly allowed the treatment to commence. Anna had not returned to Hill Street until this present hour.

A knot of women were clustered around a doorway halfway up the street, and as Anna neared them, they fell silent. She looked from one to another of the dirty, toil-worn faces grimly regarding her, and was puzzled by their uniform hostility. She nodded, and would have passed by, but one of the women stepped out in front of her.

'Be you going up to Moll Danks?' Her manner was aggressive.

Anna frowned at her accoster. 'As it happens, I am. But I fail to see why I should answer to you for my destination.'

The other woman's decayed teeth bared, as if she were snarling. 'You'd do best to keep away from theer, Missis. You'se done harm enough to young Moll.'

'What do you mean?' Sudden anxiety caught Anna's breath.

'Her kid died two nights past. Choked to death, he did. And her man is blaming her for it, because she was atreating the nipper like you and that Scotch quack told her to.'

Dismay clutched Anna's heart, and she brushed past the woman and ran up the slope and into the gloomy dankness of the court. She hammered on the bolted hovel door. 'Molly? Molly are you in there? Open this door, it's me, Anna Coldericke, open the door, Molly.'

After a few moments the inside bolt rattled, and the door swung open.

Anna moaned softly with shocked pity. Molly Danks's face was a grotesquely swollen mass of cuts and bruises. Her one eye completely closed, and the other only a slit in the black-blue flesh.'

'Just you bugger off from me, Mrs Coldericke,' the young woman's words were slurred by her swollen lips. 'If

Edwin finds you 'ere, he'll bleedin' well swing for you.'

'But what happened?' Anna was almost begging. 'How did the child come to die?'

Moll Danks spoke as if numbed emotionally. 'His coughin' fits got wuss and wuss, and then he just choked and died. Now piss off! Afore my man comes back. I'se taken enough battering through you and your fancy man.'

'But the treatment should have cured your child,' Anna burst out. 'Are you sure that you followed my instructions?'

Molly Danks nodded dispiritedly. 'I followed 'um, Mrs Coldericke. And mebbe my kid would ha' died anyways, because the cunning woman was doing him no good. But me husband blames you and the doctor, so you'd best keep well out on his way. Because he'll bloody swing for you iffen he comes next to you.' She lifted her hand and pointed to her battered face. 'Just be thankful that he worked his fust temper out on me. And now, bugger off, and leave me in peace.'

The door slammed shut, and the bolt rattled home. Anna lifted her hand to pound on it again, then realized the futility of doing so, and made her way from the court.

The knot of women still clustered around the doorway halfway down the slope, and as Anna passed them again the one who had previously accosted her called out.

'Keep out on this street, Missis, becos Edwin Danks 'ull bloody swing for murder iffen you comes nigh his missis agen.'

Anna halted, and turned to face the women. 'I am as unhappy as anyone here that Moll Danks's boy died,' she spoke clearly and firmly, 'but I cannot be held to blame for his death, and neither can the doctor. The treatment that Doctor Royston prescribed was the most modern and effective known.'

'Ahr, that's right enough!' one of her listeners shouted. 'It killed the poor little bugger stone-dead!'

A howl of raucous, jeering laughter greeted this sally and Anna scowled her disgust. She felt a sudden need to escape

176

from the filth and the stench and the abysmal ignorant savagery of her immediate surroundings, and hurrying from the street she went down the Unicorn Hill and took the rolling track known as the Red Lane, which would take her westerly through the woods and meet the Tardebigge road where it passed through the Webheath Liberty. A few ancient wattle and daub cottages dotted the first section of her route, and the tall chimney of the brick kilns within the Muskats Wood belched smoke across the green masses of the treetops. Anna Coldericke looked at the smoke, and for a brief moment tried to imagine herself working among the kilns with the brickyard women: her hands and arms wrapped in sacking to protect her skin from the fierce heat of the fired bricks, her clothing thick with the Red Marl clay, smoking a short clay pipe like a man, and swearing, brawling and toiling like a man also.

'The life I lead must seem idyllic to those poor benighted souls,' she told herself, 'and yet I have the audacity to consider myself ill-used by life. I should feel ashamed of my self-pity.'

She walked slowly, lost in her thoughts, which inevitably turned to Lucas Royston, and where he might be at this moment.

The young man she thought of was in fact, much nearer to her than she knew. He was riding down from the very brick kilns whose chimneys belched the smoke across the woods, and he also was indulging in a bout of self-pity. His pursuit of the delicious Emma Cutler having been brought to an abrupt halt before it could truly have been said to have begun.

Her father, Josiah Cutler, the biggest coal dealer in the district, and also a select vestryman, had called on Lucas at his dingy lodgings two days previously, and had made it very clear to the young doctor that his attentions to Emma were not welcome. If his financial status should ever improve, and with it his social standing in the parish, then Josiah Cutler might reconsider his veto. But until that happy day should dawn, then Lucas Royston was to keep

177

well away from Josiah Cutler's delectable daughter.

'I must needs do something spectacular to alter my fortunes,' Lucas told himself for the hundredth time, and for the hundredth time was left with the unanswerable question: 'What?'

A vague idea concerning the child with the smallpox persisted in hovering at the back of his mind. Too nebulous to grasp, yet somehow Lucas felt that if and when he should grasp the idea fully, it would provide the solution for his problems. Deep in thought, he ambled on.

Anna crested a steep rise in the track and began the descent which would lead her past the entrance lane for the brick kilns. From that lane she saw a horsedrawn two-wheeled cart debouch onto the track, a horseman rode abreast of the cart, and a troop of sack-aproned women trailed behind its open tailgate. With a happy start she recognized the horseman as Lucas Royston, and instinctively waved to attract his attention.

Lucas Royston saw the woman further up the hill as she waved to him, and simultaneously recognized her to be Anna Coldericke. With that recognition the vague idea concerning the child at the poorhouse suddenly sprang in full solidity to the forefront of his mind.

'Goddamn me! It could work!' He gasped the words aloud, and kicking his spavined wreck of a horse into a trot he rode towards her.

She watched him approach with mixed feelings, pride battling with her desire for him. He reined in before her, forcing her to a halt. Removing his hat he bowed in the saddle.

'Good Afternoon, Anna. I trust you are well. I've sorely missed you.'

'Indeed?' she snapped frostily. 'Is that why you have not called upon me for nearly a week?' Her pride had temporarily defeated her desire.

Lucas Royston recognized that unless he acted quickly and correctly, her present mood might well create a gaping estrangement between them which would not be easily bridged. He dismounted, and pointed his hat in the direction of the approaching procession.

'There has been an accident at the kilns, and the girl is on that cart. I don't wish you to be distressed by catching sight of her without warning. The girls were stacking bricks and the stack fell upon that unfortunate creature, her chest and head are sore hurt. I have done what I can to aid her, and now it is in God's hands. But I fear that even if she lives she will be gravely afflicted, mayhap a cripple. I wish I could save her from that, but my knowledge has limitations.'

His thin face was troubled and sad, and Anna Coldericke's pride melted. '*The poor boy. How can I berate him for his neglect of me, when he has so many afflictions to deal with.*' Aloud, she told him gently. 'You must not blame yourself, Lucas. I am sure that you have done all that any human being can do.'

He grimaced joylessly. 'I still feel remiss, Anna, my love. I should know more than I do. My skills should be equal to the worst fate can inflict upon we humans. Ah well . . . ' He sighed heavily, and gnawed on his lower lip as the cart creaked by the couple. The normally rumbustious brickyard women walking in silence with downcast eyes, some weeping quietly.

Anna glanced at the pathetic motionless figure on the cart-boards and thought how much sadness she had witnessed within one brief hour of time. 'I cannot tell Lucas about the Danks's child at this moment.'

'May I walk with you for a little way, Anna,' he asked diffidently. 'I feel the need for your company.'

She lifted enquiring eyebrows at the cart, and the young man shrugged his narrow shoulders helplessly.

'There is nothing more that I can do for that poor girl at present. They are taking her home.'

In the face of his despondency, a great wave of loving sympathy flooded through Anna, and impulsively she took his arm. 'Of course you may walk with me, my dear. I am going towards the Webheath Liberty.'

'Then that suits admirably, because I am also going there. To the poorhouse.' He smiled wryly, 'My patients are such that I cannot be termed a fashionable doctor, can I?'

She pressed his arm, and told him warmly. 'You may not be a fashionable doctor, my love, but I know well that you are a very good one.'

He cuddled her arm closer to himself, and lightly touched his lips to her cheek. 'How could I exist here, without you to comfort me, Anna,' he murmured tenderly, and drew her with him along the trackway towards the Webheath Liberty.

As they walked he talked to her in tones of low-pitched urgency. He told her that he loved her, he told her that he had not called upon her because he was tender of, and caring of, her reputation, that he felt unworthy of her because he was a poor man with no social standing in the parish, he told her that he dreamed of becoming a famous and successful doctor, and that should those dreams ever come true, then he would ask her to share his life, and be his wife. And Anna Coldericke drank in his words with an avid eagerness, and believed them totally, because that was what she wanted above all else.

Their arrival at the poorhouse coincided with the return of the outdoor work gangs, and the courtyard was full of noisy paupers waiting their turn at the stone washing-trough where they prefunctorily splashed a few drops of water onto the hands and faces under the bibulous regard of Ebenezer Morris.

'Good Arternoon, Doctor, and Good Arternoon to you, ma'm.' The poorhouse master's speech was slurred, and his breath reeked of gin. He jerked his head at the trough. 'See theer, Doctor, I makes the dirty buggers keep clane.'

The censorious glare of Royston caused the man to realize his error, and he hiccuped, 'I beg your pardon, ma'm. I suppose it's not the right thing to call 'um, when a lady's in the company.'

'Mayhap it's not the right thing to call them at any time,

Master Morris.' Anna Coldericke had spoken with this man before, and had disliked him from the very first of those occasions.

His eyes hardened resentfully, but he made no reply. Only shouted at the paupers. 'Keep your noise down, damn you! A man can't hear hisself speaking wi' all that bloody rattle coming from you.'

The hubbub quietened fractionally, and the master turned to Lucas Royston. 'Well Doctor, what is it brings you here at this hour? I can't recollect sending for you to come.' Drink always brought out the bully in Ebenezer Morris, and overlayed his normal obsequiousness with an aggressive Dutch courage.

'Do you not recollect that I've patients here, Master Morris,' Lucas's fiery Scots spirit resented the other's insolent manner, 'and I need to monitor their progress.'

'The Widow Coldericke's not a doctor,' the man commented sourly. 'So why is she here with you?'

With an effort, Lucas Royston held back the hot retort that sprang to his tongue. He realized that he still needed the co-operation of the master, because despite their financial agreement, he had no powers over the man.

'Mrs Coldericke has come here at my request, Master Morris,' he explained with a laboured politeness. 'I trusted that in view of our private understanding, you might hold no objection.'

Anna Coldericke's agile brain had weighed the situation, and now she intervened smiling brilliantly at the poor-house master, 'I am sure you can have no objection to my being here, Master Morris,' she talked in tones of intimacy at Morris's cadaverous features, now flushed and loose-lipped before her, 'after all, you know well that I have close connections with Reverend the Lord Aston, through the family of my dear departed husband. In fact it was His Lordship who suggested that I should accompany the Doctor here. Of course, Master Morris, if you would prefer me to leave, then I will do so, even though I fear that my doing so would most certainly disappoint his Lordship, who has a most particular interest in what we intend here this day.'

Instant wariness narrowed Morris's eyes. Reverend the Lord Aston was a very powerful man indeed. One adverse word from Lord Aston into the ears of the select vestrymen, and Ebenezer Morris might just as well pack his traps and leave the district, for of a certainty he would never again find any employment locally. Ebenezer Morris was no blind horse, he knew very well the difference between wink and nod. Now, he lifted his tall black hat and essayed a clumsy bow.

'But o' course youm always welcome to visit here, Mrs Coldericke. It's well known to me and the vestry, that youm a good friend to the poor,' he leered ingratiatingly. 'And though I says it meself, you wun't find a better conducted establishment in the whole o' Worcestershire, or Warwick, come to that.'

Anna smiled, and rested her hand on his arm. 'Indeed, Master Morris. I was myself remarking on that fact to Lord Aston, not a sennight since.'

Upon hearing this, the man became expansively generous. 'Well, I'm most gratified to hear that, Mrs Coldericke. Now, if there's any little thing I can do to accommodate you whiles youm here, then you needs only to ask. Would you care to take a dish o' tay?'

'Mayhap later, Master Morris, I thank you.' She gently squeezed his arm before dropping her hand back to her side. As she turned away, she saw Lucas Royston staring bemusedly at her, and she winked, then said, 'Please show me your patients now, Doctor. I'll take your arm.'

He led her away from the smirking poorhouse master, and as soon as they were out of earshot, said wonderingly. 'I declare, Anna Coldericke, you never cease to amaze me. I would never have believed you capable of acting so like some mischievous hoyden.'

She smiled happily, and whispered. 'I'm enjoying myself immensely, Doctor. At times I may appear to act completely at odds with the character that the world

182

perceives as being my true one, but there is a streak of wilful giddiness buried deep within me, that must at times break the surface, or cause me to explode.'

Her mood sobered abruptly when they entered the room where little Davy Crawford was quarantined. The child moved restlessly, and whimpered loudly. His breathing was shallow and rapid, and his thickly pustuled skin burned with fever.

'Poor child,' Anna murmured. 'Poor poor child!'

Lucas Royston went to the side of the bed and felt for the pulse in the delicate wrist. He studied the pustules and pursed his lips as he noted a sprinkling of livid, purplish spots among the general rashes.

'How is he?' Anna Coldericke questioned, and the young man told her gravely.

'The petechiae is beginning to appear,' he pointed to the darker spots. 'That is a bad sign. I'll have to dose him strongly, and perhaps bleed him to see if I can disperse the petechiae, and instead raise the laudable pus into the vesicles. This is the secondary fever that has gripped him, and now begins the crucial time. If I do not act with all due haste, and utilize my skills to the utmost, then the child will most assuredly die.'

Anna sniffed sharply. 'There is a most peculiar smell. What is it?'

He bent until his nose almost touched the child's face, then straightened to tell her. 'It is the pustules that smell so offensive to you. But it is of no matter, it is normal. If the petechiae had not appeared, then I would have been gratified by that smell. It shows that the pustules are ripe and ready to be opened. It means that the pox is erupting and leaving the body. If the eruptions were to subside, or as the cunning women term it, ''Strike In'', before the pustules had reached the stage of ripe maturity, then the danger to life would be very great indeed, and I fear there would be little enough that I could do. This child is in danger, I admit, but I feel confident now that I can save him.' He smiled at her grave expression. 'Now pray don't regard me with such sternness, I shall do my utmost for the child, and believe me, our modern methods are often miraculously effective. In the meantime I can use the laudable pus which has gathered to good effect. I can carry out inoculations.'

The sound of hurrying footsteps echoed on the plank flooring of the corridor, and the pale, drawn face of Tildy Crawford appeared in the doorway.

'Ahhh, it's you, Crawford,' Lucas greeted her, and told Anna Coldericke. 'This is the child's mother, and also my new nurse here. I'm training her in my methods, and she is adapting herself most admirably to them.'

Tildy stared hungrily at the bed. 'Is my Davy alright?' she questioned eagerly. 'I've listened to him crying these last hours, but Mistress Morris wouldn't unlock the door and give me entry.'

'And rightly so, Crawford,' Lucas Royston told her sharply. 'I have impressed upon you the utmost importance of staying away from your child to guard against contagion.' He saw the dark rings under her worried eyes, and softened his manner. 'Your child does well enough, Crawford. He is seriously ill, I'll not lie to you about that, but then, this disease is a most serious affliction, is it not. However, I am doing my utmost for him, and am confident that I shall bring him back to full health . . . Now I wish you to go to the apothecary in Redditch. I shall give you a written note to present to him, and he will make up a medicine for you to bring back to me. You must make all haste, because I want the child to begin taking the doses as soon as possible. While you are gone I shall bleed him from the left arm. So do not disturb the bandage when you see it. Fetch me pen, ink and paper, if you please.'

The girl ran off, and Lucas smiled at his companion.

'Did you note how clean and neat she is, Anna? That was one of the factors that decided me upon training her as my nurse. She is a good little creature, and surprisingly intelligent, although completely illiterate.'

A perverse imp of jealousy prompted Anna to add, 'And

she is also exceptionally pretty, even though a trifle pallid and hollow-eyed, is she not, Lucas?'

He coloured slightly. 'I really had not noticed her in that way . . . ' he began, then could not help but grin. 'How damnably pompous I sound. Of course she is pretty! But not to my taste, I do assure you.' His grin broadened. 'Have I not already given sufficient proof, that it is a lady of my own class who commands my devotion?'

It was Anna Coldericke's turn to colour . . .

Chapter Eighteen

The elderly apothecary wore a long green apron which covered the front of his clothing from neck to feet. Green protective sleeves stretched from wrist to elbow, and a tasselled skullcap adorned his egg-bald head.

His tiny shop was crammed with shelves full of white-glazed jars containing the substances of his medicines. Their exotic names lettered in ornate gilt script: *Aloes, Angelica, Asarabacca, Balsalms of Canada, Capivi* and *Tolu, Mixtures of Colocynth, Cantharides, Castor, Dandelion, Dragon's Blood and Dill* and countless herbs, seeds, spirits, juices, gums, roots, resins, salts, syrups, tinctures, waxes, woods and wines. Great flasks of glass stood in his windows filled with shining cordials, red, blue, gold, black, green and purple. And the smell was a mysterious compound of bitter-sweet scents that made the unwary feel slightly giddy until they became accustomed.

The dewdrop on the end of the old man's long thin nose trembled as he took the slip of paper from Tildy's fingers and briefly scanned it, then lifted one of the glazed jars from the shelf behind him, and tipped several pieces of dark, dried substance onto his tall mahogany counter.

'This is the Peruvian bark, and you can tell Doctor Royston that it's the finest quality that can be got,' he muttered to Tildy, and putting the pieces into a thick porcelain mortar used a pestle to crush them to a fine powder. The age-rheumed eyes squinted accusingly at the girl.

'D'ye have any simple cinnamon water at the poor'us?' She shook her head.

'D'ye have syrops of orange or lemon?' She shook her head.

'D'ye have the spirits of vitriol?' She shook her head.

'God blast my eyes! D'ye have anything at all in that blasted poor'us except a rake o' bloody useless paupers?' he snarled furiously.

'Would I stand here and be shouted at by you, if we already had medicines?' Tildy was stung to reply.

'Doon't you be so saucy, young 'ooman,' the Apothecary growled, and grumbling under his breath rummaged beneath his counter to produce small black bottles containing the named fluids. He wrapped the powdered bark in folded paper and pushed the articles towards her. 'Now remember what I'm agoing to tell you, young 'ooman,' he squinted at her. 'What's this lot for?'

'It's for a twelve-month boy,' Tildy answered, willing the man to hurry, so that she could begin her two-mile journey back to Webheath without further delay.

'Right then. Youm to mix two drachms o' the powdered bark wi' three ounces o' common water, one ounce of cinnamon water, and two ounces o' syrop o' lemon. Sharpen it wi' the spirits o' vitriol and dose the child wi' it every hour. A good full tablespoonful each time. Take care you don't trifle wi' this medicine, it's not a glass o' beer. But you must make sure to keep on giving it to the child just as long as his stomach can stand it. And as well as that, you must gi' him plenty o' drink. Port wine, or a strong negus, and acidulate them wi' the spirits o' vitriol as well. And you'll need to feed the brat only wi' boiled or roasted apples, cherry preserves, plums and suchlike . . . D'ye understand all that?'

Tildy nodded, and snatched up the bottles and folded paper. She was out of the shop when the latter part of his instructions sank home: cherry preserves? port wine? negus? Where was she to obtain those luxuries? Or even fresh apples and plums come to that? Her steps slowed and halted, and she felt despair creeping over her. Little Davy's illness had taken a heavy toll of her strength and her nerves, because she had not been able to rest knowing that her child fought for his life behind locked doors, and she could not go to him and help him in that unequal battle. 'And now I can't even help Davy by buying the foods and wine that he needs.' Sudden rage swept through her. 'Damn this life! Damn being a pauper! Damn the day I was ever born!'

In front of her above the crooked gabled rooftops the sun was setting, its rays gilding the cupola of St Stephen's Chapel turning the lead sheeting to gold. 'Gold! That's what counts for all in this life. To have gold. With enough of it you can buy anything, even health.'

Her thoughts were bitter, and for a brief while she mused on what relief it would be to go to sleep right at this moment, and never, ever wake. 'At least the dead find peace. Naught can worry or harm them. All suffering is at an end.'

A sudden outburst of shouting and laughter brought her from her gloomy reverie. She looked for the source. It was an inn some twenty yards ahead with a weathered sign of a Red Lion hanging above its doors. From those doors a group of men and women had spilled onto the roadway, two of the men were playfully sparring, and their companions drunkenly cheered them on. They looked to be gypsies – they were wearing velveteen jackets and waistcoats, and favouring gaudily-coloured neckerchiefs, and some of them gold earrings. The women in vividly coloured skirts and shawls, bangles on their wrists and arms, their hair hanging long and wild.

The next moment Tildy caught her breath as a man came from the inn door with two girls clinging to his arms.

It was Caleb Hawkes, shirt and waistcoat open to his waist displaying his well-muscled torso, his hat crammed on the back of his head, and roaring encouragement to the boxers.

Instinctively Tildy stepped into the doorway at her side, and her emotions confused her as she saw the higgler laughing and joking with the girls on his arms. Even as she watched, one of the girls threw her arms around the higgler's neck and kissed him passionately. To her own shock of dismay, Tildy experienced a fierce pang of jealousy.

'Don't be so stupid!' she told herself forcefully. 'How can you feel any jealousy over Caleb Hawkes. He is nothing more to you than a friend.'

Yet still the pangs persisted, and with an exclamation of self-disgust Tildy left the shelter of the doorway and hurried away in the opposite direction to the noisy party.

'Tildy? Tildy? Wait on!'

Before she had taken half a dozen steps her name was shouted, and she recognized Caleb Hawkes's voice. She ignored the shouts and pressed on, then running footsteps came behind her, her arm was gripped, and she was pulled to a halt.

'Tildy, why d'you run from me like this?' his white teeth shone as he grinned down at her. He brought his head nearer to her face, and she could smell beer and tobacco on his breath. 'Come back and have a drink wi' me and me friends,' he urged.

She glared at him. 'You're drunk, Master Hawkes, and you've no need of me to keep you company. You've friends enough already, I can see.'

'Caleb? Caleb, come on now, will you, my handsome. We'em agoing to the Unicorn,' one of the girls shouted, and Tildy jerked her arm free of his grasp.

'You'd best go on back to your fancy woman, Master Hawkes,' she snapped.

He looked searchingly at her for a couple of moments, then threw back his head and roared with laughter, the cords of his muscular throat taut against the stubbled, bronzed skin.

'What is so funny, that it makes you bray like a jackass?' Tildy demanded hotly, hating herself for reacting in this way, but powerless to stop herself from doing so.

His laughter still bubbled in his throat as he smiled fondly at her. 'It's you, my lovely, that makes me laugh so. I do believe youm jealous!' Before she could muster a scathing reply, he went on, 'And believing that makes me the happiest man in Christendom, little Tildy. For it means that you returns some of what I feels for you.'

'Believe that nonsense if you will,' Tildy told him coldly, 'but I've no more time to waste talking to a drunken fool.' She swung away and walked on, and he stood looking after her.

'Tildy!' he called out, but her face remained turned from him, and her pace did not falter.

'Have it your own way, girl,' he shouted angrily. 'I'm no lovesick bumpkin to goo running arter a bit o' skirt, if she chooses to act the shrew.'

'Caleb, bist you acoming?' The gypsy girl screeched out from behind him, and with a last lingering look at Tildy's slender back, he turned and went to rejoin his friends.

Chapter Nineteen

Lucas Royston lay back upon the soft, down-filled pillows of the bed with Anna Coldericke's body a pale ghost hovering above him in the darkness. He reached out and the ghost became a reality as his hands found the erect nipples and warm heavy globes of her breasts. He tried to pull her down to him, but she pushed her arms away.

'Wait,' she whispered. 'Wait.' Anna moved so that she knelt astride her lover's legs, and still holding his arms away from her, she dipped and kissed his mouth, then slowly nuzzled his throat, his chest, his lean belly, she heard him gasp with pleasure as her mouth took his throbbing erectness into its hot, moist caress, and she moved her hands to gently cup and fondle the sensitive testicles.

'Ohhh Jesus! Ohh Jesus, that's good, Anna. That's good, sweetheart.'

Her own excitement mounted as she worked her lips and tongue, tasting his flesh, feeling its satin-smoothness pulsing in her mouth.

'Jesus that's good! Jesus that's good!' He writhed sinuously and his fingers cupped her head and he tried to impose his own rhythm upon her. But lost to all but her own needs the woman thrust his hands away and raised her body, taking his maleness and guiding it to fill her aching hunger. As he filled her body she began to pant harshly and crouched down upon his leaness, clamping her lips to his mouth, sucking, biting, sucking, immersed utterly in the driving rhythms that dominated her mind and flesh. She felt him shudder and cry out as he reached his climax, but unfulfilled she drove her hips up and down in furious staccato bursts, and then the ripplings of delight flooded through her loins, and the inner flesh of her thighs, and up through her groin and belly. Their sweating skins slithered, and sucked and slapped liquidly and Anna's breathing became a grunting, guttural moaning that rose and rose and rose and ended in a longdrawn wailing cry as exquisite sensation exploded through her, and she clutched and strained and twisted to hold that exquisite time, to entrap it, and drain it, and absorb every nuance of it into her body. And then it was gone, and she was left spent and near to bodily collapse.

Almost brutally Lucas thrust her slumped, inert body so that she rolled to lie by his side.

'I've never met a woman like you before in my life,' his voice was a curious menage of differing inflections: wonder, respect, disgust, puzzlement, even fear.

Anna Coldericke lay perfectly still. Herself inwardly examining with both fear and wonder the intensity of the sexual forces that she contained within her body, and that this man by her side seemed able to unleash by his mere proximity.

'*Could any other man unleash those forces?*' she pondered. '*My husband never did so, and I've had no other. I truly believe that no other man could affect me as Lucas does,*' she decided, and then physically trembled with dread as she thought of what it might do to her, if she were to lose him. '*I'll do anything to keep him.*' she told herself. '*Anything at all . . .*'

Lucas Royston lay staring into the darkness trying to marshal his thoughts. He briefly considered his sexual relationship with this woman by his side. '*She is too much for me,*' he readily accepted that fact. '*She is too dominant in the bed. What she really needs is some great ox of a yokel, who will overmatch her strength, because all his brains will be in his bollocks, and all his energies will be directed towards blocking her all and every night. I'm too intelligent and sensitive a man to wish to be used solely as a stallion to soothe the hot itches of a mare.*' His mind pictured Emma Cutler. '*She is what I want in my bed.*' He

192

smiled appreciatively. '*She would be shy, and sweet and tender. Submissive and passive. Not a raging ravenous beast like this one . . . I would be the master in the bed, and she the slave . . .*' He was uncomfortably aware that with Anna Coldericke that idyllic relationship was, if anything reversed. But he needed Anna Coldericke at this moment in time. Needed her desperately.

He centred all his concentration on what he must now do to further his plans, and turning on his side he gently clasped her to him, and kissed her tenderly.

'I love you, Lucas,' she told him simply.

'And I you,' he whispered. 'But if we are ever to be able to marry, then I must needs ask your help now.'

'You have only to ask,' she answered eagerly. 'I'll do anything for you, my love, my dear dear love. Anything.'

'I need to make my name locally, as a doctor,' he said quickly. 'And I have been presented with an ideal opportunity of doing so – the child at the poorhouse who has smallpox.'

'But I'm sure that you will cure him, Lucas,' Anna whispered encouragingly, and he suppressed an impatient hiss at her interrupting him.

'I know I shall, honey, but to cure one child of the smallpox will not gain me any local fame. What I wish to do is to inoculate the whole population of paupers in the parish, and by doing so prevent any outbreak of the disease recurring locally in our lifetime. The trouble is that so many of them object to being inoculated. Because of superstitious ignorance they are afraid to take it, and the master, Ebenezer Morris, is opposed to inoculation because he says it is against God's will.

'What I fear above all else, is that without inoculation the disease will spread to all those in the poorhouse who have not yet suffered from it. It is a highly infectious complaint, as you well know, sweetheart, and I do not have to tell you what a terrible scourge it is, and how many die of its effects. That is the tragedy of it, Anna! They suffer and die needlessly. The inoculation would avoid all that. If only someone of status in the parish, one of the gentry or similar could show them the way. Could lead them . . . '

He lapsed into silence, waiting for some reaction from her. But again she only murmured soothingly.

'You will prevail, my dear. I know that you will.'

'*Jesus Christ on the Cross!*' he cursed silently. '*Is she too dense-skulled to offer.*' Aloud, he sighed heavily, and said. 'It will look very bad for me, if the pox should spread among the paupers. The difficulty is that I am a foreigner here. I have told them that I myself have undergone the inoculation, and benefited. But they disregard me.

'What I need is for someone of social standing and good repute locally, to volunteer as my example. I am convinced that if this happened, that if those poor ignorant souls witnessed such a person taking the inoculation, they would then be persuaded . . . ' Again he lapsed into silence, mentally willing Anna Coldericke to volunteer herself.

She was abreast of him in this, and was already considering whether she should act thus, and demonstrate with her own body her lover's medical expertise.

'*Now then, madam,*' she challenged herself silently. '*How deeply rooted and sincere are your sentiments about your fellow creatures? How sincere your constant protestations of concern for the poor and the afflicted? Lucas offers you a chance to perform a worthy act, which would benefit the paupers and their children . . . *'

Aloud she observed. 'But this inoculation would infect me with this loathsome disease, would it not, sweetheart?'

He took her use of the first person singular as a sign of victory.

'But of course it would, my honey,' he spoke lightly to minimize any fear she might have, 'as it infected me when I carried it out on myself. But that is the entire object of the exercise. The infection is of so mild a nature, that it cannot harm you, and it renders the body immune to any further attacks.

'Of course you will have some discomfort, and of course you will find a spattering of pustules form on your skin. But none of these effects last for more than a brief time. And then you will have gained your sure and certain shield against any future onset of the disease.'

His hands moved over her hips and thighs, and brought with them fresh stirrings of desire. She thought hard for some moments: by aiding him in this way she would be creating fresh bonds between them, by showing her readiness to help him in his work, she would be binding him closer to her. She hugged him closer.

'I will serve as your example, Lucas.'

He grinned in satisfaction, and rewarded her with fervent kisses and greedy caresses.

Chapter Twenty

The cloying smell of boiled cabbage permeated throughout the house as the paupers ate their evening meal. In the quarantine room its smell even overlaid the penetrating odour of the smallpox.

Tildy had not eaten since breakfast, but she could not stomach the bowl of mutton fat and cabbage that was her ration, and placed it on the floor beside her low three-legged stool. Sitting facing her, young Hannah Knight stared hungrily at the discarded food, and Tildy nodded. 'You take it, Hannah. I've no appetite.'

In the bed little Davy stirred in unquiet sleep and whimpered softly. Tildy moved to look at him, yet even now could not bring herself to break Doctor Royston's instructions by picking him up in her arms.

'I think the medicine is doing him good, Hannah, and the bleedings.' She sought reassurance, and Hannah gave it gladly.

'Surely it is, Tildy. See how easy he rests now compared to before.'

For a moment Tildy's hands moved towards her child in silent yearning, then she drew them back guiltily.

'Won't be long now, Tildy,' Hannah told her soothingly, recognizing the fierce maternal hunger to cuddle and caress that racked her friend. 'The doctor said that only a few minutes arter you'd took the inoculation, then you'd be able to cuddle Davy agen.'

'I wonder how long the doctor will be?' Tildy remarked, her eyes still devouring her child. 'It seems like hours since

Morris asked him into the parlour.'

'Be you feared o' this inoculation, Tildy?' her friend wanted to know.

Tildy shook her head. 'Only a bit nervous, that's all. All my life I've heard people rant and rave against it. But I trust the doctor somehow. He's taught me much in the short time I've known him, and he's so clever and know-ledgeable about the modern ways of treating diseases. And apart from that, he's told me that unless I take this inoculation then it'll be weeks before I can care for Davy. So for that alone I must take it. I want to cuddle my babby again.'

'Me Mam always says that the old and tried ways are the best ones. She don't hold wi' these new-fangled doctors at all,' Hannah stated, with doubt tingeing her voice, 'but then, I'se seen Old Esther Smith, the cunning woman from over Mappleborough Green way, cast her spells to drive out the smallpox, and still the kid who had it died. Mind you, theer's a lot on 'um hereabouts who'll never take the inoculation. Katie Reeves reckons it's a terrible thing. She says that if they tries to mek her take it, she'll put a knife in their hearts. She says that Doctor Royston is atrying to kill off all the poor, by deliberately infecting 'um wi' the pox. There's a lot who agrees wi' her in that.'

'Kate Reeves is an ignorant fool!' Tildy said with conviction. 'But are you afraid of it, Hannah?'

The pert face was solemn. 'I am a bit, Tildy. But when Mrs Coldericke told you and me that she intended to be the first to have it done, then I thought that it must be safe. I mean, a lady like she is wouldn't let summat be done to her unless it was agoing to do her good, 'ud she?'

'No, I'm sure not,' Tildy answered, then groaned impatiently. 'I wish the doctor would hurry up. What can old Morris be keeping him so long about?'

In the parlour a bitter argument was taking place between the doctor and Ebenezer Morris.

197

'. . . it arn't natural, Doctor Royston. It's agen the word o' God, this inoculation business is. It's a dirty heathen practice, so it is. Besides, no matter what you say, the vestry 'ud never agree to it.'

An exasperated sigh hissed from between Lucas Royston's teeth. For almost an hour the same points had been repeated *ad nauseam*. 'I've told you already, Master Morris, that the bishops themselves have stated publicly that there is naught to contravene God's will, or to offend against Christian teachings in this practice.' He called on his lover for support. 'Is that not so, Mrs Coldericke?'

'Of course it is so,' she stated firmly. 'I can assure you Master Morris, that Reverend the Lord Aston has no objection to the practice. And that would definitely not be the case if it offended Christian beliefs, would it.'

The man scowled, feeling the trap closing about him. 'It arn't only that, that meks me tek against it, Mrs Coldericke. There's other objections.'

'What are they, man?' Lucas demanded impatiently. 'For by God, you've already given us sufficient objections, which we have dealt with and shown they have no foundations to stand upon.'

Morris stared from one to the other with a hunted expression, then cursed sibilantly. 'Bollocks to it! Why should I be hounded so. If you must know, it's the church warden, George Holyoake, that prevents it the most.'

'Why, man?' Lucas could barely hold in his temper. 'Why should he prevent you? All we are trying to do here is to safeguard people's lives. How can he have objection to that?'

'It arn't just him alone,' Morris muttered sullenly. 'It'll be all the others as well. The rest on the farmers hereabouts. You see it's nigh on harvest time, and they needs every pair o' hands they can get to clear the crops. They always takes all the able-bodied paupers and kids from here. Now if I understands correctly, then this inoculation 'ull make the people badly for a while, wunt it. And they'll be no good for work then, 'ull they. And if I can't supply a fair number o' hands from here, then George Holyoake 'ull soon be summoning the vestry, and they'll bloody well want to know what I bin adoing.'

As Anna Coldericke listened, she could not help but feel a sneaking sympathy for the man's situation. The men who appointed him to his position, and who could at will remove him from that position, expected him to supply free labour when they required it. If he failed to oblige them, then they could very quickly bring him to heel. When Lucas would have returned yet again to the attack, she spoke to forestall him.

'No, Lucas, wait a while. Master Morris has some justification for his attitude.' While the young man stared at her enquiringly, she thought over the matter. 'Might I suggest a course of action?' she requested, but in such a manner that the request was more a statement of intent. 'Master Morris has pointed out the difficulties we will encounter with the vestry, and also with the paupers themselves, because many of them are adamant in their refusal to submit to the operation. Let me then suggest a compromise . . .

'We will gather the paupers together now, and I will take the inoculation in front of them. If she be willing, then Tildy Crawford will take it also. You, Lucas, will explain fully to the gathering what the purpose of the treatment is, and they will see with their own eyes how simple and painfree it is. Then, to remove the threat of contagion from this house, I will return to my home, taking Crawford and her child with me to stay there . . .

'My servant may take leave of absence while the disease runs its course. Tildy Crawford can act as my domestic maid during that time, and thus enable us to quite easily maintain a quarantine in my house. After recovery, myself and Crawford can return here to the poorhouse, and so demonstrate upon our own persons the efficacy of the operation. By that time the harvest will have been got in will it not, and then the vestry can surely not object to your inoculating the rest of the paupers here.

199

'What say you to that, Lucas? And you, Master Morris?'

'I think it a good plan,' Lucas agreed readily, 'but still I feel that at least we should inoculate the children here. It is they, after all, who are most at risk.'

'The mothers 'ud never agree to that,' Morris told him sullenly. 'And if they did agree, then wheer's your bloody quarantine gone to?'

Lucas was reluctantly forced to concede that point, but refused to let go of the idea entirely. 'Then how about the orphans? There are three small ones here. No one would object to them being used.'

His crusading zeal had swept Anna Coldericke along with him completely. Her dull, boring life had miraculously found purpose, and she clutched at it. 'Yes, why not? I can keep those children in my home as well. Crawford and myself will manage them admirably.'

'But the vestry?' Morris protested weakly.

'Damn the vestry!' Lucas was on fire to carry out these fresh plans. 'Think of the money you will be saving yourself, man. No cost of feeding a woman and four children for as long as the quarantine lasts. It is sheer profit for you, is it not? We can say that the children had already been infected by Crawford's child, and that to avoid any danger of rendering the rest of the paupers unfit for the labour of the harvest, you prevailed upon Mrs Coldericke here, to care for those tragic children, she being well known as a good friend to the poor. You will gain kudos for it, man. The vestry will applaud you for helping them to line their own pockets by ensuring that they still have free labour.'

Further argument followed, but eventually the poorhouse master was worn down by the united pressure of the couple, and with a bad grace, gave his assent . . .

The day room was crowded, and at one end a solitary smoky-flamed lamp suspended from a ceiling beam shed a

200

weak light, which barely illuminated the faces of the paupers in the front ranks of the crowd. Directly beneath the lamp a trestle table had been set up, and on its boards little Davy squirmed and whimpered, his wrapping-shawl serving as a blanket between his naked body and the unplaned wood.

Behind the narrow table were ranged Lucas Royston, Anna Coldericke, Tildy, and three small children, two girls and a boy, none of them above four years of age. Their eyes were wide, and the small faces mirrored their fear at this new experience they were undergoing. With their backs to the door, the Morrises looked dourly on.

From his open bag on the table before him, Lucas Royston took a small sharp-bladed knife, and a roll of black sticking-plaster. He smiled at Anna Coldericke and Tildy. 'Please bare the tops of your left arms, and make ready the children likewise.'

As they obeyed, he spoke to the crowd, some of whom displayed a lively interest in what was happening. Others stood in stolid indifference, while the spattering of imbeciles and mentally ill paupers gaped with vacant eyes and dribbling mouths, or giggled and talked, absorbed in their own disordered fantasies.

'I am going to demonstrate how simple, and free of pain the operation of inoculation is,' Lucas told them confidently. 'So that you will then all realize how stupid you are in fearing something that can only bring great benefit to you.

'Are you ready, Mrs Coldericke?'

Anna nodded, and beneath the calmness of her demeanour, suppressed a tremor of nervousness.

Royston bent low over the child on the tabletop, and deftly cut into the largest of the pustules on the delicate face, allowing the released pus to smear the full length of the blade. The baby jerked frantically, and howled in anguish. Tildy involuntarily stepped forwards, her hands stretching towards her child, and the doctor was quick to reassure her.

'He'll come to no harm, Crawford. All he feels of the knife is the slightest of pressures, and in due course all of the pustules must be opened, perhaps twice or thrice to drain away the foulness. He will quickly grow accustomed to the sensation of the blade. There is naught to distress yourself over.'

Biting her lower lip, as she mentally wrestled with her doubts, Tildy moved back from the table. But her heart ached as her baby cried.

Satisfied that the blade was thickly coated with pus, Lucas Royston took hold of the soft upper arm of Anna Coldericke and lifted it towards the light. Her eyes met his, and he murmured, 'Trust me, Anna.'

She smiled at him, and he brought the knife up and lightly cut three small shallow incisions that barely penetrated the tender white skin, then smeared the blade across the area of the cuts. Laying aside the knife he tore off a strip of the black sticking plaster and laid it across the site, pressing it firmly down.

'There, it is done. Leave this plaster in place for a week and three days, and all is well.'

The entire sequence had only taken seconds.

He beckoned Tildy forwards, and she swallowed hard, quelling her fear, and closed her eyes tightly while Royston repeated the procedure of draining a pustule, and then incising her arm. All she felt was the minor discomfort of the three scratches and the pressure of his fingers.

'Open your eyes, Crawford. You still live,' he bantered gently.

'Can I hold my baby now?' she asked eagerly.

'As soon as we have done with the children,' he told her kindly, 'but mind what I say, you must not suckle him again. He must now be fully weaned.'

All three orphans screamed wildly in fright as Lucas went towards them with the knife, and it took the combined efforts of both Tildy and Anna Coldericke to hold the small wriggling bodies still, so that the incisions could be inflicted. The children's screams and struggles evoked a varying reaction among the watchers. Some laughed with a cruel enjoyment at the antics before them, others felt sympathy, and were indignant that the children should be tormented in this way. There were yet others whose thoughts took a more sinister route.

'T'is black evil, so it is,' Katie Reeves muttered to her cronies. 'To my mind these bastards be trying to kill off them kids. You mark my words well, we'll not see the little buggers alive agen arter this night. You mark what I say.'

'How can you dare say that?' Hannah Knight whispered. 'Arn't the lady, and Tildy both took the inoculation.'

Katie Reeves's swarthy features twisted in mockery. 'Youm a rare booby, you am, Hannah Knight. Why d'you think there was only the light of a single lamp? Why d'you reckon they took care that we could hardly see what was happening? I'll tell you why . . . Because the bloody doctor was only pretending to cut them two, Tildy Crawford and the lady. If you warn't such a thick-yedded chaw-bacon, you'd know what's agoing on here, right in front of your bloody blind eyes.' Her knowing air sharpened the appetites of her listeners.

'What is it that's going on then, Katie?' one woman questioned in an enthralled whisper.

The mockery became spiteful relish. 'Well I knows what I thinks, and that's that them three bastards be up to no good. It's bloody plain to see why they'm using them orphans, arn't it. Kids who've got no kin to look arter 'um, or make enquiries about 'um.'

Puzzlement and curiosity dominated the faces surrounding her, and she hissed impatiently, 'Use your brains, you thick-skulled cows! He's the surgeon to the poor, arn't he . . . and what does surgeons use to learn their trade on, and to practice with?'

She paused to let her words sink in to her listeners' minds, before continuing with low-pitched intensity.

'The cart's awaiting outside to tek Crawford and all four kids to Redditch, arn't it. Why don't they leave 'um here, like they always does? Why be they taking all the kids away, arter they's gone and infected the poor little sods wi' the smallpox? And can you name me a more certain killer than the pox?'

While she had been listening, Hannah Knight's brain had been racing. Quicker-witted than her companions, she was the first to sense what lay beyond Kate Reeves' sentences. Abruptly she gasped audibly, and an expression of fast-expanding horror marred her smooth features.

'Yes, that's it!' Kate Reeves exclaimed with satisfaction. 'You'se got my meaning, arn't you, Hannah, my duck. It's a cheap way o' doing things for that bloody surgeon theer, arn't it? It saves him a rake o' money, doon't it, and a lot o' bother. Doing it this way he don't have to find and pay the bloody resurrection men, does he?'

She glanced at each staring, horrified face in turn, and was satisfied that her words had struck home on their target . . .

The moon was a yellow sliver in the sky when the two-wheeled cart carrying Tildy and the four children lurched away from the poorhouse. Lucas Royston rode ahead, with Anna Coldericke mounted pillion behind him. As the black, forbidding mass of the house merged into the surrounding darkness, Tildy tried to comfort the orphans who, still upset by the inoculation, were now crying in their fear of the unknown destination to which they were being taken.

'Hush now, you're going to a nice house, where you'll have soft beds to lie on, and lots of nice things to eat and drink. I'll take care of you. You've no call to fret yourselves. Hush now, there's good kids.'

She drew the three closer to her, and spread her skirts to give them a little shelter from the chill air. On her lap Davy was dozing, and although he smelt badly, yet Tildy cuddled him closer, and kissed his soft hair, glorying in her first opportunity to nurse her baby after the long days and nights of separation.

'I'll bet youm glad to leave here?' Joey, the old pauper who drove the cart turned his head towards the young woman sitting on the straw behind him. For a moment Tildy considered his statement, and found to her own surprise that no great feeling of gladness pervaded her.

'No, not so much really,' she answered, 'but then, how can I feel glad for leaving, when I know that I'll be back here in two or three weeks at the outside.'

'Ahr, that might be so, Tildy, but at least youm agoing to be living on the fat o' the land until that day comes.'

She didn't reply to this, instead her mind wandered. *'How strange life was. This morning she had breakfasted on salted gruel in the poorhouse. Tomorrow she would breakfast in the house of a gentle lady.'* She smiled wryly. *'In a gentry house, yes, but I'll still only be in the kitchen. I'll not be eating breakfast in the parlour, that's for sure.'* Then a sense of thankfulness swelled within her. *'But Davy will soon get well there. I'll be able to give him good things to eat and drink, things that'll nourish and strengthen him. It'll be good for these other poor little souls as well. I'll take good care that they get the best I can get for them. The doctor promised that we should live like fighting cocks, and that he and Anna Coldericke would eventually get money from the parish for us. So we shall not be taking advantage of Mrs Coldericke's kindness in any way.'* The thought of Anna Coldericke sent Tildy's musing off at a tangent.

'What an unusual person. Taking a poorhouse woman and four poorhouse kids into her own home, and behaving as if it were nothing extraordinary in the slightest.'

The gossip engendered among the inhabitants by Anna Coldericke's appearance in the poorhouse had been faithfully related to Tildy by her friend Hannah, and Tildy knew a surprising amount concerning the Coldericke woman already. 'They say that she goes her own way, and nothing nor nobody can ever prevent her doing what she will. They say her knowledge is the equal of any school-teacher in the County. They say she loved her husband so much, that when he died she near went out of her mind, and lived for years like a hermit. They say that no other man has ever known her body. They say she teaches the young ladies of the town all sorts of wickedness against the King and the great lords of the nation . . . ' Tildy giggled to herself. 'They say that Anna Coldericke says that all men have big cannons and small brains and that they shoot all their strength and thought through the first . . . '

Perched behind Lucas Royston, her arms wrapped about his lean waist, feeling the warmth of his body penetrating through the layers of cloth that divided them, and the rough texture of his coat against her cheek, Anna Colder-ricke was at peace with the world. All her loneliness and boredom had been almost miraculously banished, and her mind was full of delightful visual fantasies about her future. Those fantasies each containing one focal point, Lucas Royston . . .

Lucas Royston was also enjoying his fantasies. Fantasies of the personal triumph he would achieve when the success of his containment of the smallpox was known throughout the parish. 'Josiah Cutler will see me in a very different light then, I'll wager on that. I'll be considered a fitting suitor for Emma then . . . ' He dwelt on his mental image of the young girl, and a smile of contentment curved his lips . . .

The little cavalcade ambled on, each immersed in their own thoughts, unsuspecting of what lay ahead for them in the days to come.

Chapter Twenty-One

James Bray's throat was troubling him badly. It hurt him to swallow and the soreness created an irritation which made him cough frequently. A strong sense of injustice oppressed his normally ebullient spirits as he walked towards the crossroads of Redditch Green, and the morning's freshness did nothing to cheer him. Coming to a halt in the very centre of the crossroads he rang his handbell vigorously, and steeling himself against the pain, bellowed hoarsely.

'Oyez . . . Oyezzz . . . Oyezzzzz . . . There is an auction sale to be held this day at Twelve o' the Clock, Noontime, of farming stock, implements of husbandry, household furniture and effects of Mr William Purcell of Astwood Lane Farm in the Parish of Feckenham . . . ' Again he rang his handbell. 'Oyez . . . Oyezzz . . . Oyezzz . . . Fresh meat! Fresh meat! Fresh meat! Butcher Vincent has killed a fine bullock. Fresh meat! Fresh meat! Fresh meat!' The bell jangled furiously. 'Oyez . . . Oyezz . . . Oyezzz . . . Prevailing articles of the very latest London fashions be now ready for inspection at the premises of the Misses Nicholls and Provost . . . '

Tildy opened her eyes and for a brief moment thought she was dreaming as she saw the neat curtains, the pictures on the walls, and smelt lavender water on her sheets, and rose-petal scent on her soft lawn pillows.

'Oyez . . . Oyezz . . . Oyezzz . . . There is an auction sale to be held . . . '

The hoarse shouting was muffled by the closed

207

casements, and Tildy rose from the bed and went to open the leaded panes and let the fresh warm air fill her lungs. She looked down at the crier, admiring the splendid figure he cut in his gold-laced tricorn hat, full-skirted canary yellow coat, plum breeches and white stockings ending in silver-buckled shoes. Tildy smiled at the antics of the group of urchins with their barking mongrel dogs who cavorted around the crier, begging him to let them ring his bell. Then her smile died abruptly, as she realized the lateness of the hour.

'What will the lady think of me? Lying in my bed like a lazy slut 'til this hour, and no doubt the kids are awake and crying for their breakfasts.'

Hurriedly she dressed herself and went down the three flights of stairs that separated her attic room from the ground floor. Even as she came down the final flight, Anna Coldericke called from the rear of the house. 'Come here, Crawford.'

Tildy followed the voice through the passage and so came to the kitchen. A high-ceilinged room, made welcoming by the fire crackling in the gleaming black-iron cooking range. All round the walls copper and brass vessels cast burnished reflections of the flames, while a huge dresser covered one entire wall, with blue and white glazed plates, jugs, bowls, dishes, saucers and cups ranged upon its myriad shelves.

Anna Coldericke was seated at the big white-scrubbed table in the centre of the room, and standing facing her was the servant, Mrs Bray.

The woman glanced sourly at Tildy, her eyes narrowing upon the red pauper's badge on the girl's right shoulder. 'This 'ull be the poor'us woman then, ma'am,' the servant sniffed indignantly. 'I canna think what the old master and mistress would say, if they was alive, I'm sure. Filling the house with paupers and their brats like this. God only knows what they'll bring in wi' 'um.'

'That is enough, Mrs Bray,' Anna Coldericke silenced her sharply. 'And you will have no reason to worry about what they bring into this house with them.'

The woman's round pink face became instantly suspicious. 'How can that be, ma'am? Iffen I'm working here then I'll have good reason to worry, wun't I.'

'You will not be here, Mrs Bray. At least, not within this house. All I shall require from you for approximately a sennight, is to go to market, and carry out any other errands I need of you. We shall be making a quarantine of the house for that length of time.'

'Making a what, ma'am?' the woman gaped blankly.

'A quarantine, Mrs Bray,' Anna Coldericke repeated, and went on to explain what had happened the previous evening. As she did so her servant's features expressed a gamut of emotions, of which doubt and fearful disapproval were the dominant themes.

'So you see, Mrs Bray. To avoid exposing you to any risk of infection, I shall not permit you within the house. We can pass messages, and baskets, etcetera, through the kitchen window here.'

'And what about your classes, ma'am? What's to be done about the young ladies. You canna expect them to come to a house that's full o' paupers and disease.'

'There will be no classes for this period of time,' Anna Coldericke explained with strained patience. 'I shall write notes giving the reason for the cancellations, and you shall deliver them. Meanwhile, here is a list of necessaries I have need of. Go to the shops, and when you return I shall give you further instructions.' She paused for a moment looking at the woman's sour face. 'Come now, Mrs Bray, let's have no more petulance from you. Your looks would curdle cream. You will not lose any wages because of this, and Crawford and I are quite capable of managing the house for a sennight, I'm sure. Now be off with you, and do the shopping.'

With doleful shaking of her head, the servant took up her withy basket and left. Anna Coldericke smiled happily at Tildy.

'Pay no heed to Mrs Bray, Crawford. Like all old servants, she imagines she is the mistress of the house, and her employer is only there to be bullied. I declare, I'm enjoying all this. It is an adventure, is it not?'

'Yes, ma'am,' Tildy nodded dutifully, but could not resist adding, 'but there are parts of it that I could well do without.'

The other woman laughed appreciatively. 'I see you have a sense of humour, Crawford. Good! I like that. I feel that you and I shall agree very well. Now, let us to business. You rouse the children and I will prepare bowls of bread and milk for them.' She looked disapprovingly at Tildy's shabby grey dress with its red badge. 'I am not enamoured of that dress and badge, Crawford. After breakfast we shall see what clothing there is in my chests. I'm sure there will be something there to fit you . . . '

Chapter Twenty-Two

From the Chapel Green, the Fish Hill fell sharply away to the north, leading towards the distant city of Birmingham. At the bottom of the hill, on the corner of a lane and over-shadowed by its needle mill neighbour, was an ancient, half-timbered tavern, the Royal Oak. Its gabled front facing up the Fish Hill, and its ground floor doors and windows some three feet below the level of the roadway.

Tommy Green was the landlord, a man so short and fat that he seemed to be all head, belly and topboots. He was an old friend of the crier, James Bray, and now both men stood sharing a flagon of beer across the tall counter of the tap room, and watched a group of needle pointers from the mill next door, playing a noisy game of dominoes. Hands raising brass counters high and slamming them down onto the tabletop. Argument and challenge and jeer creating a constant barrage of accompaniment to the play.

Phoebe Bray, the crier's wife and Anna Coldericke's servant, came into the tap room and scowled at her husband.

'I guessed I'd find you here. Why arn't you acrying round Ipsley and Studley? Butcher Vincent wants to know what he's apaying for? He says he arn't apaying you to stand and cry his meat in the bloody Royal Oak.'

'Doon't talk sarft, 'ooman,' her husband croaked. 'Wi' me throat like this nobody can bleedin' hear me. I've cried the Green, Pigeon's Bridge and Bredon, and I was just on me way to Holyoakefield when me voice went all together.

I couldn't get a squeak out, ne'er mind bloody Vincent's rotten mate.'

'Youm talking well enough now,' his irate wife challenged.

The altercation attracted the attention of the group of pointers. Richie Bint poked his elbow into Rammer Perks' ribs and winked broadly, then said loudly.

'You tell him, Phoebe. The bugger's bin here aswilling beer wi' Tommy Green for a good two hours or more, and we'se all bin able to hear him spaking clear enough, arn't that so, Lads?'

The other four pointers agreed vociferously.

'O' course that's so, Rich.'

'It's no wonder we'em so bloody ignorant o' the world, wi' a lazy bloody hound like him for crier.'

'He never spreads more than one day's news in a bloody month.'

'That's true! He didn't cry about Waterloo until two weeks afore last Christmas.'

'Yes, I thought Boney was still the Emperor o' the Frogs.'

'You shut your mouths, and mind your own business!' The woman screeched at her tormentors, 'Youm bloody ignorant o' the world, because youm born and bred ignorant. It arn't my poor Jimmy's fault that he's bin took badly in his throat.'

'Oh my Gawd! Look how she fights for him. She loves his bones, doon't you Phoebe, my duck.'

'Doon't you call me duck, Richie Bint. I arn't your duck, and never 'ud be. I got too much pride to lower me'sen to your level.'

The brawny pointer's big yellowed teeth bared in a delighted howl.

'How can you say that, Phoebe? Jesus bloody Christ! I'm a yed taller than your man sitting down on me arse. How did you ever manage to lower yourself to his level? You must have had trouble getting him inside you on wet nights when you was acourting. Or did you allus take a leather blanket wi' you to lie down on?'

'She used to take some bricks for Jimmy to stand on, didn't you, Phoebe?' Rammer Perks chortled.

Tommy Green began to laugh, and pushed his flagon towards Phoebe Bray. 'Here, have a sup o' this, my wench. The lads be only having a bit o' fun.'

She refused to be mollified so easily. 'Ahr, that's all very well for them to make sport o' me. But I knows summat that 'ud tek the silly grins off their faces.'

'How can you know anything, Phoebe?' Richard Bint asked in mock wonder. 'How can anybody in this town know anything what wi' our noble crier here not able to shout the price o' two-pennorth o' stale mate, ne'er mind any fresh news.'

'That's right, Phoebe,' Rammer Perks was quick to back up his friend's continued teasing. 'You ought to tek your man to bed and sweat the badness out on him. If he doon't get well, we'll never know nothing ever agen.'

'Ahr, my buck, you can laugh,' the woman nodded jerkily, her pink cheeks hot with resentment at being teased. 'You can mock at my Jimmy, because he's bin took badly, but you might easy be laughing on the other side o' your face shortly.'

'Why so?' Richard Bint asked.

'Yes, Phoebe, why so?' Tommy Green was curious, because he sensed that the woman did indeed have some information which could concern them all.

Satisfied that she had temporarily gained a dominance over the room, Phoebe Bray made the most of her advantage, and took a drink of beer while several of them urged her to tell her news. Finally her own desire to tell overcame her, and she gabbled rapidly. 'It's that silly cow of a mistress o' mine. Her's filled her home wi' pauper brats from the poor'us at Webheath, and told me to keep away.'

'Well? How's that going to make us laugh on the other sides of our faces?' Richard Bint was scathing. 'You bin give the sack, don't make any odds to any of us, barring your man, does it now, Phoebe?'

'You arn't understood me, Richie Bint.' Again her head

213

began to nod erratically. 'Her's not gi' me the sack. Her's told me to keep away, because all the kids she's brought to the house has got the smallpox. And her's got it as well, and a young 'ooman name o' Tildy Crawford, that her's fetched down from the poor'us as well.'

'The pox!' Tommy Green exclaimed. 'That's bad tidings, that is. Spreads like a bloody plague sometimes, so it does.'

'Ahr, and it can kill like a bloody plague, as well,' James Bray added solemnly.

Phoebe Bray's sense of triumph swelled. 'That's wiped the grins off your faces, arn't it,' she crowed over them, 'but you arn't heard all on it yet.'

'Come on, Phoebe, spit it out a bit sharpish, 'ull you.' Tommy Green had lost his first three children to the smallpox and had three more young children whom he loved very dearly. 'You knows how I feels about the pox. It's served me and mine evil enough. I hates to hear of any poor cratur getting it, and the pity is, as you all well knows, it spreads through the air and can grip ahold of anybody in its neighbourhood. I don't want to lose any more o' my nippers to the bloody stinking thing.'

Like a consummate actress, now that she had her audience hanging on her every word, Phoebe Bray lowered her voice to little above a whisper. 'That Anna Coldericke is a raving bloody loony. When she told me in the kitchen this morning what her 'ud done, I just couldn't believe me ears.'

'What had she done?' Tommy Green asked eagerly, and his mates shushed him to silence.

'Her took the pox deliberately, and so did that poor'us woman who's wi' her in the house. They did it because that bloody newcome Doctor Royston talked 'um into it. He's got some power over 'um, that's what I reckons . . . and worse nor that, was what the three on 'um did together . . . ' she stared at the rapt faces surrounding her, and knew the sweetness of complete triumph over her tormentors when she noted in some of their eyes the first flickerings of fear.

214

'The kids they got wi' 'um now, be poor orphan kids, that they infected wi' the pox as well.'

A concerted gasp of outrage greeted her, and her head jerked erratically. 'May God above strike me dead, if it arn't the truth, boys,' she mouthed dramatically. 'Anna Coldericke told me herself, what they'd done. I'll tell you, her poor old feyther and mother 'ud turn in their graves iffen they knew what their daughter had done. Her must be stark staring mad!'

'She bloody well must be!' Tommy Green agreed emphatically. 'But then, her went a bit funny in the yed when her man got killed in Spain, didn't her.'

'That's right enough,' Richard Bint remarked thoughtfully. 'Mind you, the pox doon't bother me, because I'se had it already, when I was a kid.'

'That's alright for you then, arn't it,' Tommy Green spluttered angrily, 'but think of all the ones in the town who arn't had the stinking bastard. Think on all the kiddies who could be in danger o' catching it now. And all because one bleedin' mad'ooman has gone and brought it among us. And another thing, arn't Edwin Danks bin saying that it was Coldericke and the bloody Scotchman who caused his nipper to die.'

Phoebe Bray felt the first stirrings of apprehension, as she looked at the gathering anger on the faces around her. She began to wonder if it might not have been a wiser thing to have kept her mouth shut.

'The Coldericke woman had got no right to do this thing,' James Bray croaked indignantly. 'It might well be her that's caused me throat to be so badly.'

'And who's to tell her about her rights. And who's to say her, Nay? Not you, you little worm.' Phoebe Bray was not prepared to allow her hen-pecked husband to criticize her mistress. 'She's Gentry, so she is, and can do what she pleases.'

'I don't give a bugger if her's bloody royalty!' the crier blustered. 'Her's got no right to risk our well-being, or our lives, by doing what her's done.'

215

'Oh can't she?' His wife moved swiftly to crush this unusual spasm of defiant rebellion from her meek and submissive spouse. 'Well, she can do as she pleases for all that the likes o' you would ever dare do to stop her. Besides, who'se to say that she's risking anybody's life? She's a book-learned woman, and she told me that so long as she keeps in that quarantine thing, then nobody else in the town can ever take the pox from Ivy House.'

'I don't gi' a bollocks, what her said to you!' James Bray's croak became a throat-straining bellow, and the woman's eyes opened wide. The worm had finally turned. 'So you just hold your tongue, missis, because I'se heard too bleedin' much on it today.'

Phoebe Bray was stunned into silence, and her husband took a long swallow of beer to soothe his throat, then went on. 'I've a mind to goo and see the vestrymen about this. It just arn't Christian to do what that bloody mad 'ooman has done. I mean, if the pox gets among you in the normal sort o' way, then that's the will o' God, and we can't do aught else but accept it, and pray for His mercy. But, to infect kids and spread the bloody thing deliberate, well . . .'

'That's the Devil's work!' Tommy Green finished his friend's sentence for him.

'It's no use you aseeing the vestrymen,' Richard Bint was positive. 'They'm just a load of arse-creepers to the gentry. Besides, what can they do about it? Anna Colder-icke is a friend o' the bloody parson, and she's in her own house. She arn't no poor woman that can be put on a cart and wheeled out of the parish. Anyway, like I said afore, the pox doon't frighten me, no matter who brings it here, God or Coldericke.'

'Well it frightens me,' Tommy Green snarled, and glanced around him at the others. 'And by the looks on it, it frightens the rest on us who'se got wives and childer to think on.'

A rumble of assent sounded out.

'I'se got little 'uns, Richie,' Rammer Perks youthfully handsome face was grim. 'And I'll tell you now that if one on 'um takes the pox in the next weeks, then I'll know for certain who brought it down on 'um.' He broke off, to stare hard at the crier. 'And I wunt think o' going to see the vestrymen, Jimmy. I'll not waste me time like that . . . No.' He shook his head emphatically. 'No, I'll take revenge in me own way. I'll burn that Coldericke bitch's house down, wi' her inside it.'

The threat excited Tommy Green. 'And I'll help you do it, Rammer. I swear on me babbies' graves, I'll be wi' you.'

Richard Bint decided to reassert his normal position of leadership among the group. He grinned ferociously. 'Well now, Rammer, my buck. You'se always stood a good mate to me, so I'll tell you what we'll do. We'll spread the word around town about what's going on at Ivy House. Then we'll wait, and if any cratur hereabouts takes the pox in the weeks to come, then we'll all bring torches to light the bonfire. Only we'll have three Guy Fawkeses instead o' one only. Youm forgetting that the bloody Scotch doctor and the poor'us woman be just as much to blame as Coldericke. So, what say you to that idea?'

A roar of agreement filled the room, and Tommy Green shouted as he lifted a bottle of rum from beneath the counter. 'Come on, lads, give us your pots over. We'll drink to that wi' a drop of the good stuff. And I'll stand treat.'

Phoebe Bray was by now thoroughly frightened. 'You can't mean to do that,' she protested. 'Mrs Coldericke told me that it was safe. That nobody else could take the pox because of her. Youm all bloody mad, so you am!'

Her husband's face was that of a stranger as he turned furiously upon her. 'I told you to keep your bloody mouth shut, you cow!' His arm swung wildly, his knuckles crashing against her mouth.

It was the sheer surprise of the blow rather than the weight or pain of it which caused her to cower back from him and scurry out of the tavern, holding her apron to her bleeding lips.

'Good on you, Jimmy,' Tommy Green applauded, 'you ought to have done that years since.'

Shocked by what he had done, James Bray could only stand staring unbelievingly at his clenched fist.

Chapter Twenty-Three

From the doorway Tildy smiled in pleasure at the sight of the three small heads bending low over great crock bowls of steaming chicken broth, ranged side by side along one edge of the kitchen table.

From the opposite end of the room Anna Coldericke smiled also as she watched the pewter spoons rising and falling in such urgent rhythm.

'Is Davy sleeping?' she asked.

Tildy nodded. 'He seems much relieved now that the scabs are formed. Doctor Royston says that the crisis is passed, and that now he will most certainly get well again.'

The doctor had followed Tildy down the stairs, and now he came past her and into the kitchen. 'Yes, he will most certainly get well, but you must still maintain the utmost vigilance for two or three weeks more.' He patted the shining clean hair of the orphans as he walked behind the bench they sat on. 'I declare Anna, you feed these little creatures like veritable fighting cocks. You will ruin their palates for poorhouse rations. But remember, as soon as the smallpox takes hold none of you must eat any red meat at all. A little white meat on occasion, but no red.'

A shadow passed across the woman's grey eyes. 'The pity is that they should ever have to return to the poorhouse. Look at them now, after only five days in my home. Do you not see the improvement?'

'Indeed I would have to be a blind man, and lacking a sense of smell, not to perceive improvement, Anna. They are gaining weight, and the pauper-sores are fast disappearing from their skins.'

The children seemed oblivious to the conversation above their heads, all that concerned them apparently was to cram as much of the savoury broth as possible into their stomachs.

Impelled by something beyond her conscious will, Anna Coldericke pointed at Tildy. 'And how about Crawford, Doctor Lucas Royston? Do you not think that she also is looking much improved?'

The man looked back at Tildy, then turned so that he faced her fully. His eyes dropped to the dainty slippers peeping out from beneath the folds of her dark-blue dress, and slowly travelled upwards. Past the rounded hips, the high gathered waistline, the creamy globes of breasts displayed to advantage by the low cut of the bodice. The softly dimpled throat, the oval face framed by glossy dark hair. The open admiration in his expression embarrassed Tildy, who flushed and dropped her eyes as he said quietly,

'Indeed, Anna, you have worked a veritable miracle here. Five days ago she appeared a toil-worn pauper woman. You have transformed her into a beautiful young lady.'

It was the fervency in his tone more than the actual words he spoke that stung Anna Coldericke.

'*You have only yourself to blame,*' she acknowledged inwardly. '*You continually draw his attention to the girl, and then feel torment because he finds her beautiful. Why must you bring this hurt upon yourself, you pathetic fool.*' Despite the tumult of her thoughts, Anna Coldericke's smile never faltered, as she answered aloud. 'Yes, I fully agree, Lucas. That dress quite remarkably becomes her.' She turned her smile on Tildy, 'Come Crawford, you must take your supper now.'

Still with eyes downcast, Tildy ladled out a bowl of broth and seated herself at the table facing the children. As she ate her mind dwelt on the incident that had just occurred. Tildy was shrewd enough to realize that Anna Coldericke was besotted with the doctor, and ravaged by jealousy.

'*I wonder how long it will be before her goodwill towards me turns to ill? She suffers inner torments constantly, the poor woman.*'

Tildy was becoming genuinely fond of Anna Coldericke. During the five days she had lived at Ivy House the woman had demonstrated her goodness of heart, and had been kindness itself to the children.

'*And to me also. I wish she were not so in love with Lucas Royston. He has a hardness and a selfishness within him, that I'm sure of, although he keeps it well hidden. He may return some of her feelings for him, but I can't help but think that his are of a more self-serving nature, than a self-giving.*' A sadness momentarily swept over Tildy. '*I have begun to find contentment and stability here at Ivy House. Even allowing myself to hope that there might be some way in which I could have stayed in service here after the pox has run its course. But I fear that cannot be if Anna Coldericke is to continue tormenting herself by urging the doctor's attention towards me, instead of keeping it centred upon herself.*' It was not vanity that caused Tildy to think in this manner, but purely a subjective recognition of fact. In sexual matters men's appetites usually centred on youth and beauty, and those two ephemeral attributes could temporarily overwhelm any attraction of character and personality possessed by older, plainer women.

'Doctor Lucas is leaving now, Crawford,' Anna Coldericke's voice broke into her thoughts, and Tildy dutifully rose and went to stand by the front door with his top hat in her hands.

'Are you sure that I cannot prevail upon you to stay and eat with me, Lucas. I have so much that I wish to talk with you about,' Anna smiled invitingly, inwardly begging him to accept.

He smilingly demurred. 'I have a previous engagement, Anna.'

He took her hand, and she successfully resisted the temptation to ask him who that engagement was with. Struggling to keep her tone light, she forced a smile.

'Oh very well, but do try and keep yourself free for tomorrow evening, Lucas. You seem to dash in and out of Ivy House with all the speed of a comet. If you could but stay an hour or so, it would give me much pleasure.'

His striking eyes regarded her closely, and seemed to glow with an inner satisfaction, as if they gloried in what they found. 'I bid you goodnight, Anna.'

At the front entrance he took his hat from Tildy, and casually chucked her beneath her chin. 'What a pity that there will be spots on that pretty face, Crawford. But never mind them, they'll soon disappear.'

She bobbed a curtsey, and would have closed the door behind him, but Anna Coldericke came to stand by it.

'Leave it, Crawford, I need a breath of air. Go and finish your supper.'

Tildy left the older woman staring after the tall slender figure of Lucas Royston.

'Turn back,' Anna willed him. 'Only turn back and wave even.'

The man went quickly on without a backward glance, and out from her sight. She sighed and closed the door gently, then went in to her living room. An old hand-mirror was laying on a small table set into the window recess, and Anna lifted it and tilted her face towards the light, studying what the mirror showed her.

Her complexion was pale, innocent of rouge or powder, and for a thirty-year old woman, surprisingly free of blemish.

'But still, there is no mistaking it for anything other than thirty years old flesh,' she smiled wryly, noting critically that her teeth were a trifle too long, but at least were sound and white. 'I could perhaps term myself as handsome,' with her fingers she traced the strong lines of cheeks, mouth, nose and jaw, 'but certainly I could not term myself a sweetly feminine rosebud.'

Her body she was secretly proud of. Knowing that her breasts were still high and firm, her waist trim, and that she carried no rolls of fat around stomach, hips or thighs. 'Lucas can find no fault with me in that respect, I'm sure of that. But apart from that, what else have I to offer a younger man, who is handsome, gallant and charming. With a first-class mind that will undoubtedly bring him to prominence and success in his profession. I am a thirty-years-old widowed school-marm, with no money, and no property other than this ramshackle house; and have the reputation among local society of being a half-insane, blue-stocking,' acute despair whelmed. 'The town is full of wealthy young girls. Some of them pretty. Some of them accomplished. And some of them both those things. Their families and connections would ensure a most lucrative practice for Lucas. Their dowry would provide for him the wherewithal to travel and to study. He would be able to pursue all his own theories of medicine without any other cares to distract him. I must truly be mad if I think that he would want me for his wife, when there are so many younger, prettier, richer matches available in this town . . . ' She welcomed the distraction of soft tapping on the door. 'Come!'

At her call, the door opened and Tildy Crawford entered, balancing a large tray on which a plate of cold meats kept company with salad bowls, white bread and a dish of fresh butter. 'I've brought your supper, ma'am.'

Anna Coldericke experienced a rush of shame that she should feel jealousy of Lucas Royston's obvious admiration for this young woman's undoubted good looks. How could the girl help it?

Tildy placed the tray on a table close to the fireplace. 'I'll fetch your pot of tea in directly, ma'am.' In only seconds she was back with the silver tea-set on its silver tray.

Anna watched the girl lay out the meal, and her sense of shame intensified. Impulsively she stretched out a hand to prevent Tildy leaving the room. 'Wait, Crawford, I wish to ask you something.'

Tildy regarded her curiously. 'Yes, ma'am?'

'Tell me, Crawford,' Anna searched for words. 'Tell me, if there was anything that was in my power to do for you, what would you choose for me to so do?' She had deliberately introduced a jovial note into her voice, as though she meant her question to be taken purely as a hypothetical one.

Tildy smiled, but took the question seriously. 'You've already done too much for me, ma'am, that I could never repay. You've given me clothes, and a fine bed to lie on, and good food, the chance to care really well for my Davy and those other poor little souls. I would say you've already done sufficient.'

The older woman shook her head in sharp negation. 'Come now, Crawford, I'll not accept that for answer. Now tell me what you would choose me to do. Find you a handsome husband, perhaps?'

Tildy laughed with genuine amusement. 'Oh God, no ma'am! Someone once chose one of them for me, and I'm still married to him although he's a runaway.' Her lustrous dark brown eyes swept the room, lingering upon the serried red, blue, brown and green Moroccan spines with their gold lettering that shone dully behind the glass of the bookcases. 'To speak truly, ma'am. If I could choose anything at all then I'd choose book-learning.'

The answer startled Anna Coldericke. 'Book-learning?'

Tildy nodded firmly. 'Oh yes, ma'am, book-learning. I'd have you teach me to read and to write, and to do the proper arithmetic,' enthusiasm heightened her colour, 'and then I'd ask you to point the way for me. To tell me the best books to read, so that I might gain a knowledge of many things. Instead of being so ignorant, as I am now.'

'And what would you do with this knowledge, once you had gained it?' Anna was touched by this unexpected reaction to her question.

'That's easy answered, ma'am. I'd use it to give my Davy a better chance in life. I'd try and use it to gain money, so that he could become a gentleman.'

'To have money does not guarantee that a man is a gentleman, Crawford,' Anna spoke curtly. 'Some of the greatest blackguards I know of are wealthy men, but I personally would never term them gentlemen.'

For the first time in the conversation bitterness crept into Tildy's eyes and throbbed in her voice. 'To lack money does guarantee that a man or woman is regarded by the rich as being on a level with the beasts of the fields, and treated accordingly, I know that only too well. At least if my son had wealth, he would then have the chance of being either blackguard or gentleman. Without money, he will only ever be pauper scum in the eyes of his self-styled betters.' Abruptly aware that her words could be construed as a personal attack by Anna Coldericke, Tildy flushed and bobbed a curtsey. 'Mayhap my tongue is over-sharp for my station in life, ma'am. I mean no offence to you personally. I'll go now, shall I, and put the children abed.'

Anna Coldericke regarded her gravely. 'Yes, Crawford, your tongue is indeed over-sharp for your station in life. You would do well to curb it.'

Tildy bit her lip to hold back the hasty retort that sprang to them. Reminding herself of this woman's kindness to her and the children. She bobbed another curtsey. 'I'll try to curb my tongue, ma'am. But whether I will be able to, I don't rightly know, to speak honestly.'

The older woman's lips compressed into a thin hard line. Then she said. 'Go now and complete your chores, Crawford. Then come back here to me.' A smile spread across her stern features. 'We will begin your book-learning, this very night.'

The wax candle had burned to a stub. Been replaced. Burned to a stub, and been replaced twice more, but Tildy felt no fatigue. Only elation and a brimming over of energies. To her this introduction to the mysteries of writing and reading, of deciphering the meanings of symbols, of beginning to understand how the combinations of those symbols reproduced the spoken word, was a magical pathway along which would be found an enchanted future.

For Anna Coldericke also the hours had flown. She was both impressed and excited. Impressed by the quickness with which this ignorant girl had grasped what she was striving to impart, and excited because she sensed that within this girl's delicately shaped head there pulsated a brain of quite remarkable capability. For the first time in Anna Coldericke's life, she had experienced the profound joy of being a teacher.

The grandfather clock in its shadowed corner clicked, whirred and chimed the strokes of midnight. Anna Coldericke sat back on her chair and smiled at Tildy. 'It is very late, Craw . . . ' Her tongue hovered, and her smile widened. 'I think it more fitting that from now on I call you by your Christian name. You are my pupil now, and no longer a mere servant. You shall be Tildy to me, and I shall be Anna, to you.' She noted the girl's instant expression of doubt, and laughed softly. 'At least, when we are alone, my dear,' she qualified. 'When others are present, then it must continue to be Crawford, and ma'am, for that is the way of our world, and although I have the reputation of being a madly eccentric blue-stocking, there are those who would resent very strongly our using such terms of familiarity. And some of them might try to make your life difficult because of it.'

Tildy understood what the woman meant. Indeed, she knew that even when they were alone, she would have difficulty in calling this gentlewoman by her Christian name. The conditioning process of inculcating servility begun at birth and continued all her life would not be easily halted and turned back upon itself.

'We have studied enough for tonight, Tildy. Now do not look so sulky, we shall continue at each and every opportunity. It is a rare pleasure for me to have such an eager and apt pupil.'

'Oh, ma'am,' Tildy burst out. 'I'm so grateful to you for this. It's wonderful! It's like a dream.'

Anna Coldericke was moved by the obvious sincerity with which the words were spoken. 'If it be a dream, Tildy, then be assured that it is a dream that you will wake from and find it true to life.' She mock-frowned, 'But do not call me ma'am when we are alone. My name is Anna. Now say it.'

226

Tildy smiled, and replied, 'It shall be Anna then, but only when no others are present.'

'Good!' The older woman patted Tildy's hand. 'And now I think it is time that we went to our beds, Tildy.'

They both rose, and Tildy collected the primers in a neat pile, and wiped the quill pens she had been using to form the letters of the alphabet. From the road outside came the gentle soughing of the night wind, and born on that wind the discordance of men's voices raised in song.

Anna Coldericke went to the casement and using her hands to shield her eyes from the room-light, peered out into the darkness. Another outcry of voices came on the wind, and she clucked her tongue against the roof of her mouth.

'Drunken sots!' she exclaimed disgustedly. 'Probably they are pointers. It is only they who have sufficient money to get soddened with drink night after night.' She turned to look at Tildy, 'No, my dear, I do not begrudge the labouring classes their pleasures, but I see what happens to the wives and children of those men. They get swinish drunk and they argue and brawl like wild animals among themselves, and then go back to their homes with the madness still in them, and inflict terror and brutal beatings upon their families. The pointers are not as other men, Tildy. Their work kills them within scant years, and because of that they care naught for any of the decencies of life.'

She sighed, and again clucked her tongue. 'I declare, I sound like a ranting killjoy, do I not. But it is only that I wish those men would consider the happiness and well-being of their families, before throwing all that cruelly-earned money across the counters of the beershops.'

She stepped towards the table in the room's centre, and Tildy straightened, and said.

'There, Anna, all is ready for tomorrow's lesson.'

She lifted the candlestick, and a window-pane smashed inwards.

Anna Coldericke screamed out in shock, and as her

227

scream died, a man's voice bawled outside the house. 'That's a warning to you bloody child-killers. Gerron out o' this town, and take the stinkin' pox wi' you.'

'Oh my God!' Anna Coldericke's face was chalk-white, her eyes grotesquely staring. 'What is he shouting?'

Tildy was looking down at the shattered pieces of glass and the lumps of brick strewn across the carpet. Her mind flashed back to other glass smashing, and flames exploding, and men shouting, and her baby screaming. Her body began to shake uncontrollably, and her teeth ground together as old terrors savaged her once more.

'What is he shouting? What does he say?' Anna Coldericke screeched hysterically, and Tildy stared at the other woman, and the sight of that hysteria paradoxically enabled Tildy to begin to fight to control her own rampaging fear.

'Don't be frightened, ma'am.' She stepped forwards and clutched the older woman's trembling arm.

More missiles crashed against the casement and more shards of glass and brickbats exploded into the room.

Anna Coldericke screamed out in fright again, and Tildy blew out her candle plunging the room into darkness. Fiercely she shook the other's arms.

'Calm yourself, for pity's sake calm yourself.' She urged through clenched teeth. 'I've stopped the light so that they can not see us now.' Her earlier terror was rapidly ebbing, and the memories that had initially unmanned her, now gave her strength. 'I've had similar to this happen to me afore, ma'am. They didn't kill me then, and they'll not kill us now. Just don't let the fear beat you, that's all you must do. Not let the fear beat you . . . '

The wind gusted through the shattered panes of the casement, billowing the curtains, and Tildy drew Anna Coldericke deeper into the room. 'They can't see us, ma'am,' she whispered soothingly, 'and they'll not dare stay about the road. They know that the noise will bring the neighbours out.'

The other woman was whimpering now. Muttering

228

meaningless threads of sentences. Tildy felt a mingling of pity and contempt for her companion. The pity won out, and she put her arms about Anna Coldericke as if she were a frightened child.

'There now, there now, I'll not let them hurt you. They've gone now . . . No one is outside. I'll look after you, so don't distress yourself anymore.'

A distant shout sounded faintly, and Tildy vented a long shuddering sigh of relief.

'They've gone, Anna. They've truly gone . . . '

Chapter Twenty-Four

William Smallwood, needle master and factor to the trade, was a blunt-spoken man who believed in calling a spade a spade. 'To speak plain, Doctor Royston, I regards you as an arrogant, swollen-yedded puppy, and by God above, I'm tempted to take a bloody whip to your back.'

Lucas Royston faced the burly blustering man with his own fiery spirit in open display. 'Feel free to try, Master Smallwood. Feel free to try.'

'Gentlemen! Gentlemen! Let us remember that we are in God's House,' the Reverend John Clayton remonstrated with both disputants. 'Kindly be seated, Master Smallwood, and let us conduct ourselves in an orderly manner, as befits gentlemen.'

After a moment of indecision the needle master slumped down upon his chair, muttering angrily to himself, and John Clayton lifted his wooden hammer and brought it sharply down upon the table around which he and two select vestrymen were seated in the small vestry room of St Stephen's Chapel.

Lucas Royston remained standing facing them, his hat held before him in fingers that trembled slightly, betraying his extreme agitation.

The second vestryman, Josiah Cutler, looked at the young doctor as if he were regarding a piece of rotting, stinking fish. 'By what rights did you take them childer out from the poor'us, Royston? And by what rights did you tell the master that you'd got permission to inoculate 'um, from Reverend the Lord Aston?'

'By the right of my profession to save lives,' Lucas told him defiantly.

'Save lives, you say?' William Smallwood could not restrain himself. 'Save lives? How the bloody hell d'you save lives by deliberately giving the pox to women and kids? That sounds a peculiar way o' saving lives, if you asks me.'

'Gentlemen!' John Clayton once more slammed his hammer against the tabletop, and now his own features were reddening with vexation. 'What is done, is done, and we shall achieve nothing by continually harping on it. We must concentrate on making our decisions as to a course of future action.'

'That's easy decided.' Josiah Cutler bore no physical resemblance to his beautiful daughter, he was dark-visaged, lean-bodied and ugly. 'We hands Royston his sack.'

'I'll second that,' William Smallwood eagerly supported his colleague.

The clergyman shook his head. 'I do not think that to be the solution. I believe that Doctor Royston acted in good faith. The practice of inoculation is widely known, and is used by other physicians in this country. It is recognized . . . '

'But not accepted!' Smallwood interrupted vehemently. 'At least not in these parts. And it arn't that alone which is angering me, Reverend. It's the bloody high-handedness of this young puppy here, in removing paupers from the poorhouse wi'out so much as a by-your-leave, to we who has the charge o' them paupers.'

'Reverend Clayton, I acted as any responsible physician would have acted in this matter,' Lucas defended forcefully. 'Smallpox requires to be quarantined, and that is what I have done in this case. Created a quarantine.'

'Created a bloody spreading o' disease, more like it.' The vestryman spluttered irately. 'Deliberately infecting them soddin' kids, and then setting 'um smack bang in the middle o' the bloody town. I always thought that bloody Coldericke woman was mad. Now's her's proven it wi'out

231

any doubt. Serves her bloody right that her winders got smashed in. I hopes it's her bloody yed next time.'

'Master Smallwood, I will not countenance such talk in this chapel, or anywhere else I may be present,' John Clayton was really roused. 'The lady to whom you are referring may well act eccentrically on occasion, but she has the welfare of the poor at heart, and I am convinced that she acted on this present occasion solely with good intent.'

Joseph Cashmore, who was guarding the vestry door, now opened it and poked his head into the room. 'If you please, Reverend Clayton, it's Master Holyoake come.'

John Clayton nodded. 'Very well, Cashmore, I thank you.' He looked at the other two vestrymen. 'So gentlemen, with Master Holyoake here, that constitutes a Quorum. We can now decide and put into execution what we will.'

George Holyoake stamped in, his weather-beaten features stern and set. 'I bid you good morning, gentlemen.' He greeted them gruffly, and drew a chair up to the table. He jerked his thumb at Lucas Royston. 'What's this I bin hearing about what this bloody fool has done? Theer's bloody ructions agoing on up at the poor'us. The bloody paupers be crying blue murder.'

Lucas's temper flared, and he moved forwards and grabbed the farmer's shoulder. 'Call me fool again, and I'll break your head for you,' he gritted out.

The older man sprang to his feet, fists clenched, but before any blows could be struck John Clayton's muscular bulk interposed between the pair. 'There will be no fisticuffs while I am present,' he warned grimly, and told Lucas, 'You'd best leave, Doctor Royston. I am fully cognisant of the reasons for your actions, and I will defend your interests. But I fear that while you remain present, then there will be only bad blood created at this meeting. Please go now, I shall personally hasten to inform you of the vestry's decisions concerning what has occurred.'

Lucas was tempted to stand and argue his case, but realized the truth of what the clergyman said, and bowed curtly. 'Very well, Reverend Clayton. I will await you at my house.'

In the event he did not have long to wait. Within the hour John Clayton was facing him. 'The vestry has made the decision that you are to be suspended, Lucas.'

'Suspended? What in Hell's name does that mean?'

'Precisely what it denotes,' Clayton was brusque, irked by the other's attitude. 'They wished to cancel your contract, but I have prevailed upon them to merely suspend it temporarily, until the results of the inoculations are known. If the women and children take no lasting harm, and if no cases of smallpox occur in the town which can be in any way attributed to your actions, then you may resume practice as the surgeon to the parish poor.'

'And if I refuse to accept such a suspension?' Lucas asked.

The clergyman's broad shoulders lifted as he spread his arms, palms outwards. 'Then the vestry cancels your contract, Lucas. Of course, there is nothing to prevent you practising in the parish in a private capacity. But I doubt very much whether you would be able to earn sufficient for your needs in such a case. However, there is nothing to prevent you.'

Lucas chuckled mirthlessly. 'Naught but three other doctors, and a dearth of patients able to pay.'

'Well, what is it to be?' Clayton wanted to know.

The younger man grinned at him. 'I'll sleep on it, my friend, and let you know my decision in the morning.'

Clayton did not return the grin. 'No, I'm sorry Lucas, but that will not serve. I have to know now.'

Lucas Royston went to the window, and for a while silently gazed out at the squalid street. Then slowly turned, and again the grin flickered across his thin face. He jerked his head to indicate the street outside.

'Hardly the best of neighbourhoods, Reverend Sir, but it holds a certain charm for connoisseurs of the picaresque. You may tell the gentlemen of the vestry to tear the contract in pieces and shove it up their separate arses . . .'

Chapter Twenty-Five

'What ails you, Caleb? You'se never bin like this afore?' The woman's voice held both disappointment and vexation. 'You must be getting old, Cully.'

Caleb Hawkes levered himself off the warm naked body beneath him and rolled so that he sat on the edge of the bed facing the damp-mottled walls, with his bare feet upon the warped floor planks.

'Don't be angry wi' me, sweetheart,' soft arms twined around his shoulders, soft breasts pressed into his back, and soft moist lips nuzzled his ear. 'I was only kidding you on, Caleb. Don't be roiled at me. Come and lie down agen, and I'll soo ha' you panting for it.'

He shrugged his powerful shoulders to loosen her grip, and moved his head away from her searching lips. 'I'm not angry wi' you, Peggy,' he told her. 'It arn't your fault that I'm this way. T'is naught to do wi' you.' He stood up, and taking his clothes from the top of the battered old chest began to dress.

The woman displayed a flash of temper. 'Wheer be you agoing? You promised you'd stay all day wi' me.'

He chuckled mirthlessly. 'God strike me, girl! I bin here wi' you since last night. Arn't that time enough?'

'Oh yes, that's time enough alright,' she tossed her head petulantly. 'You bin here wi' me all night, and half the morning, and for all the good you'se done me, I might as well ha' bin by meself. Better if I had bin, come to that. Me hand could ha' managed what your prick couldn't.'

'I've already said that it's my fault,' he told her placatingly. 'And I'm sorry for it. But there's nothing I can do about it.' With that he left her, and as he clumped down the rickety stairs, her shout followed him.

'You'll mayhap be alright later on, Caleb. Come back then, I'll wait for you.'

'Don't do that, Peg,' he called back, and carried on down the three more flights that led to the street level of the lodging house, which was situated in the Silver Square.

Mother Readman was standing in the doorway of her establishment, and she turned at the sound of his descent. A gigantically fat, scar-featured old harridan whose eyes had seen too much of life ever to be surprised or shocked by anything ever again.

'Now then, higgler, youm leaving early. Did Peg wear you out so that you had to run away from her.'

Caleb, who liked the old woman for her tough independence, smiled into the great moon of her dirty face. 'You could say that, mother.'

He noticed a discoloured swelling around her right eye on which a small cut was weeping blood, which she periodically dabbed away with the corner of her grubby shawl. 'What happened to you? Who gave you the shiner? Been battling again wi' Mother Shipman, have you?' This was her rival who owned another lodging house close by.

Mother Readman spat in scornful denial. 'Course not. That old cow couldn't black my eye, not if I give her three full hits at it wi' a bloody great club,' she laughed, and her pendulous cheeks wobbled as her grey frizzed hair fell about them. 'No Caleb, it warn't that old bitch. I had a bit of an upset wi' one o' them Paddy harvesters earlier on this morning. The bastard was trying to slope off and give leg bail for his reckoning.' She tapped misshapen knuckles against the cloth bag hanging between her massive shapeless breasts. It clinked dully and she grinned, disclosing jagged stubs of brown teeth. 'He settled it alright, arter I took a piece out of his bleedin' earhole, and had him screaming out to the bloody Pope for a fresh set o' knackers.' Again the pendulous cheeks wobbled as she wagged her head from side to side in sad commentary on the world's wickedness. 'What hurted me most though was that I'd let the bugger share me own bed. Because I was full up here last night, but couldn't be hard-hearted enough to turn the bugger away into the cold and wet. I'm too soft for me own good, higgler.'

'Yes, you've the good heart, mother,' Caleb laughed. 'Though I sometimes wonder if there's a man in this town that you couldn't beat in a rough and tumble.'

She winked her undamaged eye, and cackled uproariously. 'Theer's bin many a one try to beat me, and none have succeeded yet, my old cock. Why, does you know when I was a young 'ooman I once toed the mark wi' a professional pug, and I held me own too, and that's no lie.'

'I know it's not,' Caleb agreed, knowing that what she told him was indeed the truth. The woman was almost legendary in the district for her fighting ability.

'I'll be off, mother.' Caleb handed some coins to the woman. 'There's Peg's rent for the week. It's best I give it straight to you. If I give it to her she'll drink it all away before nightfall.'

'I dunno why you wants to waste your money on that slut, higgler,' the gigantic woman scolded.

'Because she never asks me for it, mother,' he answered, and sauntered off. As he neared the Red Lion arch a man spoke out from the low doorway of one of the hovels.

'How bist, Master Hawkes?'

'How bist, Bocker?' Caleb halted.

Bocker Duggins was short and stocky, and although not yet twenty, looked like a man of forty years. His face was lined and covered with a mass of tiny scars under its layers of deep-grimed dirt. His teeth were black and rotting, his hair greasy and lank, and his clothes mere rags.

'Be you still wanting me to handle for you at the match, Master Hawkes?' he asked eagerly.

'Surely,' the higgler answered, and a slight frown creased his forehead. 'Why are you asking that, Bocker? Is summat gone wrong wi' the dog?'

Without waiting for a reply he pushed the man aside and entered the hovel. The air was thick and acrid with the hot smell of pent-up dogs. Its single long room was packed with rows of hutches in tiers one upon the other, fronted with grills of needle-wire, and in each hutch was a dog.

As Caleb moved along the tiers the animals erupted, barking frantically and hurling themselves at the wire grills, and the room became a canine bedlam. Bocker Duggins came running, slamming the palms of his hands against the grills, roaring the dogs to silence, sending them cowering back at the rear of their hutches.

Caleb opened a hutch on one of the topmost tiers and lifted out a brindled brown and white bull terrier. The dog recognized his master's voice and came docilely to rest in his arms while he checked its mouth and gums. Satisfied that all was well he replaced the dog, and secured the hutch.

Bocker Duggins was quick to pounce. 'Theer now, Master Hawkes, I told you all was well, didn't I. I dunno why you can't trust me.'

'I know why I can't trust you,' Caleb was half-grim, half-jovial. 'Because youm a drunken thievin' bastard, who'd sell his own Mam for a glass o' gin. I arn't forgot the money you cost me last year, when I left you in charge of a good dog, and come back to find the bugger cankered in its mouth.'

The other's reddened eyes became shifty. 'That's in the past, that is, Master Hawkes. I'se not neglected any beast o' yourn since, have I? And I've handled well for you, arn't I? And it's well known that I'm the best handler o' dogs in the bloody county.'

'I don't know about that, Bocker,' Caleb teased. 'I've met some real good lads over in the Black Country.'

'What be you telling me?' Bocker was scathingly dismissive. 'Them Black Country bastards couldn't handle my droppings.'

Caleb chuckled harshly. 'Neither could old Nick himself handle 'um, once he'd took sight o' you. Anyway, be up at the Navigation by six o' the clock next Saturday. There's a lot of rhino can be made. When I was in Droitwich yesterday I heard that the bargees were bringing a dog up from Gloucester that's a prime ratter,' he winked. 'It's supposed to be a secret, how good this dog is. But I reckon my dog's got the beating of him.'

He left Bocker Duggins chortling happily at the prospect of good pickings for himself, and went on to the Red Lion.

For more than an hour Caleb sat alone in the bar parlour, deep in thought. A pot of beer remaining almost untouched on the table beside him, and great clouds of smoke swirling around his head from the long church-warden pipe in his mouth. During that time he arrived at certain conclusions, and forced himself to admit to certain truths. He was infatuated with, in love with, besotted with, that poorhouse woman. So much so that he could not successfully bed any other female. Hence his failure last night, and on previous nights with a variety of willing partners. His feelings for Tildy Crawford were also affecting his other affairs as well, because he found that no matter where he was, or what he was doing, he could only wish that she were there with him, and be discontented and restless because she was not.

Until his return late the previous night to Redditch, he had been travelling around the county, and so had not heard any of the gossip now circulating the town concerning Ivy House. He still thought that Tildy Crawford was at the Webheath poorhouse.

'I'll go up there now,' he decided. 'I'll go up there and talk with her. Try to make her realize how much I care for her.' His mind ranged ahead. 'I'll take a house for myself instead of living here at the Lion. I can well afford to buy a place. Tildy can bring her baby with her and live with me. If she's unwilling to share my bed, then she need only be my housekeeper. Once she's living with me in the same house, and she sees that I really do love her, then she'll soften to me quick enough, and forget all that nonsense about living in a state o' sin. God blast me, her man might even be dead for all we know, and her a widow. I could have enquiries made for the bugger at any road. I've got sufficient contacts in London to track him down, if that's wheer he is.

'I'd like to see him for meself. Just to see what sort of a cove he is. Tildy reckons he served her badly, but then, most women say that when the man does a runaway on them.

'Ne'er mind, he's not wi' her now, and that's all that matters to me. Because she's going to belong to me, that's one thing I'm determined on, no matter what it takes me to achieve it.'

He puffed a last cloud of smoke from his mouth, and laid the pipe aside. 'I'm going to Webheath to see her. I know I'm acting like a love-sick bumpkin but Bollocks to it! That's what I am these days. A lovesick bumpkin!'

Caleb decided to take a detour through the Headless Cross on his way to Webheath, and call into the White Hart Inn at the crossroads there. A local prizefighter, Nail Styler, was the landlord of the inn. A one-time needle pointer who had decided that innkeeping was healthier for his lungs than pointing. Caleb had many dealings with the man, and now hoped that Styler might know of a suitable house for sale in the neighbourhood.

The innkeeper was a likeable rogue who was a thorn in the sides of the local constables. By a peculiarity of the ancient parish boundaries, the dividing line between the Ipsley and Tardebigge parishes cut through the expanding eastern edges of Redditch and the two Crosses, Headless and Crabbs. The White Hart stood in a small salient of Ipsley while the neighbouring buildings to its north south and west, were in Tardebigge parish.

Joseph Cashmore had cursed this fact many many times, for it meant that he had no jurisdiction over the inn itself, although his mandate covered its neighbours, some only a few yards away from its sprawling outbuildings. It was this fact that Nail Styler took constant delight in pointing

239

out to the Tardebigge parish constable at each and every opportunity. Such as the one that had now presented itself.

'And I'm atelling you to piss-off, Cashmore. I can do what I wants in me own place. There's bin no complaint made by me own constable.'

The two men were on the gravelled foreyard of the inn beneath the shade of the wide-branched trees which fronted the building.

The Tardebigge constable lifted his crowned staff and pointed its head into the innkeeper's face. 'I'll not piss-off, Styler. I'm here in me line o' duty. I'm going to tell you agen that there's bin complaints made to me by your neighbours that there was singing, dancing and fighting fit to wake the dead agoing on in your premises 'til past dawn this morning. That's agen the law.'

'What bleedin' law?' The other deliberately thumbed his flattened nose. 'That's what I says to your law, because it don't apply to me. I'm in Ipsley Parish, not Tardebigge. Ipsley, where we knows how to pleasure ourselves. So I'll tell you agen to piss-off, afore I takes that bloody pole o' yourn and shoves it up your arsehole.'

'That'll be a new experience for you, Joseph. You might come to enjoy it.'

Unnoticed by the antagonists Caleb Hawkes had walked his horse onto the foreyard.

Cashmore frowned at the newcomer. 'You might not think it so funny, higgler, if you had to be up from your bed and at work by crack o' light.' He indicated the nearby cottages with a swing of his staff. 'The people in them houses are hard-working Christians who need their rest, and this bugger here keeps 'um awake night arter night with the bloody rioting he has in this pub. Last night he had a load o' travelling navvies up here, and they brought every whore from miles about wi' them. They was shouting and blarting and fighting all soddin' night.'

'I know,' Caleb grinned at the irate constable, 'I was here myself later on for a while.'

A dull red flush darkened the constable's sullen features.

'Was you now?' he growled the words. 'And I suppose your poor'us doxy come creeping out to join you, did she?'

'Which one d' you mean, Joseph?' Caleb baited, hiding the instant shock of reaction that the reference to Tildy had evoked inside him.

'You knows which one I means alright,' the thin-lipped mouth twisted spitefully. 'There arn't much I misses in this town, higgler. I knows all about you and her. Well, you'd best make hay while the sun shines wi' that 'un, because from what I'm hearing she'll not be in this parish much longer.' He noted the startled gleam shoot across Caleb's eyes. 'O' course, I was forgetting,' he exclaimed, 'you've bin away for a few days arn't you. So you'se bin missing all the fun! Well, higgler, like I say, your doxy 'ull not be in these parts much longer, I'm thinking. She'll be drove out, back to the hole she comes from. And I'll not lift a hand to stop them what does it. So laugh that off.'

Caleb's heart began to pound, and all his relaxed easiness left him abruptly as his body visibly tautened. He swung down from his saddle and led his mount a few paces to tie its reins to the hitching post, then came back to stand face to face with Cashmore.

'That's right, Joseph, I've bin away for a few days, so I'm not getting your meaning. So how about telling me exactly what youm getting at?'

Satisfied that he had hit home successfully, Cashmore chuckled, and answered only. 'You find out yourself, higgler. No doubt your mate here 'ull be able to tell you.' He turned to Nail Styler, 'And I'll tell you, Styler, that I'm agoing down to Ipsley Mill now to have a word wi' Edward Ashwin. Since he's the Ipsley constable, mayhap he can do summat about you, as a favour to me.'

Nail Styler laughed uproariously. 'You do that, Cashmore. I knows for a fact that Ashwin wouldn't drop even a fart as a favour to you.'

'We'll see,' Cashmore told him. Before he walked away he spoke once more to Caleb Hawkes, 'No doubt you'll be at the Navigation on Saturday night, higgler. I'll be there meself. I've got a dog that I fancy 'ull have the measure o' yourn.'

Caleb was burning to ask the man again what he had meant during their previous exchanges, but he bit the question back, rather than give his enemy any further satisfaction. He forced himself to grin and reply pleasantly.

'Bring your dog up then. Mind you, if it's anything like its master, it'll be all bark and no bite.'

'We'll see, higgler. We'll see.' Cashmore swaggered away, conscious that he took with him an advantage over one of the pair at least. The moment he was out of earshot, Caleb gripped Nail Styler's thick-muscled shoulder.

'What was that bastard on about, Nail, when he was talking about my poorhouse woman?'

'Which 'ooman is that?' Styler blinked bleary, heavy-lidded eyes. 'You'll have to make it clear to me, Caleb. I've not had a wink 'o sleep yet, and me yed is buzzing like a hive.'

'Ne'er mind it,' Caleb snapped impatiently. 'I'll see you later.' He unhitched his horse and mounted.

'Wheer be you off to?' his friend wanted to know, 'I've just broached a prime barrel o' fresh.'

'Later,' Caleb waved, and kicked his horse into a canter towards the Webheath Liberty.

At the poorhouse he sought out Anna Morris. As he listened to what she told him, he was torn between laughter and angry curses.

'Are they really saying that?' he questioned incredulously.

'Yes, and no matter what I tells 'um to the contrary, Katie Reeves has got half o' the women in here believing that them three tramper kids has been deliberately infected wi' the smallpox, so that they'll die, and the doctor 'ull have use on 'um for his work. Do you know what they calls Royston and the two women in here. They calls 'um the "Bodysnatchers". And they calls Royston, Doctor Resurrection.'

Caleb Hawkes couldn't help smiling. 'Doctor

242

Resurrection! It's good that. But it's hard to believe arn't it, that in this day and age people can still be so bloody ignorant. I thought that everybody had heard about that inoculation thing. I knew a lot o' coves who had it done to them when I was in the army. I never bothered wi' it meself, because I had a touch o' the pox when I was younger. Anyway, you say that there's bad feeling in the town as well against Anna Coldericke and Tildy?'

Again the woman nodded. 'So I'm told, higgler. I've not bin down town meself for a while. What wi' the harvest being started around here, there's a sight too much for me to do, to be able to go gallivanting to Redditch. But I sends a couple o' the women down to market, and they been telling me that the windows at Ivy House was put in a few nights back, and that some o' the locals has sworn that if any take the pox in Redditch, then they'll burn Ivy House to the ground, and it'll be God help anybody who'se inside the place when they puts it to the torch.' She sniffed expressively. 'Mind you, talks always cheap, arn't it. And things gets blown up to be more than they am. I reckon meself that our women have been stirring it just as much as they can when they'm down town. They does it just for badness, God rot them!'

'And I'll bet that I can lay a name to the one who'se doing the most stirring as well, Mistress Morris,' Caleb Hawkes said solemnly. 'It'll be Katie Reeves, wi'out a doubt.'

Anna Morris tightened her lips. 'I arn't saying, higgler. I've no wish to be involved in others' quarrels. I've troubles enough of me own, what wi' Morris half-mad wi' the drink these last days. The bugger was trying to get into bed wi' the women in their sleeping room last night, and I had to goo and pull him out o' theer by his scruff. It was the women who egged him on to go into them as well, just so they could have the laugh o' me.' For a moment the tight lips quivered, and Caleb felt sympathy for this hard, bitter-faced woman, whom he knew did her best to care for the sick and old paupers, and the children, and whose

243

husband's derelictions constantly humiliated her in the eyes of the parish.

'Ah well, we've all got our crosses to bear, my duck, and Morris is yourn. I'll ride on down to Redditch, and see if I can get a few words wi' Tildy.'

He took his leave, and had mounted his horse in the courtyard, when Anna Morris came out after him. She crossed to his side and rested her hand briefly on his knee.

'I hope that you means well towards Tildy Crawford, higgler, and that she arn't just another of your passing fancies. She's a good wench, and deserves better luck than she's had in her life.'

Caleb Hawkes was very serious. 'Believe me, if she'll only let me, I'll prove the best luck to that wench that she'll ever meet with . . .'

Chapter Twenty-Six

During the days and nights that followed the window-smashing at Ivy House life for Tildy had been a strange contrast of delight and discontent. The delight had come from her rapid progress in reading and writing. The discontent was occasioned by the siege mentality displayed by Anna Coldericke. The woman had been a fearless rebel against the mores of her society up to that incident of violence. Like many other such intellectual rebels, the encounter with a violent reality so far removed from the mannered verbal conflicts that Anna Coldericke had indulged in, had completely unnerved the woman. Her fears had communicated themselves to the children, disturbing them and rendering them peevish and fractious. To make matters worse Mrs Bray had returned once to collect the notes for Anna's pupils, and then had kept away completely. Lucas Royston had not been to Ivy House even once.

Tildy had nailed planks across the broken casements, since no glazier would come near them, so that the living room was now in permanent darkness, and consequently most of the days were spent in the kitchen. Anna Coldericke would not permit the children to play in the garden, because she feared that that might provoke further attacks, and Tildy had been forced to argue long and loud even to be permitted to hang washing out to dry in the garden at the rear of the house.

'If we remain inside and do not show ourselves, or draw attention to ourselves in any other way, then the people hereabouts will forget all about us, and leave us alone,' was the gist of Anna Coldericke's reasoning.

Sometimes as she listened to the woman, Tildy felt immeasurably older and wiser than her educated companion, because for all the woman's undoubted erudition, her knowledge of human nature seemed sadly lacking.

'But you cannot leave the house!' Anna Coldericke was horrified by Tildy's present suggestion.

Tildy drew a deep breath. 'Listen to me for a moment, Anna. We've no milk, no bread or flour, no lard, no butter, no eggs, no meat and no vegetables other than half a cabbage and some potatoes. We need candles, soap and oil for light and cooking. It's plain to see that no one will come near us, so I must go out for our necessaries, or we'll starve here in the house.'

The older woman was lying on her four-poster bed with the room's curtains drawn against the daylight. She was complaining of headache, and from what Lucas Royston had told Tildy, she guessed that the older woman's headache was the advance guard of the smallpox. She herself felt feverish and dry-throated, with aching back-muscles and a throbbing head. It was these symptoms which now impelled her to override the other's objections, when Anna continued.

'But Tildy, if they see you outside, then that will provoke them to further violence. If we stay quietly inside, then we'll be safe.'

'Don't talk nonsense, Anna. If someone has a mind to attack us, then they'll do so, no matter how we try to hide from them. And we are both starting to take fever and head pains, arn't we. That means that the pox is taking hold. If I don't get out now and buy what we need, then I may be too unwell to go abroad later.'

'Lucas promised to take care of all arrangements. He is going to provide a nurse for us if it should become necessary. She will be able to go out for whatever is needed.'

'Lucas Royston's promises are worthless, Anna.' Tildy's

patience momentarily snapped. 'Cannot you yet see that we are only regarded by him as creatures he is using for his experiments? And judging by his absence of late, he has lost interest in the experiment.'

'How dare you voice such wickedness?' The other woman sat bolt upright in the bed, staring with shock-widened eyes. 'I declare, Tildy, you fill me with horror at times.'

'That's as maybe, Anna, but I can't help thinking that way, and we still need candles, oil, bread, flour, lard, milk, eggs . . .'

Anna Coldericke groaned dramatically, and slumped back on her pillows. 'Ohhhh, my poor head. My poor poor head. Stop harrassing me, for pity's sake, I feel so unwell.' She waved her arms weakly. 'Do what you will, girl. There is money in the top drawer of my bureau, take what is needed and go. I am too ill to care what may become of us.'

Tildy hurried to the desk and took some coins from the drawer before the other could change her mind, then left the bedroom struggling against the feeling of contempt for the weakness of Anna Coldericke in acting as if she were dying for the sake of a headache. 'The gentry are a different breed,' she told herself, 'they are not raised hard like us.'

She went into the children's bedroom to check that they were alright.

'I'll not be long away, honey,' she told the eldest girl. 'I'm going to buy food and milk. Stay here in the bedroom all of you, and be very very good and quiet. The lady is feeling poorly, and you mustn't disturb her.'

'I feels badly too, Aunt Tildy,' the eldest girl told her, and Tildy felt her cheeks and forehead, which were hot and dry to the touch. She smiled down at the anxious little face. 'It's a touch of fever, honey, and naught to worry about. We're all of us going to feel a bit poorly in the next few days, and we'll all of us have spots on our faces, and on our hands and feet as well.'

'Like Davy's got?' the child asked interestedly.

'Yes, honey.' Tildy gently hugged the thin little body. 'Yes, honey, just like Davy's got, only perhaps not so many. Now you lie on your bed and rest yourself for a while.'

The two other children were playing with a rag doll that Tildy had sewed for them with scraps of cloth, and before she left she checked them also for fever, but found none.

'Play very quietly, kids. I'll bring you all some sweet-suck when I come back.'

Downstairs she found the large withy basket, and the cans for oil and milk, and arranged her shawl about her head and shoulders.

'If I go gently out through the bottom of the back garden and cut along to the shops by that way, then no one will know what house I've come from. I'm not known in the town, and I've no spots on me, so who'll be able to recognize me.' The disturbing thought that she might be a means of spreading contagion did occur to her. But she dismissed it. 'Until the spots come, then the pox hasn't gripped me properly. So I can't spread what I haven't got.' Satisfied by her own logic, she left the house.

For the shopkeepers it was the quiet period of the day. Most of the inhabitants were at their work and the house-wives had generally done their shopping early in the morning, and so the shopmen and women were free to come to the doors of their establishments, to enjoy the sunlight and exchange gossip. Today it was hot again, one of the hottest days of what had been up to now a remarkably fine summer. It was this heat that caused Tildy to throw her shawl back onto her shoulders and go bareheaded. She walked slowly along the main street of the town, comparing prices and deliberating over her purchases. As the weight in her basket increased, so did the aching of the muscles in her shoulders and back increase, and the throbbing in her head metamorphized into sharp pulses of pain.

Apart from the odd glance of curiosity caused by a new face in a small town, and the occasional lingering look of an admiring male, she attracted little attention, and was grateful for that fact. Because although she had presented a brave face to Anna Coldericke and the children, Tildy too was afraid of possible assault if someone should recognize her as coming from Ivy House.

At last, to her relief, all her purchases were made except for milk and cheese, and these she could not buy in this chandler's shop.

'Where can I buy fresh milk?' she asked, and involuntarily winced as a bolt of pain lanced through the frontal lobes of her head.

Thomas Abbot, the chandler, considered the young woman through his square-rimmed eye-glasses as he brought the filled oilcan to the counter, and began wrapping the candles she had bought in a twirl of brown paper. 'Milk? Fresh milk?'

'Yes, I want to buy milk, and cheese as well,' she repeated.

'Well I don't sell it,' the chandler snapped pettishly, and his mean, pinched features momentarily smoothed, as if the fact that he did not sell milk, soothed him immensely.

'I know that,' Tildy was dreading the onslaught of another slash of pain through her head, and spoke softly in an effort to avoid any unnecessary jarring of her senses. 'Where can I buy some?'

'From the milkman, I shouldn't wonder.' Thomas Abbot followed his answer with a question, 'What's your name, young 'ooman? I arn't seen you hereabouts afore. Be you in service here?'

Tildy opened her mouth to tell him her name, and abruptly closed it again. For all she knew he could be one of those who had smashed in the windows of Ivy House. She held out her hand for the candles, and with her other hand hooked the full oilcan onto the side of the basket. 'Please, where is there a milkman's shop?'

Abbot passed the paper-wrapped candles to her, and his eyes magnified by the thick lenses, reminded Tildy irresistibly of the eyes of a dead fish.

'You'd best try Ben Waring, down by the big pool. He's the main cheese and milk dealer in the town.'

'Many thanks,' Tildy hurried out of the greasy den, glad to escape the man's questing eyes. A few paces along the street she stopped, drawing her breath in sharply as once more the bolt of pain seared through her head, leaving her feeling giddy and disorientated. For a few moments she was tempted to hurry back to Ivy House, but then thought of the children.

'They all need milk, especially Davy. Besides, it'll not take long to get it.'

She walked along the main street and turned right when she reached the Chapel Green, then continued eastwards. She smelt the big pool for some distance before she came to it. The stench of the stagnant water, the reek of sewage and rotting refuse, the putridity of gas-bloated carcasses floating soggily among the other debris on the pool's black-green scummed surface hung heavy in the air.

As she skirted its noisome banks Tildy thought of the irony of the situation wherein the local people feared Ivy House as containing a threat to their health, and yet appeared uncaring of this disease-ridden cess-pit which lay only yards from their dwelling places, and allowed their small children to splash and play in its shallows.

Across the road from the big pool was the Horse and Jockey public house, with its adjoining stocks, where on her wedding day her husband had been imprisoned and bombarded with refuse from the pool. Tildy thrust the memories from her mind.

Ben Waring's shop was a little way beyond the pool on the road that led down to Bredon and Ipsley. It was merely the front room of an old cottage, and his dairy and cowshed lay just behind the shop. He was a big, ruddy, bucolic man who wore the smock and canvas gaiters of a farm-worker, and he smelled of hay and cow-dung. His two grown daughters were with him as Tildy entered, plump, fresh-faced girls, their brown gowns bunched up on their large rumps to display yellow and pink underskirts.

250

Ben Waring had an eye for pretty women, and he greeted Tildy with a rustic gallantry. 'Now here's a pretty cratur come to see me. How can I best serve you, my sweetheart?'

Tildy was feeling increasingly unwell, but she managed to return his smile. 'I'd like some milk, if you please.'

'Milk, is it? I'd hoped it was me you wanted. Still, you've come to the right man, my sweetheart. I'll draw you the creamiest, sweetest milk you ever tasted in your life, fresh from the tits o' the finest cows in the county.'

One of the girls giggled, and told Tildy. 'Pay no heed to the silly old sod, my duck. The sun's touched him agen today.' She took Tildy's can and went out to the rear of the building, and through the door she left ajar came the soft sounds of lowing cows.

'Hark to my ladies singing, my sweetheart.' Ben Waring's eyes twinkled as he drew Tildy's attention to the sound. 'That's because they'm so happy and contented. They knows it'll soon be time for milking, and they'm looking forwards to feeling Ben Waring's gentle touch.'

The other daughter now giggled and told Tildy. 'He's a bloody loony, arn't he. He drives me poor Mam mad wi' his nonsense. I'll be glad when the bugger gets too old to come into the shop. He makes me goo red wi' shame, some o' the things he says to folk.'

Tildy was warmed by the obvious affection of the family for each other, and not for the first time wished that she had been part of such a family.

'Newcome to Redditch, be you?' the girl asked.

Tildy nodded. 'Yes, that's so.' Inwardly she fidgeted for the other daughter to come back with the can of milk, so that she might leave without being subjected to a series of probing questions. It was the way of the country and the small town and village. A stranger had to account for themself. It was not like the cities where anonymity was the accustomed norm. Here, there was a carefully structured social order, and any stranger had to be identified and their strata in that social order established to the locals' satisfaction.

'Wheer be you living, my sweetheart?' The man asked point-blank. 'Only my girls does the rounds fust thing in the morning, and agen at eventide, every day except the sabbath. They can deliver your milk to your house for you. It saves you acarrying such weight.'

'By coming here, I save them carrying extra weight,' Tildy attempted to turn aside his question with a smile.

The man winked mischievously. 'That might be so, my sweetheart, but a dainty cratur like you be far less able to manage the weight, than these bloody great heifers o' mine.'

'You saucy old bugger, I 'eard that,' the first daughter had returned with the milk, and she slapped her father resoundingly on his broad buttocks. 'I'd lay me hand across his yed, but where there's no sense, there's no feeling,' she told Tildy jokingly, and put the can on the narrow counter. 'That'll be a penny-ha'penny, my duck. Is there ought else you need?' She pointed to the racks of yellow, saffron, orange, cream and red-skinned cheeses that permeated the shop with their rich, heavy scents. 'Got some beauties theer. Ripe as peaches, so they am. We'em reckoned to make the best cheeses in the whole o' Worcester, Warwick and Stafford, so we am. Only nine-pence the pound, as well. But seeing as how youm a new customer, I'll sell to you for eightpence.'

'I'll take a pound and a half of the cream-skin.' Tildy heard her own words as if they were coming from a great distance. Her tongue felt swollen and clumsy in her mouth, and the dull throbbing ache in her head suddenly swelled and burst with a violent force that sent her reeling and instinctively reaching out for support.

'Be you alright, duck?'

Tildy could hear the anxious voice, but could not formulate any reply. The head pains intensified excruci-atingly, and as she fought to stifle a cry of anguish, she felt her stomach heave and a hot surge in her throat, and tasted acrid bile in her mouth. Stumbling from the shop Tildy leaned against the outside wall, then bent low to retch and vomit uncontrollably until her heaving stomach was empty and nothing more could be voided. The head pain receded to the dull throbbing ache, and gasping for breath, Tildy wiped her mouth with her shawl, and felt hands lifting her upright.

'You'd best come and sit for a spell, duck.' It was Waring's daughters.

'You'se probably got a touch o' sunstroke.'

'That's what it 'ull be alright, a touch o' sun.'

'You sit awhile.'

'Yes, sit and rest, you'll be better in a minute or so.'

A stool was placed beneath her thighs, and she was gently seated on it.

'When youm able to move we'll take you home.'

'Wheer do you live, duck?'

Their kind, concerned voices waxed and waned in Tildy's ears, and she was so disorientated that she answered. 'Ivy House. I live in Ivy House.'

She sensed the instant drawing back of those around her, and as the full realization of what she had unwittingly told them came home to her, so with dismay did she see the kindly concerned faces about her transform themselves into hostile masks.

'She's that bloody poor'us woman!'

By now others were joining the little knot of people surrounding her, and as each newcomer arrived with eager questions as to who she was, so the answer was repeated time and time again.

'She's that bloody poor'us woman from Ivy House.'

'It arn't the sun that's affecting her like this, it's the bloody smallpox!' Ben Waring's jocular voice was now harsh, and his words created a perceptible widening of the semi-circle around the seated girl.

'The smallpox!'

'It's the smallpox!'

'Her's got smallpox!'

'Her's got no rights to be parading around the town like this. Her could spread the pox to all on us.' A woman

253

shrilled indignantly, and a small child who had ventured within the circle to study Tildy closely, suddenly howled in pain as his mother smacked his ear and pulled him back. 'Come here you little bleeder, and keep away from her.'

The short rest had helped Tildy to regain some strength and to reorientate herself. 'There's no call for you to be afraid,' she told those surrounding her. 'I've not fully took the pox yet, so I can't spread it to anybody.'

'Oh no?' a man challenged angrily. 'If you arn't took the pox, then what's them bloody things on your face and hands?'

Automatically Tildy's fingers went to her cheeks and forehead, and there she felt small clusters of minute nodules. She stared at her hands and arms and moaned softly in dismay, the clusters of nodules, tiny red pimples, had appeared there also.

'Here, girl.' Ben Waring had fetched her basket and cans from inside the shop, and now he banged them down at her feet. 'You take your goods and get away from here, just as quick as you can move yourself.'

'We ought to drive her out from the town,' the tall, thin, lantern-jawed man who had seen Tildy's rash said aggressively. 'She's a wicked bitch, so she is, spreading the pox deliberate to kids.'

A chorus of assent greeted his words.

'You'll do no driving of anybody, Benton,' Ben Waring warned. 'Youm too fond o' beating women who can't fight back. If I sees you lift a hand agen this wench, then it'll be me you'll be fighting, not her.'

The man shuffled backwards, protesting weakly. 'I was only thinking o' the rest, Ben. I wouldn't want to see them taking the pox from this bitch here.'

Waring ignored him, and told Tildy, 'Come on, girl. On your feet.'

She rose awkwardly, and winced as the blood pounded in her head. Then lifted her basket and feeling sick and giddy, walked slowly and painfully away towards the green.

'I'll follow you,' Ben Waring called after her retreating

back. 'And make sure that nobody tries to ill use you.' He waved his hand dismissively at the onlookers, 'You lot gerron about your business, and leave that poor little wench be.'

Now that his initial fright had subsided a little, Waring was feeling more than a trifle ashamed of himself for the way he had treated Tildy. But still that fear held him back from aiding her in any way other than giving a distant protection.

The sun burned down and to Tildy it seemed that the heated air could not satisfy her desperate need for oxygen. She panted heavily as she went on, and waves of giddiness caused her to stumble frequently. Ill though she was, she was still painfully and shamedly aware of the avid interest her halting progress through the town was creating. Men, women and children came running to stare hungrily at her, and Ben Waring repeatedly shouted.

'Let her pass, and leave her be. Let her pass, her's got the smallpox.'

Tildy felt soiled and leprous, and now knew how bitter was the taste of complete rejection. She felt truly that she was a pariah.

'Let her pass, her's got smallpox . . . smallpox . . . small-pox . . . ' Ben Waring's deep voice hit the walls and rico-chetted along the streets, and silent, grim-featured onlookers drew back as the slender figure stumbled past them, her eyes fixed straight ahead, her hands and arms straining from the weight of the full basket and its dangling, clunking, liquid-swishing cans.

The windows of St Stephen's chapel glinted in the light as Tildy passed them, and she welcomed the leaf-thrown shadows of its yard-trees to shield her throbbing head and sore, gritty eyes from the white glare of the merciless sun. Another lance of pain jolted her head back on her shoulders and she swayed violently as her senses swam. She feared that she would fall, and to avoid that she slumped onto her knees in the dust of the road, and covered her burning face with her hands, and in that instant she was overwhelmed by

255

the deepest desolation of loneliness that she had ever known.

'Will no one ever help me?' she muttered miserably. 'Will I always be so alone?' By a supreme effort of will she mastered the all-pervading urge to give in to her weakness, and again her stubborn pride asserted itself. 'I need no one to help me. I am strong enough to stand alone. In a moment I'll get up, and go on. In just a moment I'll do it . . . And I can. I can do it.'

Strong fingers clasped her arms and lifted her bodily. She found herself looking into the face of the higgler, Caleb Hawkes.

'Give me the basket, and lean on my arm, Tildy,' he urged her softly, 'I'll take you home . . . '

For a moment she wanted only to obey his urgings. But then the memory of their last meeting flooded her mind, and she saw again the gypsy girl embracing him. 'I can manage well enough by myself.' She tried to free herself from his grasp.

'Don't talk so silly,' Caleb told her roughly. 'Youm ill. You'll most likely fall flat on your face iffen I lets you go.'

'I'll not fall,' she answered determinedly, and from the deepest reserves of her body she summoned strength enough to break free of him, and stand firmly erect with her head held high.

His mouth hardened, and he snatched the basket and cans from the dust and walked on ahead of her. 'I'm carrying this to Ivy House,' he spoke over his shoulder, and she had no choice but to follow him.

'I don't need your help,' she said stubbornly.

'Well youm getting it, whether you want it or not.' He strode on, and she was forced to hurry her own steps to keep close behind him. Her emotions were a peculiar ferment of gladness and resentment, and she was so caught up in them that the pain and giddiness were thrust into the background of her consciousness, and she covered the short distance remaining without undue distress.

At the front door of Ivy House Caleb turned and faced

her. 'Who did this?' he nodded towards the boarded-up windows.

Tildy shook her head. 'I don't know.'

'Did you fetch the constable?'

Again she shook her head.

'Why not?'

She shrugged. 'Anna Coldericke thought it was best to leave things lie.'

'Did she.' The higgler's eyes were hot and angry, but he kept his voice low and controlled. 'I see by your face that the pox has taken hold. How about the Widow Coldericke and the kids?'

'Yes, they've taken it too.' By now her sense of gladness had outweighed her resentment. This man did not look upon her as something unclean, something wicked. She reached for the basket. 'I'd best take that, and my thanks to you,' she paused, and could not hold back a smile. 'And you'd best leave me, I've no wish to contaminate you.'

He made an impatient gesture of dismissal. 'I'm immune to the pox, Tildy, but I'm not immune to you. I know you think badly of me, but I wasn't lying when I said that I cared for you, and I'll not stand by and let things like this happen to you.' Again he indicated the boarded-up windows. 'And who's to look arter you now that youm badly?'

'I can look after myself,' she answered.

For the first time he smiled at her, and his light-blue eyes softened as he stared at her face. 'Youm a regular little hard-chaw, arn't you, girl. Well let me put this to you. If youm badly, who'll care for Coldericke and the kids?'

'We'll manage somehow,' her stubborn pride would not permit her to show any weakness to this man. She feared his attraction for her, and feared that that attraction could come to dominate her if she permitted it to extend its hold.

Caleb Hawkes sensed that this girl was fighting against the feelings that impelled her towards him. He admired that pride that enabled her to face so bravely a largely hostile world. But he could not prevent his frustration bursting out.

'God blast it, Tildy! Why won't you let me be a friend to you? I arn't got horns and a forked tail. Theer's no call for you to be so stupid-proud wi' me, I only wants to act for your good. By Christ, girl! The way you acts anybody 'ud think you was bloody gentry, instead o' being only a bloody poor'us woman. You makes me mad so you do.'

'Then just leave me be!' her eyes darkened and she snatched the basket from him. The cans clanked together, and some of their contents spilled from them. 'There! Now look what you've made me do?' she accused angrily, and she turned and pushing the door open darted inside. He reached out his hand towards her, but his fingertips met only the wooden panels as the door slammed shut behind her. For a few moments he stared angrily at the blue weather-faded paintwork, then walked slowly away, his hands thrust deep into the pockets of his breeches, his head low on his chest.

Inside the dark hallway Tildy leant with her back against the front door, her mind a maelstrom of conflicting emotions.

'Tildy? Tildy?' Anna Coldericke's petulant shouts echoed through the house, and Tildy blocked all thoughts of Caleb Hawkes from her mind, and hurried upstairs.

The woman was still lying on her bed, and when she saw Tildy she moaned piteously. 'Oh Tildy, I feel so ill. My head burns and the pustules are forming. I fear I'm gravely ill. The inoculation has gone badly for me.'

The younger woman, sick and ill herself, knew then that she could expect no help from Anna Coldericke. The woman lacked Tildy's own courage.

'So be it,' she thought determinedly. 'Then I'll manage by myself.'

She struggled to disregard the throbbing in her own head and body, and to remember what Lucas Royston had taught her, concerning the actions she must take. Fortunately they were simple . . . 'Keep the body gently purged.

258

Bathe the body in luke-warm water daily, and bathe the legs and feet thrice daily. Keep the body cool. Drink plenty of liquids of a cooling nature. Eat only light foods, and avoid red meats . . . ' Closing her eyes she waited until a sudden surge of nausea that had assailed her should recede. But all the time she wracked her brains in case she had forgotten anything. 'Ah yes . . . If the pulse should become too fast and strong, then bleed from the arm . . . If the fever should rise too high, then do the same . . . Open the pustules at least three times after the pus has filled them, and keep them drained and washed . . . I'll cover them with red flannel as well, like Mistress Morris advised, to avoid the scarring. She has much experience, so I'm sure that will be a good course to follow. There, I think that will suffice. If any of their conditions become unmanageable, then I'll go to the Apothecary and get the medicine that Davy was dosed with. But Lucas Royston was sure that no difficulties would arise with this inoculation. We will all of us only suffer mild attacks.'

Another pounding agony exploded in her skull, and wincing, she set her teeth and forced herself to endure without further complaint until the pounding agony lessened and died away.

'Bleeding? Will I be able to do that?' she asked herself, and experienced a nervous elation, as she thought of the challenge that faced her. 'Yes, I can do that, and anything else that's needful,' she spoke aloud, and Anna Coldericke looked curiously at her, but Tildy only smiled. 'You lie back and relax, Anna. I'll take care of you, all will be well. Only trust me, Anna, and all will be well.'

'Why does not Lucas come?' The older woman's grey eyes were tear filled. 'Why does he not come when he knows that I need him so badly? I love him, Tildy. Do you know that? I love him, and he does not come to me when I need him.'

A pang of sympathy struck Tildy, but she could not bring herself to mouth empty words of reassurance and comfort. Lucas Royston's neglect was merely the confir-

mation of her earlier opinion of his relationship with Anna
Coldericke.

'*He was only using you, Anna,*' she wanted to tell the other.
'*As he has used me and the children.*' Strangely, she felt no
urge to recriminate for the latter usage. '*I have learned much
from him,*' she told herself, and again that nervous elation
flooded through her, '*and now he has given me the opportunity to
put that learning into practice . . .*'

Chapter Twenty-Seven

The hammering on the door resounded louder and louder. Lengthening in duration and becoming so insistent that at last Lucas Royston dragged himself off his narrow bed and answered the summons. He blinked, bleary-eyed, at his irate uncle.

Alexander Pratt stumped into the room his expression deepening in disgust as he smelt the fumes of stale gin and beer that clung to his nephew's soiled, rumpled clothing.

'I want you gone from the parish,' he stated without preamble, and Lucas ran his drink-furred tongue across the hot sticky interior of his mouth, and grimaced at its foul taste.

'Well? Are you deaf, boy? Did you not hear me?' Pratt demanded.

His nephew peered through blood-shot eyes, turned his back and went into the bedroom. Groaning, he bent low and rummaged under the mattress, then grunted with satisfaction and pulled out a corked black bottle. Biting on the cork with his teeth, he drew it and spat it onto the floor, then uptilted the bottle to his mouth. Once, twice, three times, four times the glottle in his slender throat bobbed, and then the bottle was drained and with a curse he pitched it from him. It hit the wall, shattering into tiny glittering shards. The young man came back to face his uncle, and when he spoke the fumes of the fresh gin he had just drunk, gusted against Alexander Pratt's stonelike face.

'But I've no wish to go, Uncle dear. I've got good prospects here,' he sneered openly. 'I have you, do I not,

Uncle dear. You'll not be able to stand by and see one of your own flesh and blood starve, that I'm sure of. It wouldn't look well, would it. Your own nephew starving in the gutter. Your standing among the respectable inhabitants of this parish would suffer, if you should permit that to happen. Might even cost you the patronage of some of your patients, I shouldn't wonder.'

Pratt's normally sallow complexion was suffused with a dull purpling, and saliva flecked from his lips, as he spat out. 'As for that . . . I care not a damn . . . if you starve and die . . . in the middle of the damned chapel green . . . for the whole town to see and applaud.

'But, for your dead mother's sake . . . I'll give you sufficient to return to Edinburgh . . . But you will never again . . . receive a penny-piece from me . . . Here.' He tossed a leather purse onto the table. 'There is twenty-five sovereigns . . . I've already paid your stable reckoning at the Red Lion . . . Take it, and go . . . and never return here again.'

Recollection came into Lucas Royston's drink-fuddled brain. 'I cannot go at this time, Uncle. I've got patients to attend to . . . Mrs Anna Coldericke and the poorhouse woman and children.'

'Tcchaa!' Pratt ejaculated disgustedly. 'You've been swinish drunk for nigh on a week now, boy . . . I know for a fact . . . you've not been near to Ivy House during all that time . . . So spare me such a farrago . . . of damned nonsense . . . and hypocrisy. If it becomes necessary, then I shall myself attend to Ivy House . . . I want you gone from this house . . . and from this parish . . . within the hour, boy . . . If you are not . . . then I shall take measures . . . to have you pitched out . . . on your neck.' With that parting threat, and a final scowl of disgust, Pratt left his nephew swaying by the side of the table.

Lucas picked up the purse and returned again to the bedroom. He was tempted to throw himself down and try to sleep again, but the craving for more drink was tormenting him, and he knew from past experience that no sleep would be possible while that terrible craving remained unsatisfied.

His head was clearing a little, so with what water was left in the crock jug he rinsed his mouth and face to aid that clearance. He gathered together his meagre belongings, his anger constantly mounting as he thought of his uncle, and left the house without bothering to close the door behind him.

At the Red Lion stables he told the ostler to saddle his horse and left his bags with the man for safe-keeping while he went into the tap room for the drink he craved. It was Saturday afternoon and the room was packed with men. Amid the noisy hubbub in the thick atmosphere of tobacco smoke and unwashed bodies, Lucas Royston stood at the tall mahogany counter and drank gin until the tremblings of his hands steadied, and the hangover he suffered from metamorphized into a feeling of physical well-being. But his mood was still evil, and his temper ready to flare at the slightest pretext. He called for another glass of gin, and was about to lift it to his lips when a tall, scar-faced, sun-bronzed man spoke to him.

'Your pardon, but you're Doctor Royston, arn't you?'

To Lucas the man's local accent was provocation enough. This town had proved a place of humiliation for him, and he burned to extract some sort of revenge for that humiliation. He glared challengingly at his questioner, 'Who might you be?'

Caleb Hawkes recognized the sign of an aggressive drunk, and smiled placatingly. 'I mean no offence, Doctor Royston. I only wished to ask you about a young 'ooman, name of Tildy Crawford, that you'se been treating.'

'I'm treating nobody by that name,' Lucas snarled, and turned away.

Caleb Hawkes was irritated by the younger man's surly attitude, but he desperately wanted to know about Tildy. To hear if she were well, or suffering unduly from the effects of the inoculation.

'Forgive me, doctor, but I knows well that it was you

who performed the inoculation agen the smallpox on Tildy Crawford. I only wanted to ask you if she was suffering much discomfort because of it.'

The doctor took another long swig of gin, and the raw spirit finally tipped his inflamed temper over the edge of reason. He swung to confront Caleb Hawkes, and shouted.

'Will you sod off, man, and stop pestering me about that bloody poorhouse slut! I've told you once that I'm treating no one in this poxy town, so take yourself off, the stink of you offends me.'

His shout was loud enough to be heard all across the room, and a sudden hush fell as heads turned and eyes became warily watchful.

The long white scar on the higgler's face engorged to a fiery redness. 'You'll ask my pardon for calling Tildy Crawford a slut,' he grated out, and Lucas Royston spat in his face.

The higgler's sinewy hands moved in a blur of speed, and the next instant the doctor's eyes bulged and his swollen tongue protruded from his gaping mouth as his windpipe was slammed shut by cruel hooking thumbs.

'No Caleb! No!' The tap room erupted into a roaring, stamping mass of struggling, shouting men. Lucas Royston's thin body was no match for the higgler's raw-boned power and by the time the murderous hands were torn from his throat, the doctor had been choked senseless.

Richie Bint and his friends dragged the struggling Caleb Hawkes outside as he shouted, 'I'll kill you, you Scotch bastard! I swear I'll kill you!'

Herbert Willis hastened to minister to Lucas Royston. The young man came slowly and agonizingly back to awareness, retching, coughing, vomiting, and moaning in torment as the pain of his crushed throat tore at him.

'By the Christ, but youm a lucky bleeder.' Herbert Willis's plump pink face was a white mask of shock. 'Another minute and you'd ha' bin a stiff 'un. Caleb Hawkes would ha' done for you. You'd best get on your bloody horse and get out o' this town just as quick as youm able to. I reckon if the higgler spots you agen you'll not be able to leave. You'll be staying on here in a bloody wooden overcoat. He'll finish you the next time, my bucko. No doubt on that at all.'

Among the excited onlookers one man listened avidly to the innkeeper's words. A heavily-muscled, bullet-headed man, whose name was Edwin Danks . . .

Chapter Twenty-Eight

'Wheer's the higgler then, doing a bit o' poaching, is he?' Joseph Cashmore asked jeeringly, and Bocker Duggins could only scowl silently in reply.

The tap room of the Navigation was a solid mass of men and dogs, and the atmosphere was a reeking compound of beer fumes, tobacco smoke, and the sweat of humans and animals. A score of different accents filled the air with a tumult of noise. The broad vowels of Gloucester, the sing-song of Birmingham, the rustic drawl of Worcestershire, the harsh gutturals of the Black Country, all clamouring to be heard as they called for pipes and beer, greeted old friends, insulted old enemies, laughed and joked, cursed and disputed. The dogs were as varied as the men, Staffordshire Bulls, Jack Russels, Cairns, Old English, Wire-haired, Smooth-coated and mongrel breeds of terriers, their excited yaps and barks adding to the din.

'Your attention, my lords, your attention if you please.' Jimmy Shrimpton, the lanky, toothless, skeleton-bodied landlord stood on a bench to bawl across the heads of the gathering. 'The pit is ready, and I can offer you the finest collection of Little Gennulmen you've ever seen to tickle your fancies.'

Joseph Cashmore looked searchingly about the room and nudged his friend, Tom Davies, the gamekeeper. 'I see the higgler arn't come yet, Tom,' he shouted loudly. 'Lost his bottle, no doubt on it. As soon as he got challenged to wager a few guineas, the windy bastard lost his bottle.'

Bocker Duggins scowled horribly. 'He'll come. The higgler arn't afraid to bet agen any man.'

'Arn't he now?' Cashmore jeered. 'Well if that's the case, wheer is the bugger?'

Bocker subsided into silence with a muttered, 'How the fuck does I know?'

Most of the company trooped out of the main building of the inn and crossed the yard to a big ramshackle old barn. In the centre of its stone-flagged ancient threshing-floor a square edifice of boards had been erected to form a miniature arena, some nine feet in diameter and elbow height. This was what Jimmy Shrimpton called the 'Pit', and it was illuminated by a cluster of oil lamps suspended above it on a long rope, like a crude chandelier.

The light of the summer evening was fast fading and the interior of the barn was gloomy but for the area directly around the pit which caught the gleams of the smoking lamps. The men, some carrying dogs in their arms, clamoured around the wooden arena, and those at the rear stood on old benches and boxes, or climbed up to the upper levels where they sat dangling their legs, and tossing missiles at their friends below them.

Jimmy Shrimpton, perched on a very high stool, appointed himself master of ceremonies.

'Order, gennulmen, order! Let's have some hush, if you please! Keep them fucking dogs quiet, them what has 'um. Now my Lords, who wants to start the ball arolling, for here's the Little Gennulmen come.'

A ragged, long-haired youth pushed through to the pitside carrying a large wire-topped cage in his arms. A stench like hot drains came from the box, and through the wire grill could be glimpsed a dark pulsing mass of wet furry bodies.

'I'll take a dozen,' a bargee with a white and black bull terrier shouted. 'But make 'um small 'uns. My Billy's not killed afore.'

A farmer who was eyeing the dog closely offered. 'Iffen he shapes well, I'll gi' thee a bid for him.'

The ragged youth opened a small hatch in the top of the cage and without any nervous hesitation thrust his hand in amongst the furry mass to sort and draw out twelve long-tailed rats, their wet fur black in the lamplight.

'Mind them buggers, son,' Jimmy Shrimpton shouted. 'They'm straight from the cess-pits, and if they bites they'll poison you.'

The youth grinned confidently, and with a great show of casualness dropped the rats one by one into the pit. The dogs sighting them went berserk with excitement, yelping and whining and struggling to free themselves from the arms restraining them.

'Now do shut them bleedin' dogs up. A man can't hear hisself making a bet.' Jimmy Shrimpton bawled.

In the pit the terrified rats collected into one corner, their bodies trembling as they heaped one on another to form a living mound.

'Blow on 'um! Blow on 'um!' the crowd bellowed, and those nearest the small animals leaned over the sides of the pit and blew on the wet furry mass, which exploded into single particles darting to different sides to escape the man-made wind.

'Is all bets laid?' Jimmy Shrimpton questioned, staring about him, his head swaying like a serpent's upon the scrawny stalk of his neck. 'Then put your dog in to 'um, my cocker.' Lifting his stop-watch he set it in motion with a flourish. 'Time starts . . . Now!'

The bargee was in the pit, his dog emitting high-pitched kelps as its master held it close to the rats and drew it back teasingly. Then he released it and shouted. 'Get 'um, Billy! Get 'um! Get 'um! Get 'um!' Banging the sides of the pit with his hands at each shout in a thunderous drumroll.

The dog quivered, the muscles standing out in sharp relief on its lean body, then flew at the reformed mound of rats, growling as its head burrowed into them, jaws clamping savagely for their necks. Cheers filled the air as broken bodies flew across the arena, but the cheers became jeers as a rat flew at its tormentor and bit into the dog's muzzle and held there, its body hanging stretched, and jerking wildly from side to side as the howling dog shook its head and pounded the furry body against the wooden planking. The rat's teeth tore free and it went tumbling across the pit floor, and before it could recover the dog's jaws snapped its spine, and sent it somersaulting back across the pit to the plaudits of the spectators.

'He's a beauty! He's a prime 'um!' Jimmy Shrimpton bawled ecstatically. 'Worth five guineas, that 'un is.'

'Worth twenty-five, more like,' its owner bellowed back.

Within a minute it was done, and the furry bodies lay bleeding and twitching all across the pit floor. The owner snatched up his snapping, snarling, nearly frantic beast, while all round the pit men applauded wildly and bets were settled with good and bad grace.

The night wore on. Dogs snarled and bit, rats squealed and died. Men won and lost their money, and drank deep of gin and rum and ale and cider. Now and then brawls erupted and were let go on until one or other of the contestants was bloodied and beaten, and other men wagered on these brawls, and were happy that the night contained such extra diversions.

More cages of rats were brought in and instead of sixes and twelves, there were scores, fifties and hundreds at one time tipped into the pit, where in their turn they piled into living mounds that reached halfway up the barriers and squealed in pitiful terror as dogs' teeth crunched the life from them.

Joseph Cashmore's eyes constantly roved the barn, and always failed to find the man they sought. Periodically he would grab Bocker Duggins and growl, 'Wheer's he got to? Wheer's the bloody higgler?'

And Bocker Duggins would cringe and show his teeth like one of the trapped rats in the pit.

The match came to an end and Joseph Cashmore left the barn with his friend, Tom Davies. They were crossing the yard to re-enter the inn when a man ran panting up to them. He whispered long and urgently to Joseph Cashmore, and after a while the heavy, taciturn features

269

split into a grin of pure delight. He turned to Tom Davis. 'Let's go and collect some o' your lads and bring 'um with us down to Redditch, Tom. I reckon we'em finally going to have the higgler wheer we both bin wanting the bastard.'

'How's that, Joseph?' the gamekeeper questioned eagerly.

'There was trouble atween the Scotch quack and the higgler down in the Red Lion earlier today,' the constable told him happily, 'and the higgler near killed the bugger. Tried to strangle him, so Ezra here tells me, and then swore he would kill him when he next got a chance.'

'So?' the gamekeeper was unimpressed. 'You can't lock a man up for a fight in a pub. You knows as well as me, Joseph, that you'll not get a witness. The beaks 'ull laugh at a case like that.'

The grin still curved Cashmore's lips. 'Hear me out, Tom. Ezra has just told me that an hour ago him and his mate found the Scotchman lying by the side o' the Pigeon Bridge, beat so bad that he looked dead, and not a penny-piece in his pockets either. Robbery on the highway is a hanging matter, Tom. The Scotchman's lying at Alexander Pratt's now, but Ezra says he's not yet come round sufficient to name who done this to him. But for sure it's the higgler who's done the job. That's why the bastard warn't here tonight. He was alaying for the Scotchman. I'se known Caleb Hawkes all me life, Tom. He's a bad bugger when somebody crosses him. He's done this, there arn't a doubt on it.

'Come on now, let's get your lads and goo down town, and root the bugger out iffen he's still theer somewheres,' he roared with laughter, and choked out, 'What a stroke o' luck it is, Tom! We bin trying for years to nab the higgler, and he's always bin too fly for us, and now, he's handed his yed to us on a plate.'

A bystander had heard the references to Caleb Hawkes, and now he told Cashmore. 'If youm wanting to talk wi' the higgler you'd best look a bit sharpish.'

'Why's that?' Cashmore demanded.

The man grinned, and deliberately to bait the unpopular constable, made no immediate reply.

'Why's that, I asked?' Cashmore scowled warningly. 'And iffen you don't want to spend some time in my nice new lockup you'd best spit it out a bit sharpish.'

The man realized that he had better not provoke the constable further. 'Well, I was in the White Hart at Headless earlier on, and Caleb Hawkes come in for a drink. Seemed real down at the mouth he did, and said he was leaving the town for a while, and going to try his luck in London. Then he left.'

'Which road did he take?' Everything the man had said confirmed the higgler's guilt for Cashmore.

'He's gone to Evesham to spend the night. At the Black Horse theer. He's doing a bit o' business for Nail Styler theer, afore he pushes on to London.'

'That'll do for me,' Cashmore gloated, and turned to Davis. 'I'm going straight arter the bugger, Tom. He's doing a runner, no doubt on it at all.'

The gamekeeper seemed uncertain. 'You might be barking up the wrong tree, Joseph. And iffen you goes arter him wi'out any warrant from the magistrates you could get into trouble yourself for being absent from the parish wi'out permission. Suppose there was to be trouble in the town tonight, and they come for you?'

Cashmore dismissed that argument with a contemptuous wave of his hand. 'There'll be no trouble. I'm going arter that bugger. I'se waited years for a chance like this, and I'll not miss it.' He shook his head. 'There'll be no trouble here while I'm gone . . . '

Chapter Twenty-Nine

Edwin Danks pitched the thick dark rum down his throat, and shouted for more. He felt exultant as the fumes of the drink rose to his head, but still a sense of dissatisfaction nagged at him.

'I've settled accounts wi' the Scotch bastard for killing my nipper,' he told himself, 'but there's still a score to be settled wi' that Coldericke bitch.'

He put his hand into his breeches pocket and fondled the small heavy coins there. The sovereigns in Lucas Royston's pockets had been a sweet bonus, and Edwin Danks savoured the feel of them, and visualized what they would buy him in the coming days. As much rum as his stomach could hold, and good red meat to go with it as well as firm, eager young flesh to rut upon, as a welcome change from the sour-smelling, flaccid inertness of his wife.

Danks thought briefly about the man he had left lying beneath the parapet of the Pigeon Bridge earlier that night.

'He'll not murder any more kids wi' his quackery.'

Danks relished the memory of his fists caving in teeth and bones, and the shrieks of pain that had been smashed back into bloody shredded lips until they choked into dribbling whimpers. 'Tommy, gi' us a drink,' he shouted, and Tommy Green came to serve him.

The Royal Oak was full of labourers, needle pointers and artisans, among their number some of the wildest and toughest men in the parish. Their women were with them, matching them drink for drink, and oath for oath, and among them were some who were brawling hellcats, as vicious and deadly as any man.

Danks kept on pitching down the measures of rum, and while outwardly he remained stolid-featured, in his head raged a storm of wild imaginings.

'I've still got a score to settle.' The words echoed in his brain over and over again. 'I've still got a score to settle wi' the Coldericke bitch.'

The door of the room crashed open, and a young woman, wildly staring about her, shawl flung about her shoulders, stood framed in the doorway.

At a table in a corner of the room a group of needle pointers were singing a tuneless cacophony of different songs in competition to drown each others voices. The wild-eyed woman pushed across the crowded room towards them, and Richie Bint saw her coming.

'It's your missis, Rammer,' he shouted into his friend's ear.

The young man's handsome smiling face sobered as he saw his wife. 'Her's supposed to be up at her Mam's,' he muttered. 'The old girl's bin a bit badly.'

'Does her still live by the Big Pool?' Richard Bint asked, and Rammer nodded. As his wife reached him, he questioned anxiously.

'What's up wi' you, Shirley? What's wrong, my duck?'

Her face crumpled into ugly sobbing. 'It's me Mam, Rammer. It's me Mam. It arn't a fever that's making her badly, it's the bloody smallpox!'

'What?' Rammer's drunken face frowned vacuously as he tried to fully comprehend the half-choked words. 'What's that you say? Your Mam? Her's got the smallpox, has her?'

His wife's hands were at her mouth, now they dropped as she shrieked angrily. 'That's what I'se just told you, arn't I! Me Mam's took the pox!'

Edwin Danks heard her clearly, and the raging storm inside his head stilled, and like a ray of sunlight lancing through a black mass of cloud, the idea came to him.

'It's the fault o' that Coldericke bitch!' he bawled. 'It's her that's brought this pox to Redditch . . . That Coldericke bitch!'

The fears that had festered for many days in the minds of many there in the room, now exploded their poisons.

'That's right!' Tommy Green's squat body shook as he pounded his fists onto the counter. 'He's right. It's her fault. That bloody mad 'ooman! It's her that's brought the pox down on us. It's Shirley's Mam took the pox today, but who'll take it tomorrow? Tell me that, 'ull you. Who'll take it tomorrow?'

'Nobody 'ull!' Edwin Danks jumped on a stool so that all could see him. 'Nobody 'ull take the Pox tomorrow, because we'll burn the bitch who brought it here, out o' this town tonight!'

A roar of agreement greeted his words, drowning out the protests of those who dissented.

'Come on then, who'se got the balls to come wi' me.' Danks snatched the hanging-lamp and brandished it above his head. 'This is the sure cure for the smallpox· . . . Fire!'

The room exploded, 'Fire! Fire! Fire! Fire!'

Despite the lateness of the hour a candle-flame still cast its pale light across the opened book on the table in the kitchen of Ivy House.

'So King Sol-o-mon was king over all Is-ra-el, Israel . . . And these were the prin-ces wh-wh-which he had . . . ' Tildy's fingertips moved from word to word as she slowly and falteringly laboured to translate the tiny lettering into spoken words. ' . . Az-A-ri-ah . . . Aza-ri-ah . . . Aza-riah . . . Azariah, Azariah, Azariah!' With tremendous satisfaction Tildy mouthed the name again and again, pure happiness suffusing her being. ' . . . Azariah, the son of Za-dok . . . Zadok, the priest . . . '

She lifted her head as the grandfather clock in the living room chimed the hour. 'I'm winning the battle.' She smiled, with more than a hint of smugness at the pages

274

beneath her eyes. 'I can manage even the hardest words.' She hesitated, and giggled at her own conceit. 'Given a little time to dwell on them,' she qualified, 'and with your help.' She stroked the red leather covering of a book lying beside the open Bible. A book which to Tildy was an object of enchantment. A dictionary.

The chimes of the clock ceased, and all was still and silent once more. For a while Tildy relaxed against her chairback, and drank in the peace that surrounded her as if it were some life-giving fluid. Physically, she felt weak, but not particularly unwell. As Lucas Royston had promised, for her and the orphan children the attacks of induced smallpox had been mild, and the clusters of pustules sparse. She had religiously followed the instructions he had given her, and had even fashioned face-masks and long-sleeved vests of red flannel for the children to wear as protection against scarring. Her main problem with the children had been, and was, their ever-increasing restlessness.

Anna Coldericke was a different matter. Her induced smallpox appeared to have attacked her more fiercely than the others. The pustules were thickly spread, high fevers racked her, and yesterday she had lapsed into moments of delirium, during which she had raved incessantly, shouting for Lucas Royston to come to her, and at times speaking of him in terms of such sexual explicitness that the nature of their relationship was graphically demonstrated. To spare Anna Coldericke any possible future embarrassment, Tildy had kept the children as far away from the woman's bed-chamber as possible. But since earlier that evening she had mercifully quietened. Now she was sleeping uneasily, and Tildy hoped that the crisis was past, and the process of recovery had begun.

At this moment it was the problem of food and necessaries that were again entering Tildy's mind. 'I'll need to get more tomorrow. I can't stretch things any further. Mayhap I could sneak out at crack o' light and go to Alvechurch for them. No one knows me there, and I could pull my shawl well forward to hide my scabs and

275

pimples. It's not more than eight miles there and back. Surely the kids and Anna would be alright for the time I'd be away. That shouldn't be more than a couple of hours, at the most.'

'And if Anna's no better tomorrow I'd best go to the apothecary and see if I can get more of the medicine that little Davy had.' She yawned hugely, and waves of utter weariness swept over her. Caring for Anna Coldericke and the children, while suffering herself from the induced illness, had almost drained Tildy's last reserves of strength. But paradoxically, the more weary she became, the more determined to win through without calling for help from others, she became also.

She smiled wryly as she considered the difficulties she had had with Anna Coldericke during the past week. 'If I did call for help, and that help came, then I fear that the help would end by strangling poor Anna in a fit of fury.'

The woman had proven to be the very worst type of patient. Demanding, capricious, sulky and bad-tempered, and forever whining and complaining. Her constant diatribes against Lucas Royston for his abandonment of them were an added irritant for Tildy, who considered that as a once-married woman of thirty-years of age, Anna Coldericke had known well what she was about, when she had embarked on the affair.

'It takes two to make a bargain,' Tildy thought, and added, 'Yes, I know, I've become a hard-hearted bitch where love is concerned.' Her eyelids fluttered and slowly closed, and she drifted into unquiet sleep, and dreamed that Anna Coldericke was rattling a spoon against a cup and shouting for her to come.

She came awake with a start, and through the fog of tiredness heard a rapping against the window panes.

'Tildy Crawford? Tildy Crawford?' A woman's voice was whispering urgently. 'Come to the window! Come to the window, Tildy Crawford! Tildy Crawford!'

The night was black outside the glass panes, and when Tildy went to peer through them she could only distinguish an amorphous blacker denseness against the darkness. She opened the casement.

'Who is it? What do you want with me? Don't come too close, I have the smallpox.'

'It's me, Phoebe Bray,' the dark bulk moved closer, and now without the intervening barrier of glass, Tildy could just distinguish the pale blob of the woman's features.

'What do you want here at this hour, Mrs Bray?' Tildy's voice sounded unnaturally loud in the stillness of the night, and the other woman reacted with rapid frightened whispers.

'Shh! Don't shout so! No one must know I'm here. I've come to warn you and Mrs Coldericke. They'm coming wi' flaming torches to burn you out o' this house. They'm going to drive you away from this town. Run now, afore they gets here, and get away while you can, because if you waits for 'um to get here they'll likely end by killing you. I went for the constable, but he arn't at his house. So there's nobody to protect you. Get away now, and be quick about it.' With that she slipped back into the night and was lost in the darkness.

A chill of dread seized Tildy, and she slammed the casement shut, and stood with her arms wrapped around her body as if to comfort herself. Suddenly she snatched up the candle and hurried upstairs. The children were deep asleep, shining hair strewn across their pillows, tiny faces untroubled, cocooned in warm security. Tildy bit her lips and went next to Anna Coldericke's room. She also was sleeping, but sweat glistened on her pustuled face, and she tossed and turned restlessly, muttering incoherent words and phrases.

'She is too ill to be moved,' Tildy recognized, and for a brief moment her anxious fears threatened to drive her into panic. Physically trembling so that the flame of the candle she carried wavered and spluttered, Tildy fought against the rampaging fear, and gradually pressed it back into the furthermost reaches of her mind.

She hurried to her own room, but when she reached it

admitted that she did not know why she had come there. Again she went to the children's room, and again to Anna Coldericke's and even as she did so, she was berating her own indecisiveness.

'You're running about like a headless chicken, you damned fool! Now go downstairs. Sit at the table. Calm yourself down, and decide what you shall do.' Obeying her own dictates she experienced a curious sense of duality. As if one part of her being had detached itself and was standing aside, watching her physical body, and planning how to direct it.

'They are coming with torches to burn us out,' she muttered aloud. ' "They"! It is always "They", is it not. That many-headed beast that acts so bold and cruel against one alone . . . I've had trouble with "They", all my days, so it seems.' Her lips twisted with a sudden bitter quirk, 'And it seems as if I'll forever be having trouble with "They" . . . And always be the one alone,' a tiny voice whispered in her mind.

She rose to her feet and began to pace the room, then, as abruptly, sat down again at the table. 'No! No more acting like a headless chicken. I'll sit, and think out what to do. Should I take the kids and run and hide? But then, what will happen to Anna Coldericke if I leave her alone here? She's too ill for me to move her. She'll be out of her head with the fever if I wake her. I can't look after her, and the kids as well. I can't protect them all. But how can I stay here and keep the kids and Anna with me? We could all be burned alive!' Again panic whelmed, and again she fought it back into the recesses of her mind.

For long long moments she sat in deep concentration, and finally drew a long, shuddering breath. 'Damn whoever "They", may be this time.' She spoke aloud. 'I'll not run from them. I'll not force the kids or Anna Coldericke to hide like frightened animals in some ditch while "They" hunt us down. I'll not move one inch . . . '

*   *   *

John Clayton's house stood halfway down the Fish Hill, set back a little from the roadway, which his bedroom overlooked. He woke and lay staring into the darkness, wondering what had caused his unusual awakening, since he slept always without interruption. He heard noises like people shouting in the distance, and sat up to pull the heavy curtains of his bed aside so that he might hear more clearly. The noises came again, and this time Clayton was able to identify them as the shouts of men and women.

Leaving his bed he padded barefoot to the window and raised the sash high to enable him to push his upper body far enough out to view the roadway from top to bottom. The noises were coming from the bottom of the Fish Hill, where a crowd of people were milling about on the roadway. Their heads and bodies a constantly shifting, red-glared frieze among the flames of the flaring torches many of them carried. Even as Clayton watched and wondered, there came added sounds, the rattle of a drum and the shrilling of fifes.

'What in Heaven's name?' Clayton watched mystified, as the crowd formed into ragged ranks and led by the drummer and two fifers began to ascend the hill, some shouting and catcalling, some waving torches above their heads, some singing, all wild with drink. As they neared him Clayton was able to recognize some of them, and he frowned worriedly.

'Richard Bint, Rammer Perks, Edwin Danks, and more local wild men. They're up to no good with this, that's a certainty.'

As they passed beneath his window the leaders began to shout a chanting chorus in rhythm with the drum and fifes. 'No pox here! No pox here! No pox here!'

Their followers took up the chant. 'No pox here! No pox here! No pox here! No pox here!' Their battlecry shattered the peace of the night, and other windows on the Fish Hill were opened, and tangled frowsty heads peered out from them.

Having been in his bed and asleep since eight o'clock of

279

the evening, John Clayton knew nothing of the attack on Lucas Royston, but the chant made him form an instant conclusion. 'They'll be going to roust Lucas Royston, and maybe Anna Coldericke. But they must be prevented, when the drink is in, the sense is out, with those ruffians. Someone could easily get seriously hurt, or even killed.'

Without pausing to even put slippers on his feet, John Clayton ran out into the roadway, as he was, barefoot, his long night-shirt flapping around his hairy muscular legs. He sprinted to overtake the crowd, and caught Richie Bint by his coat collar. 'Hold hard, Bint. What are you about here?'

'Keep out on this, parson!' Rammer Perks warned, as the crowd swirled to a halt around the leaders.

'I'll not keep out of it!' John Clayton released Bint's collar, and stepped to confront the younger needle pointer. 'And I want to know what Devil's work you're about, creating such an unholy din on the Sabbath morning. You are offering insult to the Lord God.'

'Am I now, parson?' Rammer Perks was half-mad with the drink, 'Well I says Bollocks to your God, parson! Now piss off out o' my way!'

'How dare you address me in such a manner?' Clayton's voice was a study in furious incredulity, and he grabbed the young man's shirt front and pulled him so close that their chests were almost touching. 'How dare you?'

Perks's eyes flamed. 'I told you to piss-off, didn't I.' In a lightning motion he jerked his head back, then pistoned it forwards and downwards so that his forehead smashed into the middle of the clergyman's face.

Clayton grunted in agony as his nose was crushed, and he fell to his knees, blood spouting to saturate his white shirt-front.

'Hurrah, that's one for his nob!' Edwin Danks cheered madly, and the crowd marched on with drum rattling, fifes shrilling and voices howling. 'No pox here! No pox here! No pox here! No pox here!'

Tildy heard them coming. Her stomach turned over and

the nausea of fear made her gag in her throat.

'Oh Sweet Jesus, what will they do to us?' she moaned, and her mind locked onto the one hated word, 'They'. Every passing second the drumbeat, the fifeshrill, the shouted chant drew nearer and nearer, and the tremor in Tildy's hands became a violent shivering which spread to every limb of her body. Then, from above her in the house there came the high-pitched wailing of a frightened child. The pitiful cries filled Tildy with a fury of resentment that briefly blotted out all else.

' "They", are terrifying my kids!' The knowledge clamoured in her mind. 'They ! They ! They!' A child was weeping with terror in the night, because of 'They'. With blind instinct Tildy rose to her feet and snatching a long-bladed carving knife from the dresser, flew down the hallway.

'Theer! Look theer!' Edwin Danks shouted, and pointed at the slender figure standing in front of the neat, white-painted picket fence before the Ivy House.

The crowd vented a long-drawn atavistic howl, the fifes shrilled more wildly and the staccato rattling of the drum quickened to a frantic unceasing roll.

Tildy was once more experiencing that curious duality. One part of her being, detached, standing aside, watching the trembling, terrified physical body fronting the oncoming mob. And then that body started forwards, towards the flaming torches, towards the shrilling fifes and rolling drum, towards the gaping ferocity of the snarling mouths. The body reached the drum, the long knife rose and fell, rose and fell, rose and fell, its blade flashing like a flame in the torchlight, and suddenly the drum was silent, the drumsticks smacking shreds of leather, and Tildy was screaming at the bemused drummer. 'You're terrifying my kids with your din! You're terrifying my kids!'

Sheer amazement halted the mob in its tracks. The fifes ceased shrilling, and only the rasp of harsh breathing and the splutterings of the flaring torches broke the silence that had so suddenly descended.

281

Tildy fell back a few paces, knife held before her, its point towards the mob.

'There are four sick kids in this house, and before you put a single torch near it, you'll have to kill me . . . ' Her wild eyes went from one face to another, to another, to another, and each time that face turned away, unable to hold her gaze. 'Would you burn children in their beds?' she shouted accusingly. 'Is that the sort of people you are? Is it? The sort who would burn alive defenceless children?'

The mob began to stir uneasily. Men who would savage each other like mad dogs when they brawled, found that they had no stomach for putting the torch to children.

Edwin Danks, still thirsting for revenge, and sensing that the mob was wavering and fast losing its bloodlust, bawled out, 'How does we know that the kids be still inside theer? This is only a trick of that Coldericke bitch, to escape us.'

Before Tildy could make any reply, Shirley Perks flung her arm upwards. 'They'm inside alright. Look theer!'

A small white face framed by long hair, was pressed against the dark windowpane of the bedroom, and even at this distance the child's terror could be seen.

'Bollocks to this!' Richie Bint ejaculated, and threw his flaring torch to the ground. 'I arn't the type o' cove who makes war on kids,' he turned to face the mob. 'What about the rest on you? Be you going to burn nippers alive?'

Almost in unison, amid exclamations of self-disgust and muttered curses, the flaring torches were tossed to earth and men and women began to walk away. Edwin Danks stood his ground for some moments more, and Tildy remained rigidly confronting him. Then he also pitched his torch to the ground.

'That Coldericke bitch can thank her lucky stars that her's got you wi' her this night, girl,' he gritted out, and a note of grudging admiration entered his voice. 'Youm a real little hard-chaw, you be.' Then he also turned his back and walked away.

For long minutes Tildy stayed where she was, the flickering fallen torches casting fitful gleams across her face

282

and gown. She felt sick and spent, and was afraid to move and break her rigid posture in case she should lose her hard-maintained control of her body, and collapse.

From the direction of the Fish Hill, bloody-faced and panting, John Clayton came running at the head of a party of men, and from the direction of the chapel more men came. Tildy looked at her belated rescuers, and her eyes clouded with sudden acute sadness. She could not see Caleb Hawkes among their number.

'So, he didn't care enough to come to help me,' she told herself illogically.

'Are you alright, Crawford? Have they harmed you?' Clayton's voice was distorted by the towel he was holding to his still-bleeding nose.

'Yes, thank you, I'm alright,' she called back, and without another word went into the Ivy House to comfort the frightened children. And to wonder why Caleb Hawkes had failed to come to her when she had most needed him.

'But I can't really blame him,' she accepted sadly, 'for it was I who drove him away. But then, what else could I do? I must become my own woman. That, above all else, is what I need to be . . .'

Chapter Thirty

It was the first Monday in August, and throughout the dark hours of the previous night the gaily painted wagons of the show people had been trundling into Redditch. Sharing the roads with droves of cattle, flocks of sheep, herds of pigs and gaggles of geese, pedlars, hucksters, cheapjacks and swarms of beggars.

Dawn had come and Tildy sat at the front attic window of Ivy House watching the influx and telling the children with her, 'The Redditch Fair begins today. It lasts for three days and three nights. There'll be all sorts of high jinx here, I'll be bound.'

'Will we be able to see them, Auntie Tildy?' the small girl wanted to know.

Tildy stroked the soft blonde hair, and smiled to hide the sadness in her eyes. 'Not this year, honey. For we must go back to the poorhouse this very morning. But perhaps next year, you'll be able to see them.'

The small head nodded solemnly, 'I'll be big then, won't I, Aunt Tildy. And I'll be able to come, even though I've got nobody to bring me. I'll be big enough to come by myself, won't I.'

Tildy had a lump in her throat as she gently cuddled the thin little body to her breasts. 'Surely you will, honey. Surely you will. Oh, look there, kids.' She pointed down the roadway. 'It's a dancing bear.'

The children oohhed and ahhed in excitement, and clustered to stare eagerly at the shambling animal led on a chain by its brightly clad, ringletted gypsy master.

Little Davy was lying asleep on Tildy's bed, and as she glanced at him she breathed a prayer of thanks that all the children were fit and healthy once more.

She herself, although pale and thin, was also fully recovered and no marks of the smallpox remained on her skin.

Since the night of the mob, John Clayton had taken it upon himself to ensure that Ivy House was left in peace, and had arranged for all household necessaries to be brought to them. He had also kept them up to date with certain happenings. Lucas Royston, recovered from his beating, had left the town without divulging the identity of his attacker. But he had exculpated Caleb Hawkes from all suspicion. Which was a relief for Joseph Cashmore, because the constable had failed to find the higgler, who even now had not yet returned to the town. After Lucas Royston's departure, Anna Coldericke had also left the town. Heartbroken by her lover's desertion she had gone to a relative in far-off Devonshire to convalesce both from the smallpox and her wounded heart.

Tildy was saddened at the memory of the parting from Anna Coldericke. The woman had behaved as though it were Tildy's fault that Lucas Royston had jilted her. But despite the injustice, Tildy had held her peace, and felt a great sympathy for the woman's pain. Phoebe Bray had returned to Ivy House, but she had treated Tildy and the children kindly, so atoning for the trouble she had brought down upon them.

Today the quarantine period was ended, and now Tildy waited for the poorhouse cart which was to carry her and the children back to their bondage.

Tildy looked down at her worn grey gown, and at the red-lettered badge she wore once more on her right shoulder, and could not help but sigh heavily. 'I'd almost forgotten what it felt like to wear this,' she thought sadly, 'I was beginning to feel like a respectable woman again.'

Another regret came to weigh on her . . . Caleb Hawkes. She had not seen or heard of him since that day on the

Chapel Green when yet again her pride had forced her to repulse him. 'I fear that I wounded his pride too deeply,' she now concluded, and experienced a mixture of respect and irritation for the man. Respect that he was a man of pride. Irritation that he should allow that pride to come between them. 'I do still feel attracted towards him,' she admitted to herself. 'He exerts a powerful fascination for me . . .'

Glancing from the window she saw the poorhouse cart driven by the old pauper, Joey, lurching to a halt in front of Ivy House.

A wave of despondency assailed her. 'So, it's time to go back there. Back to degradation.' Assuming a façade of cheeriness she told the children, 'Come on, kids, we're going for a ride in a cart. It'll be great fun.'

Phoebe Bray came out to the cart as Tildy lifted the children into it.

'Here, my wench,' she handed Tildy a small cloth bag which clinked dully.

Tildy opened it and saw inside the ten gold guineas that it contained.

The other woman nodded. 'Mrs Coldericke told me that I was to give it to you on the day you left, as payment for looking arter her,' she paused, then added, 'to my mind t'is little enough reward for what you did to protect her, but theer, that's the bloody gentry for you. They always reckons that a few coins pays for all.'

Tildy gazed down at the coins, her mind working rapidly, then retied the bag and handed the coins back to the woman. 'I wasn't seeking payment for what I did, Mrs Bray.'

'But you should take the money,' Phoebe Bray protested. 'If it hadn't bin for you standing against 'um, that mob would ha' burned Ivy House to the ground that night.'

Tildy's lips curved in a rueful smile. 'I didn't stand against them only to save Ivy House, Mrs Bray.'

'Ne'er mind why you did it, Tildy Crawford. That money has bin well earned. So take it . . . If not for yourself, then take it for your babby. There's bound to be summat he'll need, arn't there.'

Tildy saw the sense in that argument, and when Mrs Bray again pressed the small bag onto her, she accepted it.

'Please give my thanks to Mrs Coldericke, when you see her again.'

She climbed into the cart, and told the old pauper, 'Come, Joey, let's be off.'

The cart lurched through the town and up the long hill known as Mount Pleasant, and while it slowly creaked on Tildy thought about the weeks that had passed since she had left the Sidemoor, and quite suddenly the despondency she had been feeling began to lift from her.

'I've learned so much,' she realized with a burgeoning pleasure. 'How to read and write. How to care for the sick. And a lot about human nature that I didn't know before...'

The despondency threatened her again as the cart creaked into the lane where the poorhouse waited, and Ebenezer Morris came out from the courtyard to meet them.

'Don't sit theer on your arse all day, Crawford,' he loured at her, 'your bloody holiday has come to a finish. Theer's work aplenty waiting for you here.'

Tildy gazed at his miserable tallowy face, and knew then that she would not tolerate her life as a pauper inmate any longer. She kissed the three orphan children. 'Run inside, kids,' she told them, and only when they had scampered out of sight did she climb down from the cart.

'I'm not staying here, Master Morris,' she said firmly. 'So I'll thank you to give me my ticket of release.'

Shock showed on the man's features, but before he could answer, Tildy took out the cloth bag with the money inside it, and clinked it beneath his long nose.

'I've money enough to support myself and my baby for a while, Master Morris. So you can't refuse to issue me with my ticket.'

She unpinned the badge that she hated, and pushed it into the pocket of his coat. 'I'll not be wearing this again, if

287

I can help it. Now, will you give me my ticket, please. Or must I go down to the vestry and apply for it.'

By this time he had recovered himself sufficiently to sneer, 'Oh I'll gi' you your ticket, Crawford. But you'll be back. And when you comes back, I'll be making you smart for this insolence.' He turned on his heel and stalked into the courtyard.

Old Joey laughed wheezily. 'That shot the bugger up his arse alright, Tildy. But wheer be you going?'

She smiled with pure happiness. 'I'm taking my baby back to Redditch. I'm going to find us a place to live, and I'm going to work as a nurse.' She suddenly laughed aloud, and told the old man. 'Do you know, until I actually said that, I didn't know myself what I was going to work at.'

The old pauper grinned toothlessly. 'But you does now, Tildy. You does now . . .'

She nodded her head slowly and firmly. 'Yes Joey, I do now . . . I surely do know now . . .'